epic!

ANIMAL RESCUE FRIENDS

JANA TROPPER

Illustrated by
GENEVIEVE KOTE
LEO TRINIDAD

Andrews McMeel
PUBLISHING®

Animal Rescue Friends created by Meika Hashimoto,
Gina Loveless, and Genevieve Kote

Animal Rescue Friends: Friends Fur-Ever text and illustrations
copyright © 2022 by Epic! Creations, Inc. All rights reserved.
Printed in China. No part of this book may be used or reproduced in any
manner whatsoever without written permission except in the case of
reprints in the context of reviews.

Andrews McMeel Publishing
a division of Andrews McMeel Universal
1130 Walnut Street, Kansas City, Missouri 64106

www.andrewsmcmeel.com

Epic! Creations, Inc.
702 Marshall Street, Suite 280
Redwood City, California 94063

www.getepic.com

23 24 25 26 27 SDB 10 9 8 7 6 5 4 3 2

Paperback ISBN: 978-1-5248-7584-8
Hardback ISBN: 978-1-5248-7937-2

Library of Congress Control Number: 2022942363

Design by Chris Gaugler

Made by:
RR Donnelley (Guangdong) Printing Solutions Company Ltd.
No. 2 Minzhu Road, Daning, Humen Town,
Dongguan City, Guangdong Province, China 523930
2nd Printing—5/15/23

ATTENTION: SCHOOLS AND BUSINESSES
Andrews McMeel books are available at quantity discounts
with bulk purchase for educational, business, or sales promotional use.
For information, please e-mail the Andrews McMeel Publishing
Special Sales Department: sales@amuniversal.com.

For my husband, Josh, who has
always believed in me and also let me
adopt a third dog.

For my editor, Meika, who helped me believe
in myself and keeps me employed so I can
afford a third dog.

—J. T.

Chapter 1

BELL, MADDIE, AND MONSTER

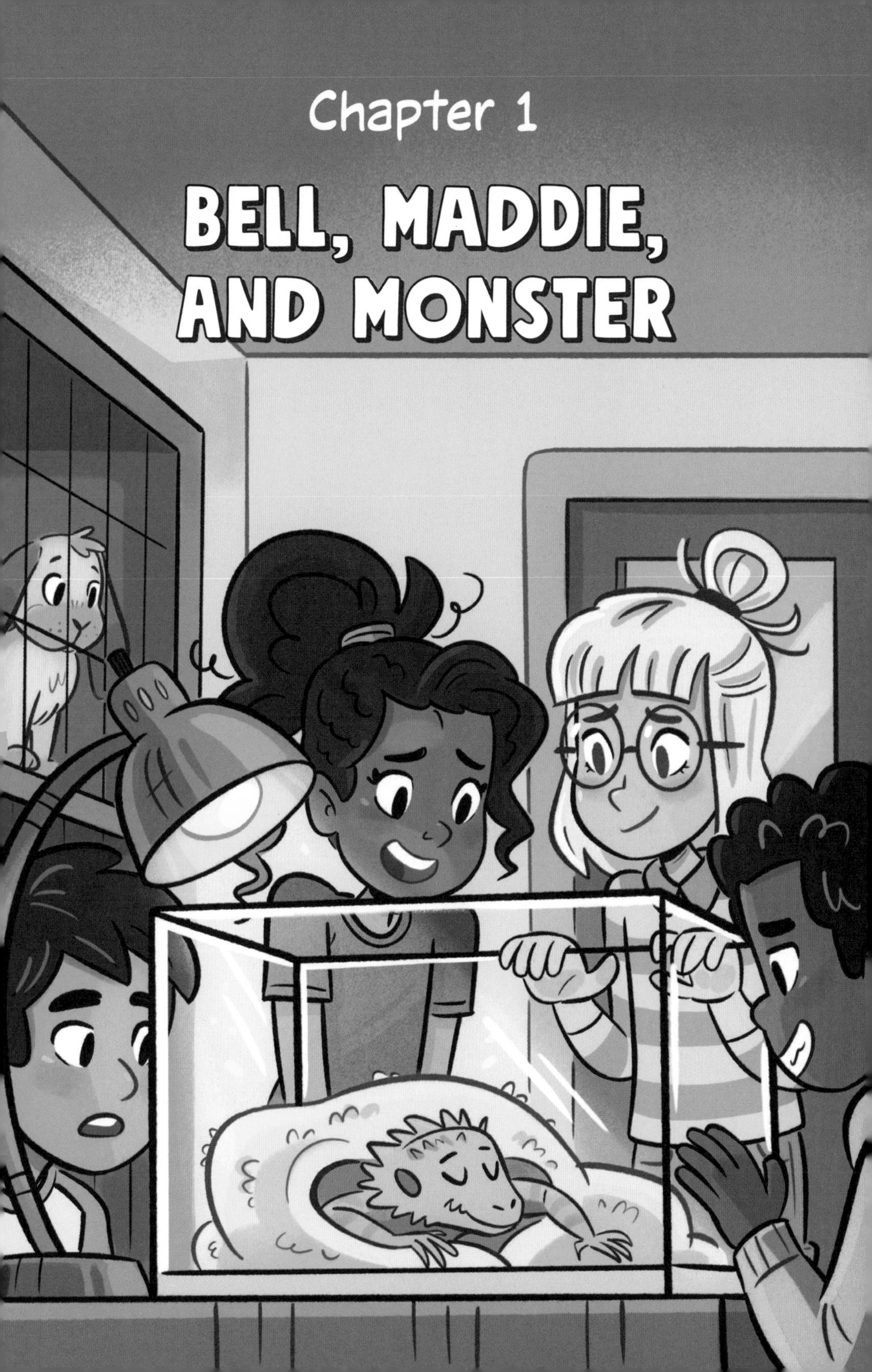

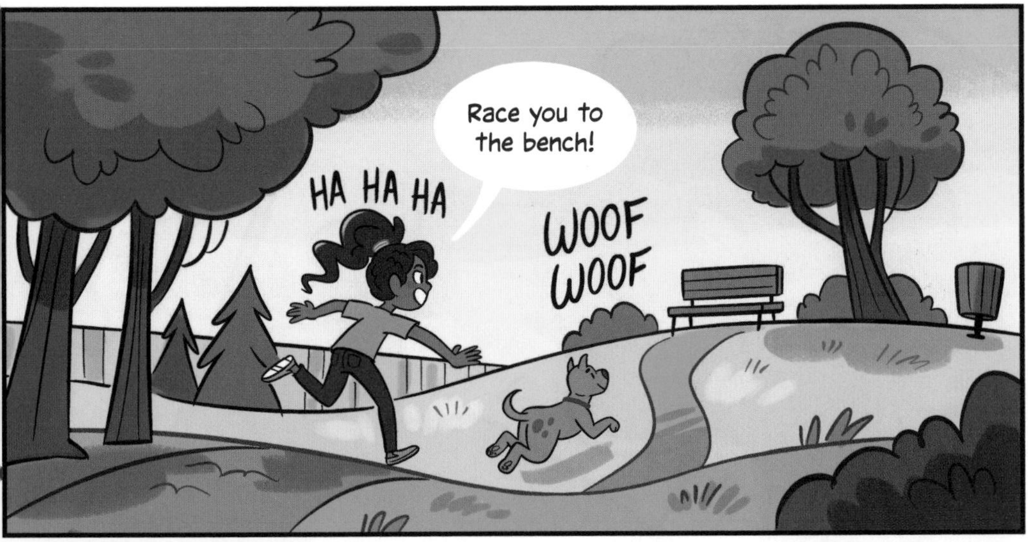
HA HA HA
Race you to the bench!
WOOF WOOF

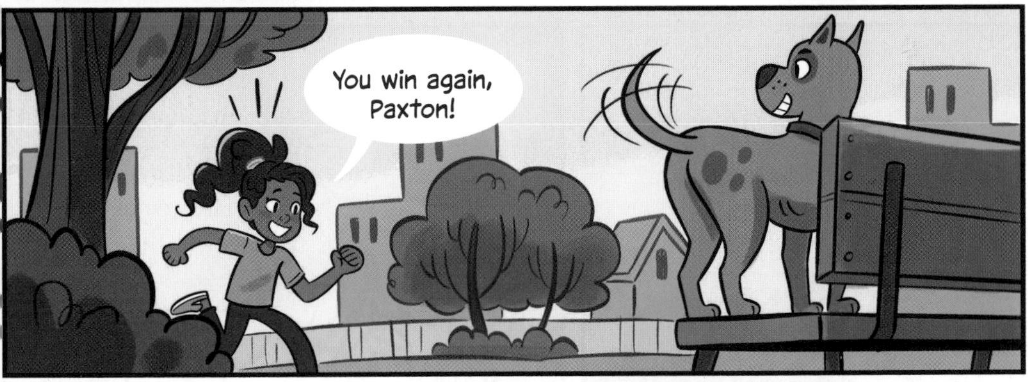
You win again, Paxton!

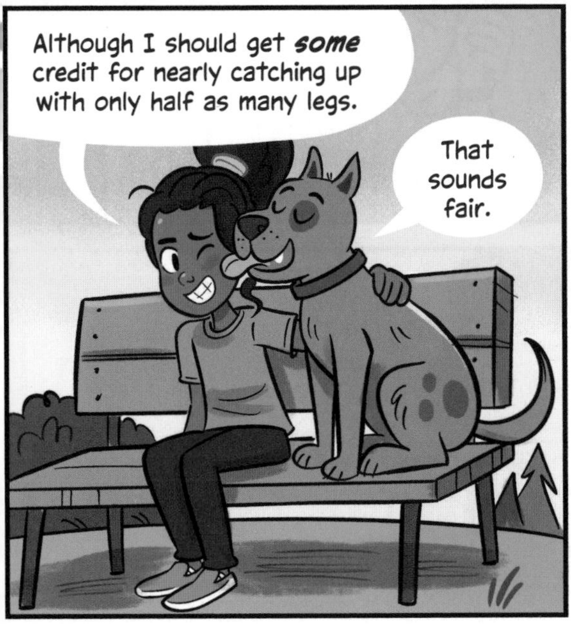
Although I should get *some* credit for nearly catching up with only half as many legs.
That sounds fair.

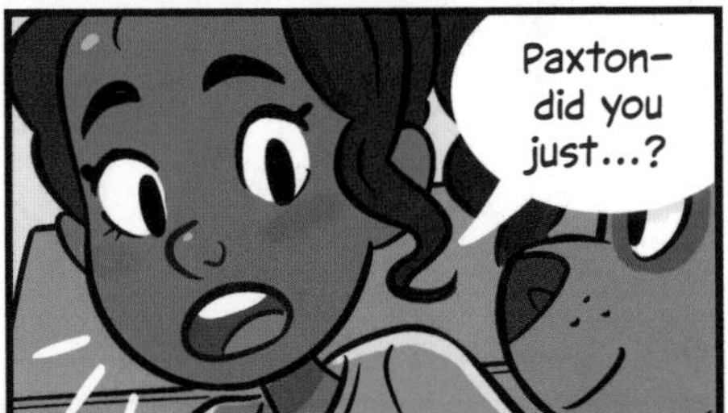
Paxton—did you just...?

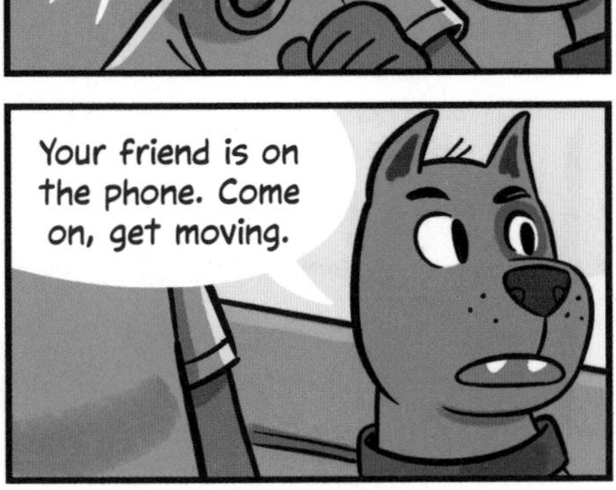
Your friend is on the phone. Come on, get moving.

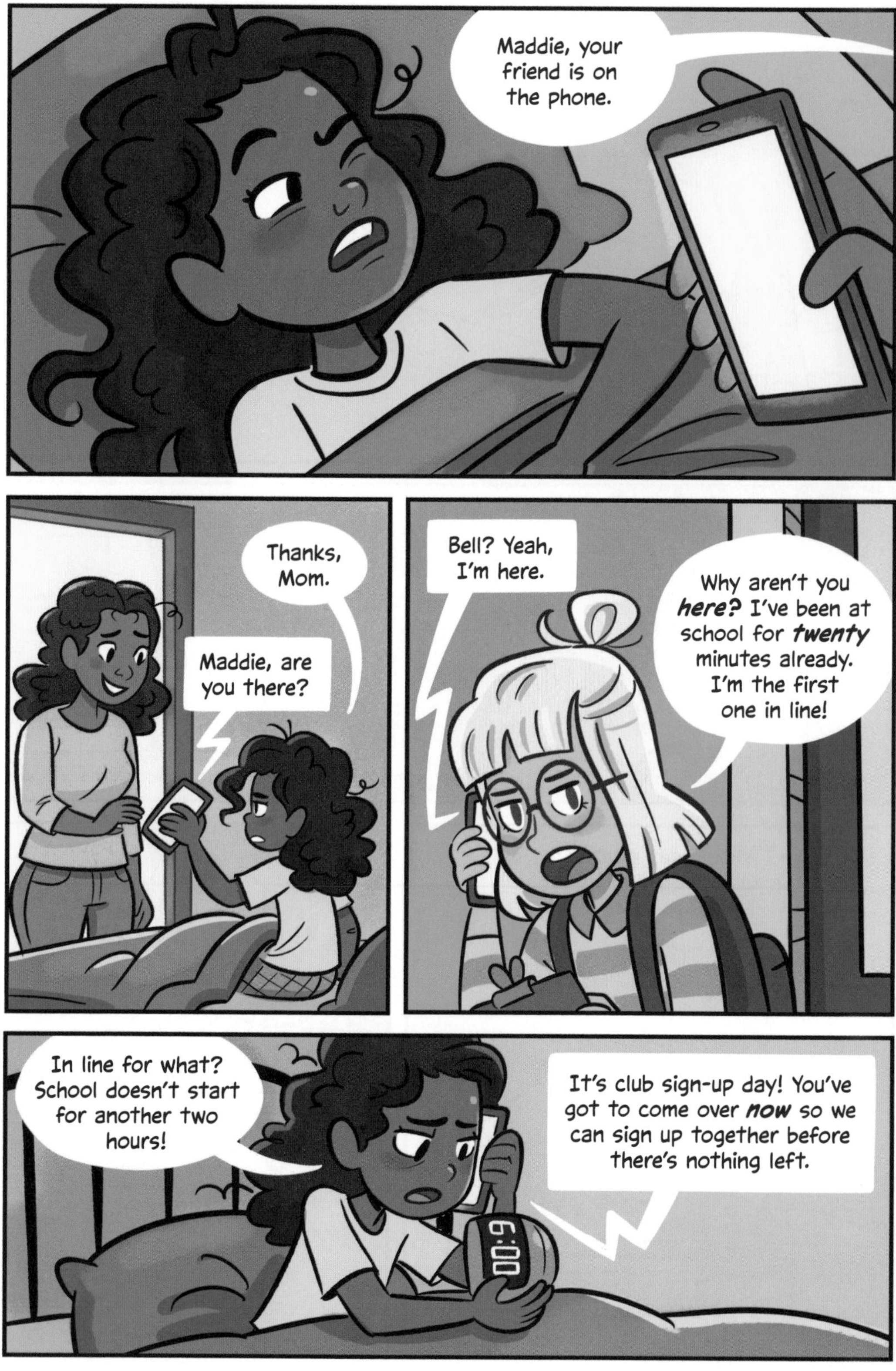
Maddie, your friend is on the phone.
Thanks, Mom.
Maddie, are you there?
Bell? Yeah, I'm here.
Why aren't you *here?* I've been at school for *twenty* minutes already. I'm the first one in line!
In line for what? School doesn't start for another two hours!
It's club sign-up day! You've got to come over *now* so we can sign up together before there's nothing left.
6:00

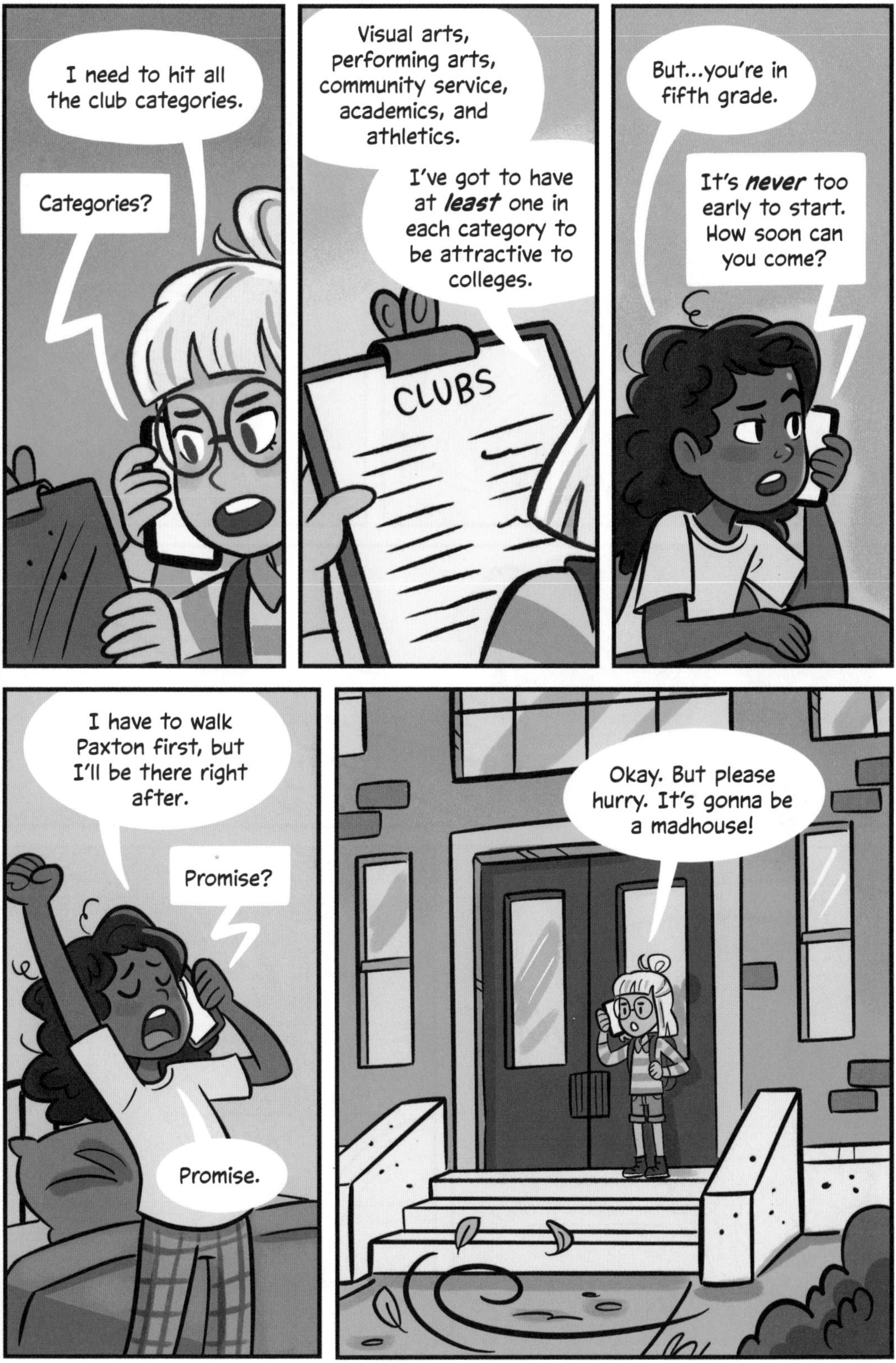
I need to hit all the club categories.
Categories?
Visual arts, performing arts, community service, academics, and athletics.
I've got to have at *least* one in each category to be attractive to colleges.
CLUBS
But...you're in fifth grade.
It's ***never*** too early to start. How soon can you come?
I have to walk Paxton first, but I'll be there right after.
Promise?
Promise.
Okay. But please hurry. It's gonna be a madhouse!

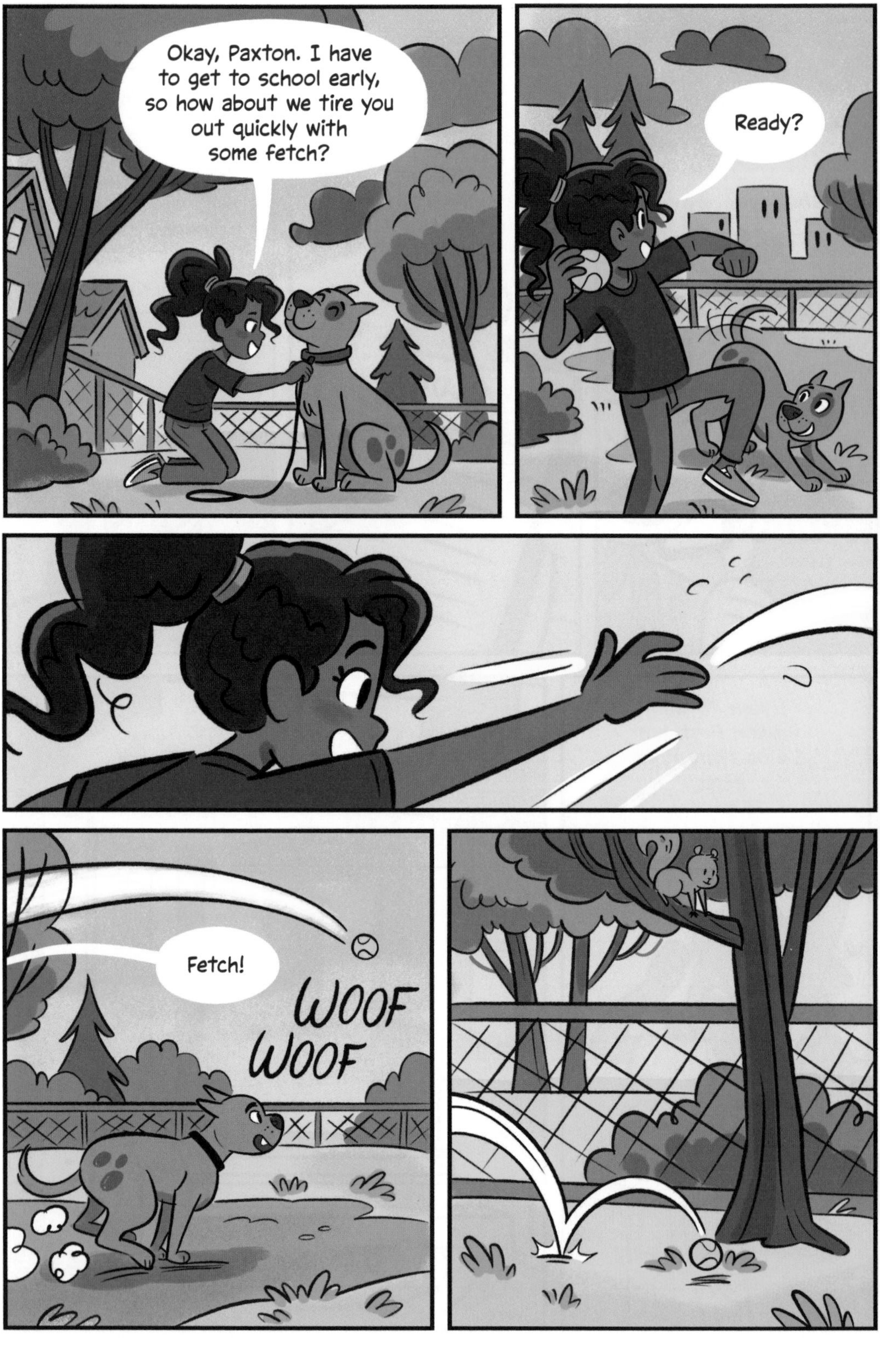
Okay, Paxton. I have to get to school early, so how about we tire you out quickly with some fetch?
Ready?
Fetch!
WOOF WOOF

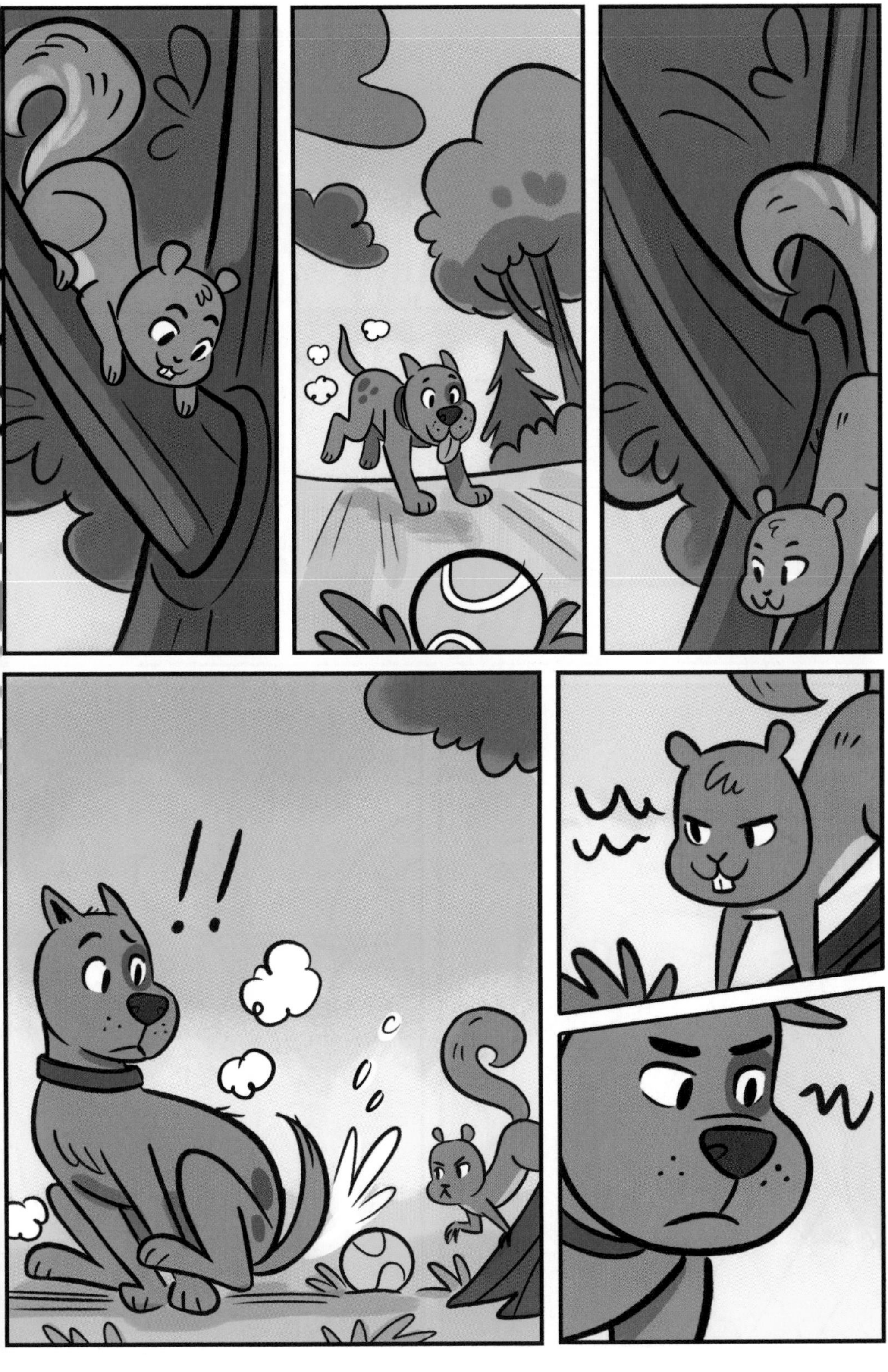
!!

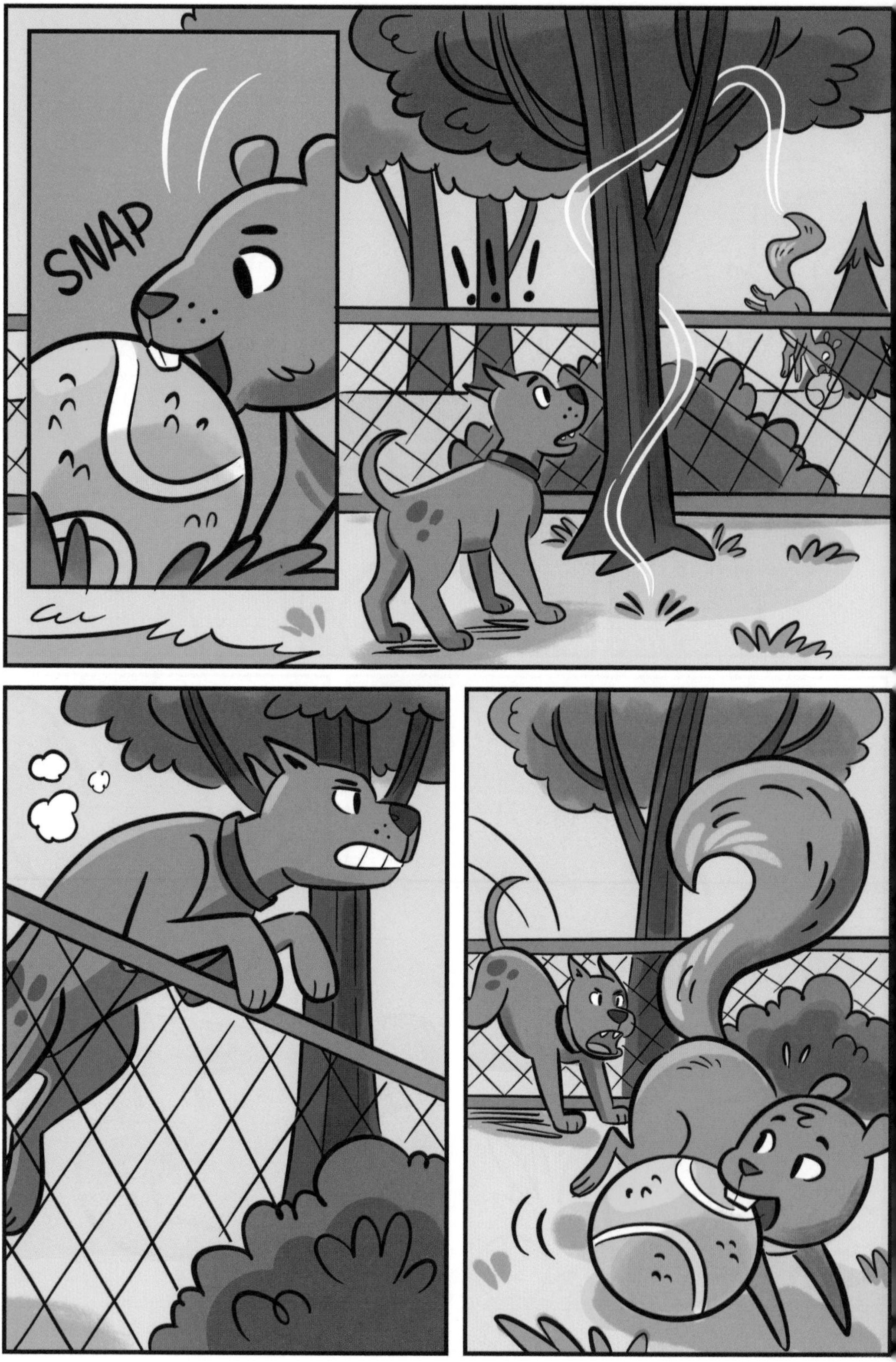
SNAP
!!!

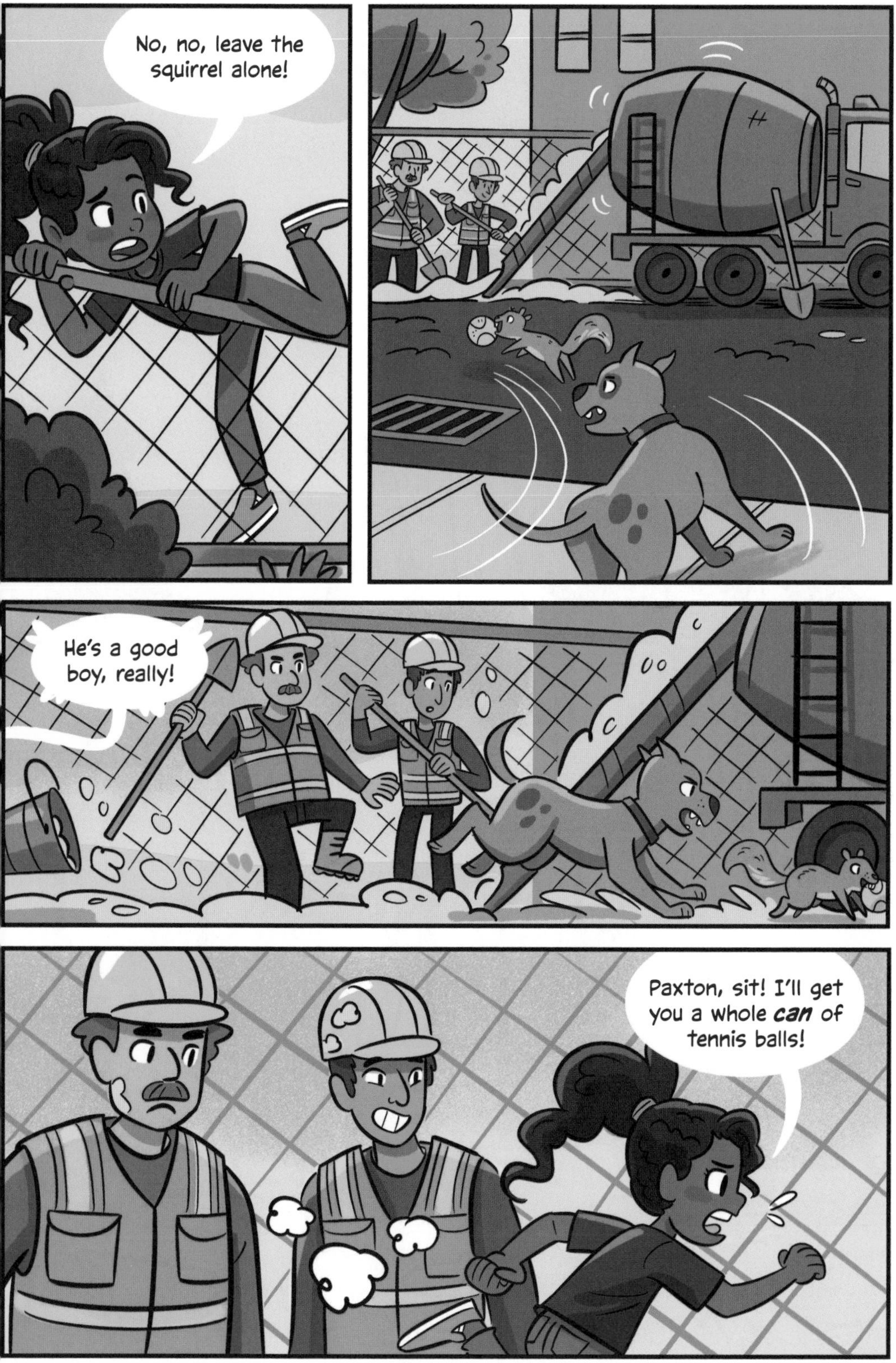
No, no, leave the squirrel alone!
He's a good boy, really!
Paxton, sit! I'll get you a whole *can* of tennis balls!

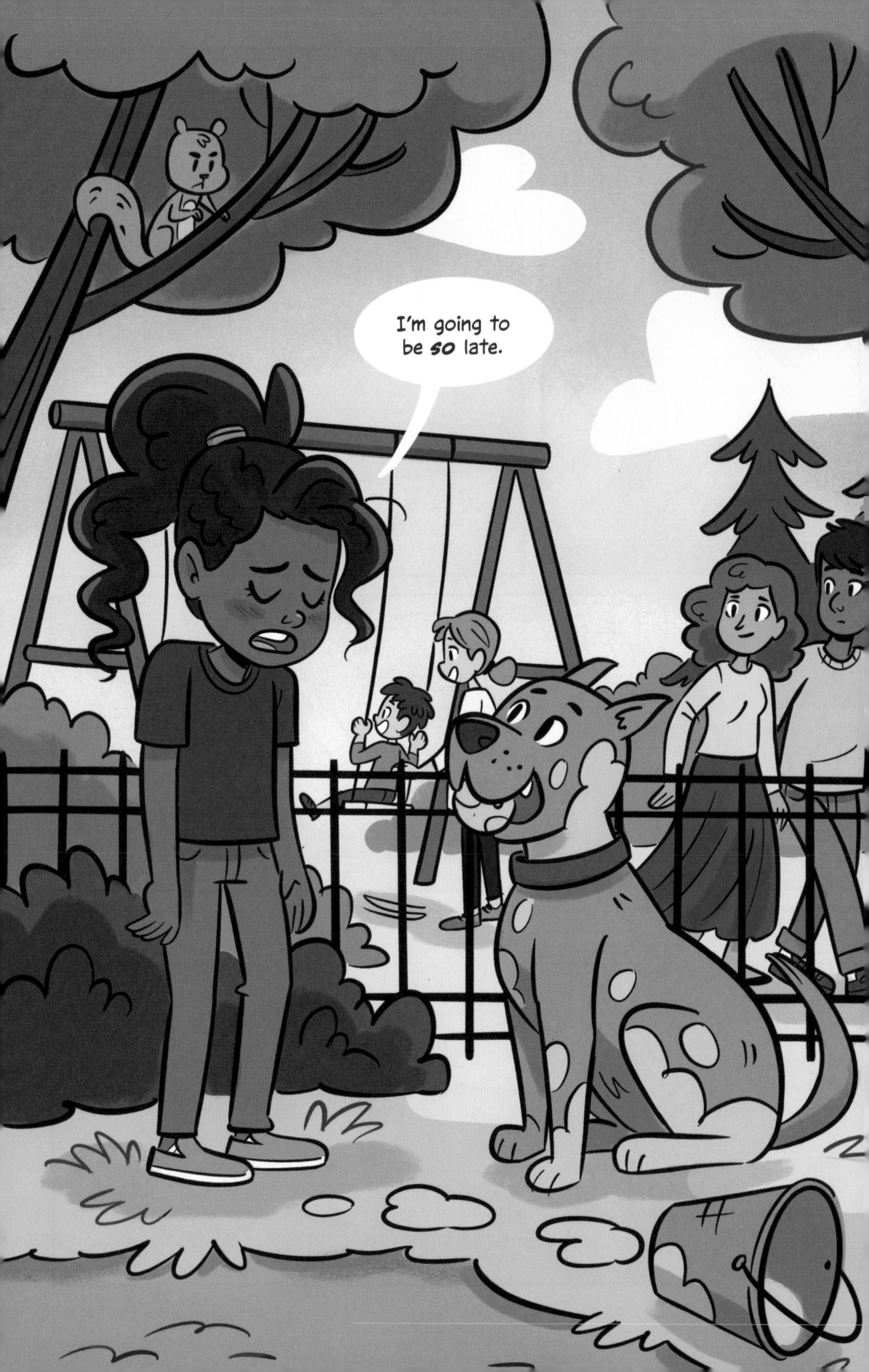
I'm going to be *so* late.

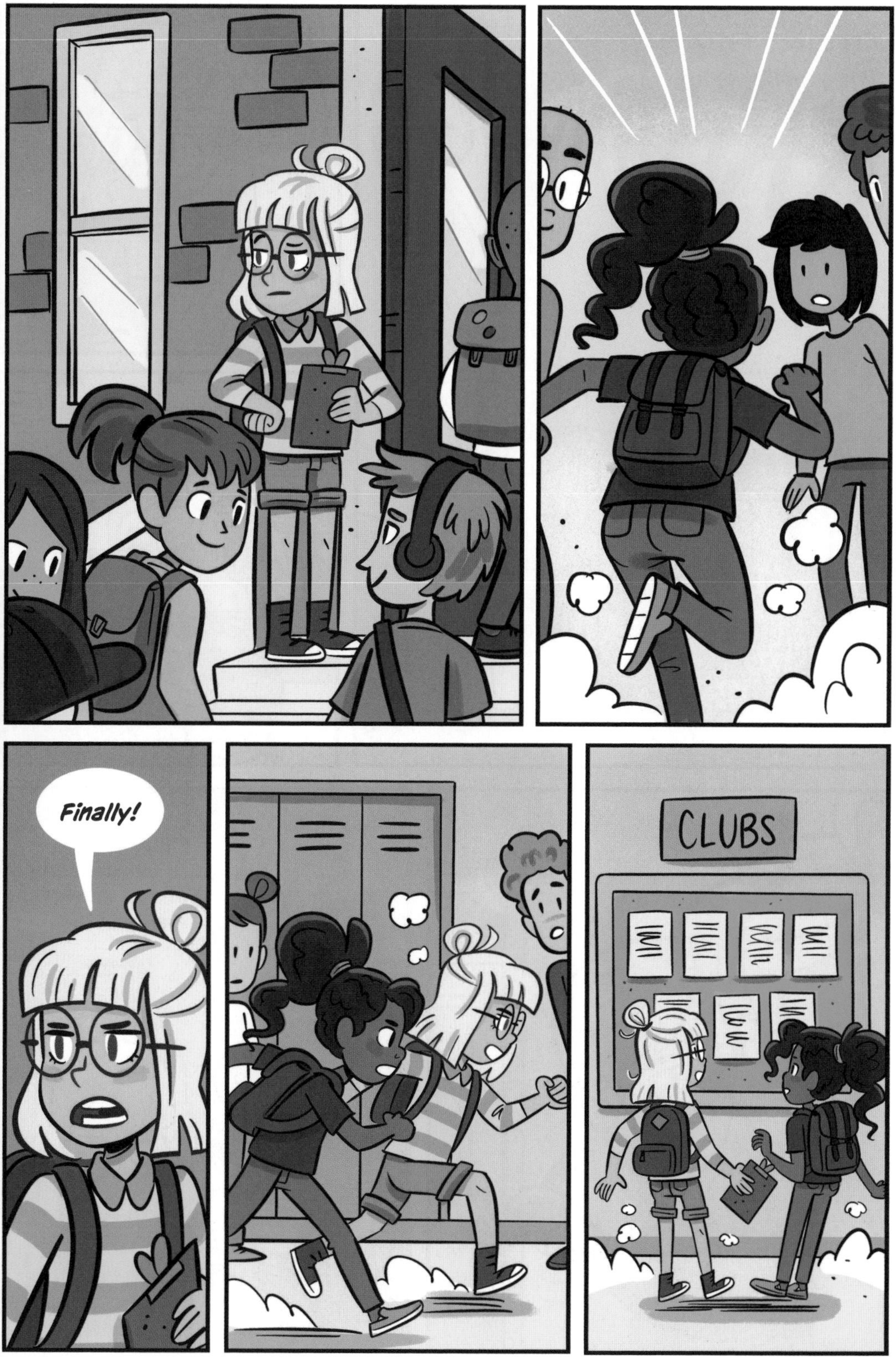
Finally!
CLUBS

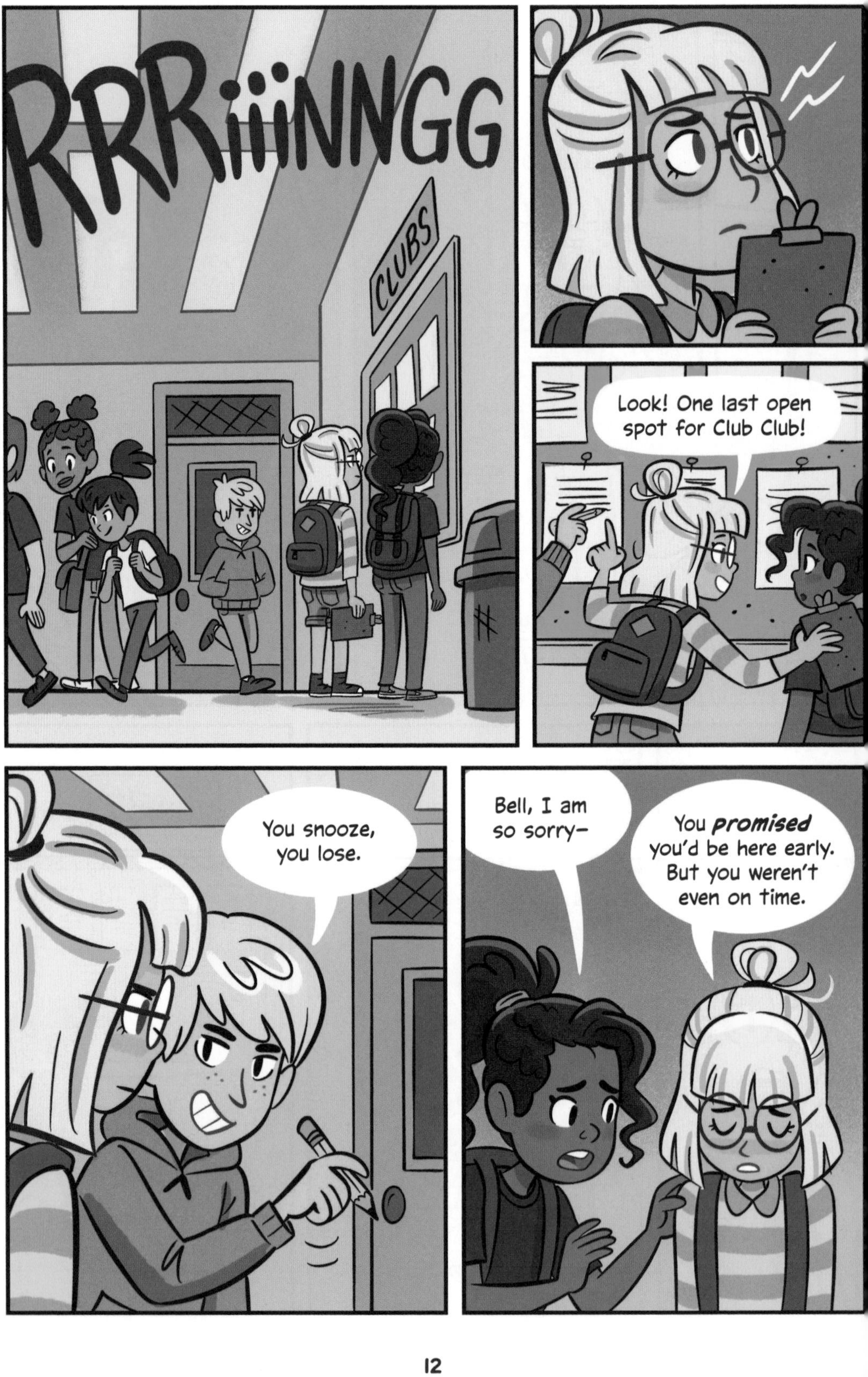
RRRiiiNNGG
CLUBS
Look! One last open spot for Club Club!
You snooze, you lose.
Bell, I am so sorry–
You ***promised*** you'd be here early. But you weren't even on time.

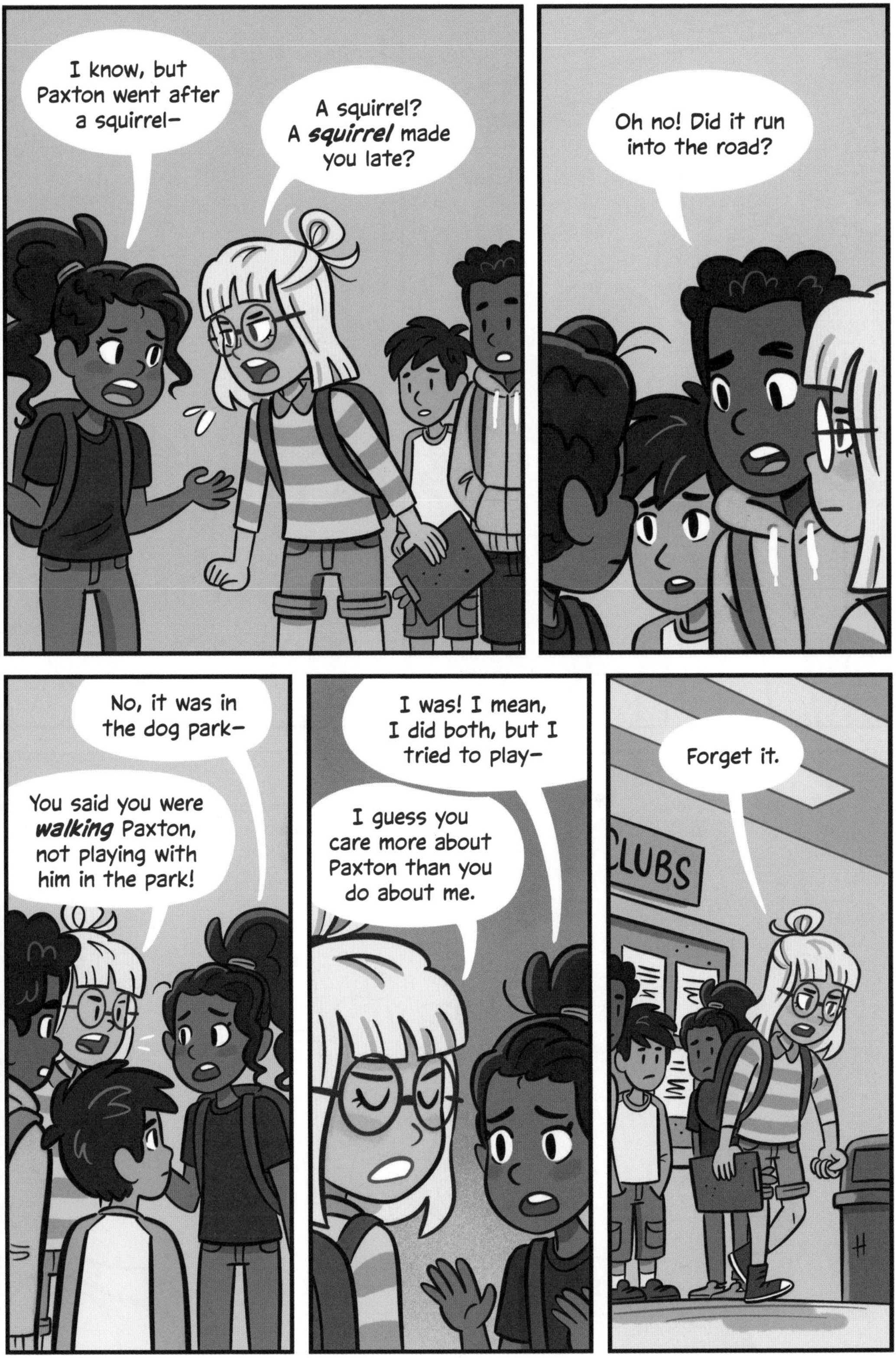
I know, but Paxton went after a squirrel—
A squirrel? A *squirrel* made you late?
Oh no! Did it run into the road?
No, it was in the dog park—
You said you were *walking* Paxton, not playing with him in the park!
I was! I mean, I did both, but I tried to play—
I guess you care more about Paxton than you do about me.
Forget it.
CLUBS

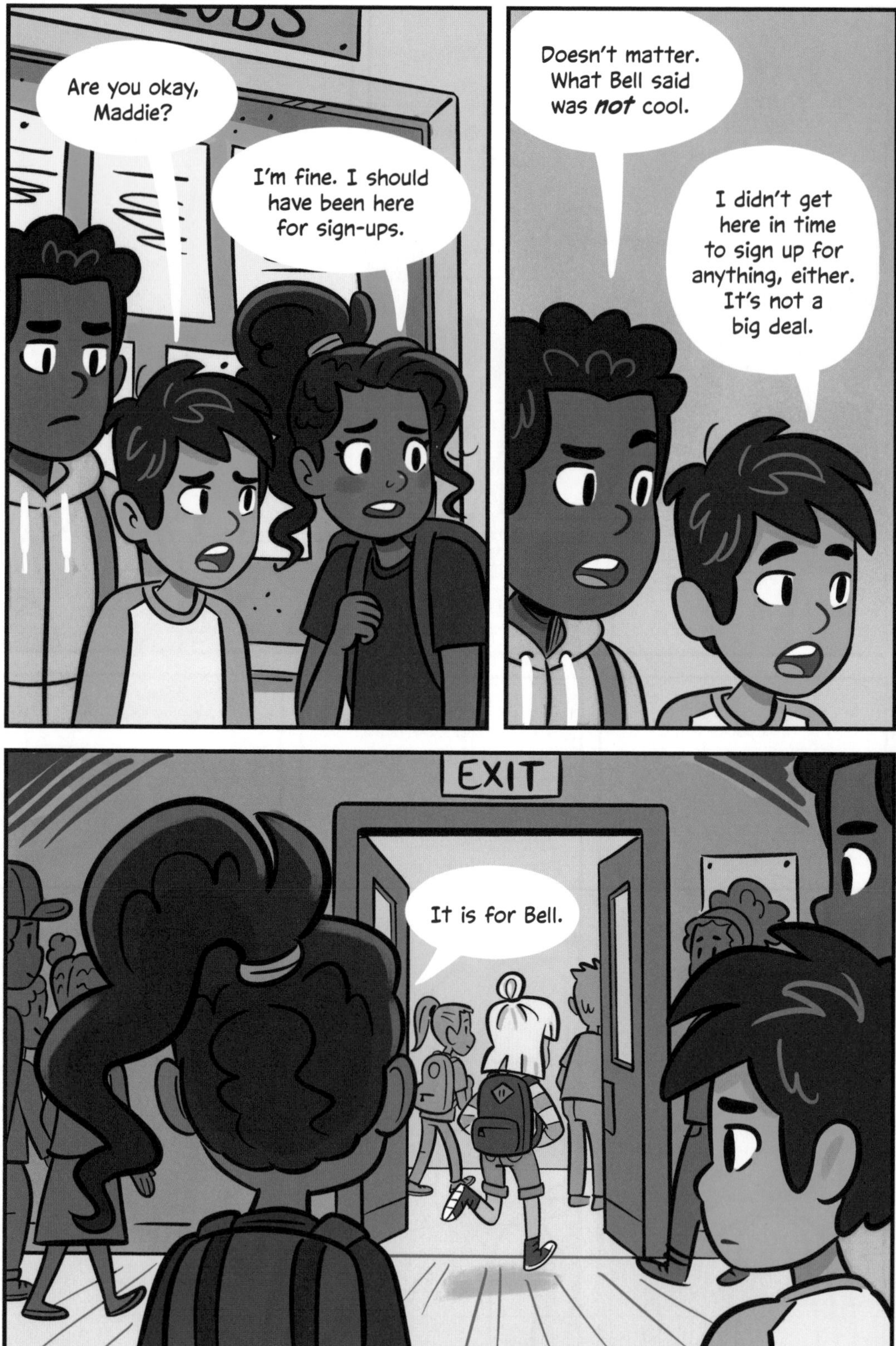
Are you okay, Maddie?
I'm fine. I should have been here for sign-ups.
Doesn't matter. What Bell said was *not* cool.
I didn't get here in time to sign up for anything, either. It's not a big deal.
EXIT
It is for Bell.

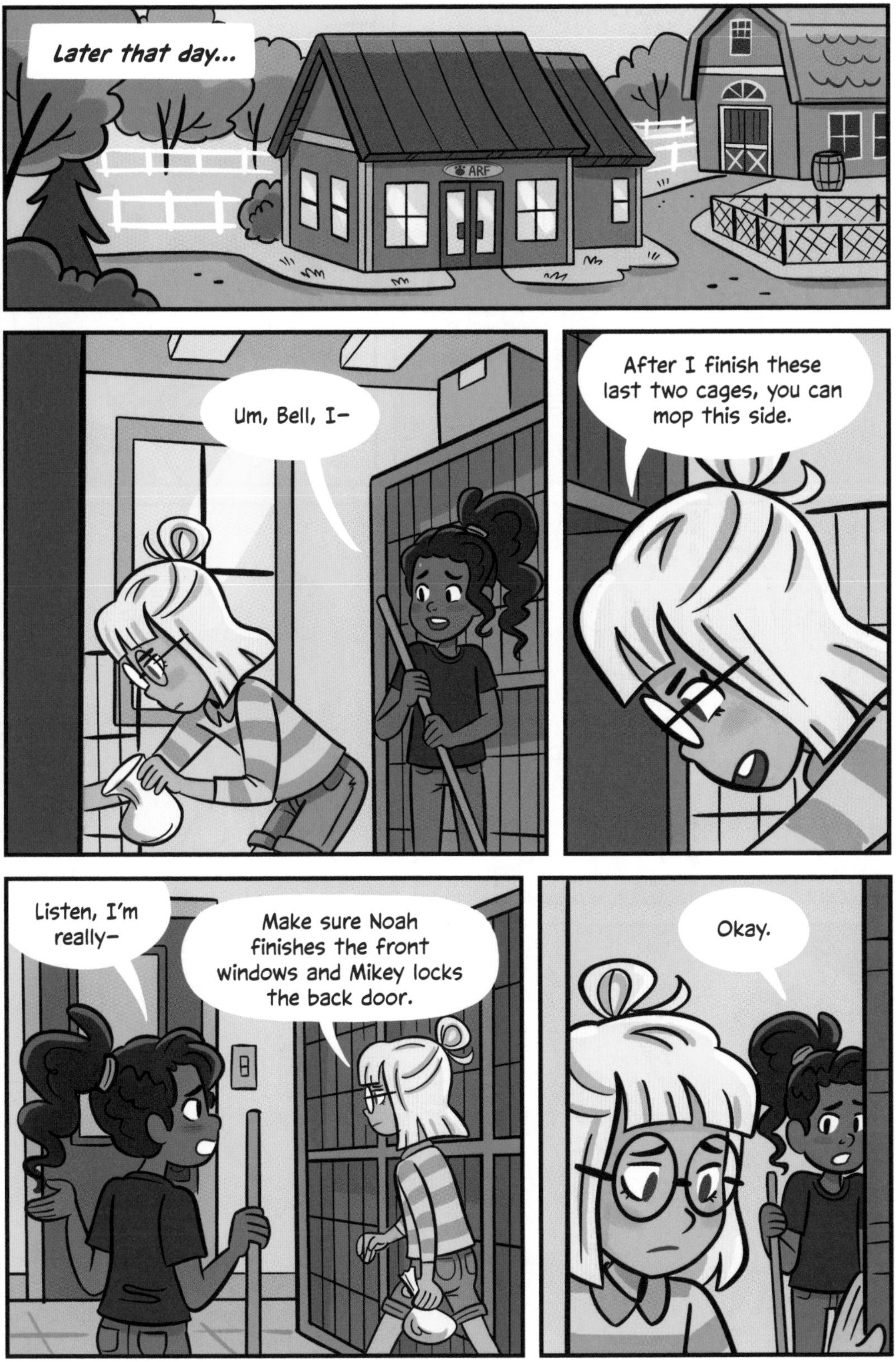
Later that day...
ARF
Um, Bell, I-
After I finish these last two cages, you can mop this side.
Listen, I'm really-
Make sure Noah finishes the front windows and Mikey locks the back door.
Okay.

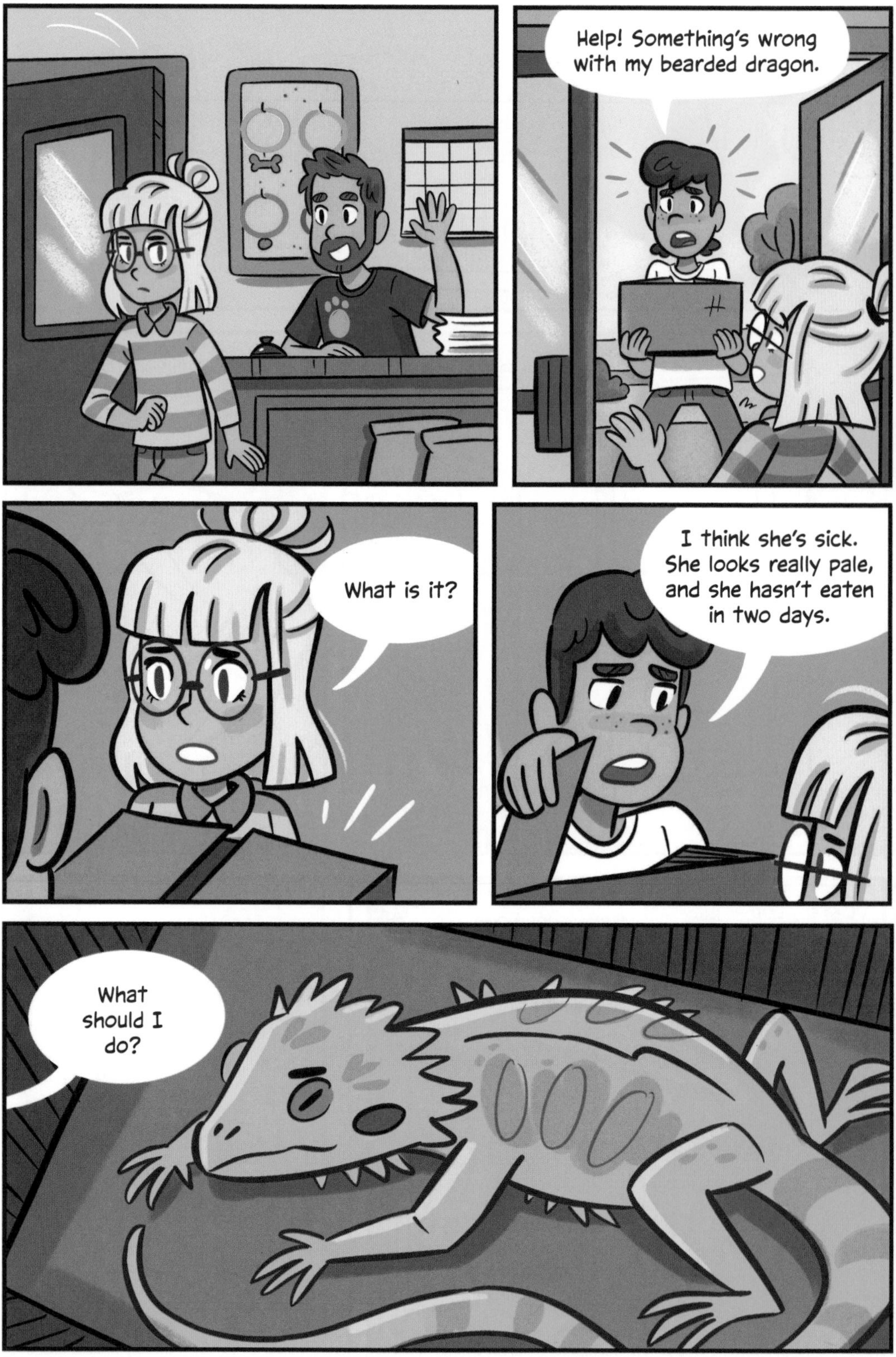
Help! Something's wrong with my bearded dragon.
What is it?
I think she's sick. She looks really pale, and she hasn't eaten in two days.
What should I do?

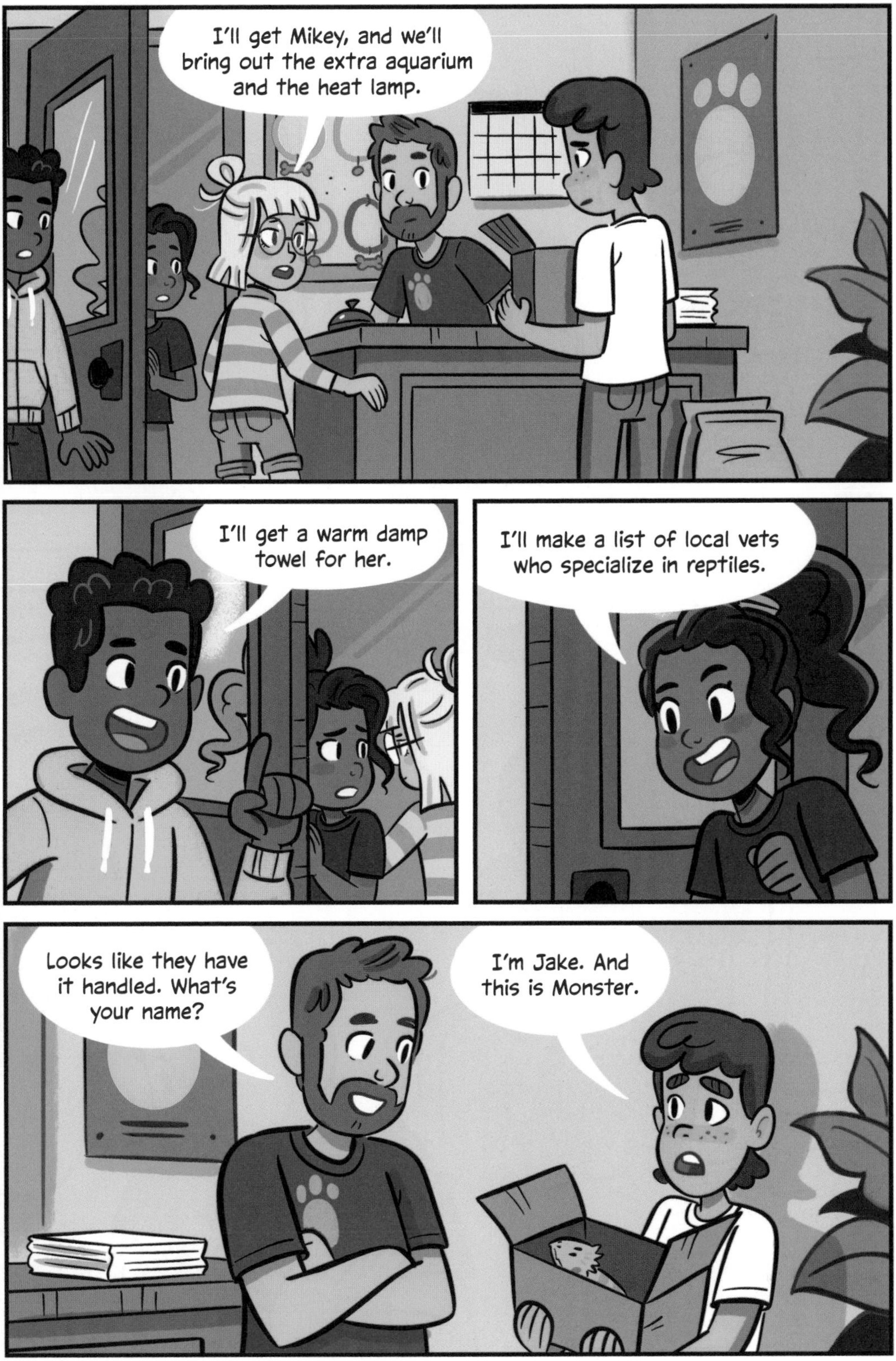
I'll get Mikey, and we'll bring out the extra aquarium and the heat lamp.
I'll get a warm damp towel for her.
I'll make a list of local vets who specialize in reptiles.
Looks like they have it handled. What's your name?
I'm Jake. And this is Monster.

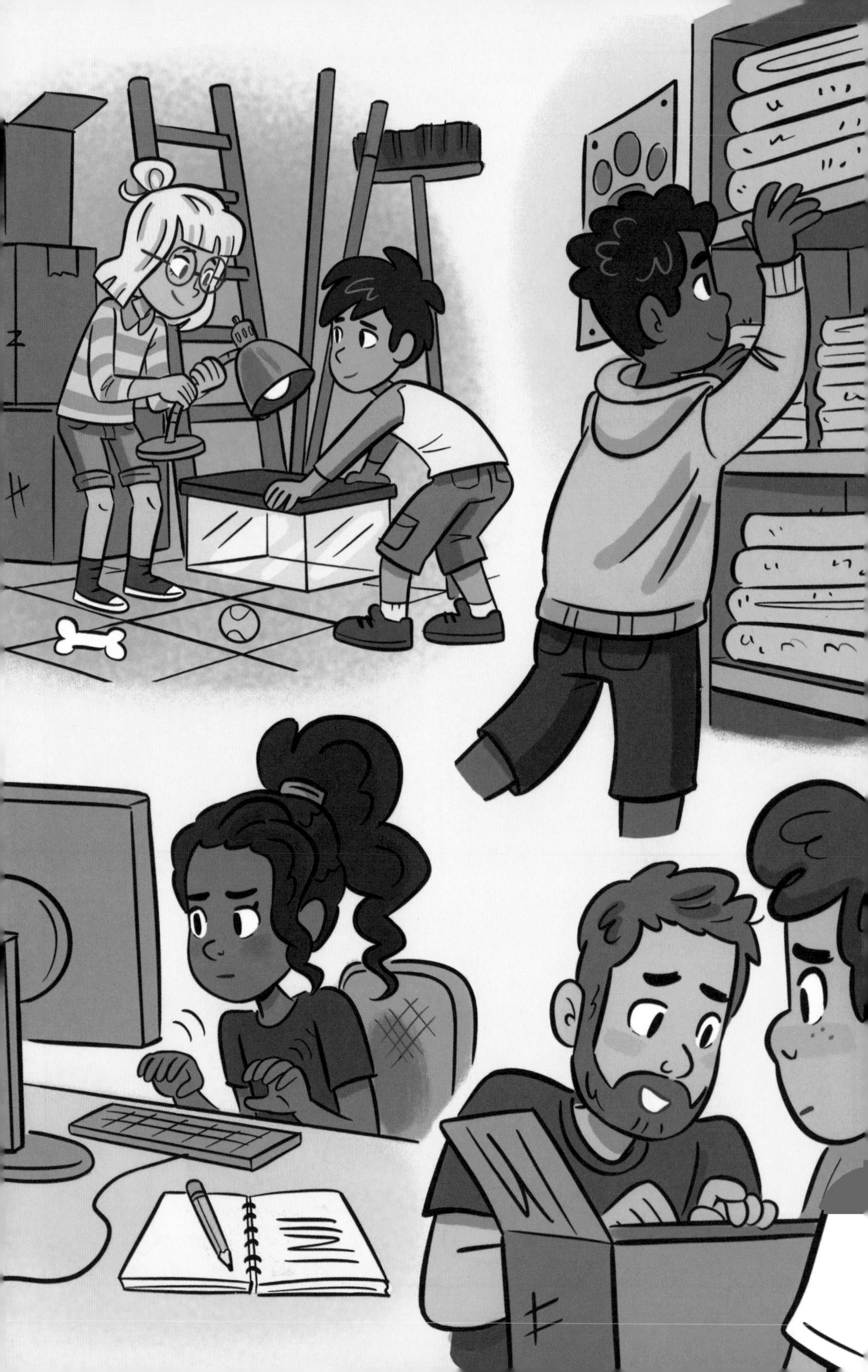

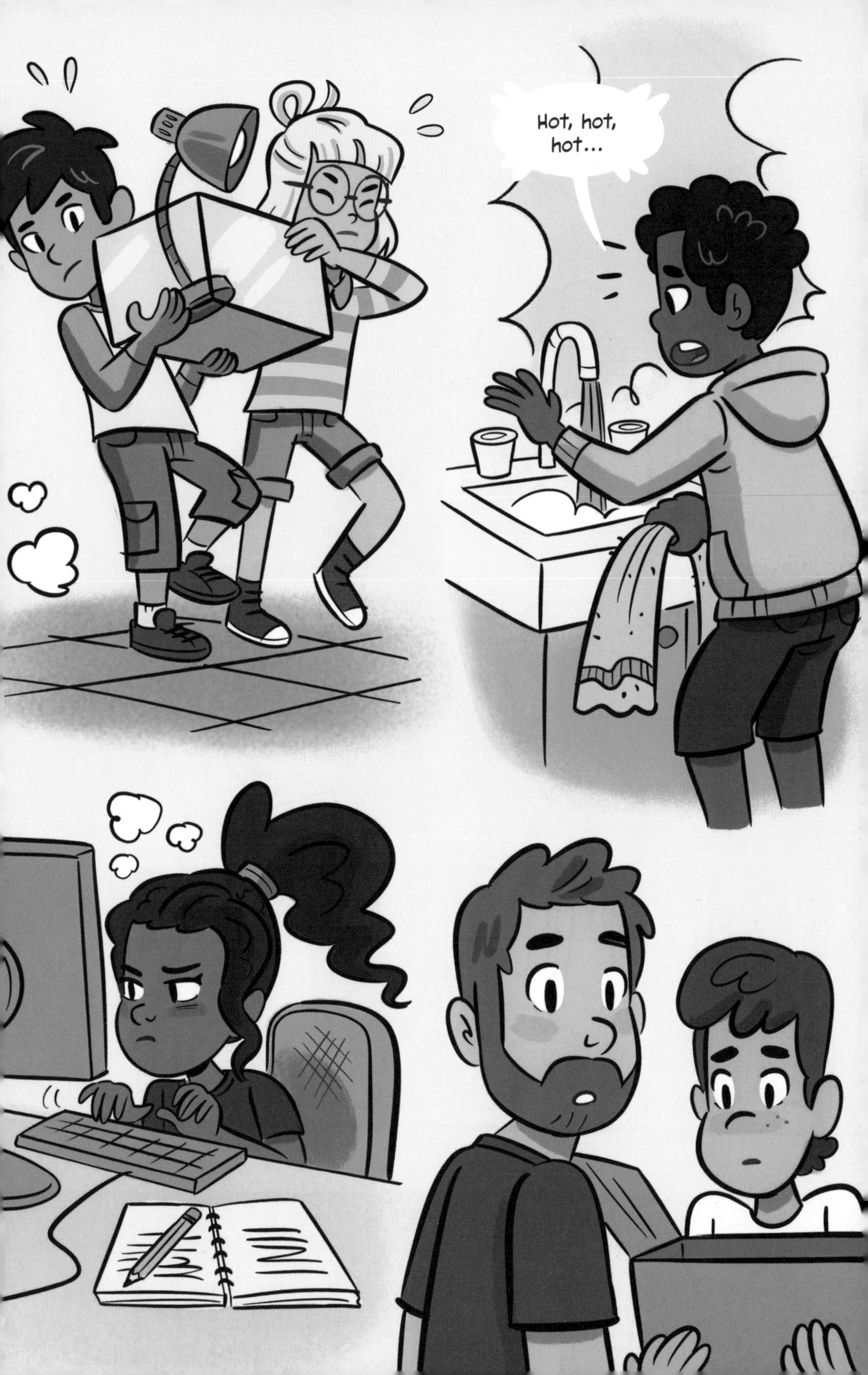
Hot, hot, hot...

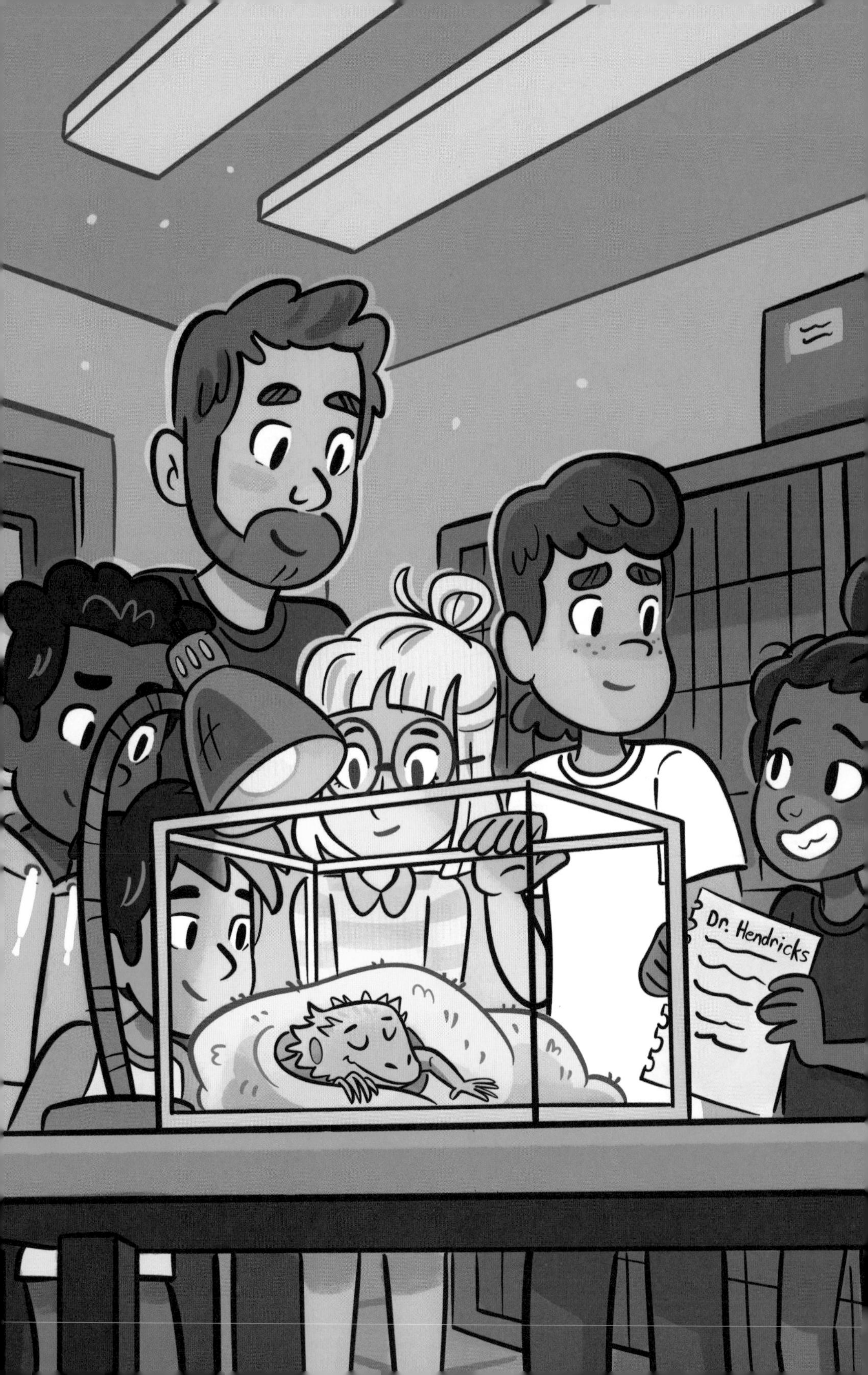
Dr. Hendricks

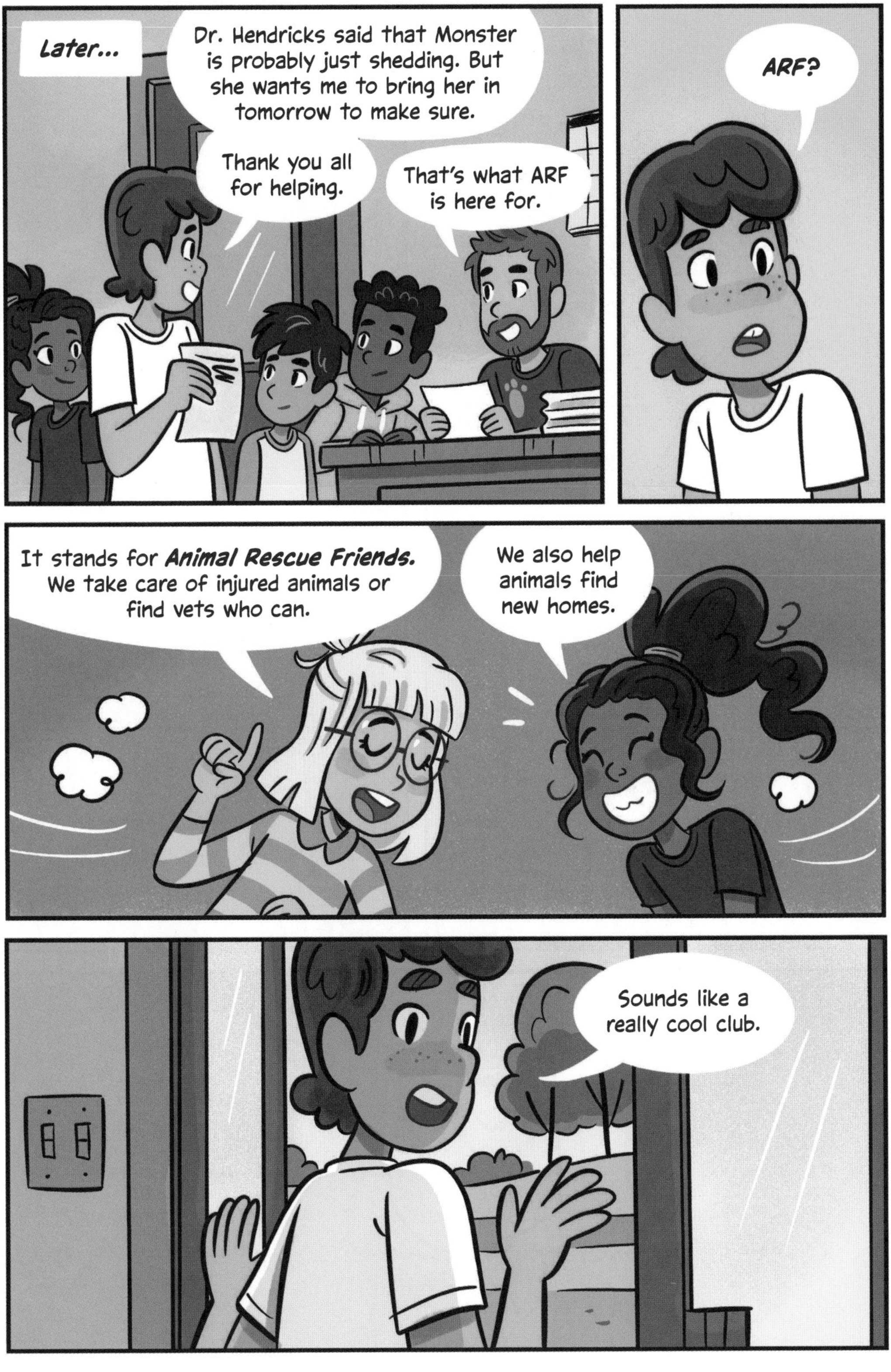
Later...
Dr. Hendricks said that Monster is probably just shedding. But she wants me to bring her in tomorrow to make sure.
Thank you all for helping.
That's what ARF is here for.
ARF?
It stands for ***Animal Rescue Friends.*** We take care of injured animals or find vets who can.
We also help animals find new homes.
Sounds like a really cool club.

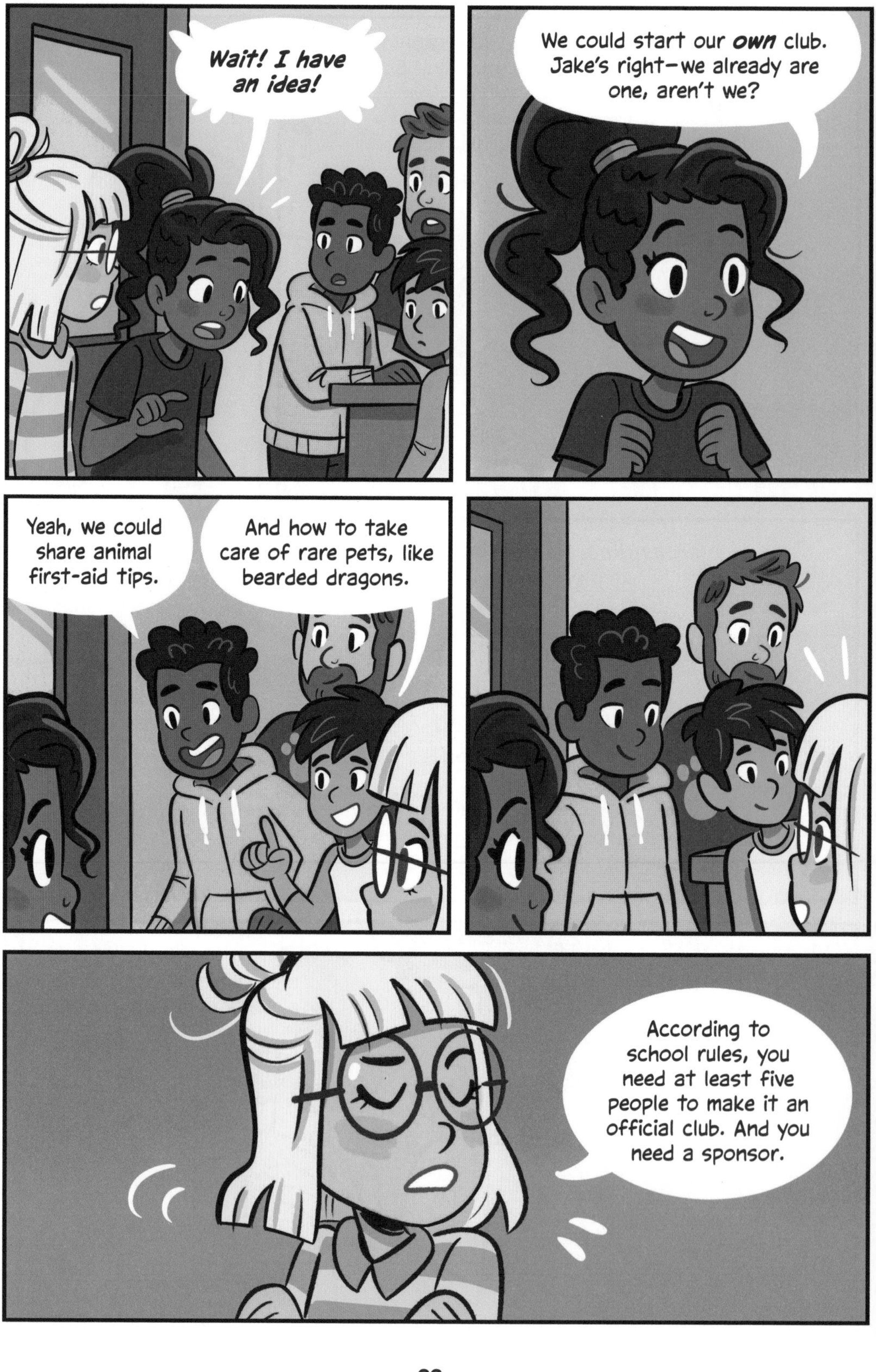
Wait! I have an idea!
We could start our own club. Jake's right—we already are one, aren't we?
Yeah, we could share animal first-aid tips.
And how to take care of rare pets, like bearded dragons.
According to school rules, you need at least five people to make it an official club. And you need a sponsor.

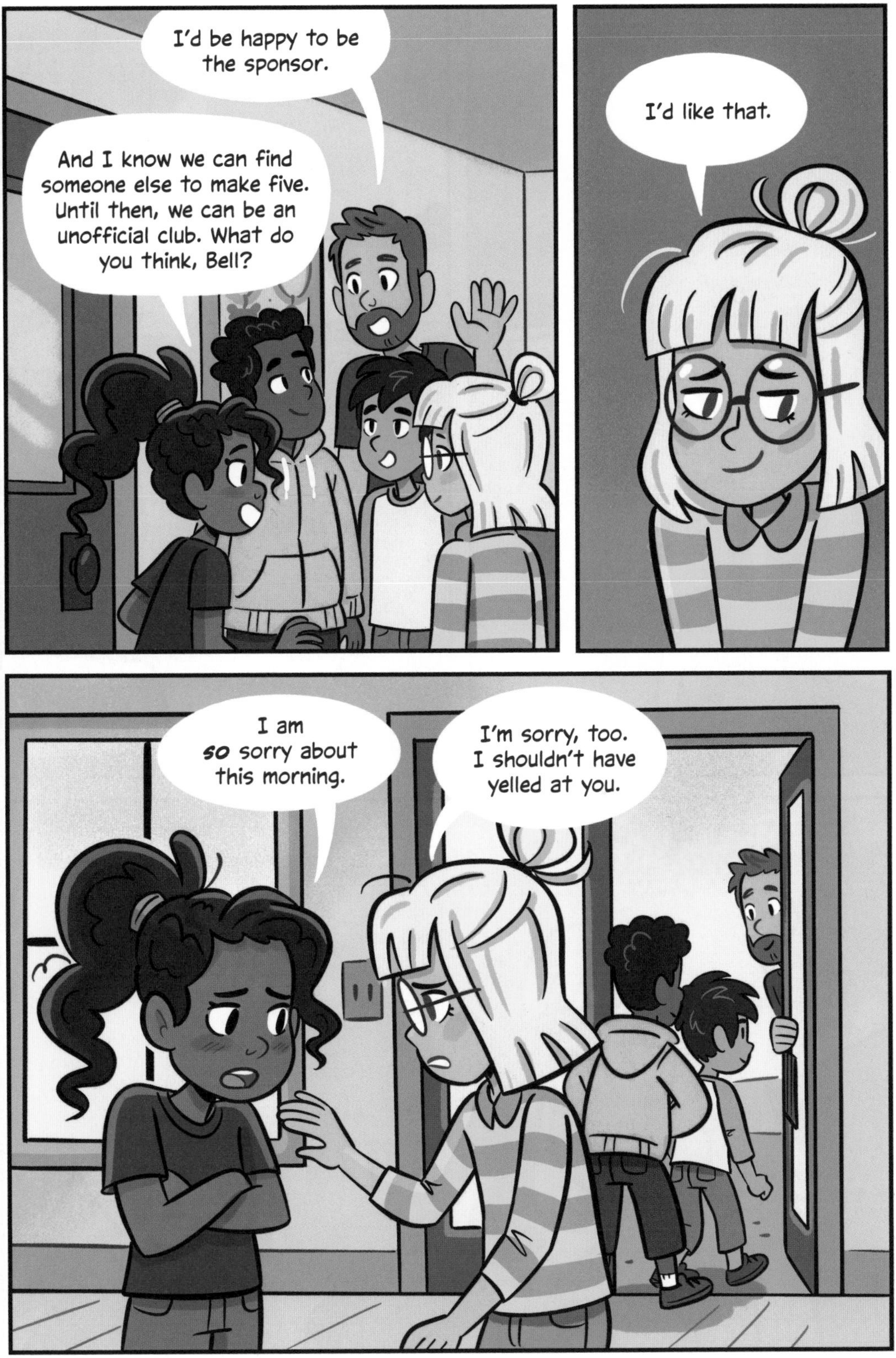
I'd be happy to be the sponsor.
And I know we can find someone else to make five. Until then, we can be an unofficial club. What do you think, Bell?
I'd like that.
I am *so* sorry about this morning.
I'm sorry, too. I shouldn't have yelled at you.

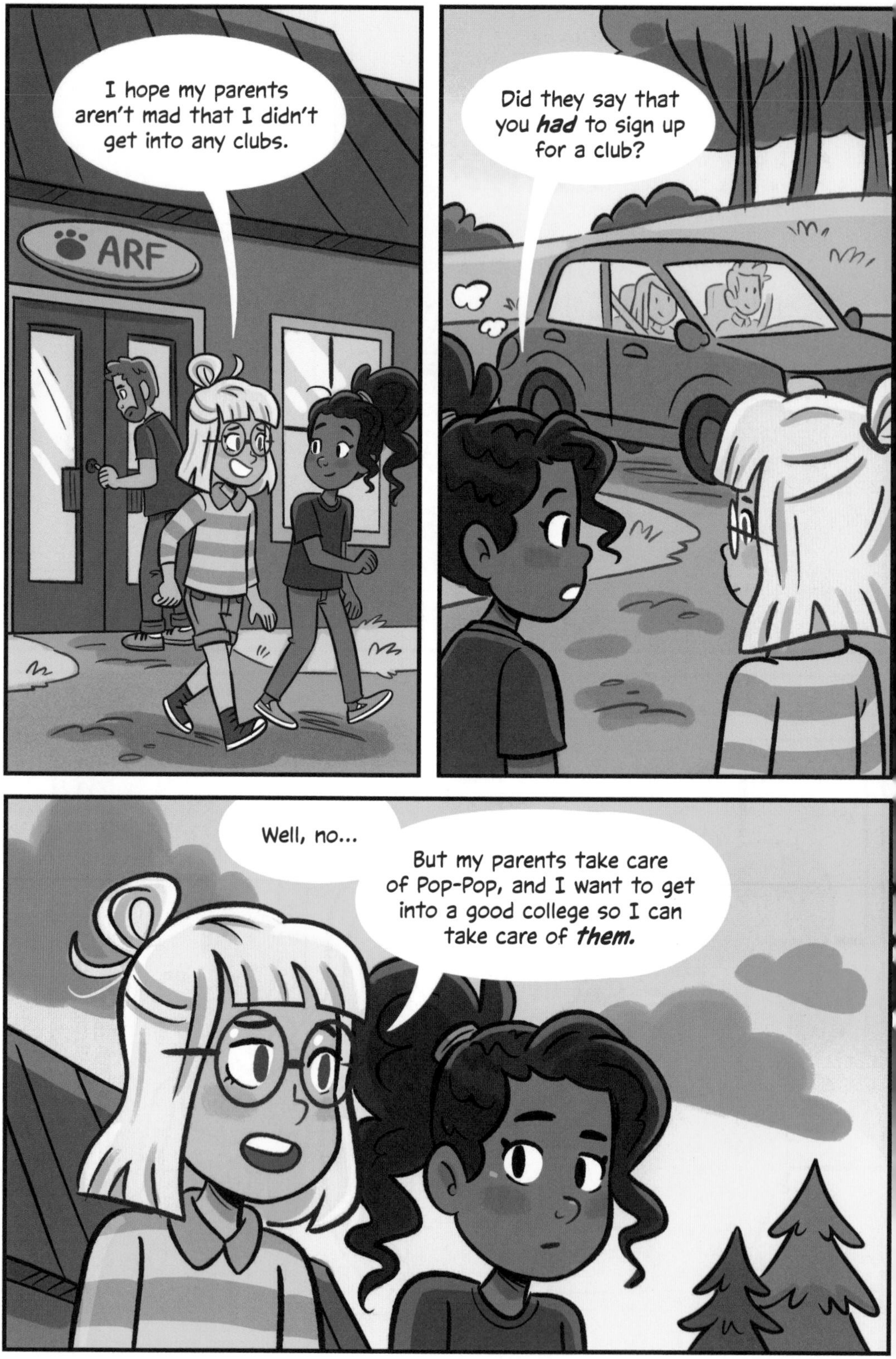
I hope my parents aren't mad that I didn't get into any clubs.
ARF
Did they say that you *had* to sign up for a club?
Well, no...
But my parents take care of Pop-Pop, and I want to get into a good college so I can take care of *them.*

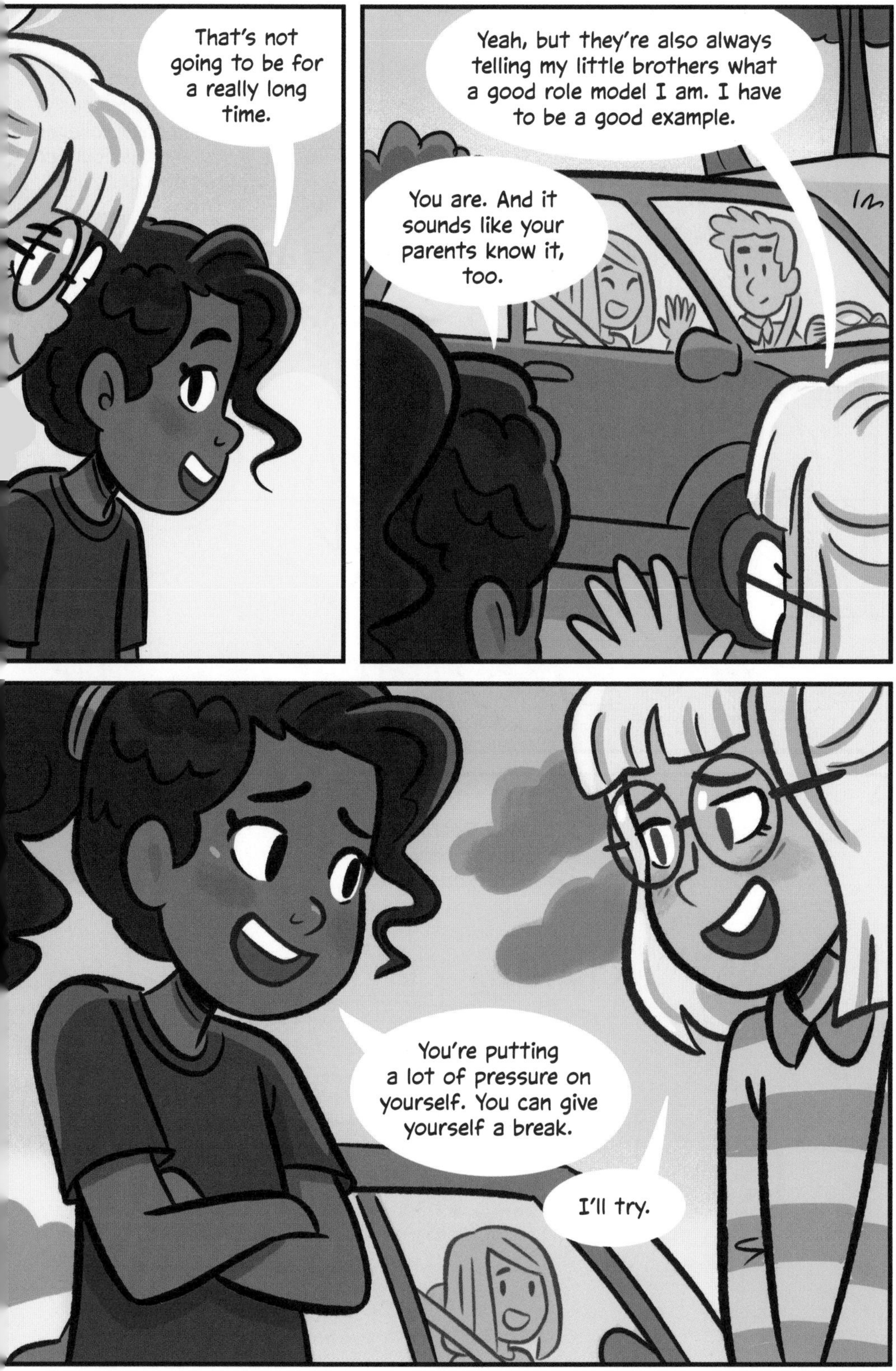
That's not going to be for a really long time.
Yeah, but they're also always telling my little brothers what a good role model I am. I have to be a good example.
You are. And it sounds like your parents know it, too.
You're putting a lot of pressure on yourself. You can give yourself a break.
I'll try.

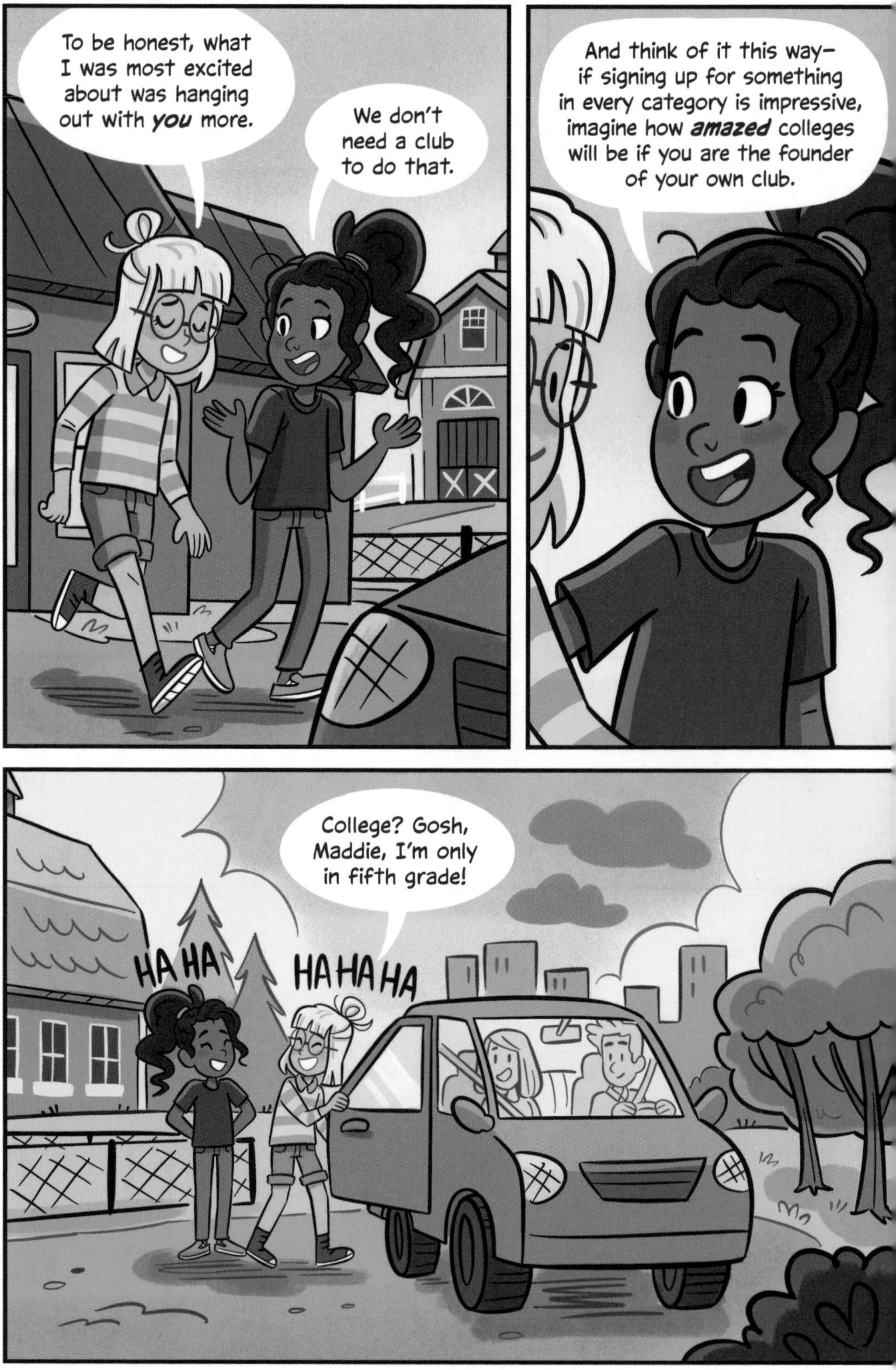
To be honest, what I was most excited about was hanging out with ***you*** more.
We don't need a club to do that.
And think of it this way–if signing up for something in every category is impressive, imagine how ***amazed*** colleges will be if you are the founder of your own club.
College? Gosh, Maddie, I'm only in fifth grade!
HA HA
HA HA HA

Chapter 2

BELL, JIMMY, AND KING JAMES POKEY McQUILLDUDE MILLER JR.

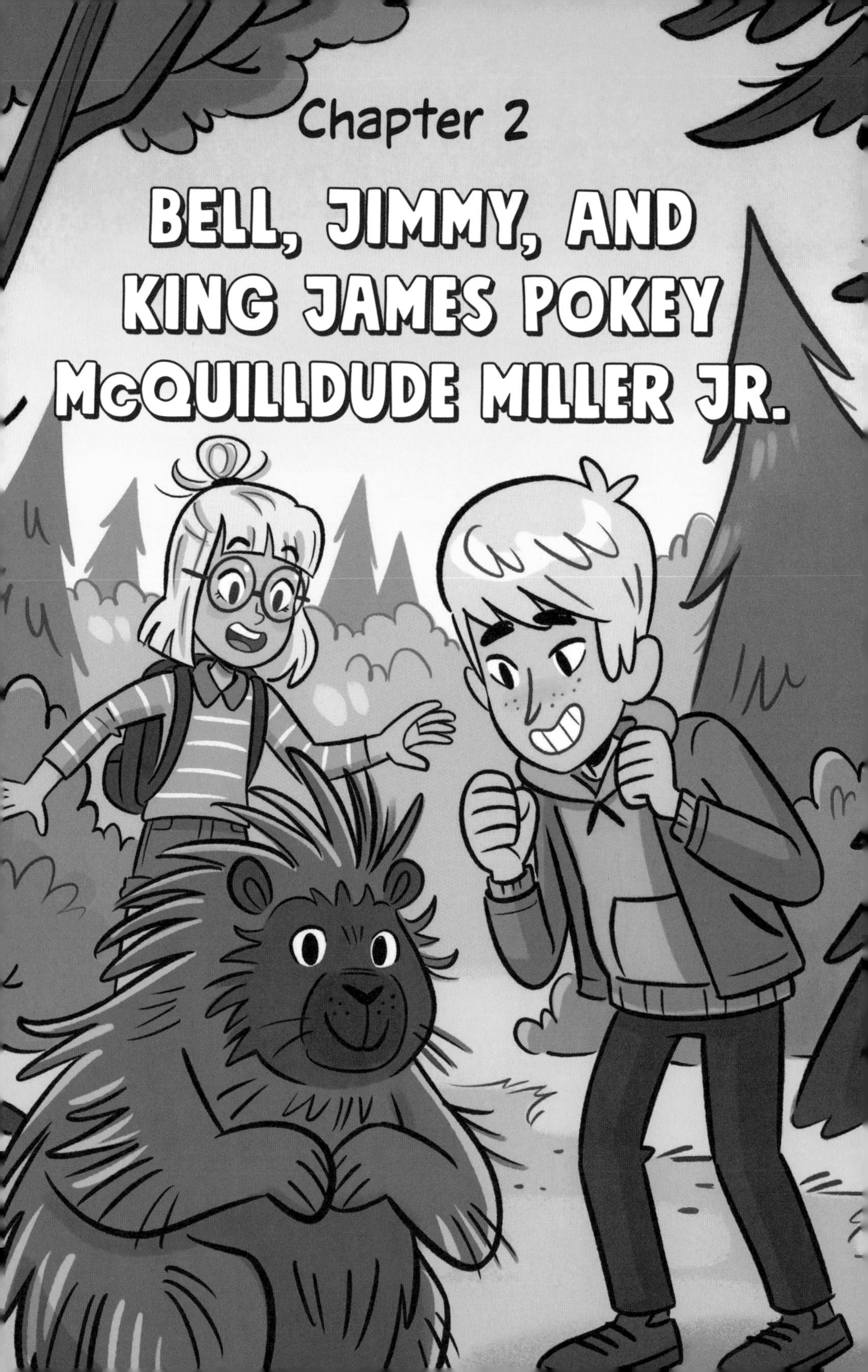

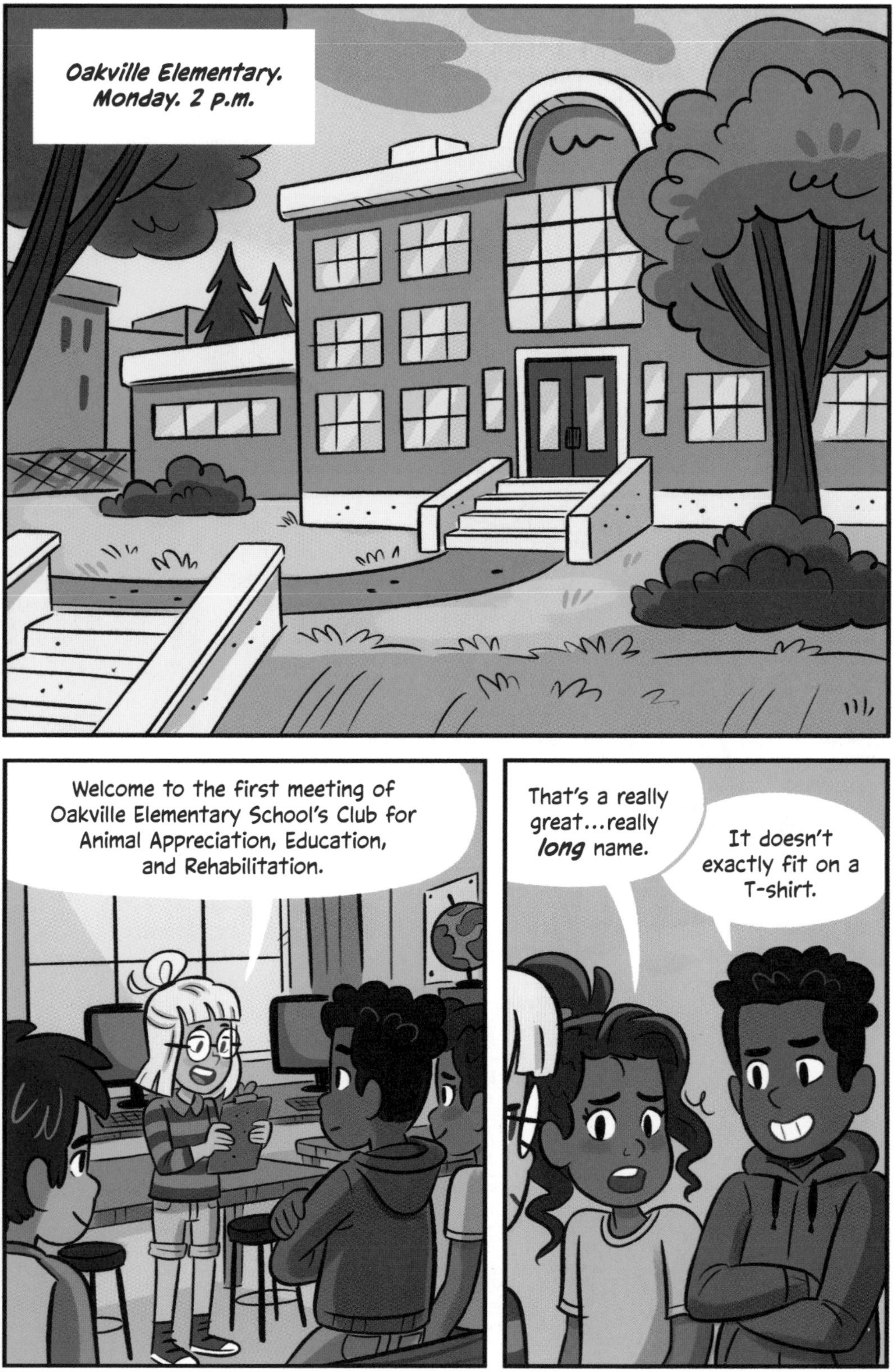
Oakville Elementary.
Monday. 2 p.m.
Welcome to the first meeting of Oakville Elementary School's Club for Animal Appreciation, Education, and Rehabilitation.
That's a really great...really *long* name.
It doesn't exactly fit on a T-shirt.

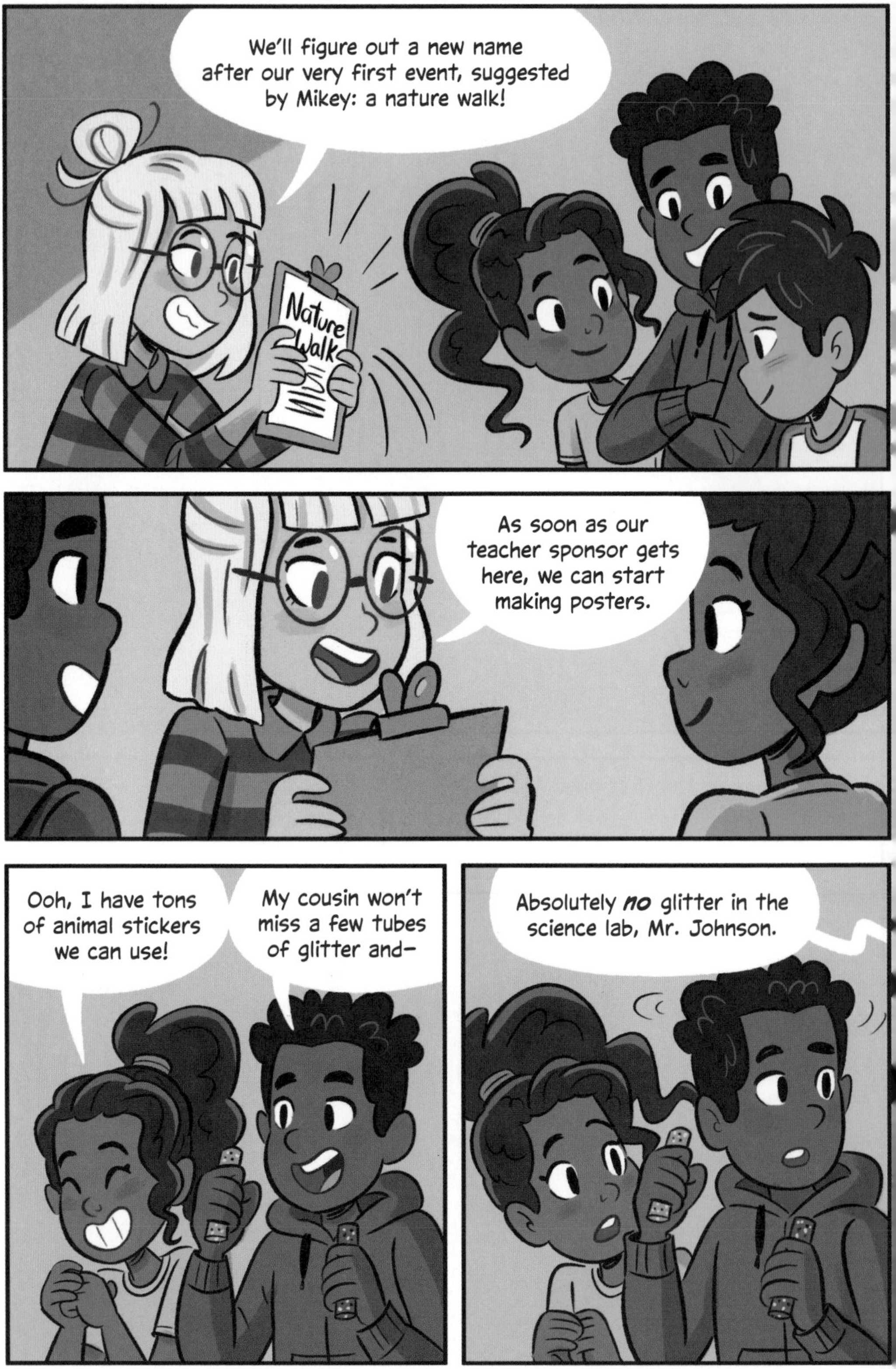
We'll figure out a new name after our very first event, suggested by Mikey: a nature walk!
Nature Walk
As soon as our teacher sponsor gets here, we can start making posters.
Ooh, I have tons of animal stickers we can use!
My cousin won't miss a few tubes of glitter and—
Absolutely *no* glitter in the science lab, Mr. Johnson.

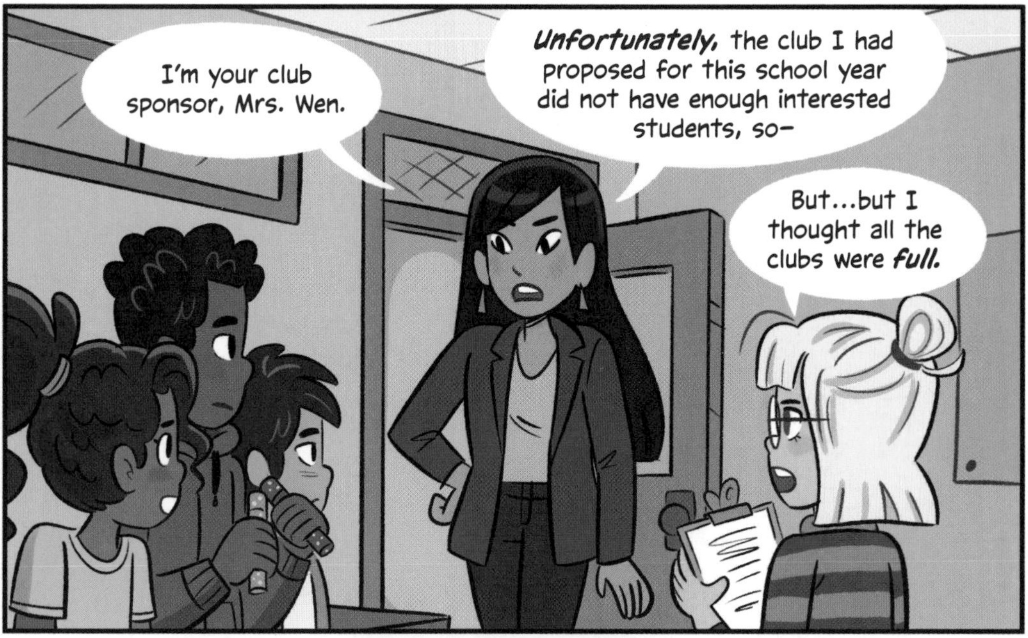
I'm your club sponsor, Mrs. Wen.
Unfortunately, the club I had proposed for this school year did not have enough interested students, so–
But...but I thought all the clubs were *full.*

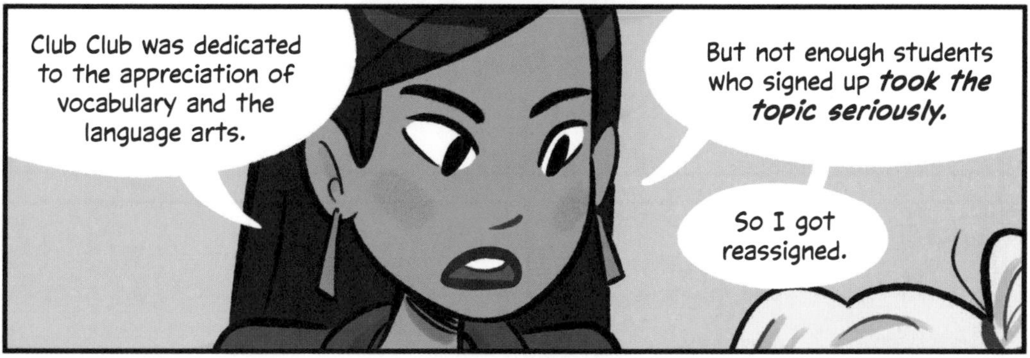
Club Club was dedicated to the appreciation of vocabulary and the language arts.
But not enough students who signed up *took the topic seriously.*
So I got reassigned.

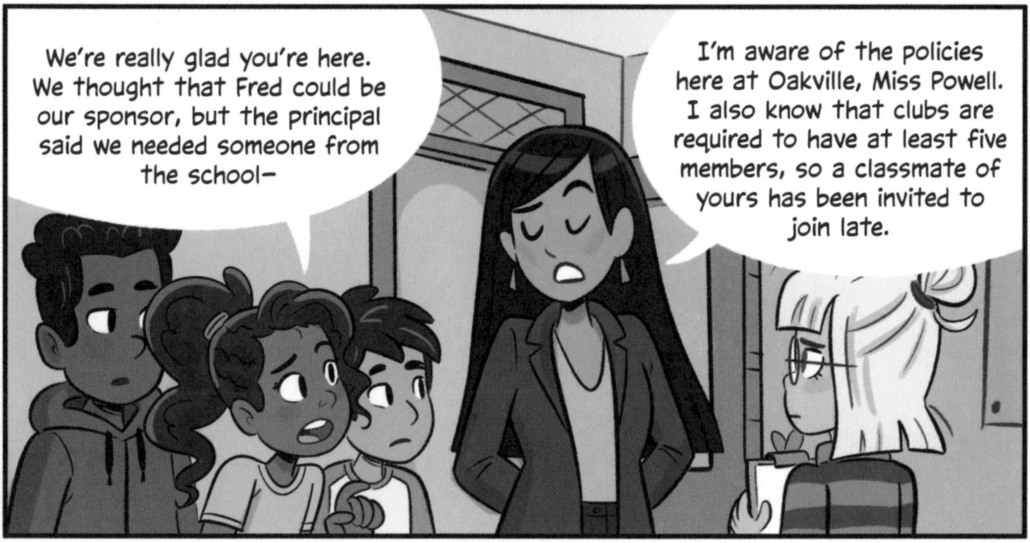
We're really glad you're here. We thought that Fred could be our sponsor, but the principal said we needed someone from the school–
I'm aware of the policies here at Oakville, Miss Powell. I also know that clubs are required to have at least five members, so a classmate of yours has been invited to join late.

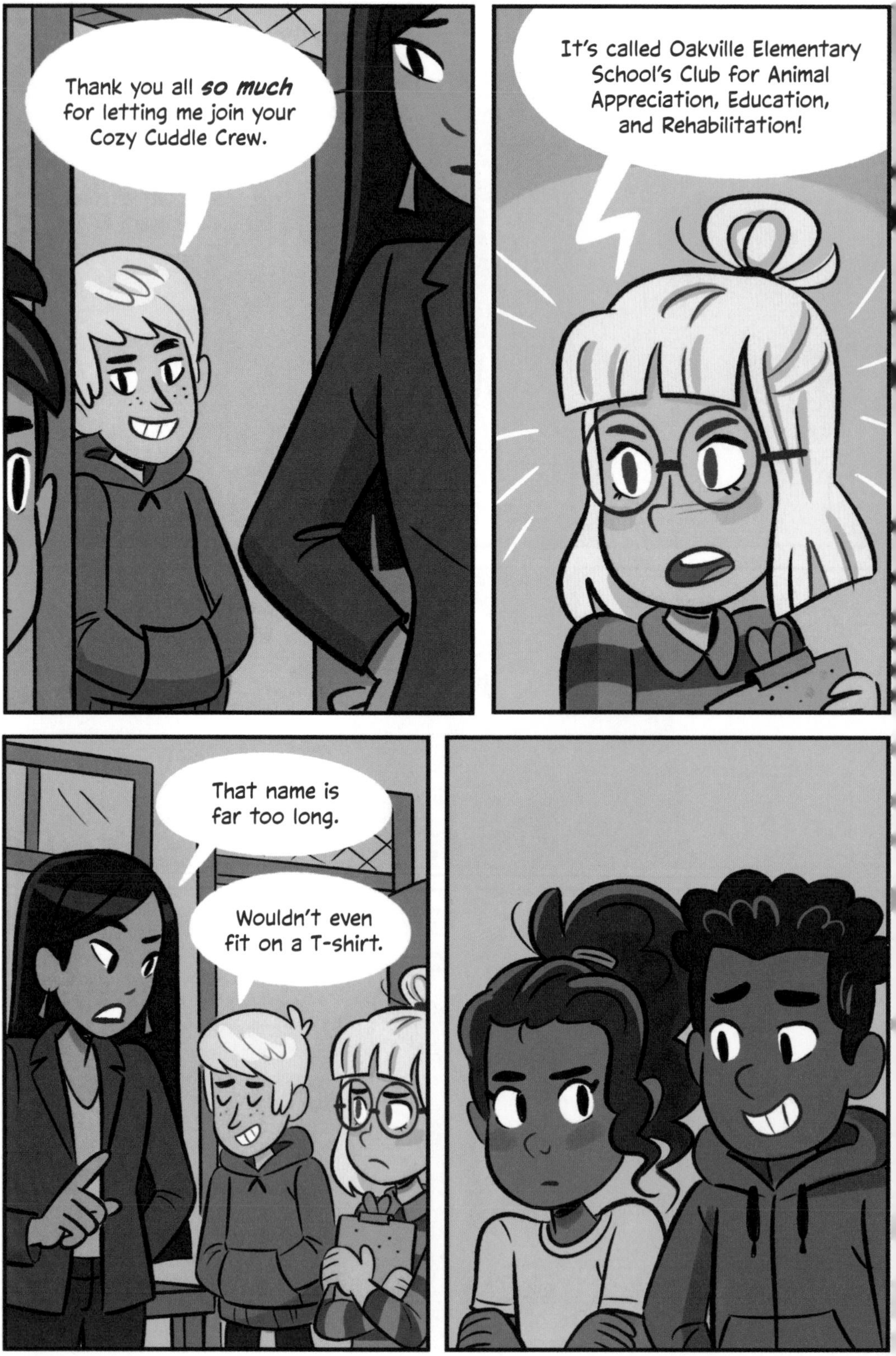
Thank you all *so much* for letting me join your Cozy Cuddle Crew.
It's called Oakville Elementary School's Club for Animal Appreciation, Education, and Rehabilitation!
That name is far too long.
Wouldn't even fit on a T-shirt.

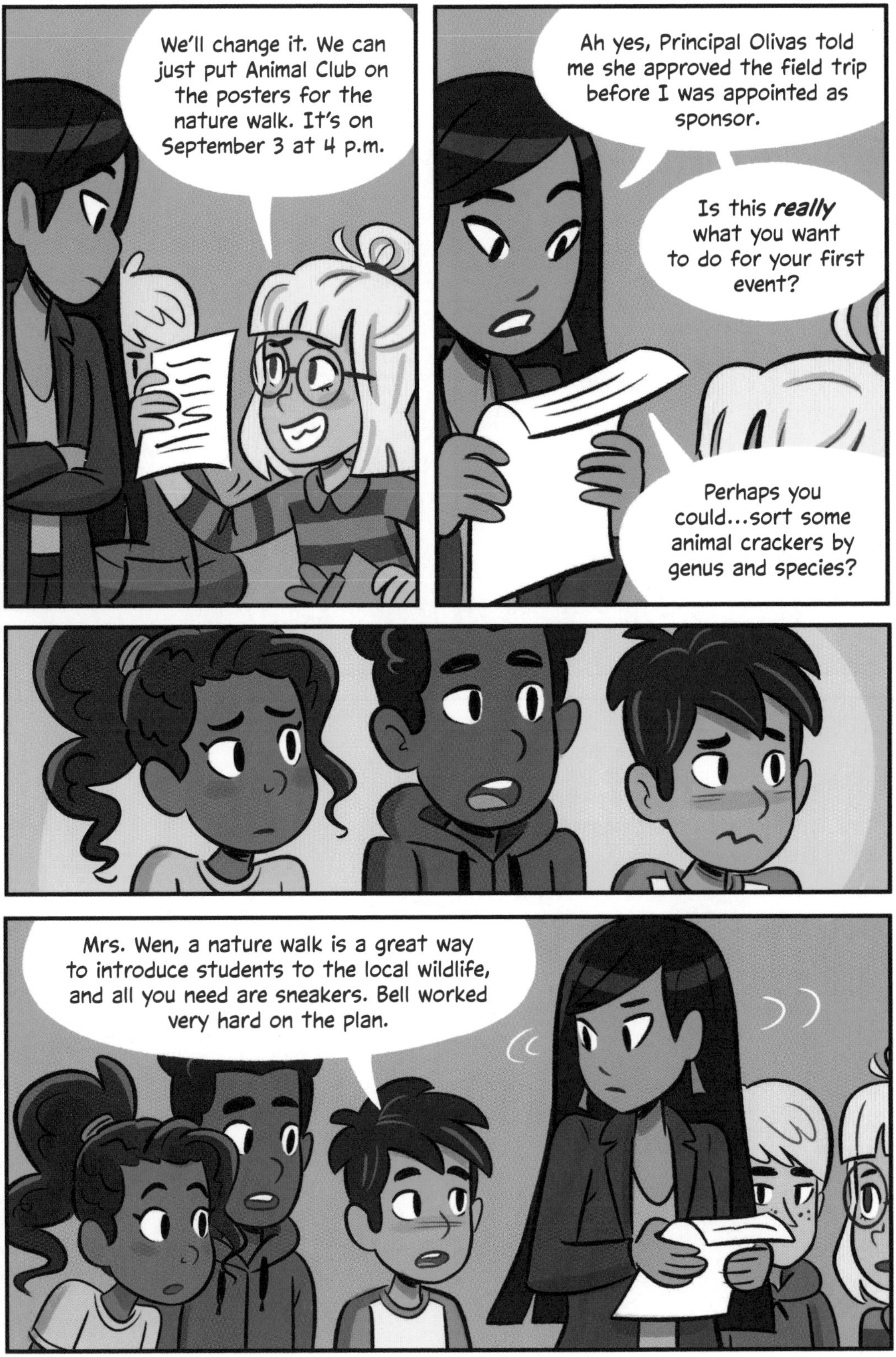
We'll change it. We can just put Animal Club on the posters for the nature walk. It's on September 3 at 4 p.m.
Ah yes, Principal Olivas told me she approved the field trip before I was appointed as sponsor.
Is this *really* what you want to do for your first event?
Perhaps you could...sort some animal crackers by genus and species?
Mrs. Wen, a nature walk is a great way to introduce students to the local wildlife, and all you need are sneakers. Bell worked very hard on the plan.

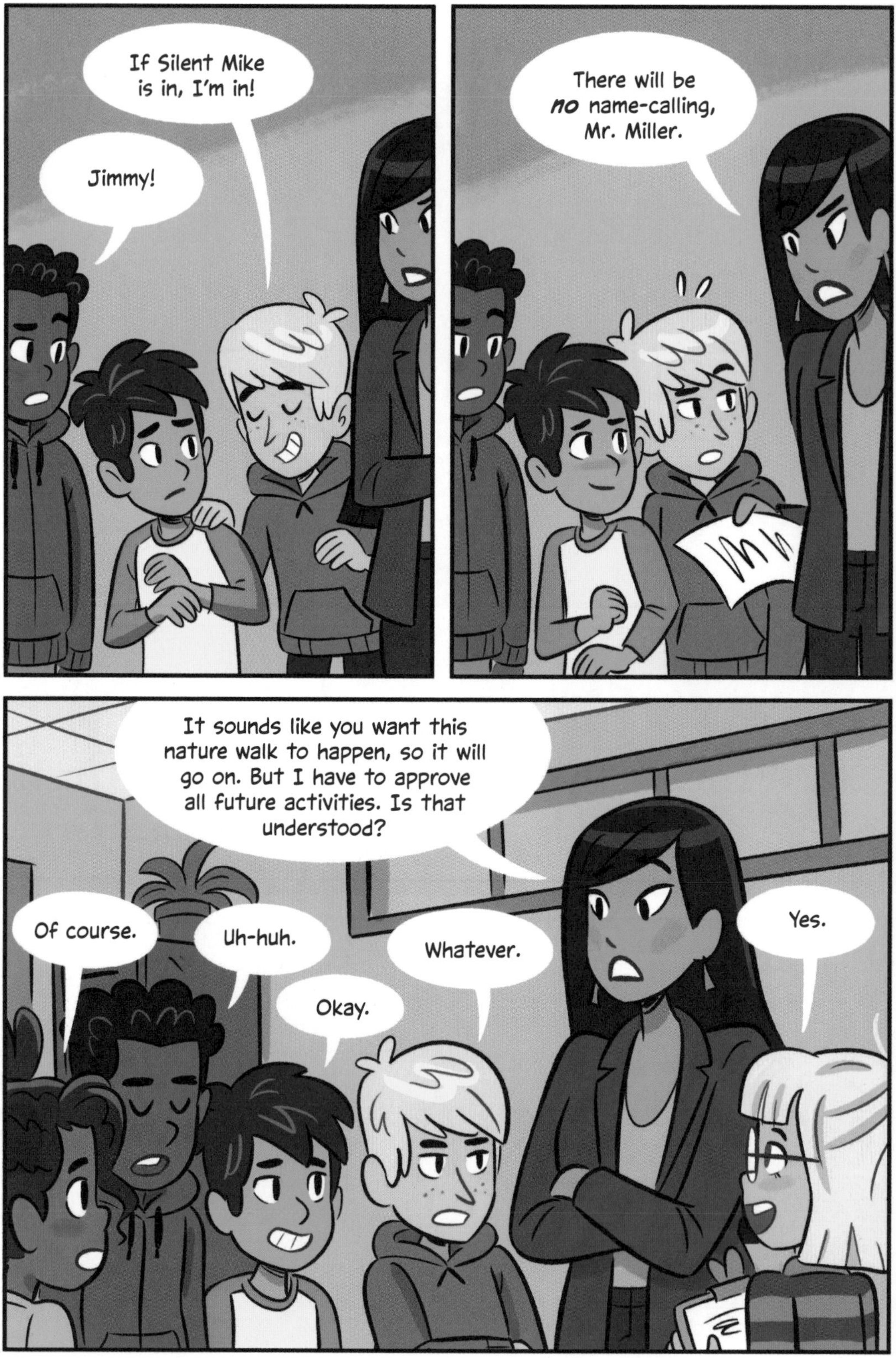
If Silent Mike is in, I'm in!
Jimmy!
There will be *no* name-calling, Mr. Miller.
It sounds like you want this nature walk to happen, so it will go on. But I have to approve all future activities. Is that understood?
Of course.
Uh-huh.
Okay.
Whatever.
Yes.

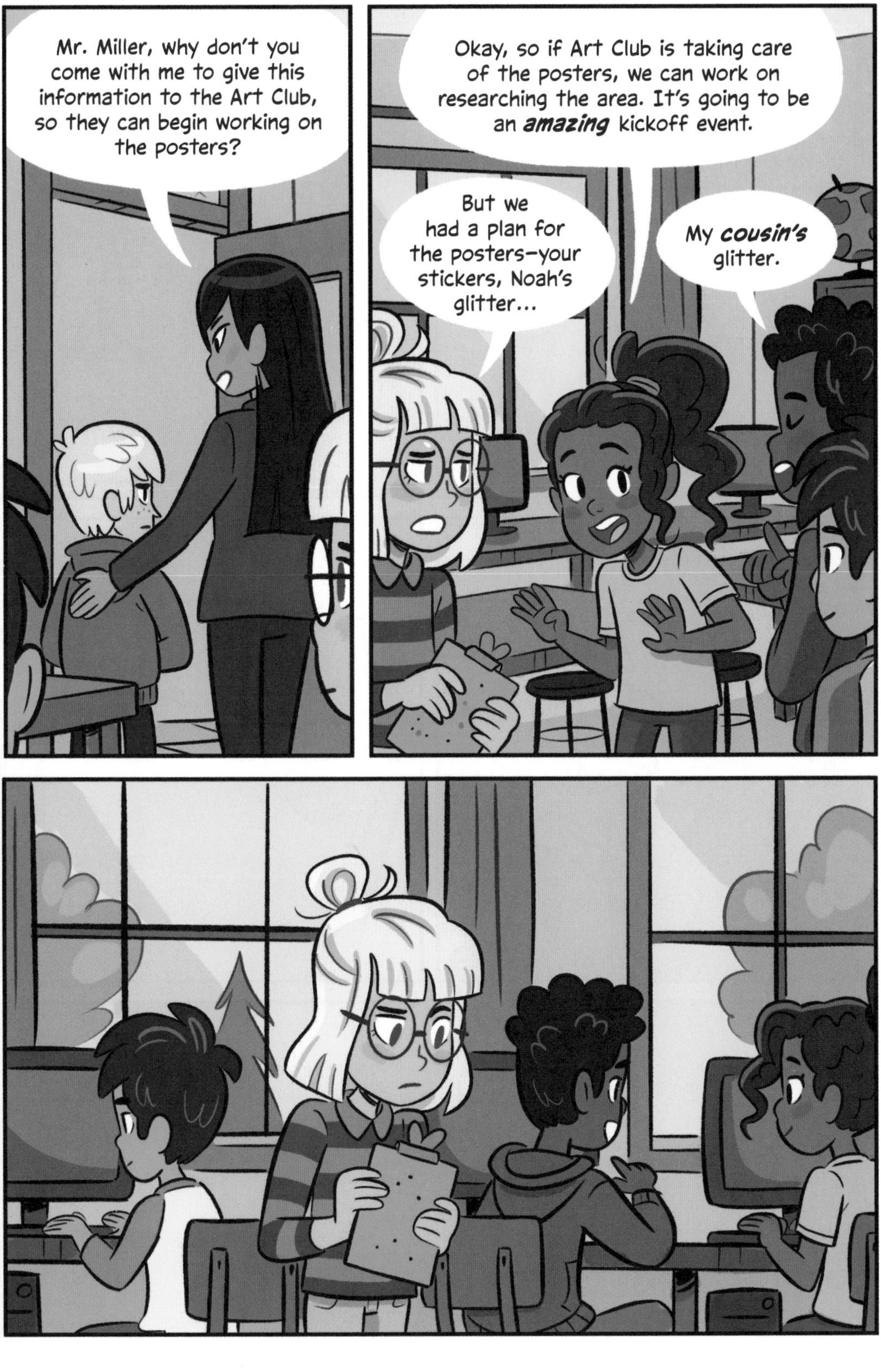
Mr. Miller, why don't you come with me to give this information to the Art Club, so they can begin working on the posters?
Okay, so if Art Club is taking care of the posters, we can work on researching the area. It's going to be an *amazing* kickoff event.
But we had a plan for the posters—your stickers, Noah's glitter...
My *cousin's* glitter.

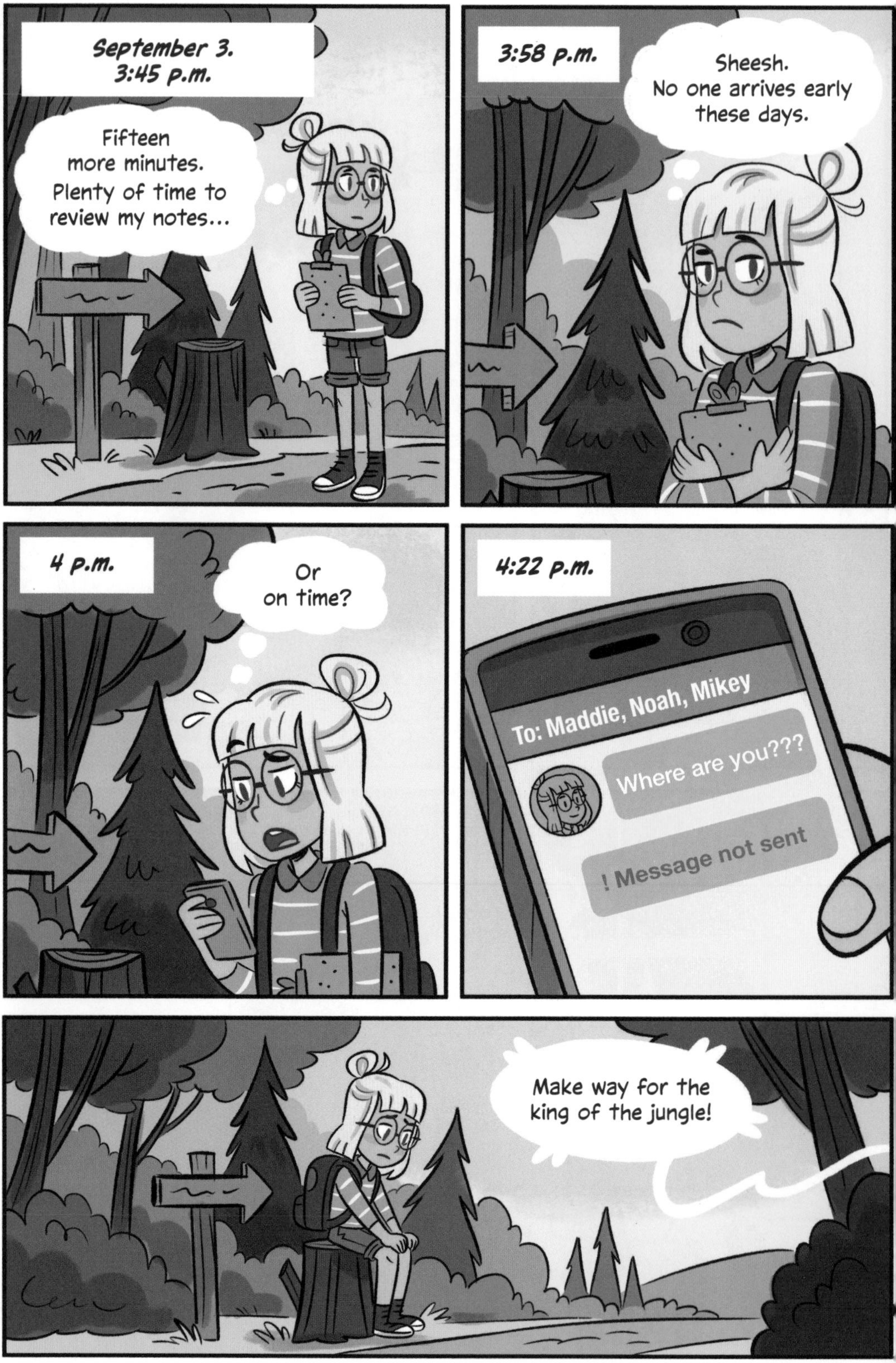
September 3.
3:45 p.m.
Fifteen more minutes. Plenty of time to review my notes...
3:58 p.m.
Sheesh. No one arrives early these days.
4 p.m.
Or on time?
4:22 p.m.
To: Maddie, Noah, Mikey
Where are you???
! Message not sent
Make way for the king of the jungle!

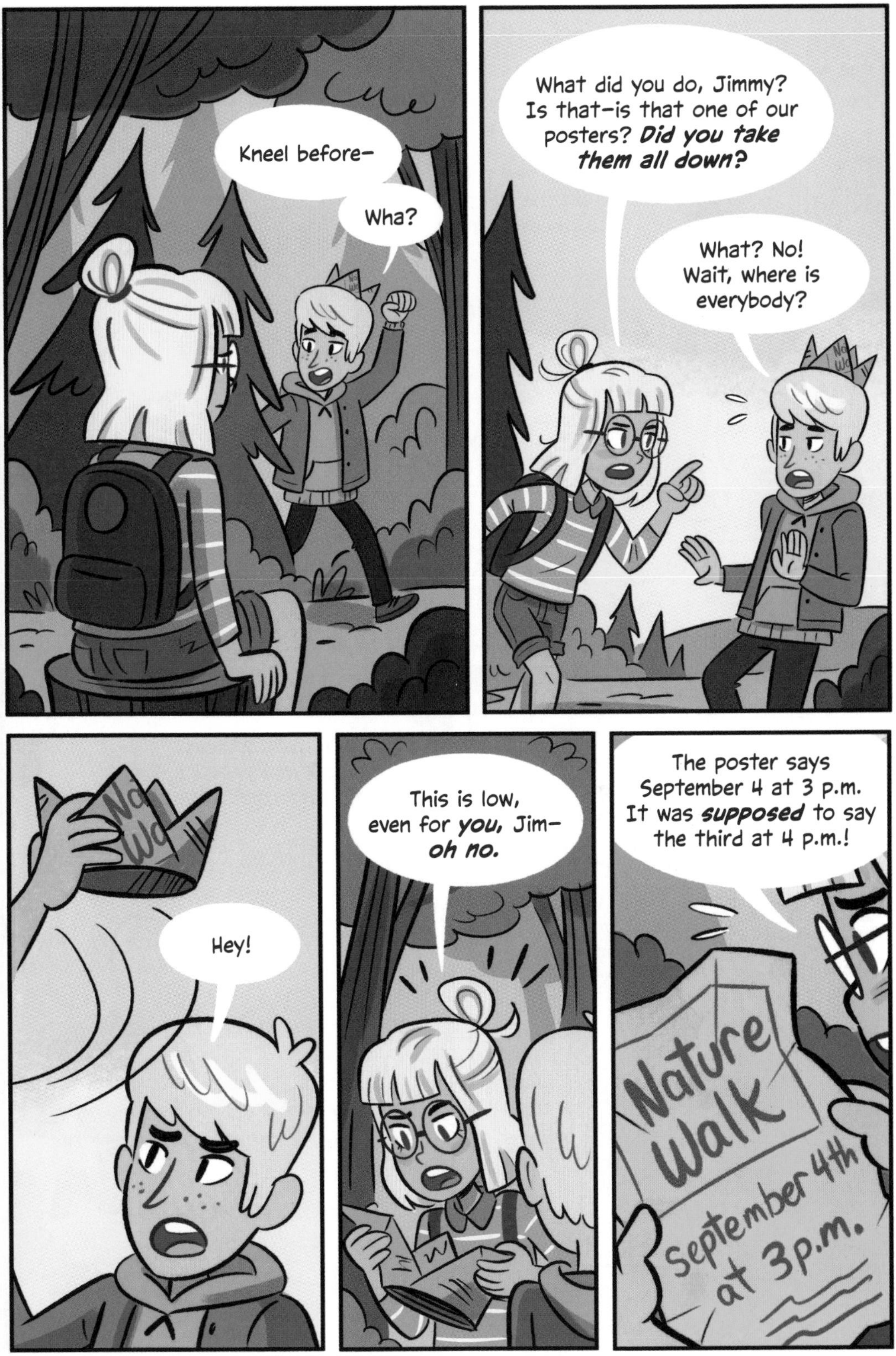
Kneel before-
Wha?
What did you do, Jimmy? Is that-is that one of our posters? ***Did you take them all down?***
What? No! Wait, where is everybody?
Hey!
This is low, even for *you,* Jim- ***oh no.***
The poster says September 4 at 3 p.m. It was ***supposed*** to say the third at 4 p.m.!
Nature Walk
September 4th at 3p.m.

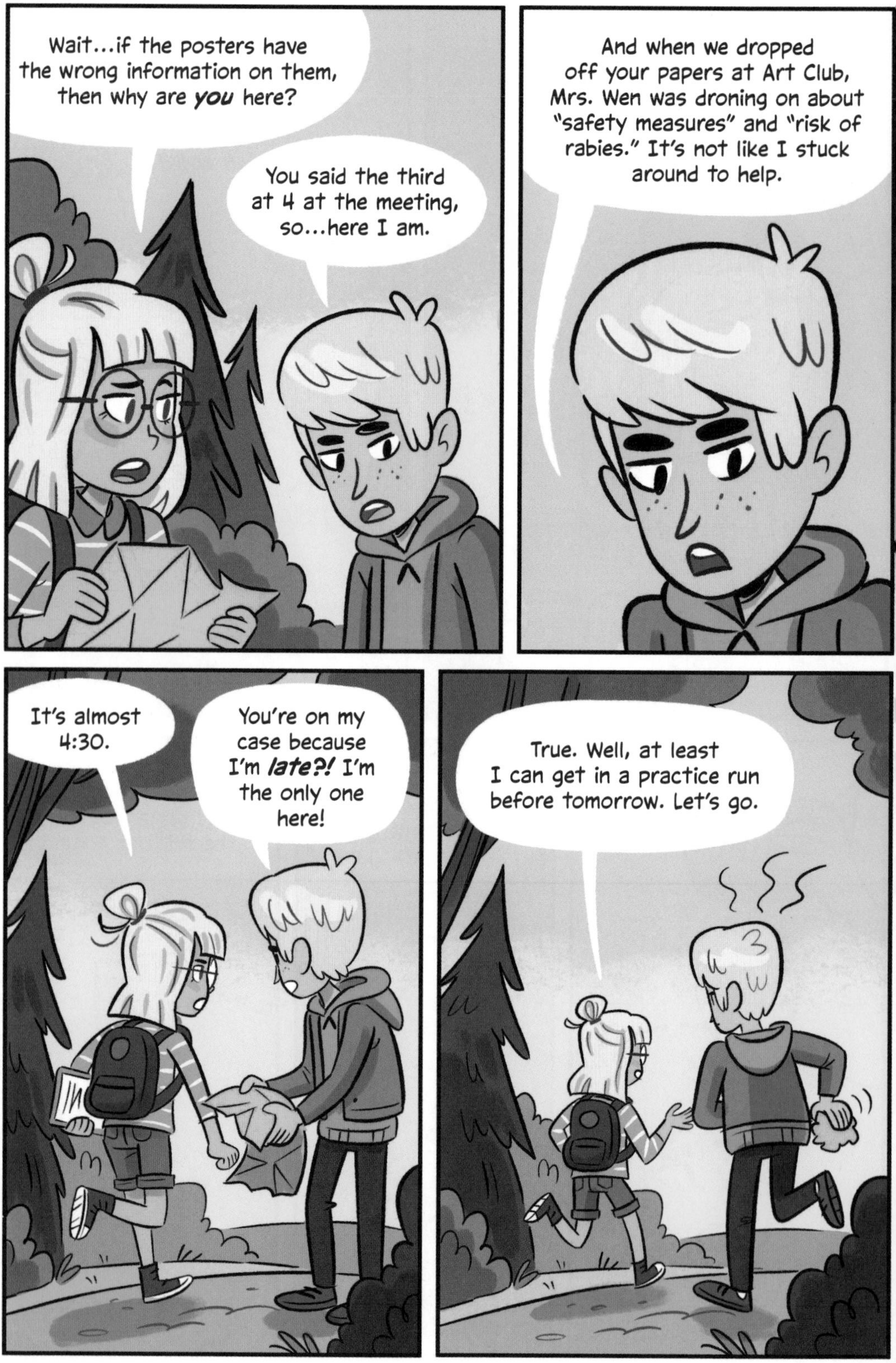
Wait...if the posters have the wrong information on them, then why are *you* here?
You said the third at 4 at the meeting, so...here I am.
And when we dropped off your papers at Art Club, Mrs. Wen was droning on about "safety measures" and "risk of rabies." It's not like I stuck around to help.
It's almost 4:30.
You're on my case because I'm *late?!* I'm the only one here!
True. Well, at least I can get in a practice run before tomorrow. Let's go.

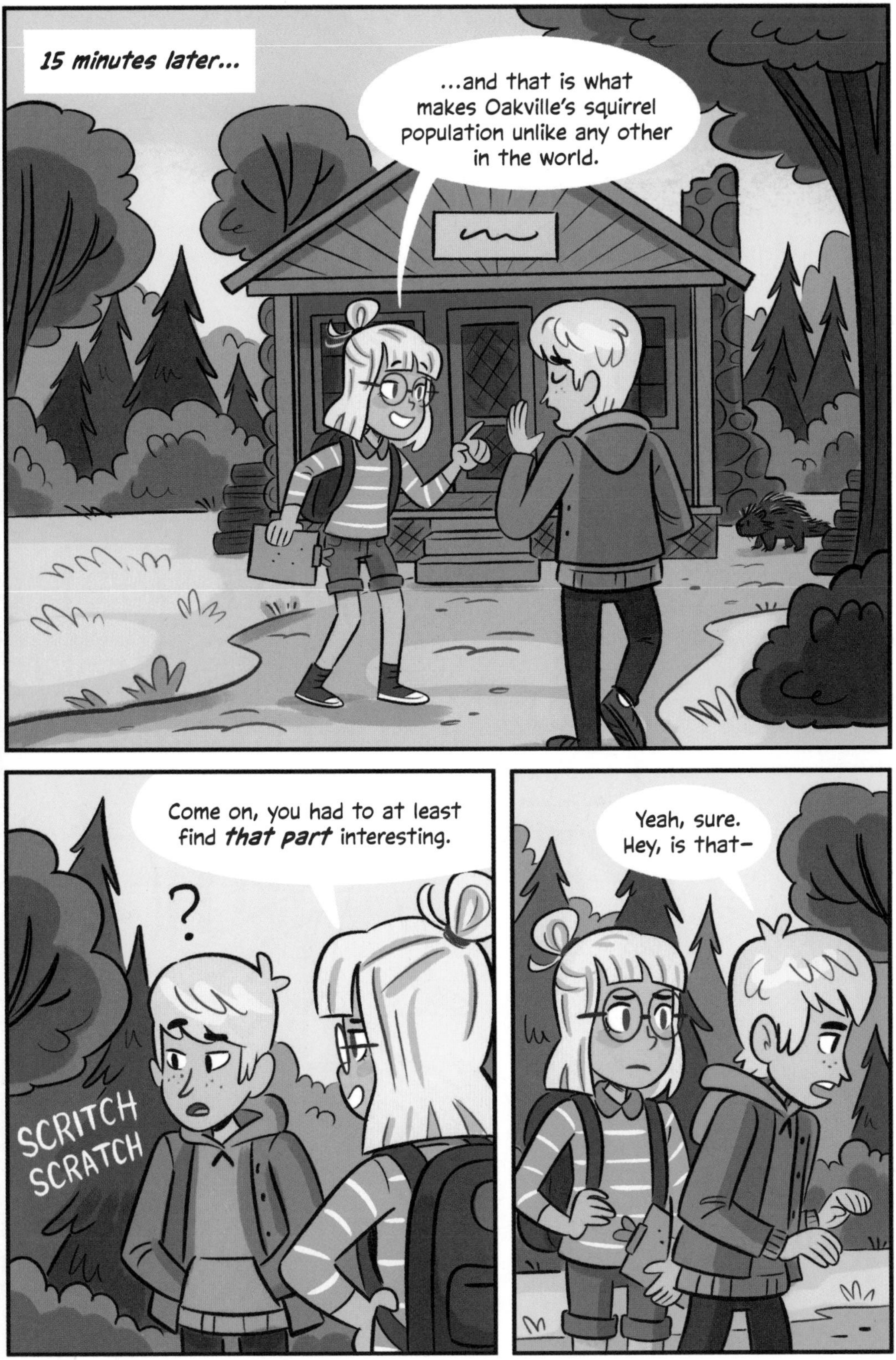

15 minutes later...
...and that is what makes Oakville's squirrel population unlike any other in the world.
Come on, you had to at least find ***that part*** interesting.
?
SCRITCH SCRATCH
Yeah, sure. Hey, is that–

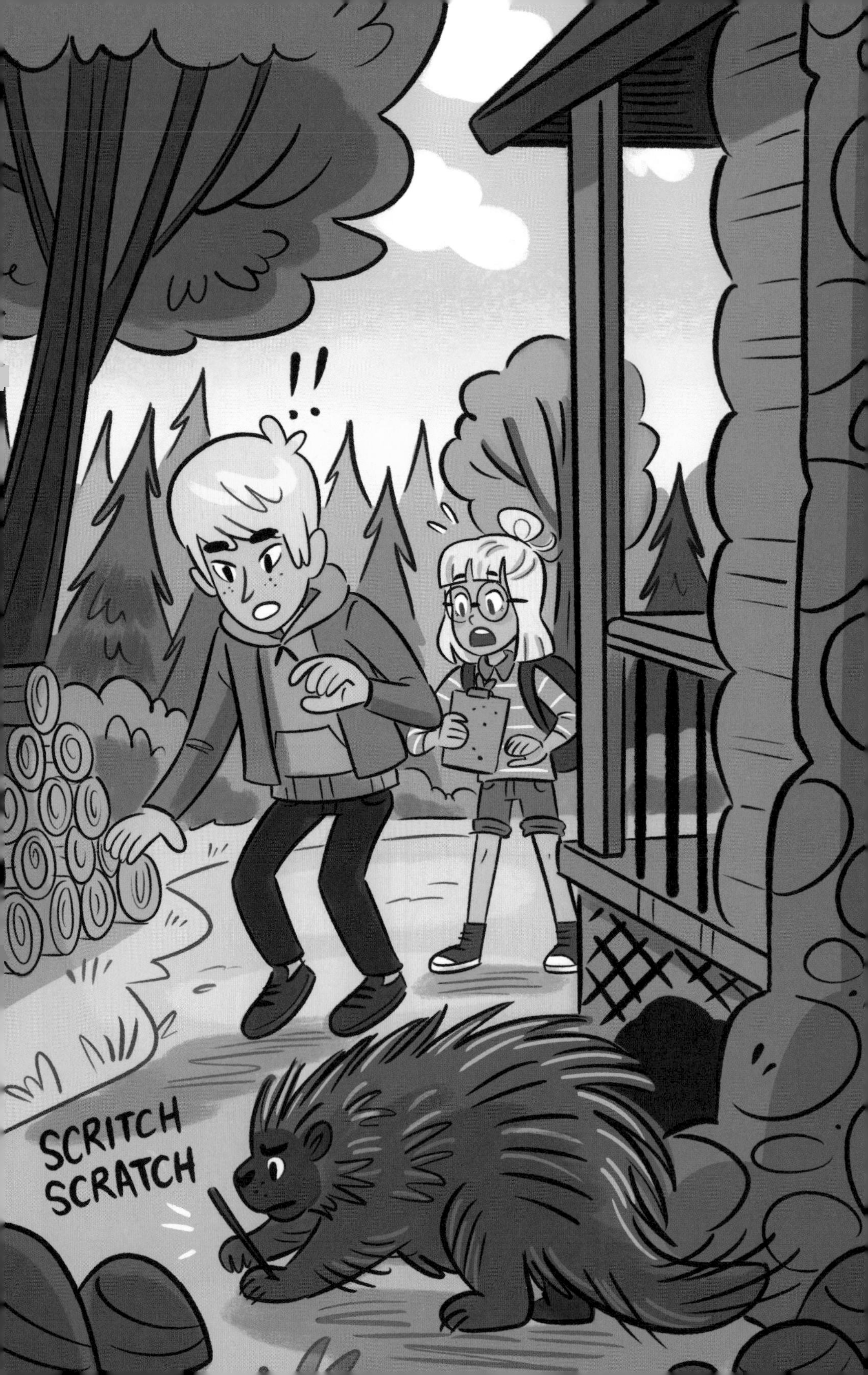
!!
SCRITCH
SCRATCH

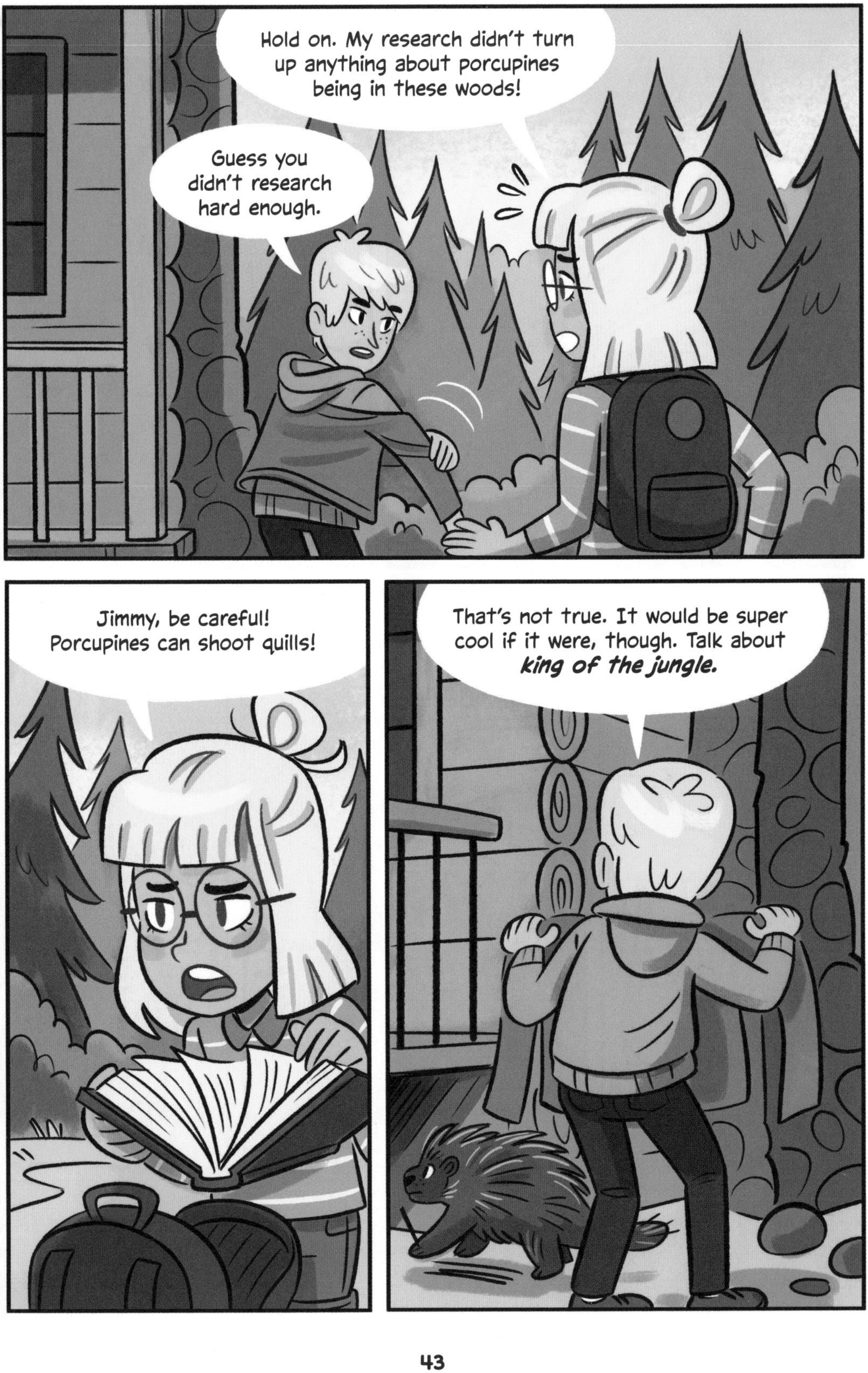
Hold on. My research didn't turn up anything about porcupines being in these woods!
Guess you didn't research hard enough.
Jimmy, be careful! Porcupines can shoot quills!
That's not true. It would be super cool if it were, though. Talk about *king of the jungle.*

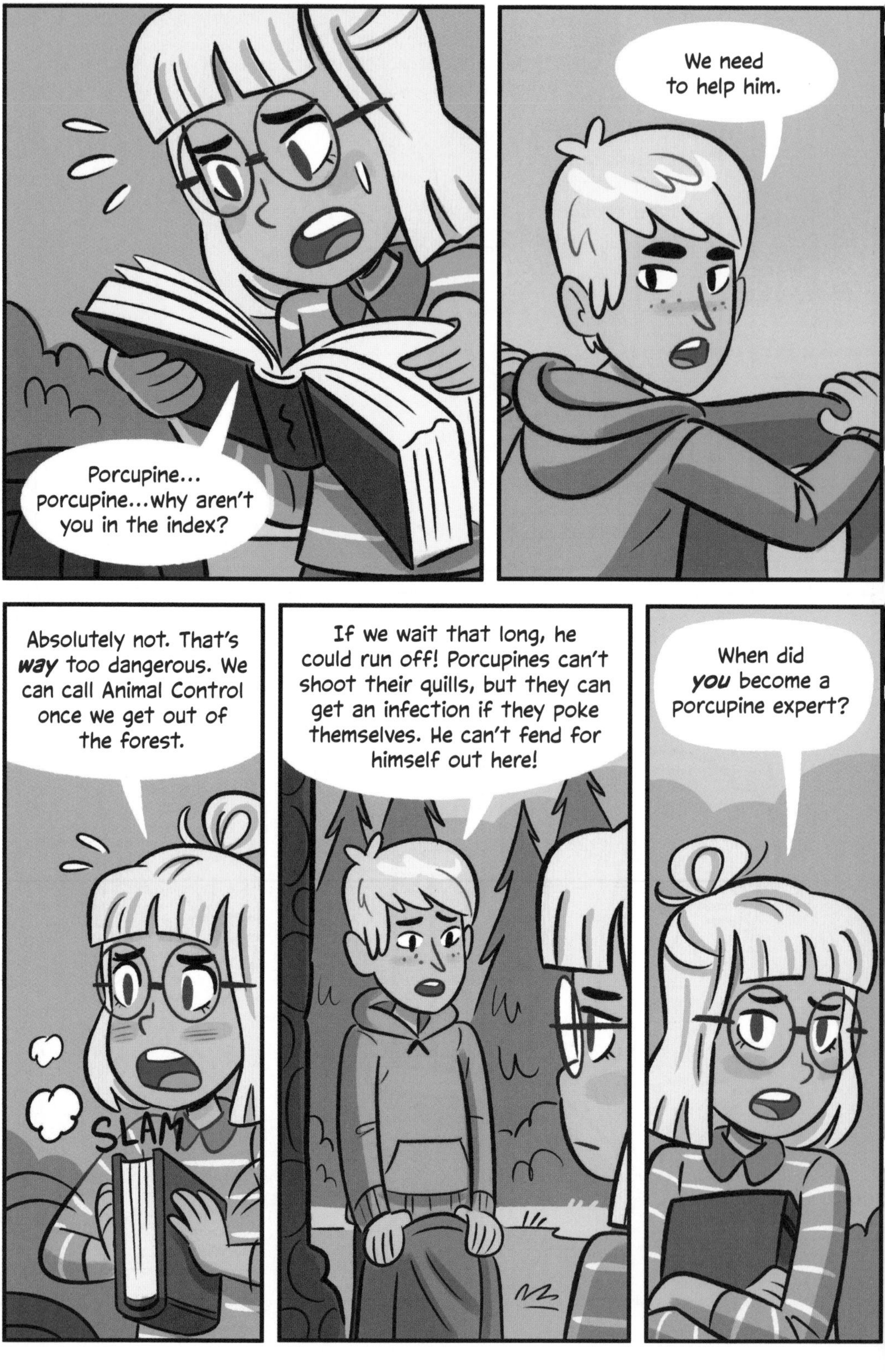
Porcupine... porcupine...why aren't you in the index?
We need to help him.
Absolutely not. That's *way* too dangerous. We can call Animal Control once we get out of the forest.
SLAM
If we wait that long, he could run off! Porcupines can't shoot their quills, but they can get an infection if they poke themselves. He can't fend for himself out here!
When did *you* become a porcupine expert?

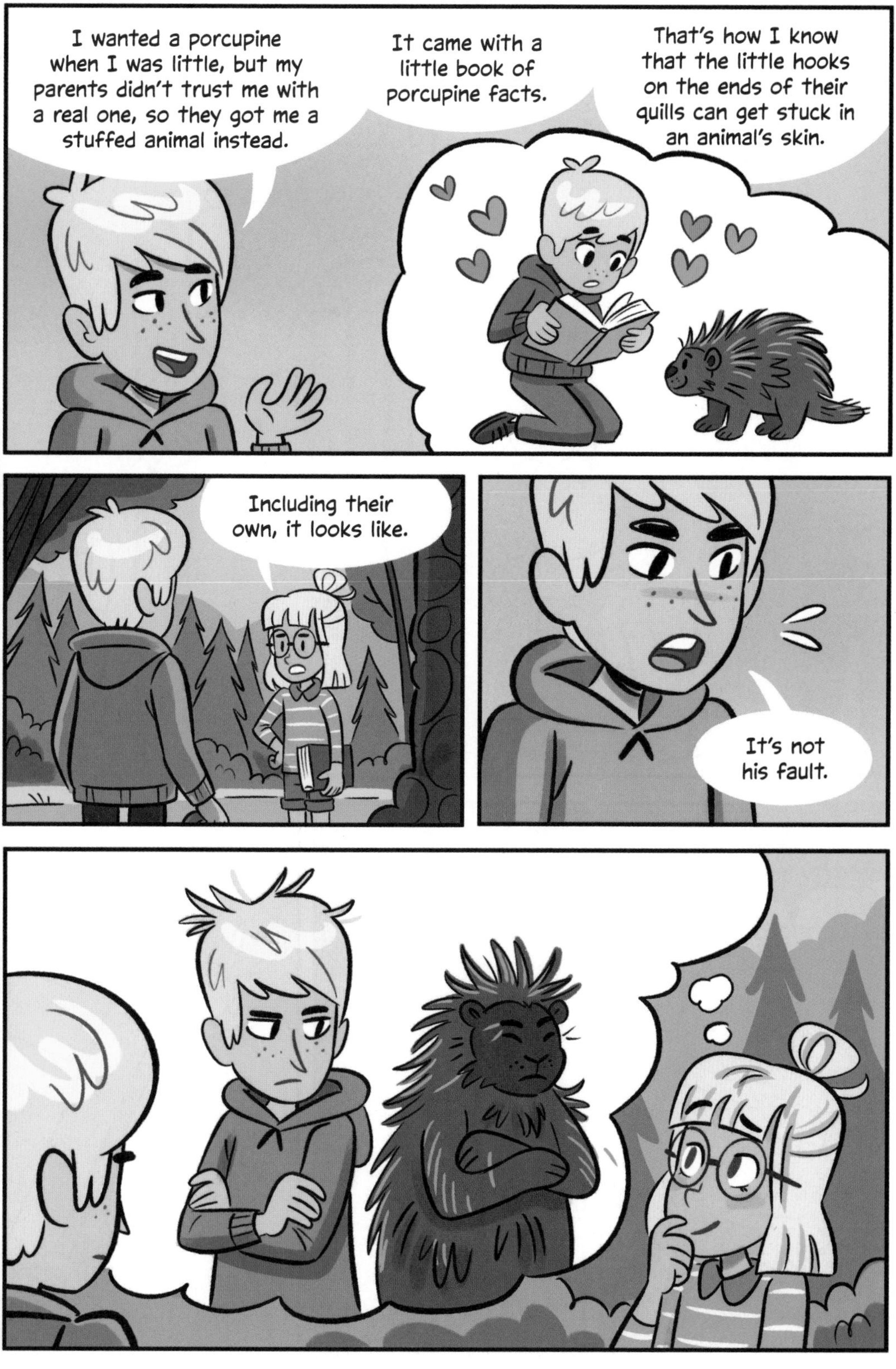
I wanted a porcupine when I was little, but my parents didn't trust me with a real one, so they got me a stuffed animal instead.
It came with a little book of porcupine facts.
That's how I know that the little hooks on the ends of their quills can get stuck in an animal's skin.
Including their own, it looks like.
It's not his fault.

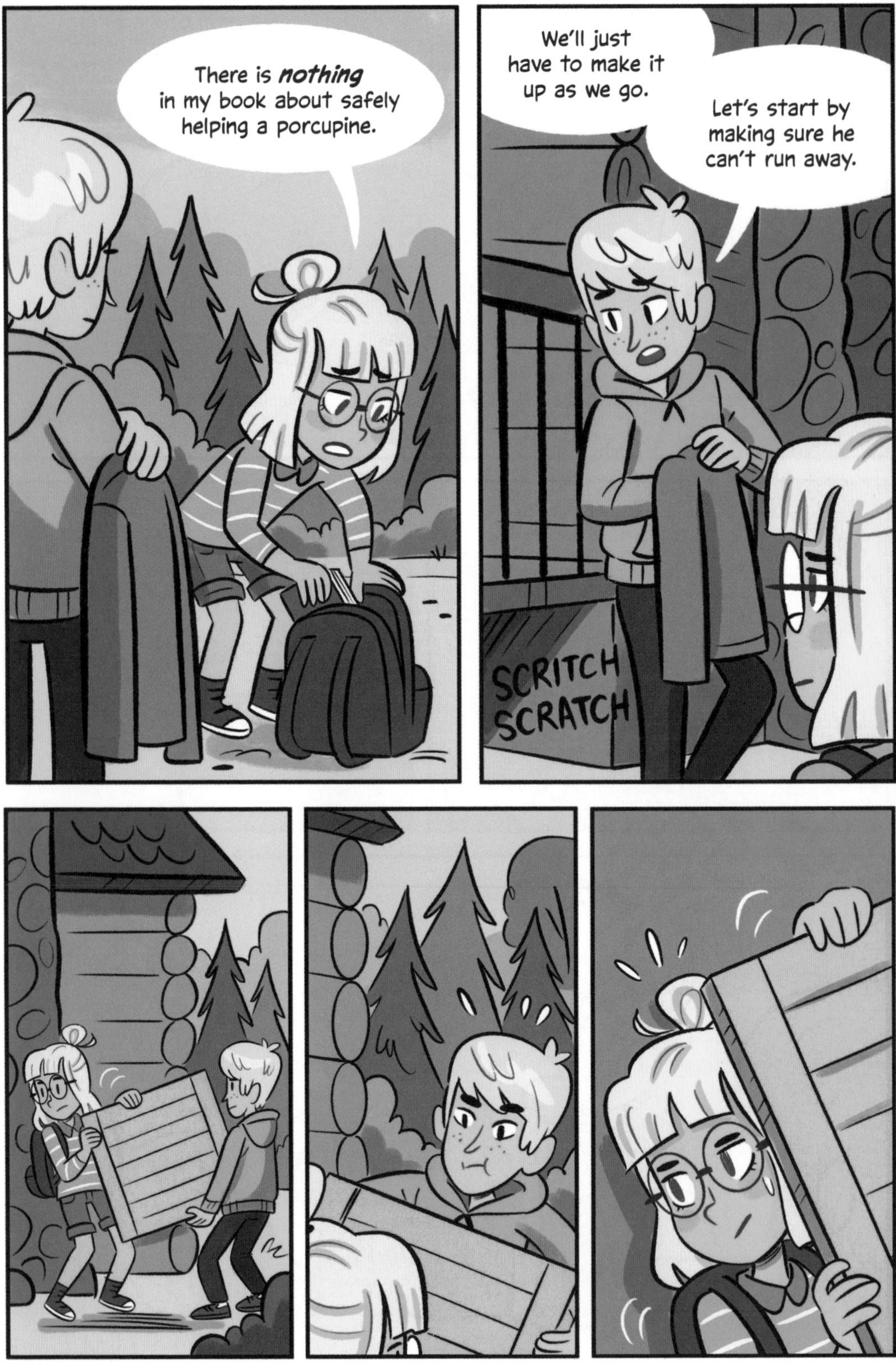
There is *nothing* in my book about safely helping a porcupine.
We'll just have to make it up as we go.
Let's start by making sure he can't run away.
SCRITCH SCRATCH

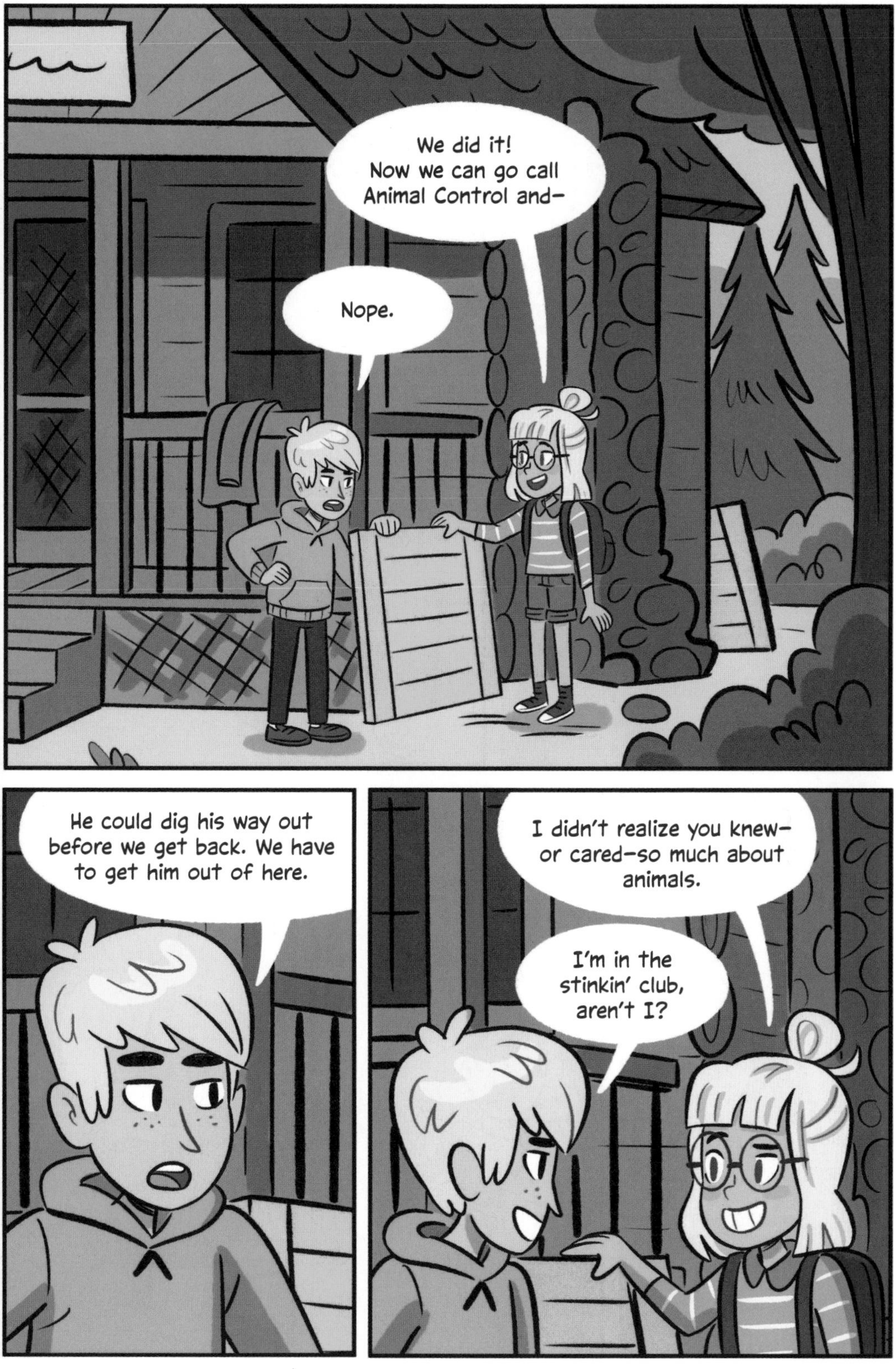
We did it!
Now we can go call
Animal Control and—
Nope.
He could dig his way out
before we get back. We have
to get him out of here.
I didn't realize you knew—
or cared—so much about
animals.
I'm in the
stinkin' club,
aren't I?

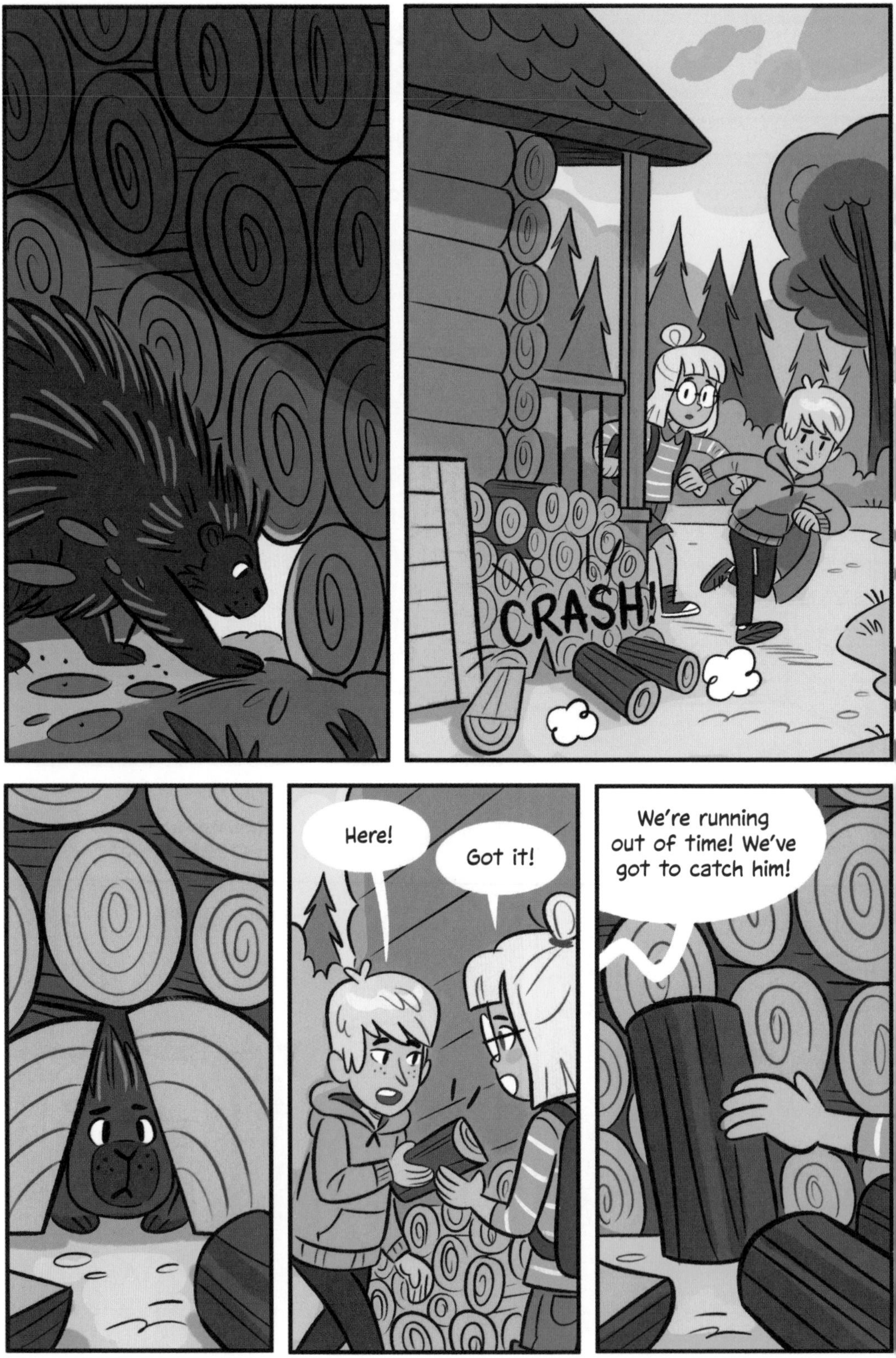
CRASH!
Here!
Got it!
We're running out of time! We've got to catch him!

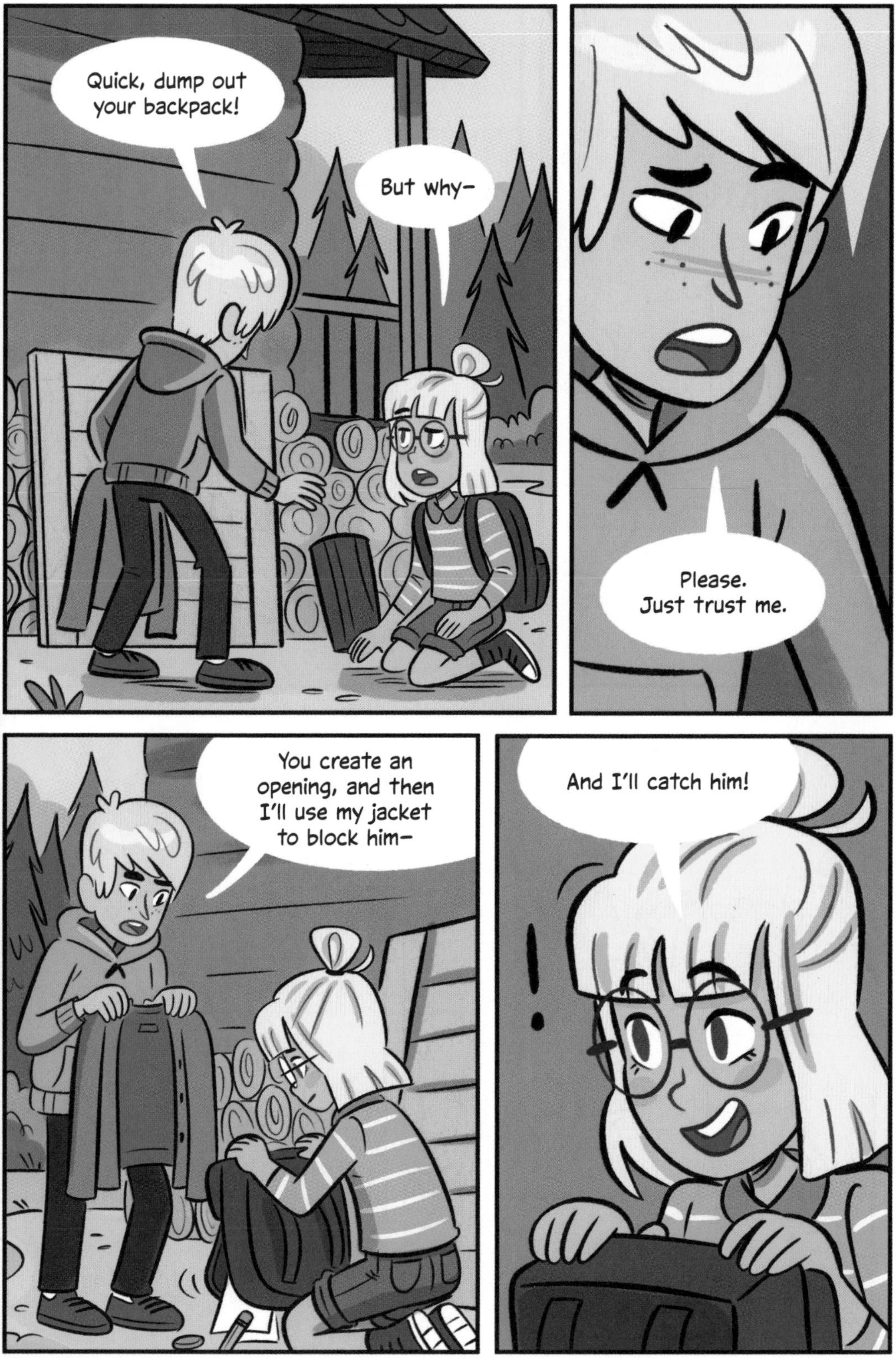
Quick, dump out your backpack!
But why–
Please. Just trust me.
You create an opening, and then I'll use my jacket to block him–
And I'll catch him!
!

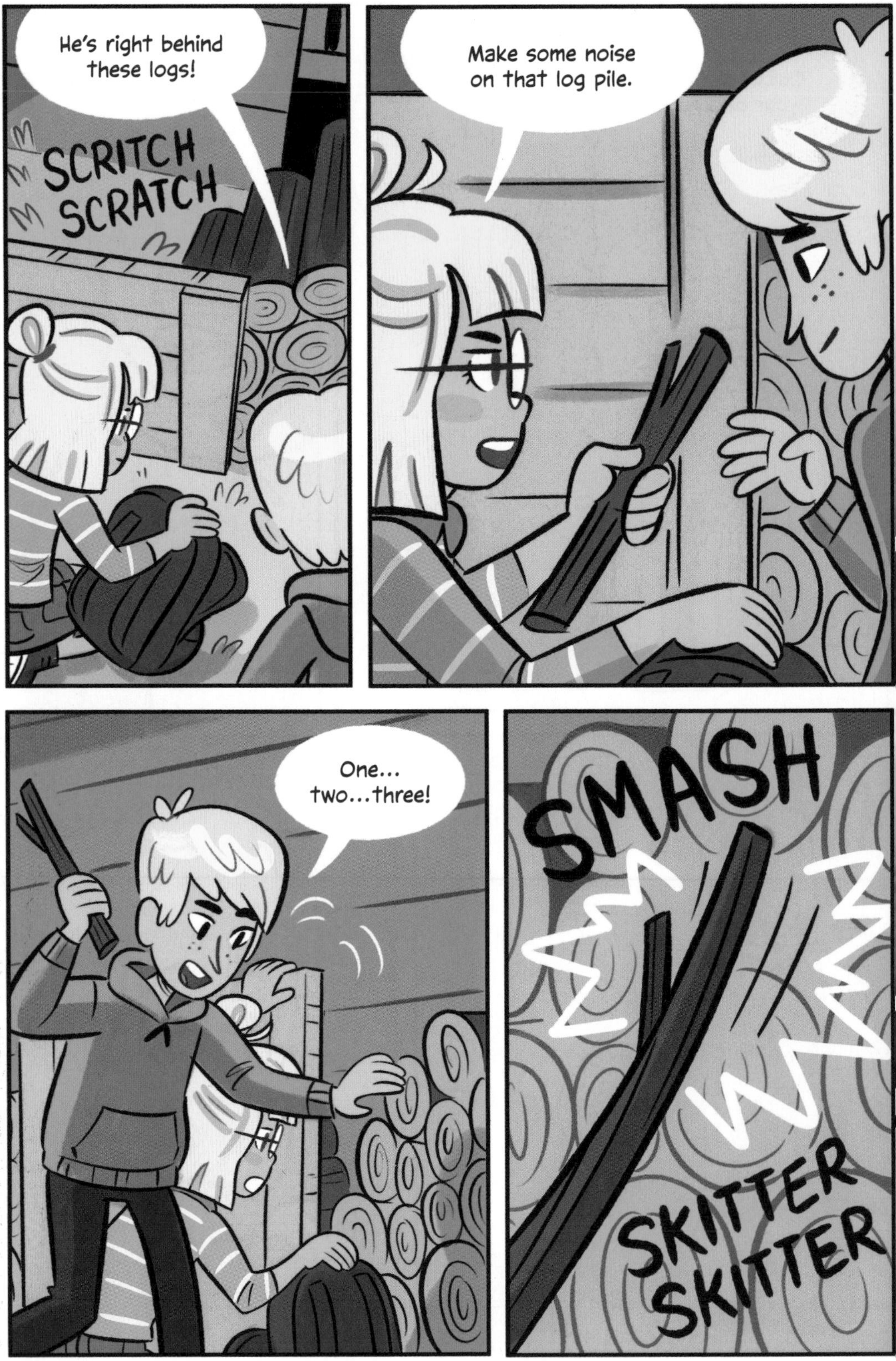
He's right behind these logs!
SCRITCH SCRATCH
Make some noise on that log pile.
One... two...three!
SMASH
SKITTER SKITTER

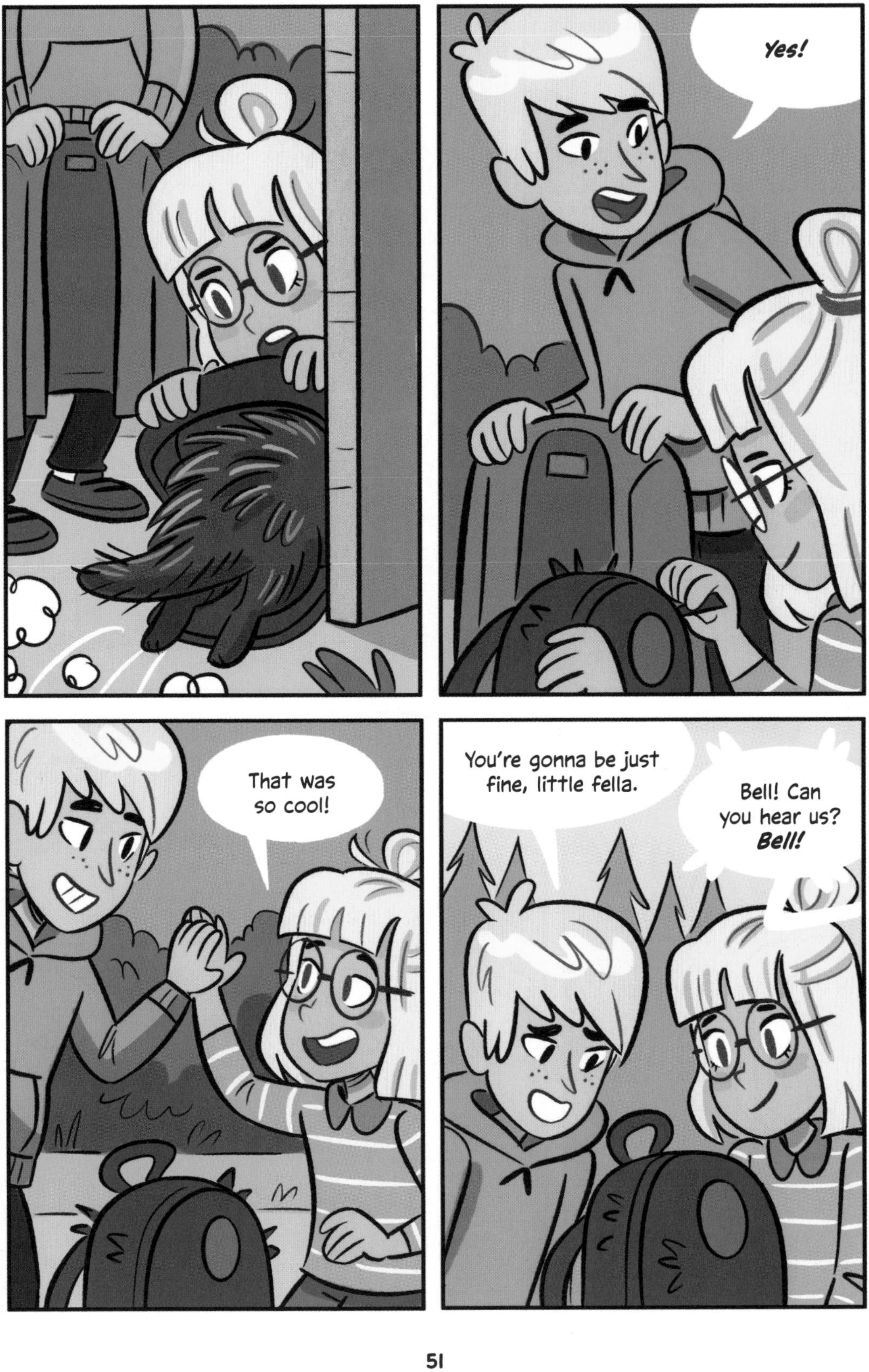
Yes!
That was so cool!
You're gonna be just fine, little fella.
Bell! Can you hear us? *Bell!*

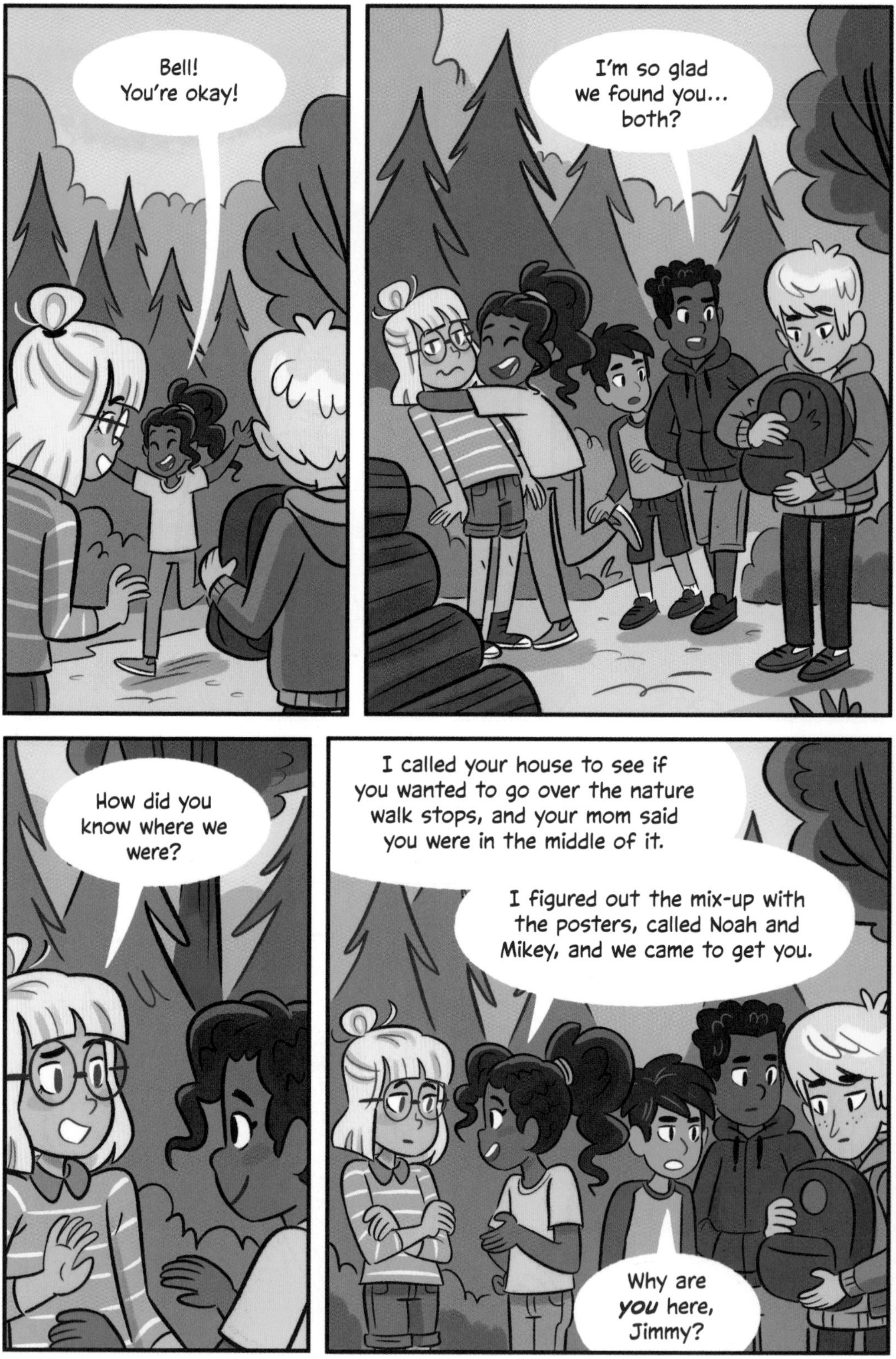
Bell!
You're okay!
I'm so glad
we found you…
both?
How did you
know where we
were?
I called your house to see if
you wanted to go over the nature
walk stops, and your mom said
you were in the middle of it.
I figured out the mix-up with
the posters, called Noah and
Mikey, and we came to get you.
Why are
you here,
Jimmy?

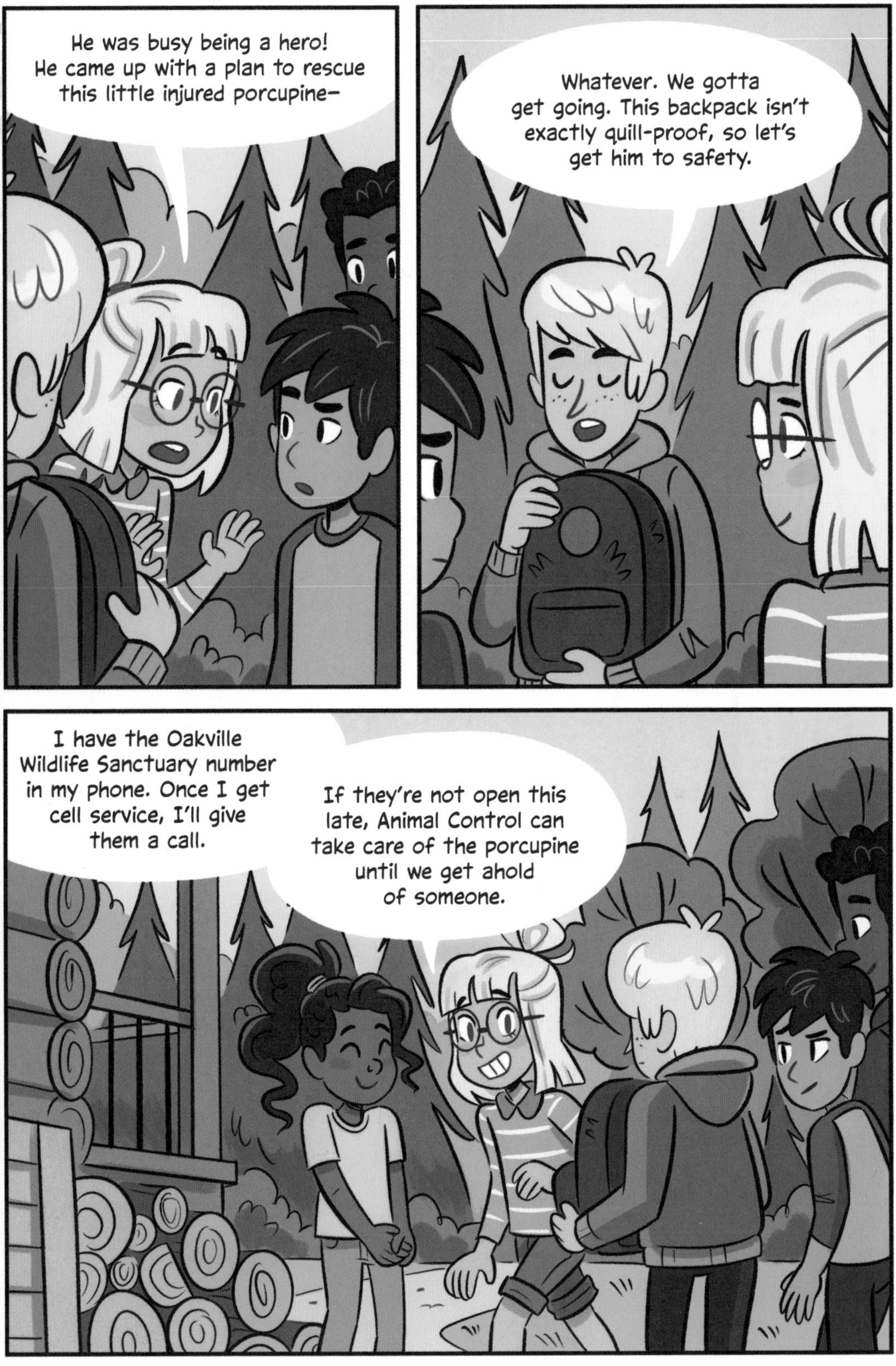
He was busy being a hero! He came up with a plan to rescue this little injured porcupine—
Whatever. We gotta get going. This backpack isn't exactly quill-proof, so let's get him to safety.
I have the Oakville Wildlife Sanctuary number in my phone. Once I get cell service, I'll give them a call.
If they're not open this late, Animal Control can take care of the porcupine until we get ahold of someone.

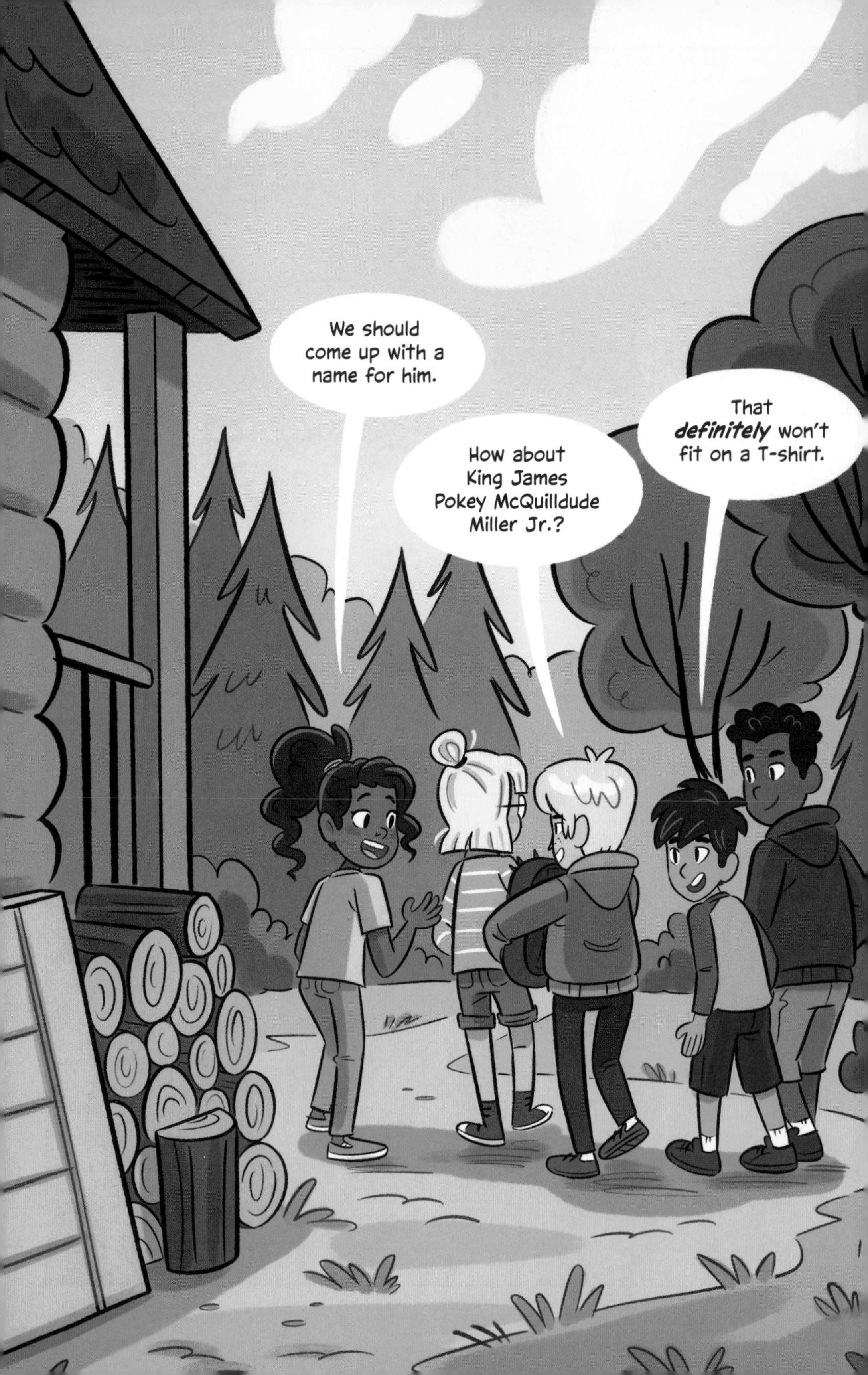
We should come up with a name for him.
How about King James Pokey McQuilldude Miller Jr.?
That *definitely* won't fit on a T-shirt.

Chapter 3

NOAH, MIKEY, HOPPER, AND COCOA

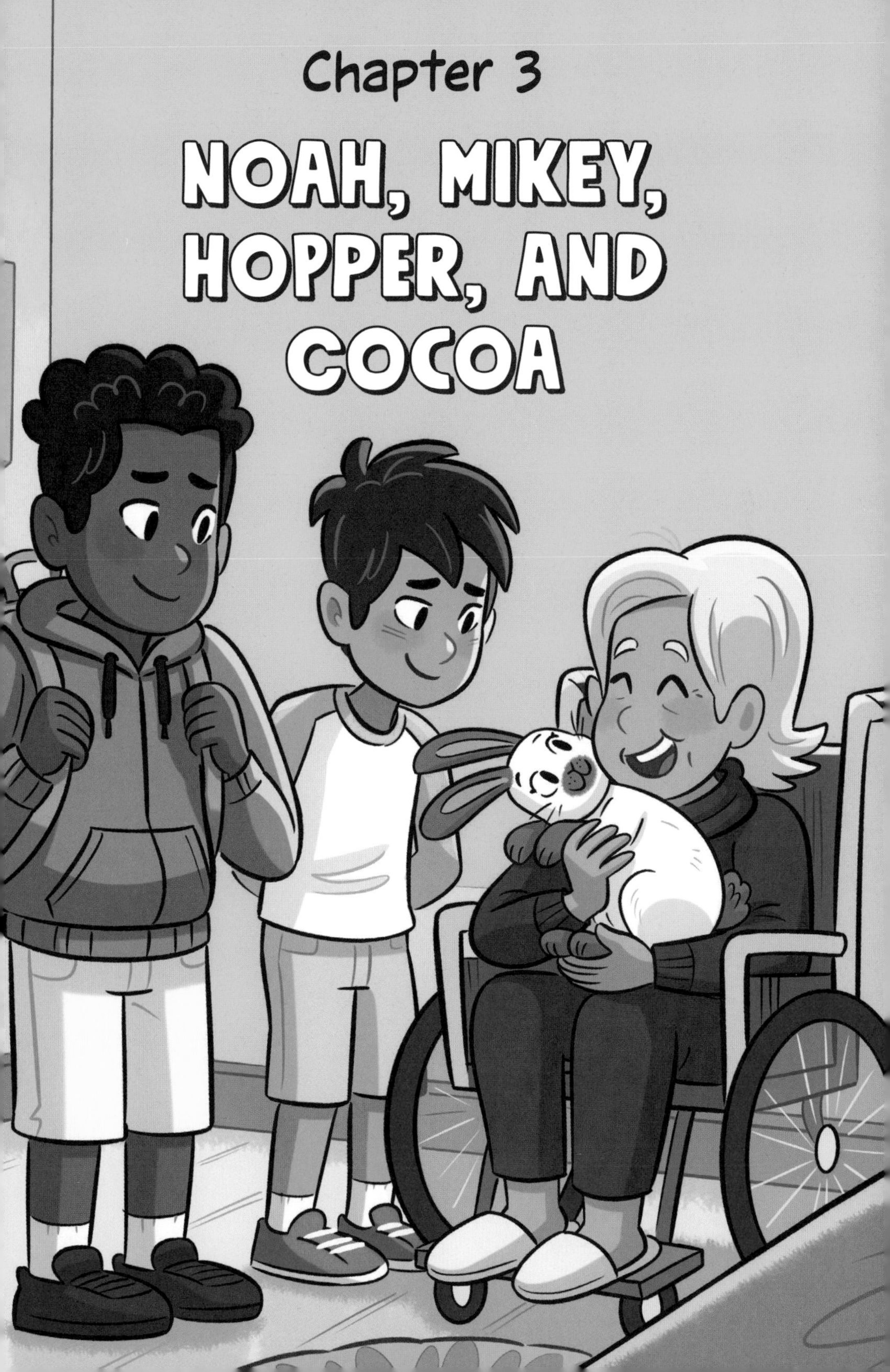

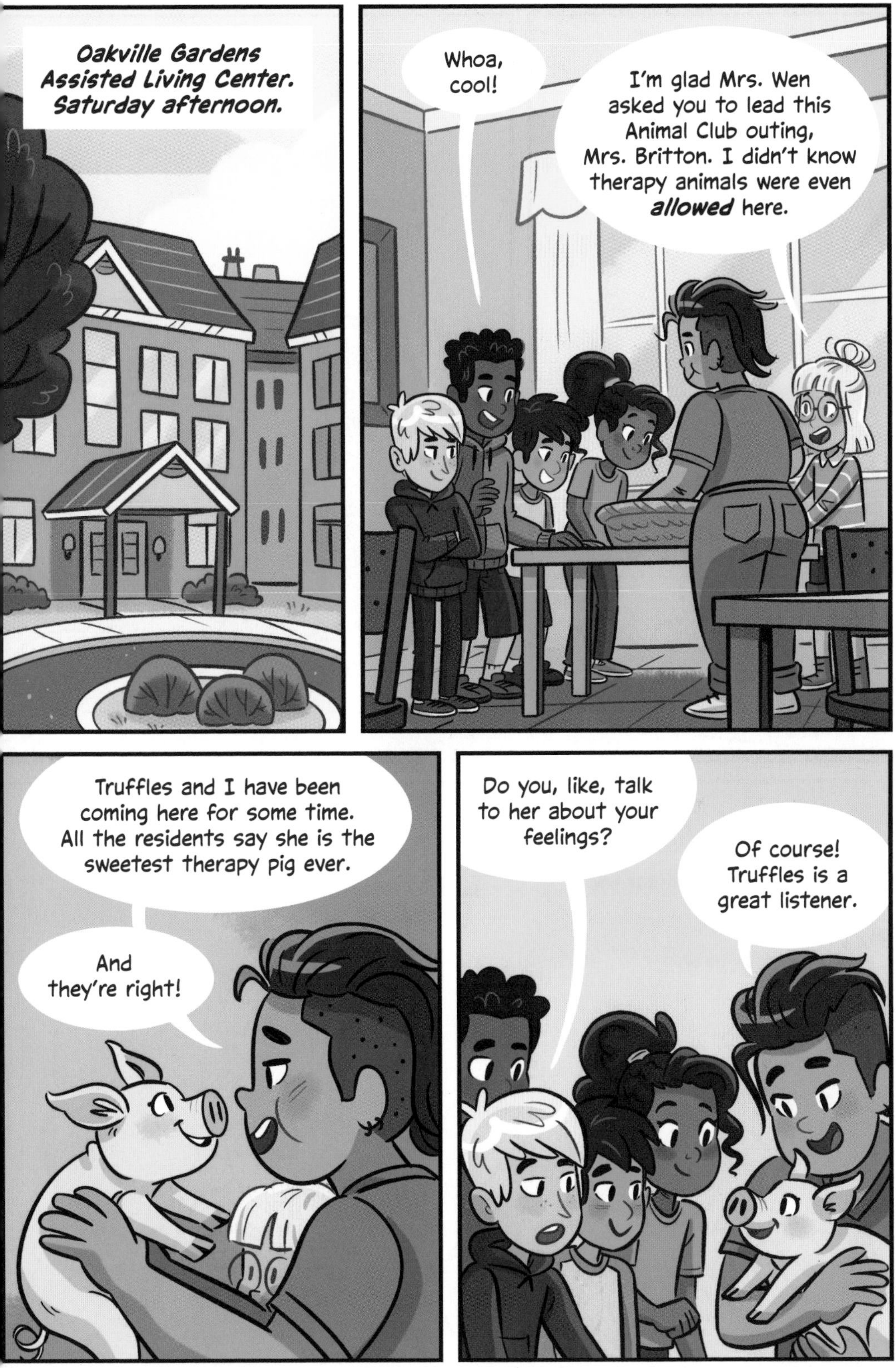
Oakville Gardens Assisted Living Center. Saturday afternoon.
Whoa, cool!
I'm glad Mrs. Wen asked you to lead this Animal Club outing, Mrs. Britton. I didn't know therapy animals were even *allowed* here.
Truffles and I have been coming here for some time. All the residents say she is the sweetest therapy pig ever.
And they're right!
Do you, like, talk to her about your feelings?
Of course! Truffles is a great listener.

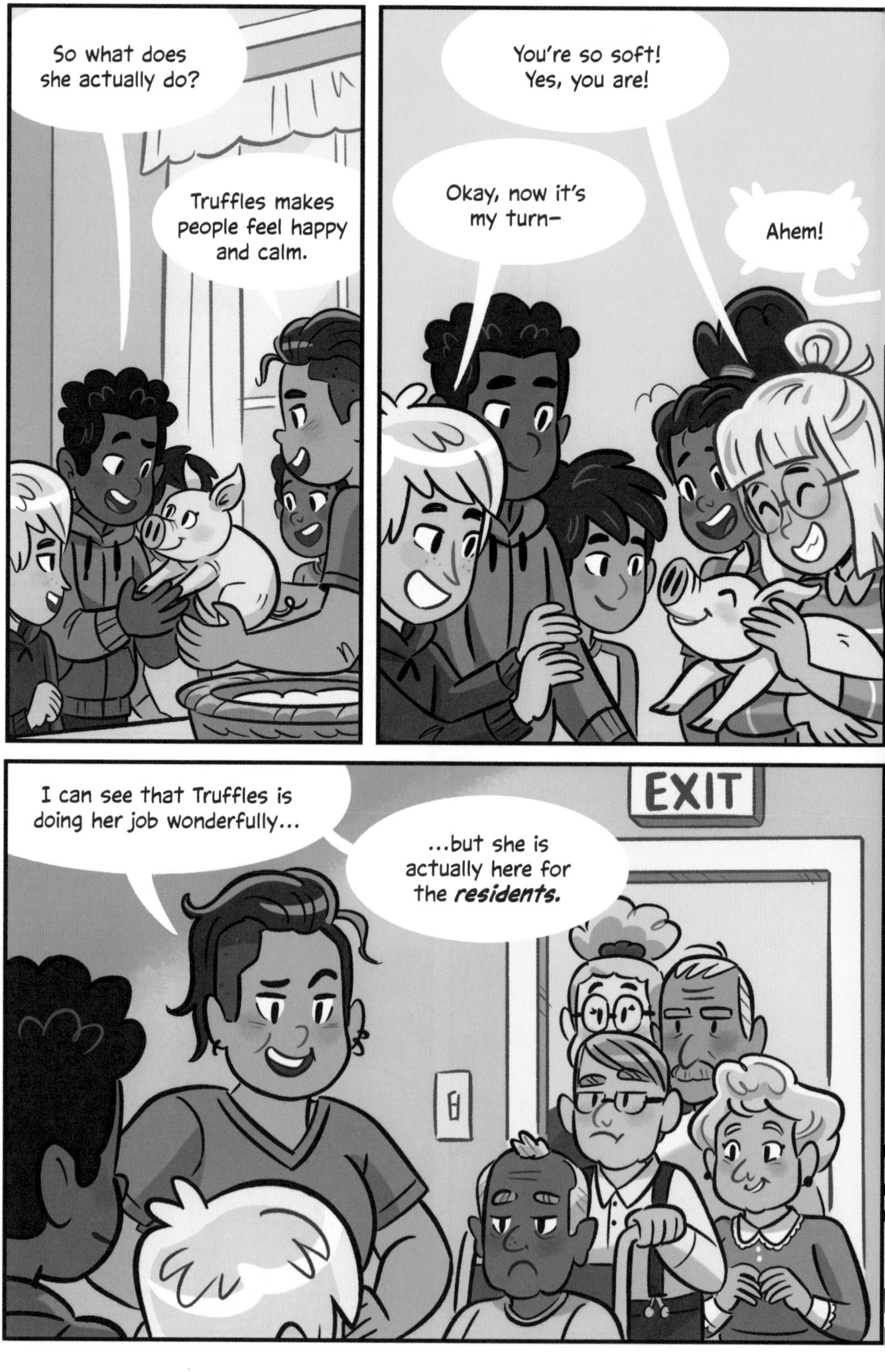
So what does she actually do?
Truffles makes people feel happy and calm.
You're so soft! Yes, you are!
Okay, now it's my turn–
Ahem!
EXIT
I can see that Truffles is doing her job wonderfully...
...but she is actually here for the *residents.*

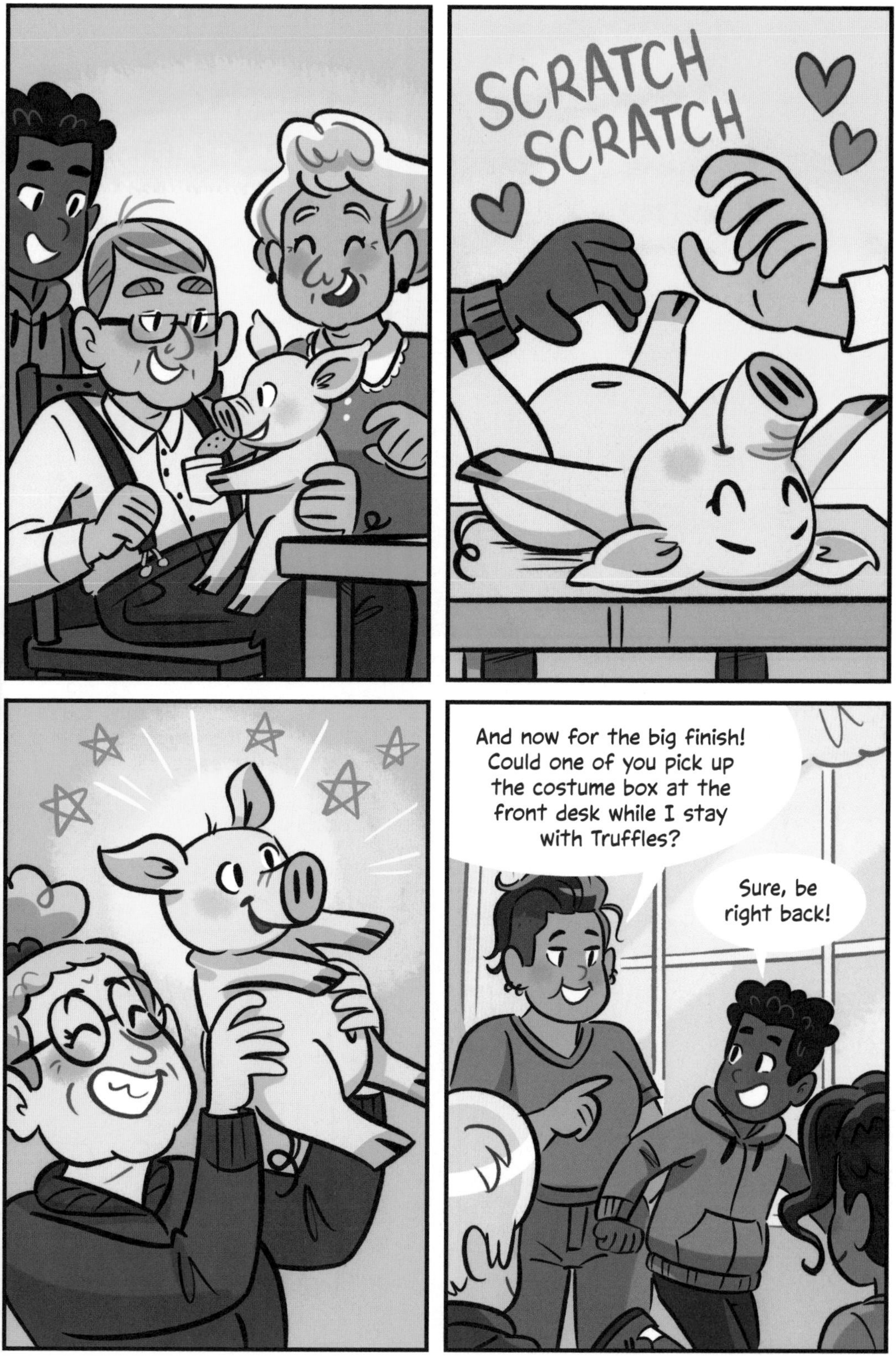
SCRATCH SCRATCH
And now for the big finish! Could one of you pick up the costume box at the front desk while I stay with Truffles?
Sure, be right back!

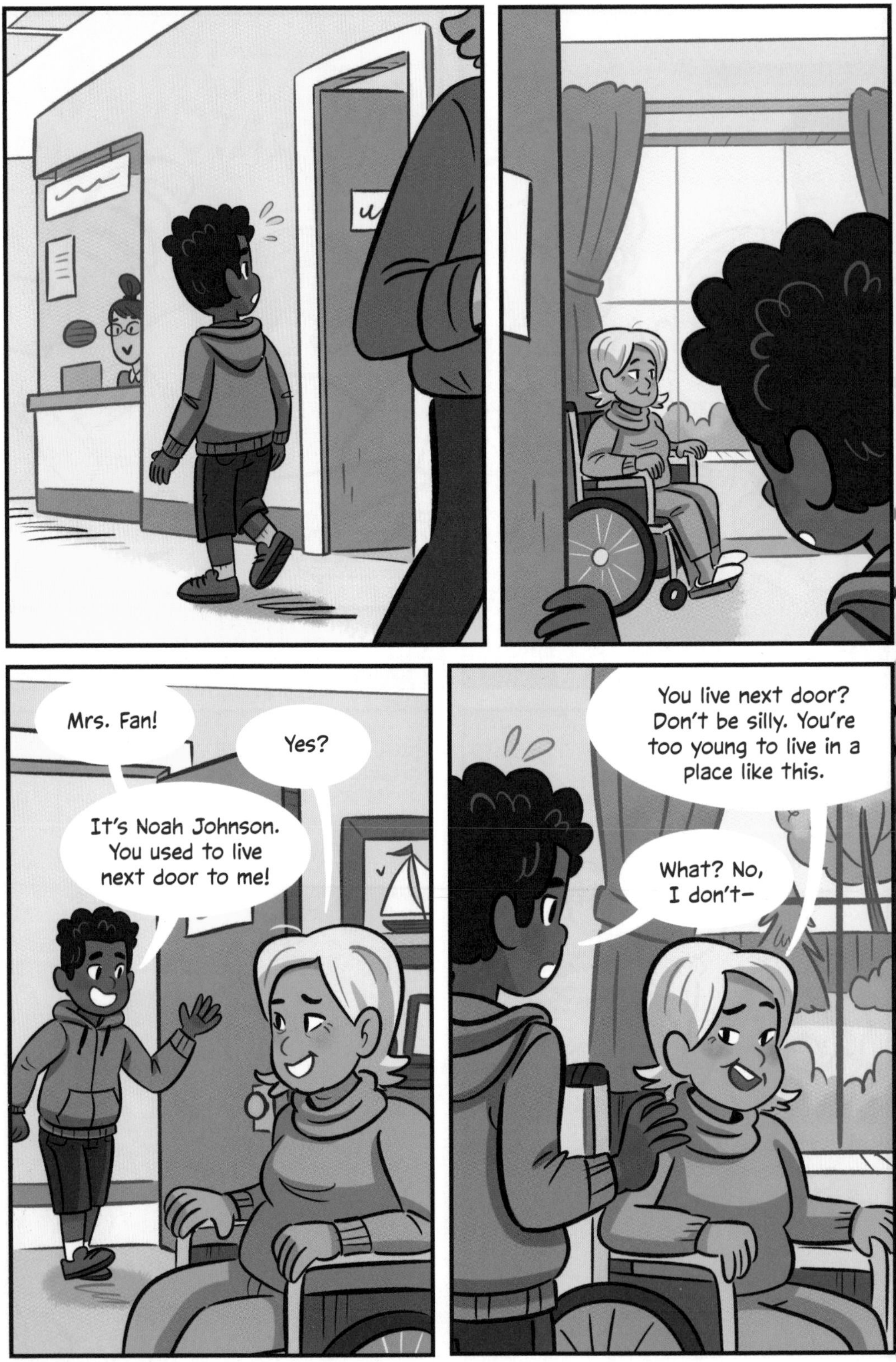
Mrs. Fan!
Yes?
It's Noah Johnson. You used to live next door to me!
You live next door? Don't be silly. You're too young to live in a place like this.
What? No, I don't–

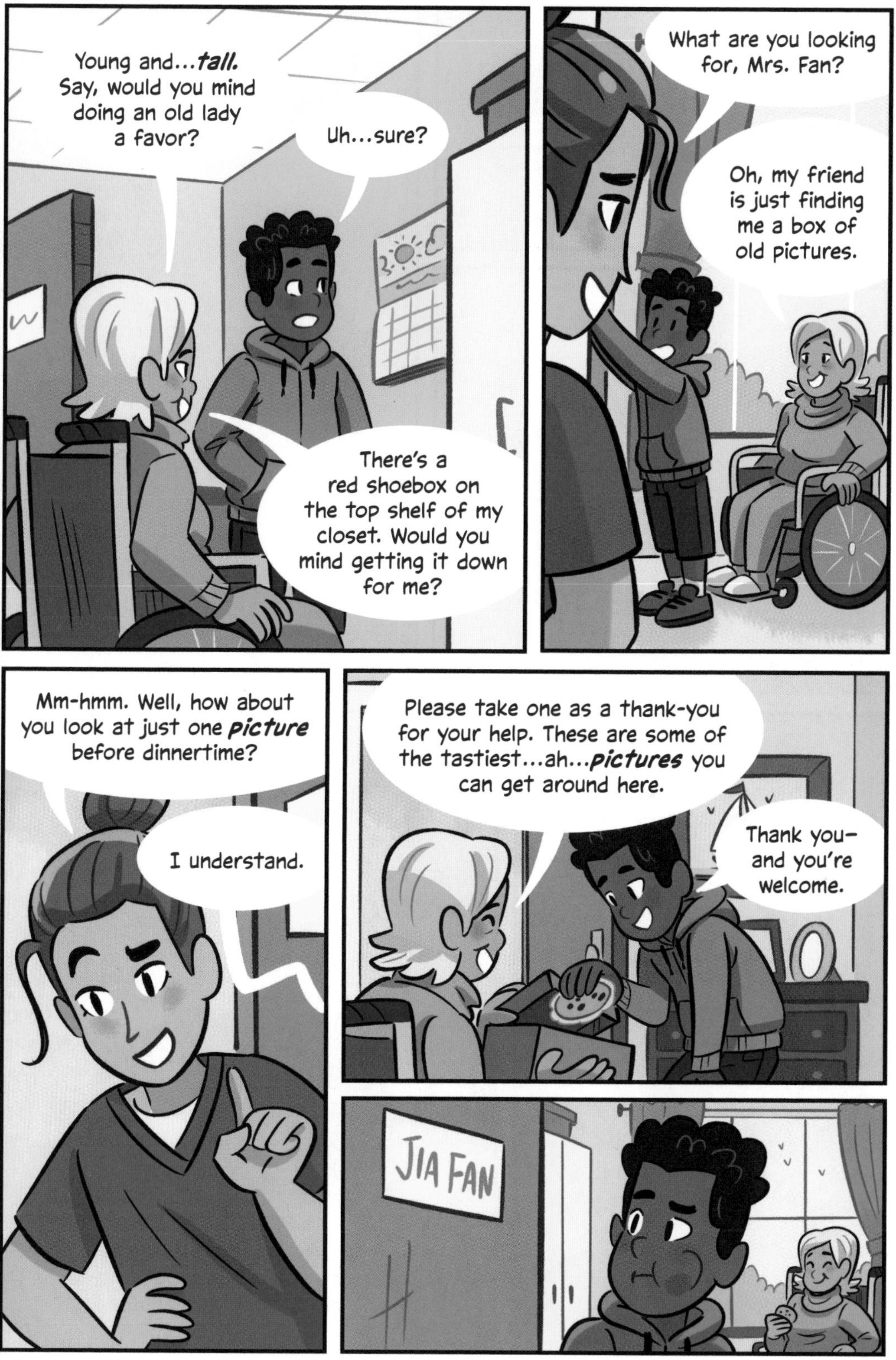
Young and...*tall.* Say, would you mind doing an old lady a favor?
Uh...sure?
There's a red shoebox on the top shelf of my closet. Would you mind getting it down for me?
What are you looking for, Mrs. Fan?
Oh, my friend is just finding me a box of old pictures.
Mm-hmm. Well, how about you look at just one *picture* before dinnertime?
I understand.
Please take one as a thank-you for your help. These are some of the tastiest...ah...*pictures* you can get around here.
Thank you- and you're welcome.
JIA FAN

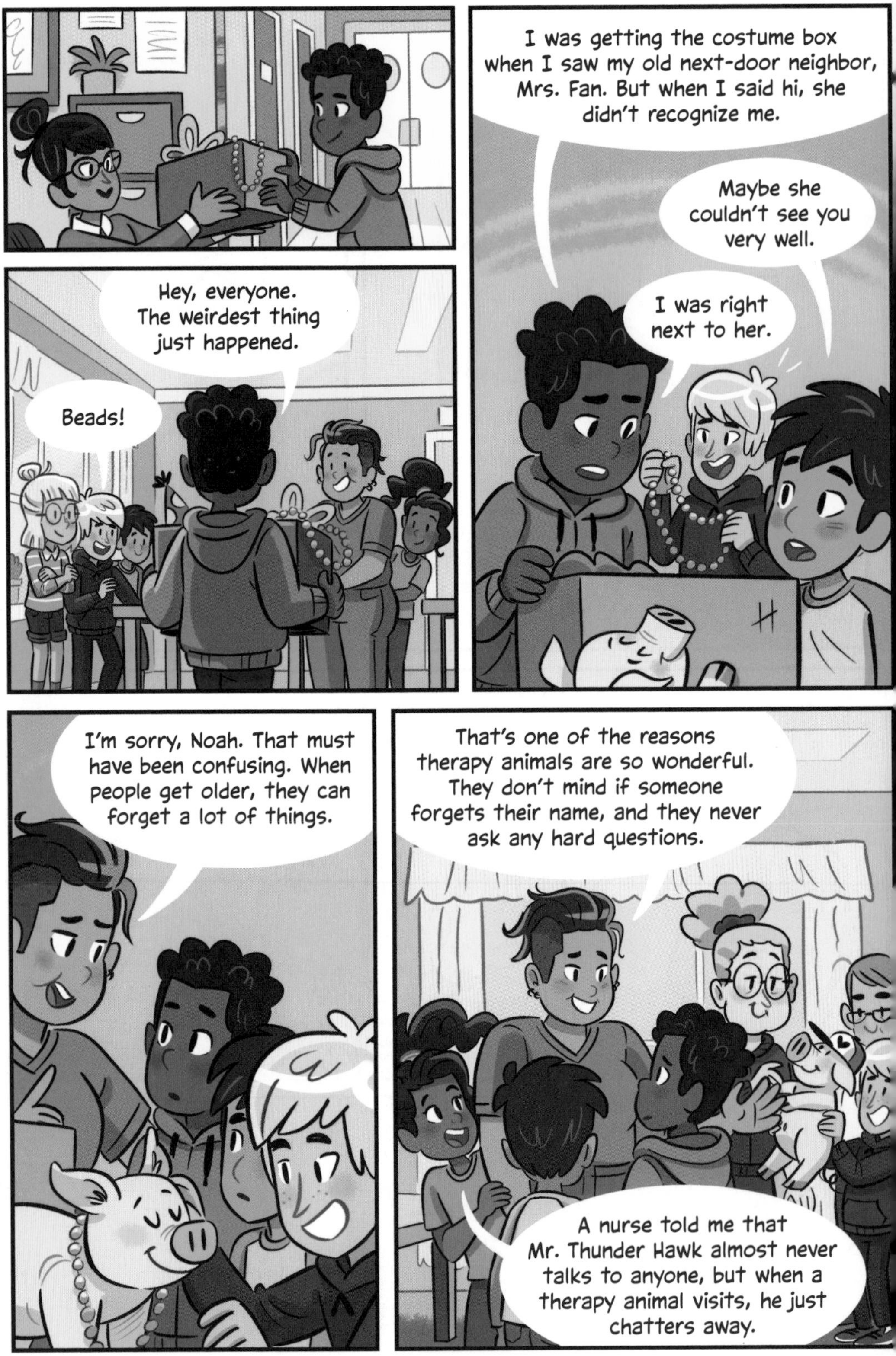
I was getting the costume box when I saw my old next-door neighbor, Mrs. Fan. But when I said hi, she didn't recognize me.
Hey, everyone. The weirdest thing just happened.
Beads!
Maybe she couldn't see you very well.
I was right next to her.
I'm sorry, Noah. That must have been confusing. When people get older, they can forget a lot of things.
That's one of the reasons therapy animals are so wonderful. They don't mind if someone forgets their name, and they never ask any hard questions.
A nurse told me that Mr. Thunder Hawk almost never talks to anyone, but when a therapy animal visits, he just chatters away.

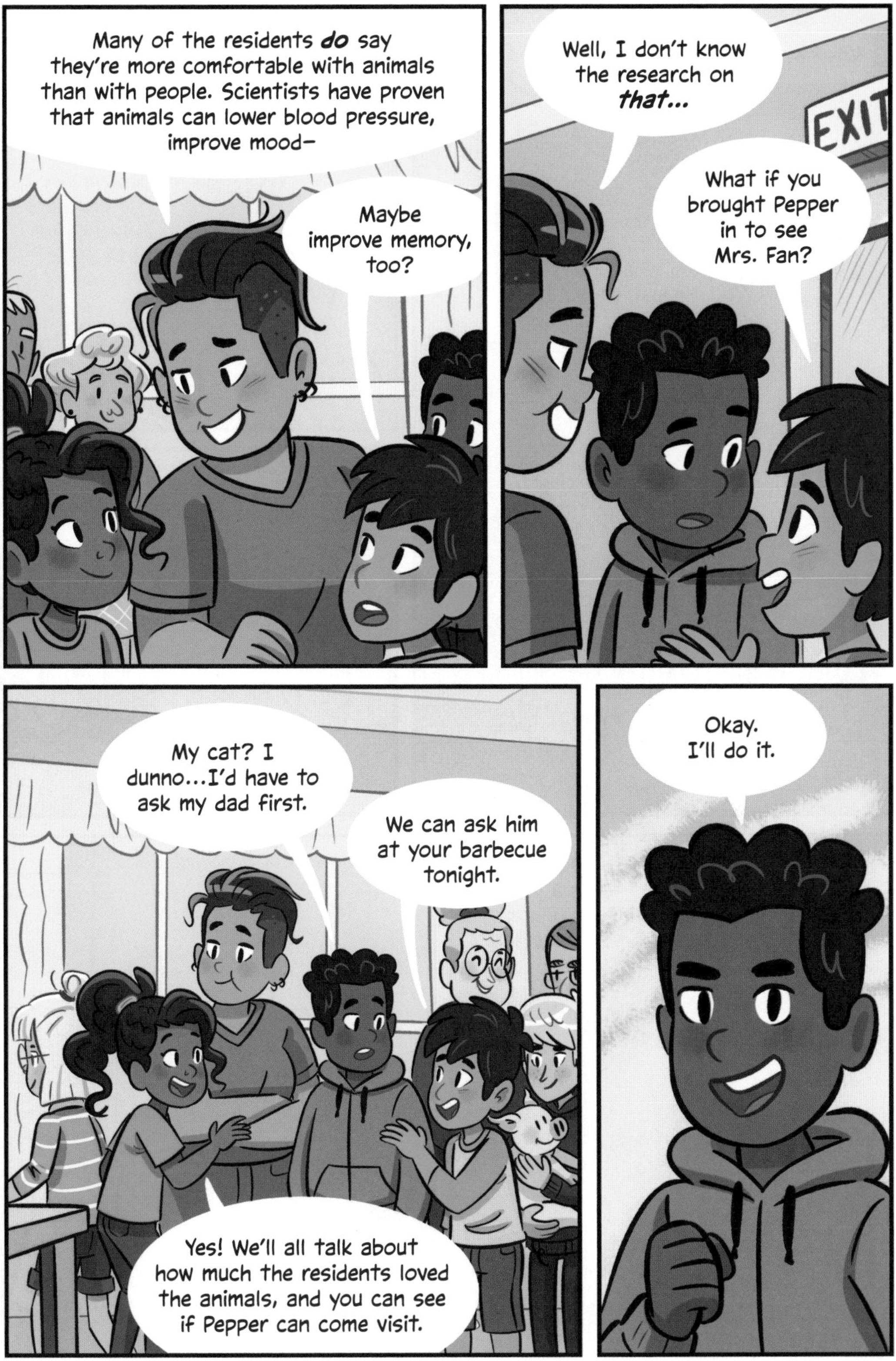
Many of the residents *do* say they're more comfortable with animals than with people. Scientists have proven that animals can lower blood pressure, improve mood–
Maybe improve memory, too?
Well, I don't know the research on *that*...
EXIT
What if you brought Pepper in to see Mrs. Fan?
My cat? I dunno...I'd have to ask my dad first.
We can ask him at your barbecue tonight.
Yes! We'll all talk about how much the residents loved the animals, and you can see if Pepper can come visit.
Okay. I'll do it.

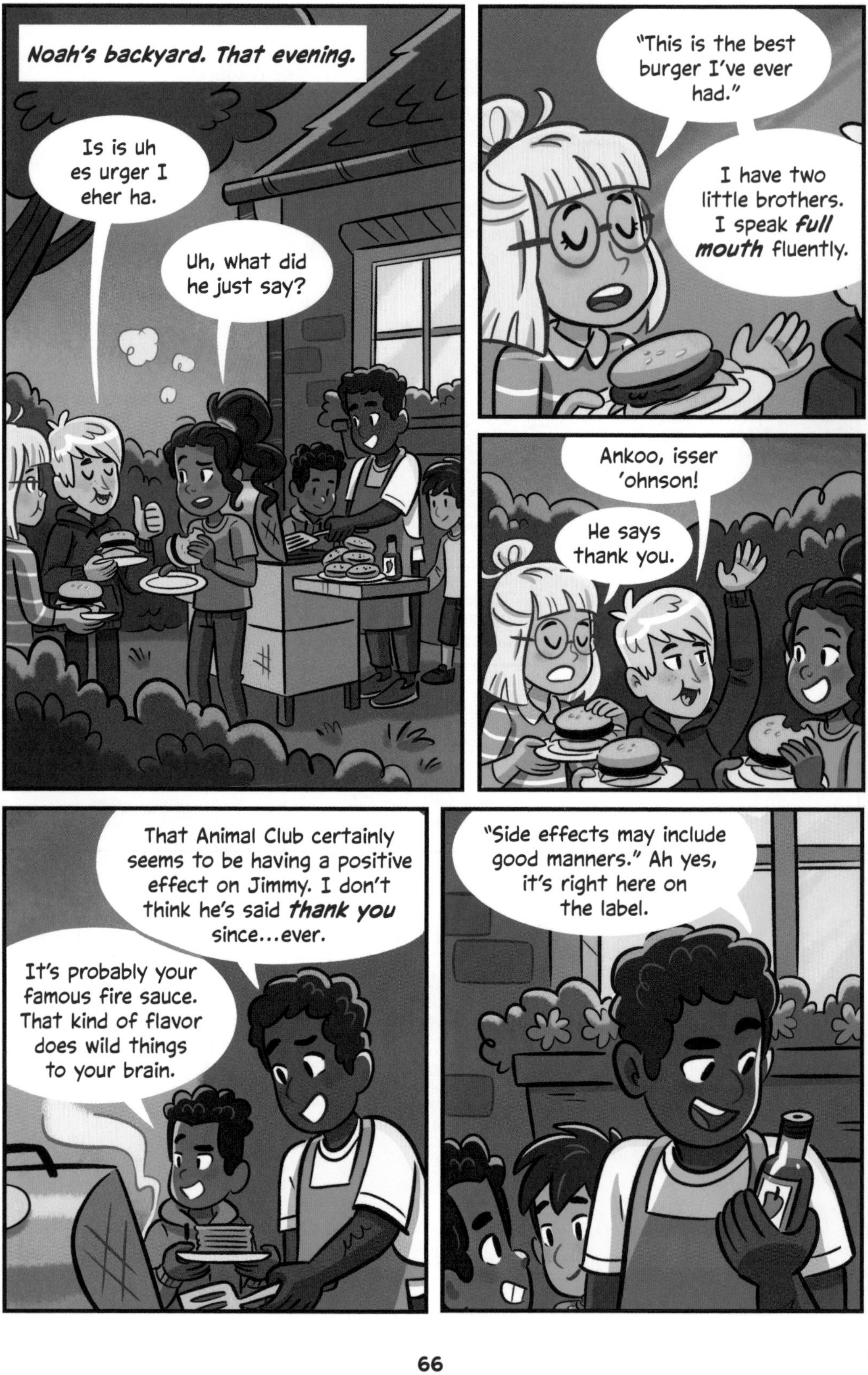
Noah's backyard. That evening.
Is is uh es urger I eher ha.
Uh, what did he just say?
"This is the best burger I've ever had."
I have two little brothers. I speak full mouth fluently.
Ankoo, isser 'ohnson!
He says thank you.
That Animal Club certainly seems to be having a positive effect on Jimmy. I don't think he's said thank you since...ever.
It's probably your famous fire sauce. That kind of flavor does wild things to your brain.
"Side effects may include good manners." Ah yes, it's right here on the label.

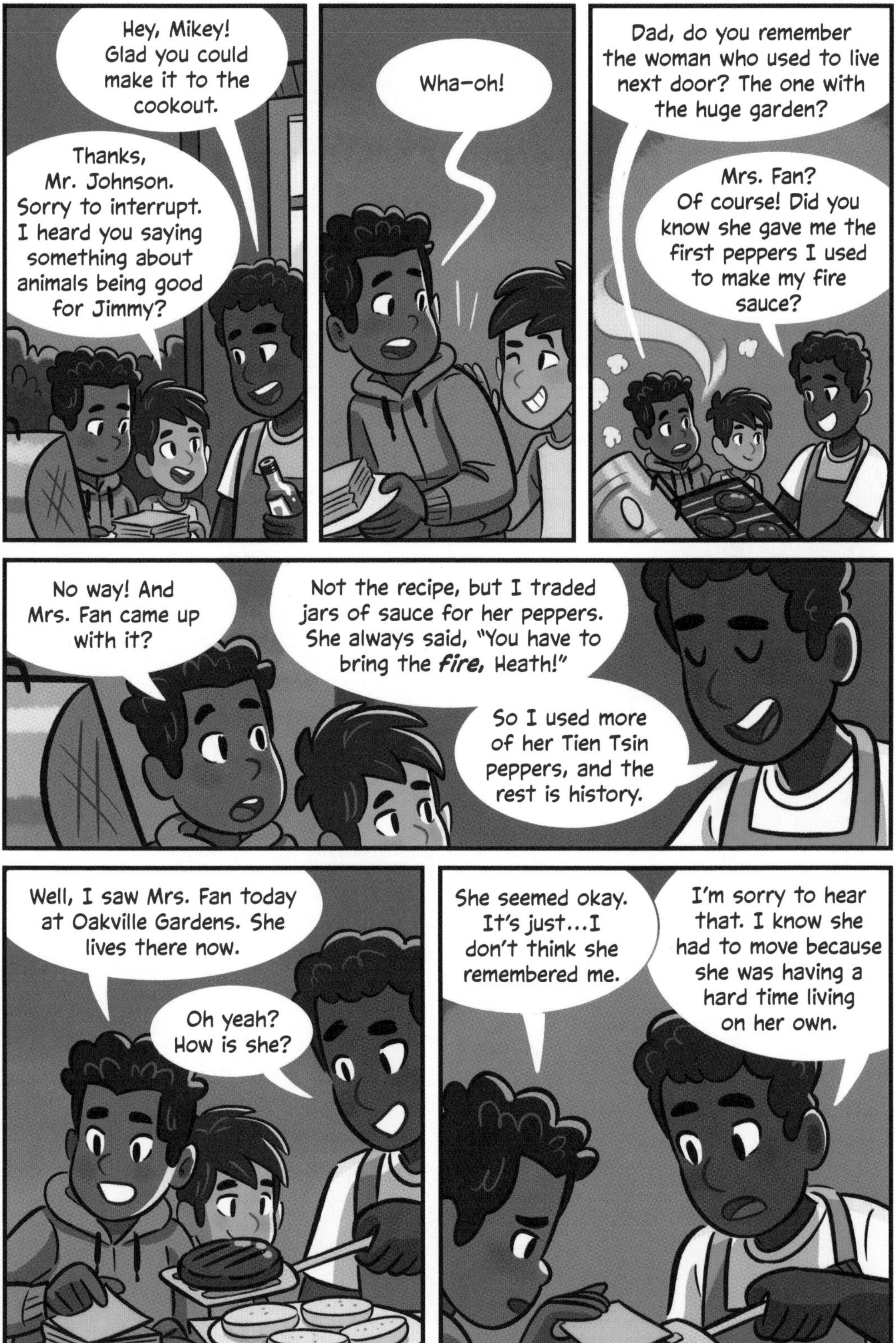
Hey, Mikey! Glad you could make it to the cookout.
Thanks, Mr. Johnson. Sorry to interrupt. I heard you saying something about animals being good for Jimmy?
Wha-oh!
Dad, do you remember the woman who used to live next door? The one with the huge garden?
Mrs. Fan? Of course! Did you know she gave me the first peppers I used to make my fire sauce?
No way! And Mrs. Fan came up with it?
Not the recipe, but I traded jars of sauce for her peppers. She always said, "You have to bring the *fire*, Heath!"
So I used more of her Tien Tsin peppers, and the rest is history.
Well, I saw Mrs. Fan today at Oakville Gardens. She lives there now.
Oh yeah? How is she?
She seemed okay. It's just...I don't think she remembered me.
I'm sorry to hear that. I know she had to move because she was having a hard time living on her own.

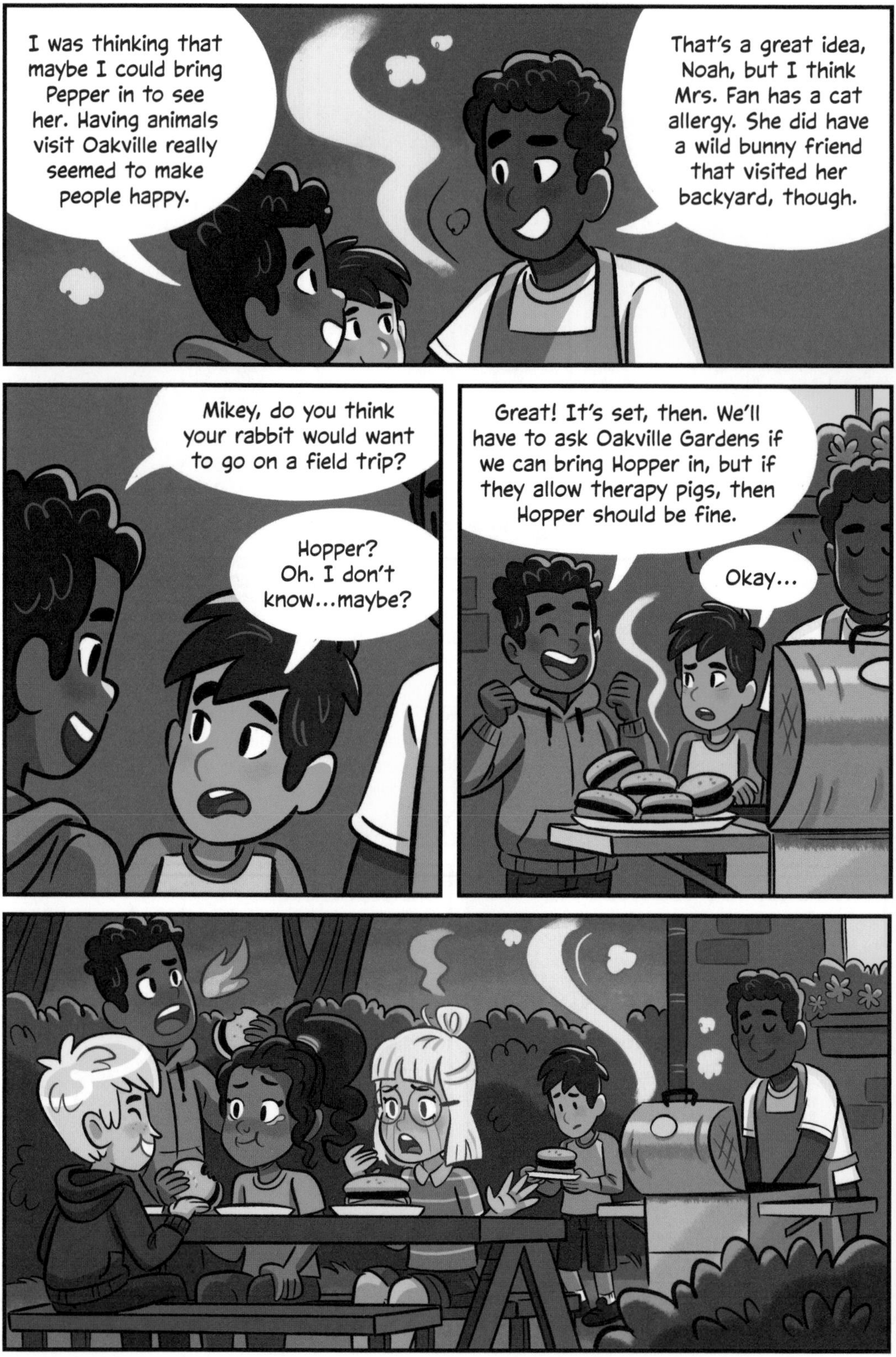

I was thinking that maybe I could bring Pepper in to see her. Having animals visit Oakville really seemed to make people happy.
That's a great idea, Noah, but I think Mrs. Fan has a cat allergy. She did have a wild bunny friend that visited her backyard, though.
Mikey, do you think your rabbit would want to go on a field trip?
Hopper? Oh. I don't know...maybe?
Great! It's set, then. We'll have to ask Oakville Gardens if we can bring Hopper in, but if they allow therapy pigs, then Hopper should be fine.
Okay...

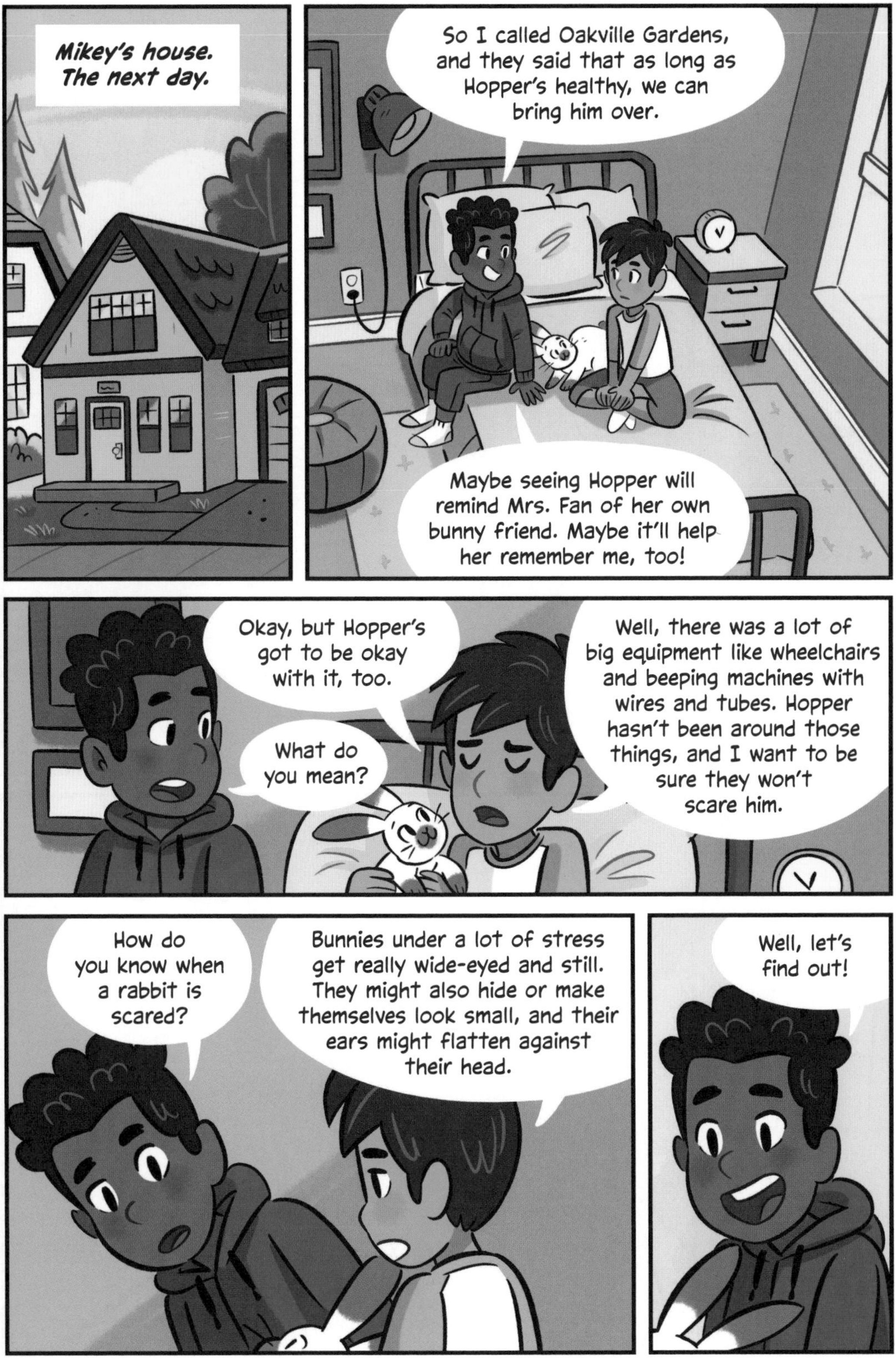
Mikey's house. The next day.
So I called Oakville Gardens, and they said that as long as Hopper's healthy, we can bring him over.
Maybe seeing Hopper will remind Mrs. Fan of her own bunny friend. Maybe it'll help her remember me, too!
Okay, but Hopper's got to be okay with it, too.
What do you mean?
Well, there was a lot of big equipment like wheelchairs and beeping machines with wires and tubes. Hopper hasn't been around those things, and I want to be sure they won't scare him.
How do you know when a rabbit is scared?
Bunnies under a lot of stress get really wide-eyed and still. They might also hide or make themselves look small, and their ears might flatten against their head.
Well, let's find out!

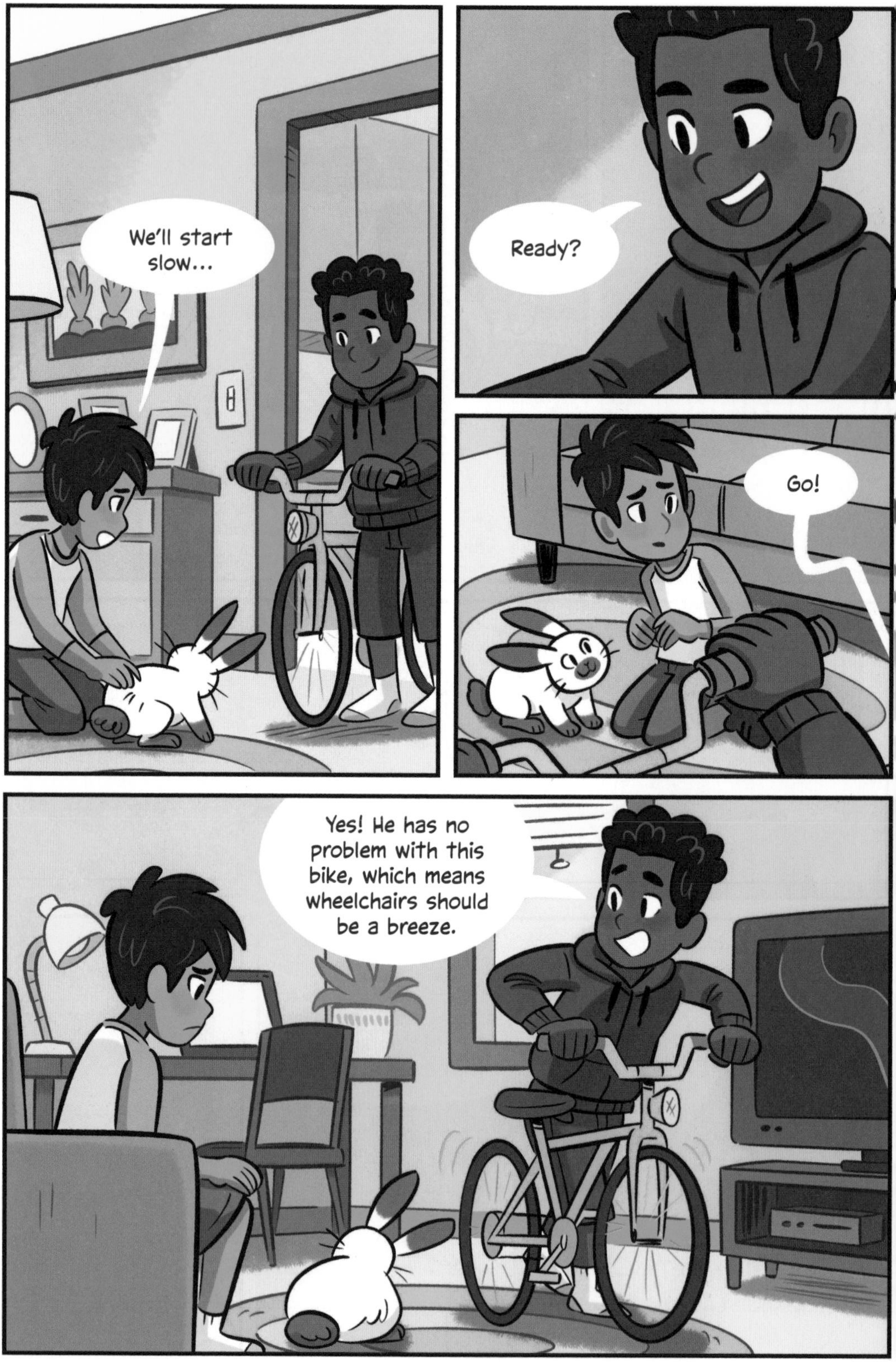
We'll start slow...
Ready?
Go!
Yes! He has no problem with this bike, which means wheelchairs should be a breeze.

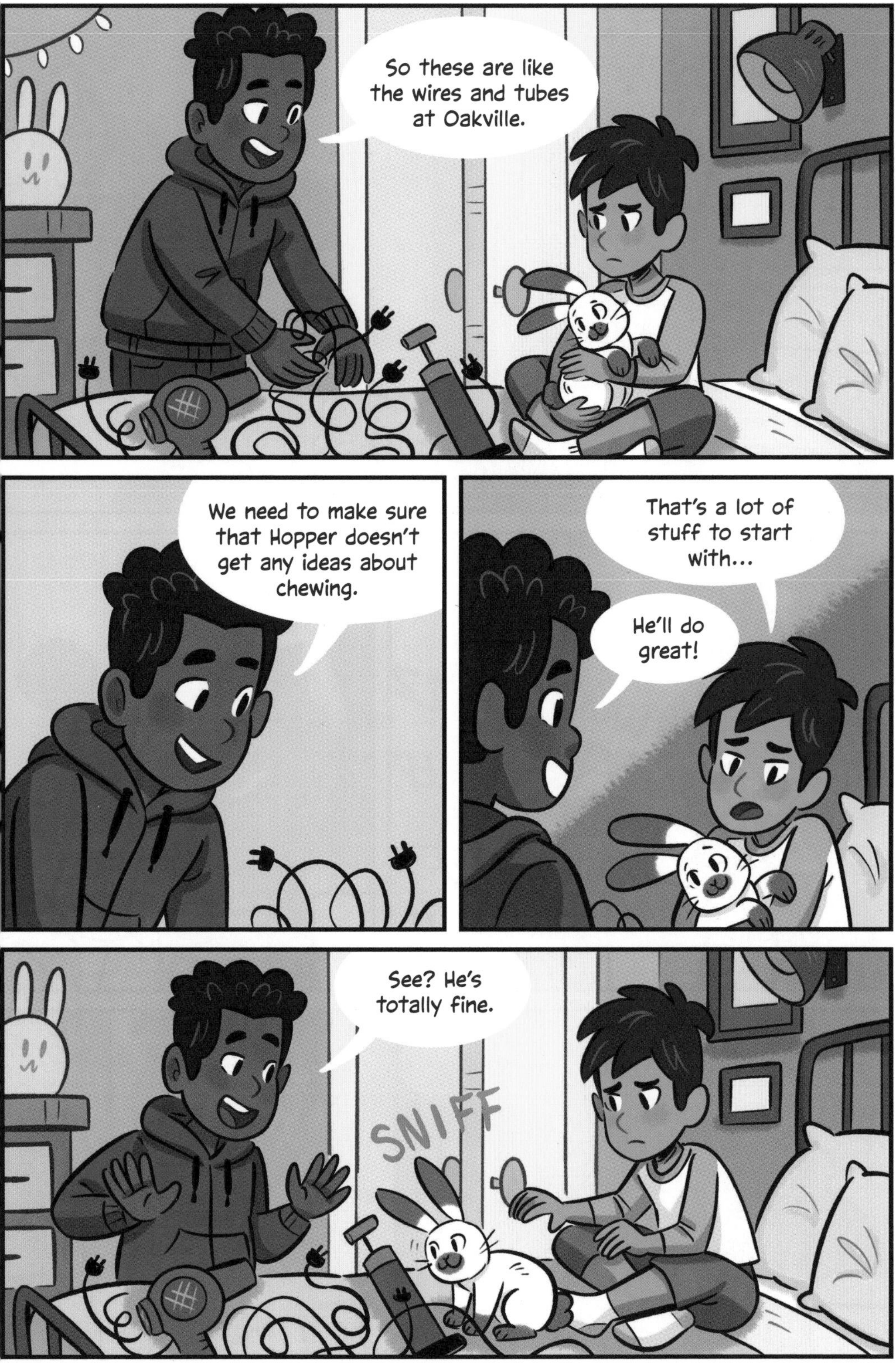
So these are like the wires and tubes at Oakville.
We need to make sure that Hopper doesn't get any ideas about chewing.
That's a lot of stuff to start with...
He'll do great!
See? He's totally fine.
SNIFF

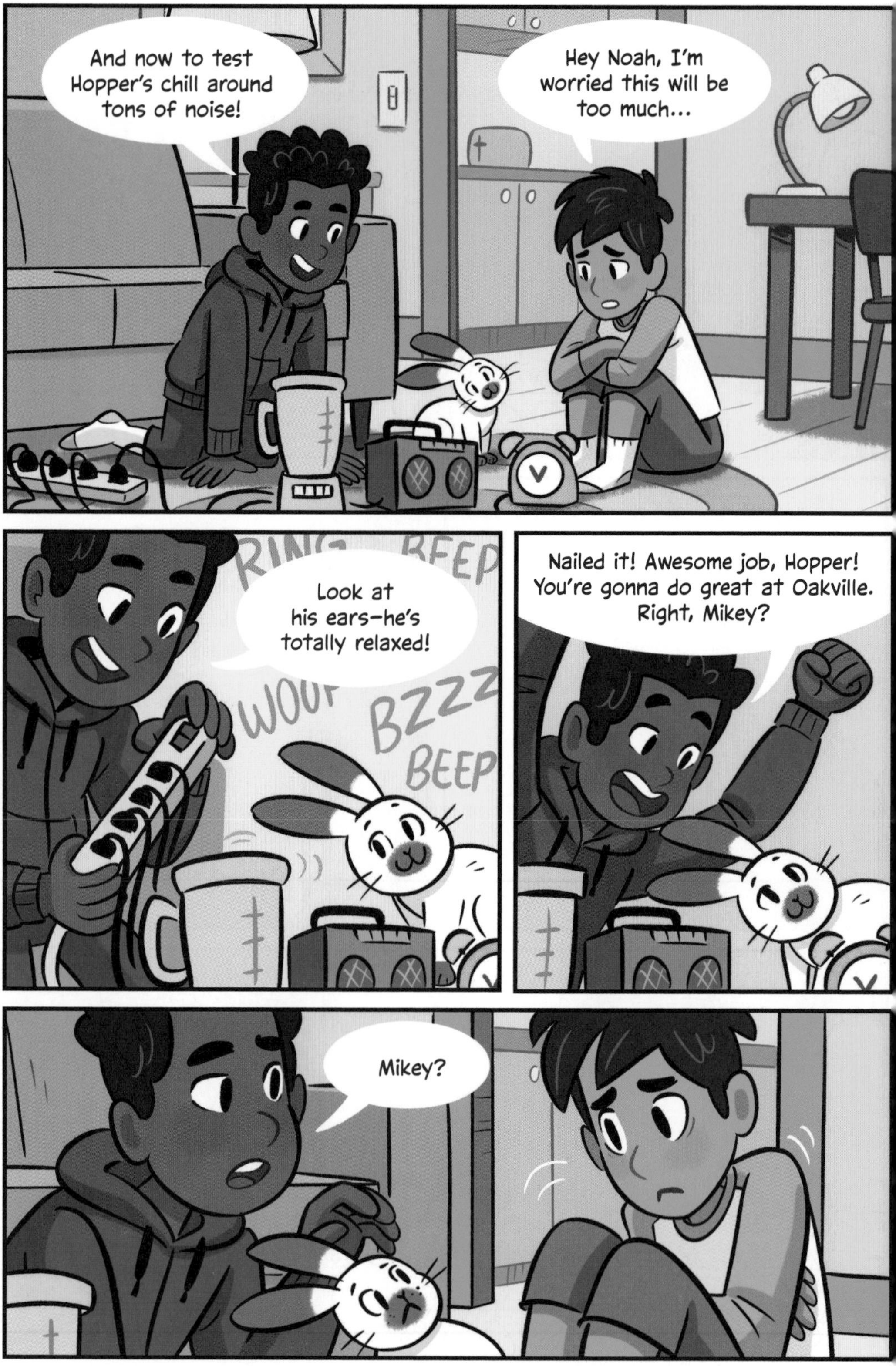
And now to test Hopper's chill around tons of noise!
Hey Noah, I'm worried this will be too much...
RING
BEEP
Look at his ears—he's totally relaxed!
BZZZ
BEEP
Nailed it! Awesome job, Hopper! You're gonna do great at Oakville. Right, Mikey?
Mikey?

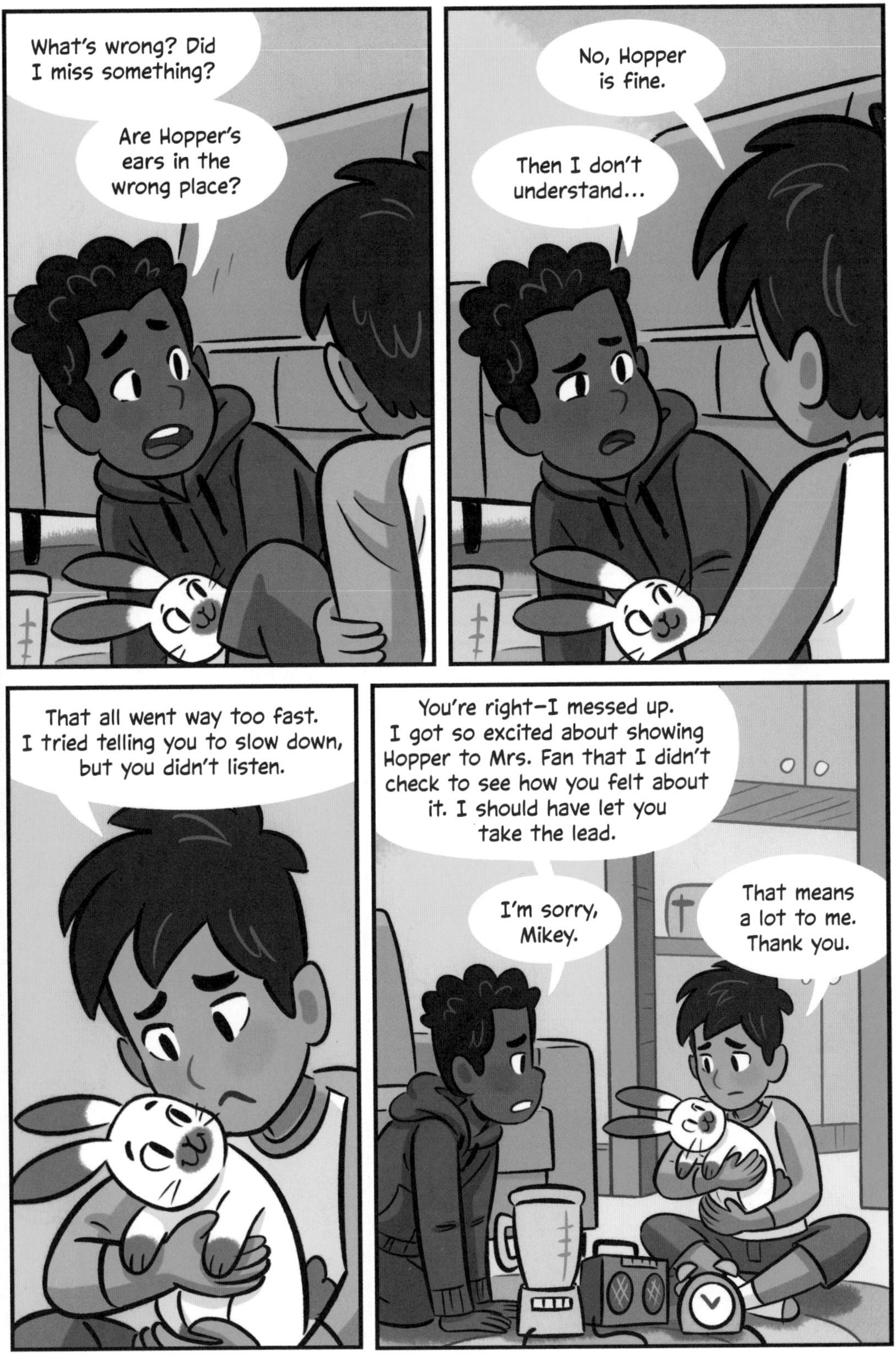
What's wrong? Did I miss something?
Are Hopper's ears in the wrong place?
No, Hopper is fine.
Then I don't understand...
That all went way too fast. I tried telling you to slow down, but you didn't listen.
You're right—I messed up. I got so excited about showing Hopper to Mrs. Fan that I didn't check to see how you felt about it. I should have let you take the lead.
I'm sorry, Mikey.
That means a lot to me. Thank you.

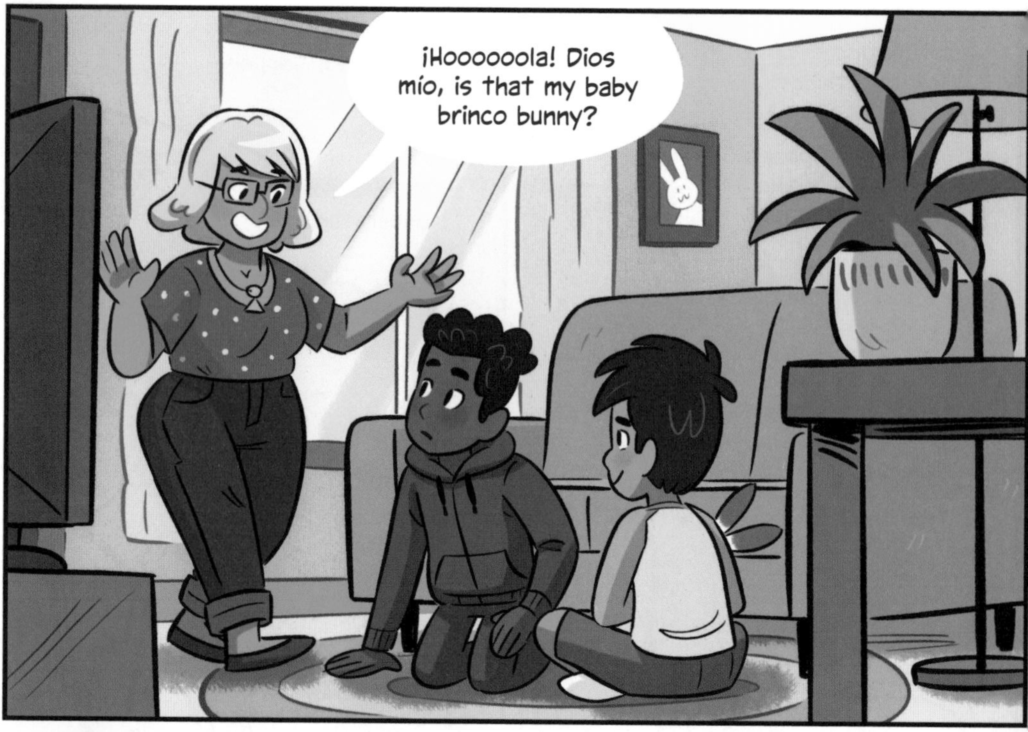
¡Hoooooola! Dios mío, is that my baby brinco bunny?

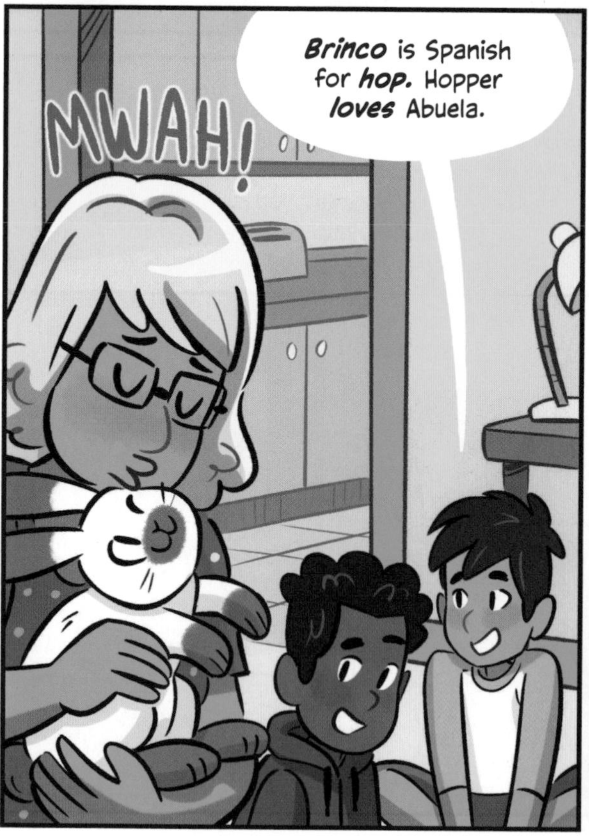
MWAH!
Brinco is Spanish for *hop.* Hopper *loves* Abuela.

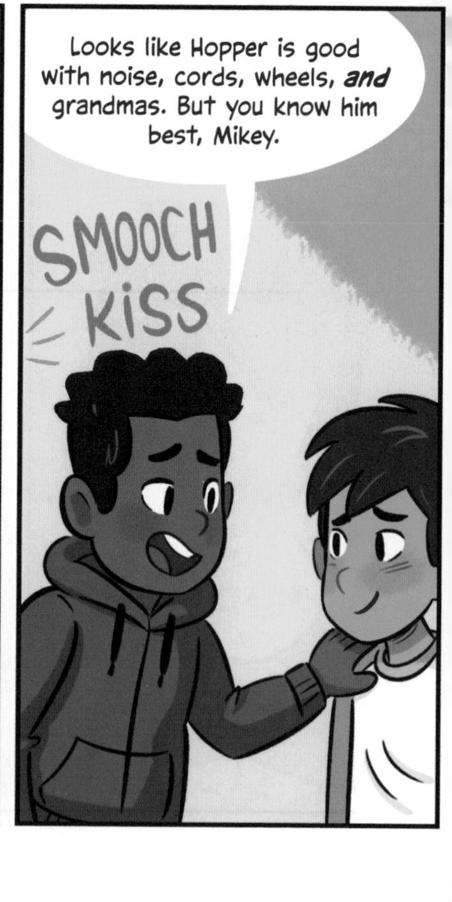
SMOOCH KISS
Looks like Hopper is good with noise, cords, wheels, *and* grandmas. But you know him best, Mikey.

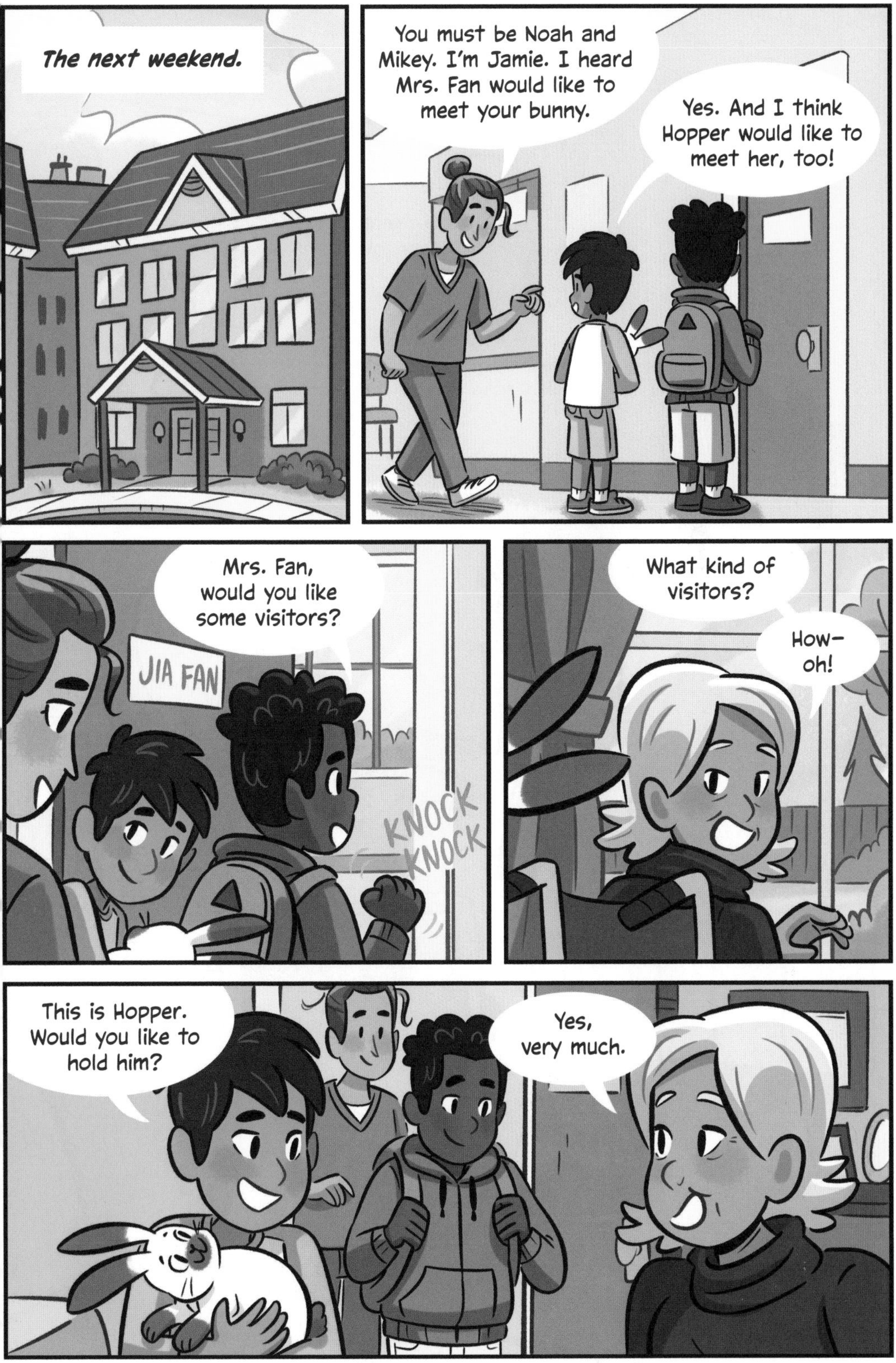
The next weekend.
You must be Noah and Mikey. I'm Jamie. I heard Mrs. Fan would like to meet your bunny.
Yes. And I think Hopper would like to meet her, too!
Mrs. Fan, would you like some visitors?
JIA FAN
KNOCK KNOCK
What kind of visitors?
How—oh!
This is Hopper. Would you like to hold him?
Yes, very much.

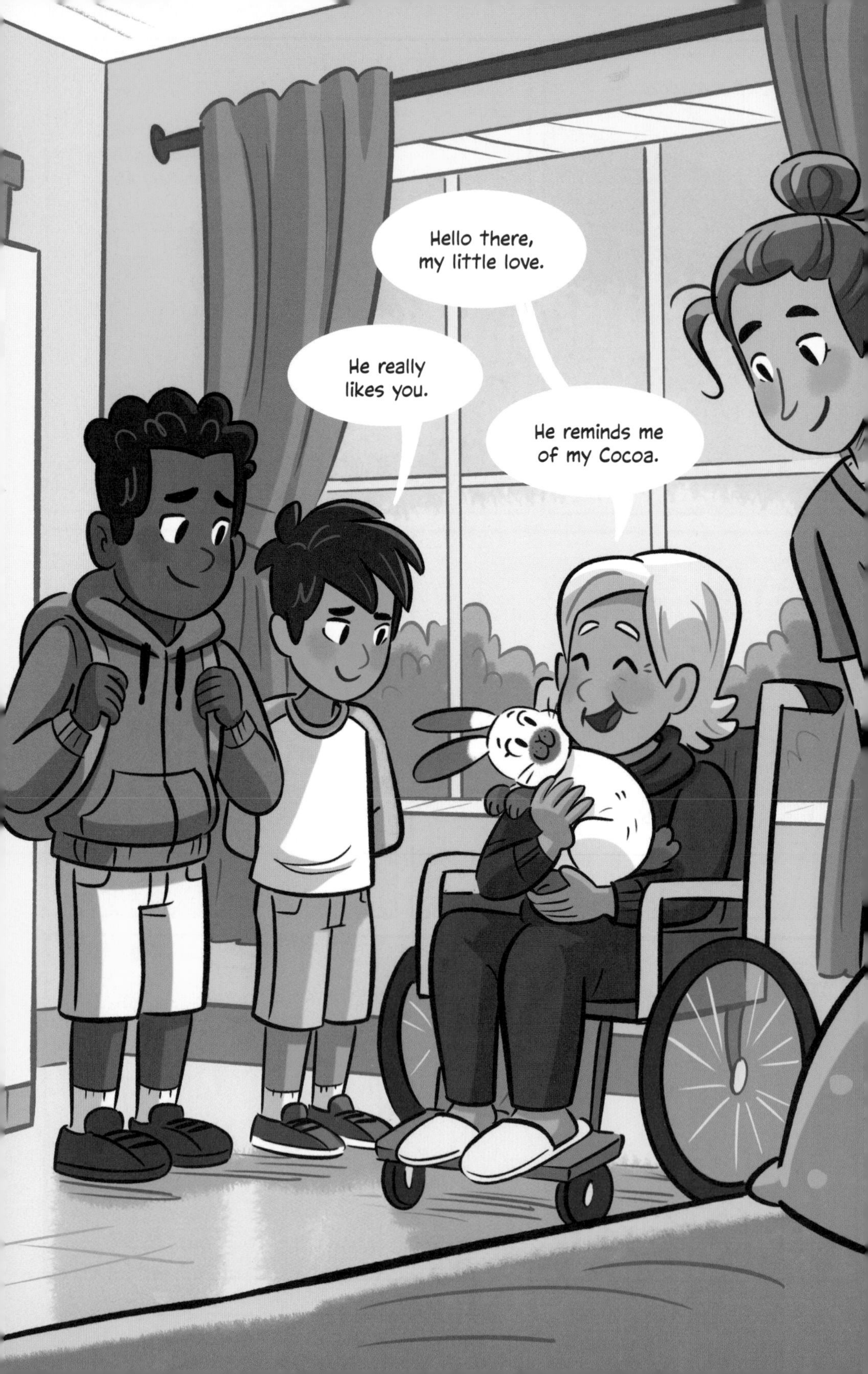
Hello there, my little love.
He really likes you.
He reminds me of my Cocoa.

"I kept a prizewinning garden for years, but one day I found that someone had come by for a snack.

"No matter what I did to protect my garden, he always found a way in.

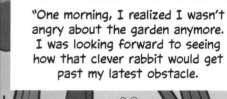

"One morning, I realized I wasn't angry about the garden anymore. I was looking forward to seeing how that clever rabbit would get past my latest obstacle.

"So I decided to try a different strategy.

COCOA'S SALAD BAR

"Once Cocoa had his *own* garden, we came to an understanding."

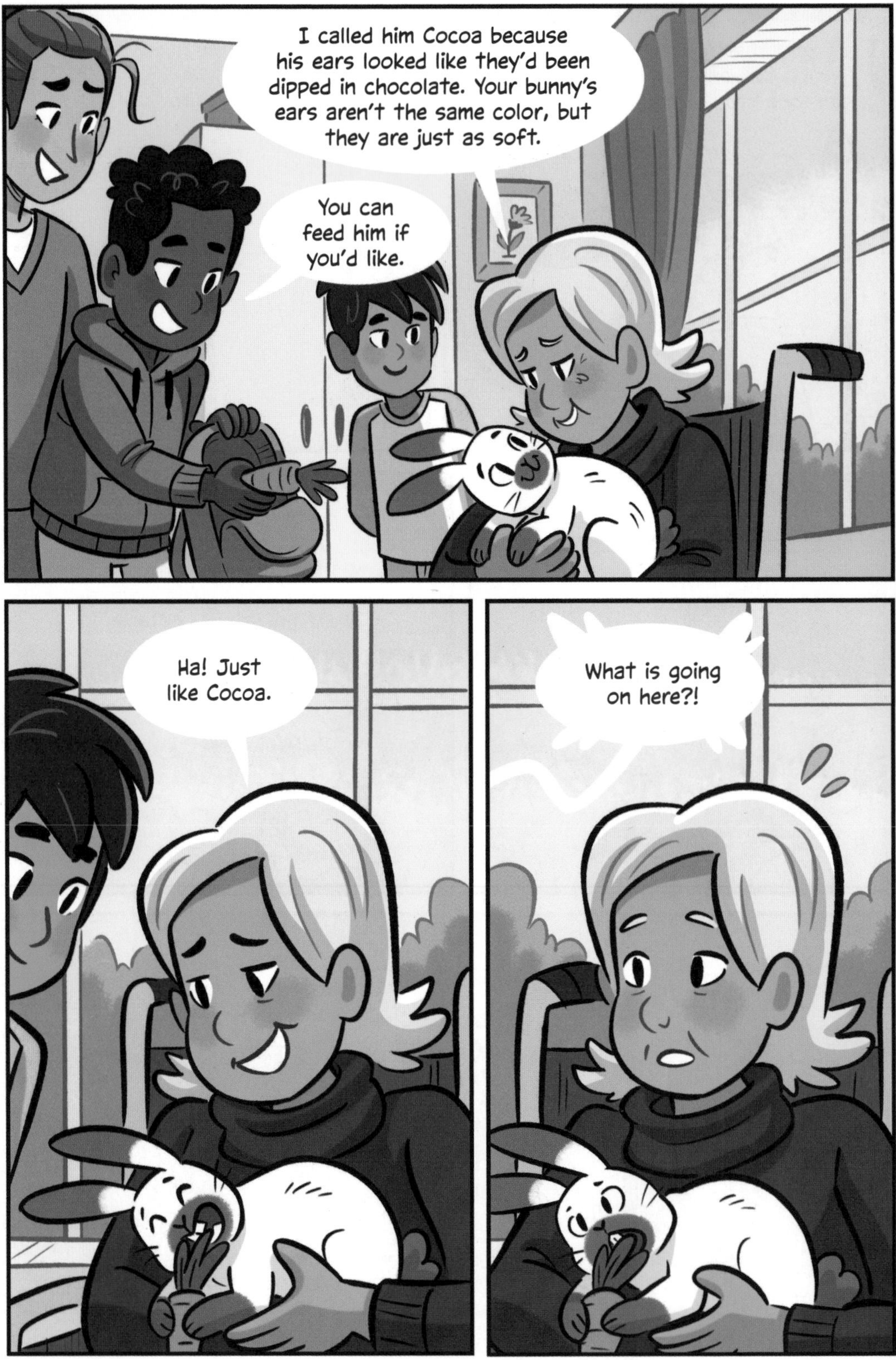
I called him Cocoa because his ears looked like they'd been dipped in chocolate. Your bunny's ears aren't the same color, but they are just as soft.
You can feed him if you'd like.
Ha! Just like Cocoa.
What is going on here?!

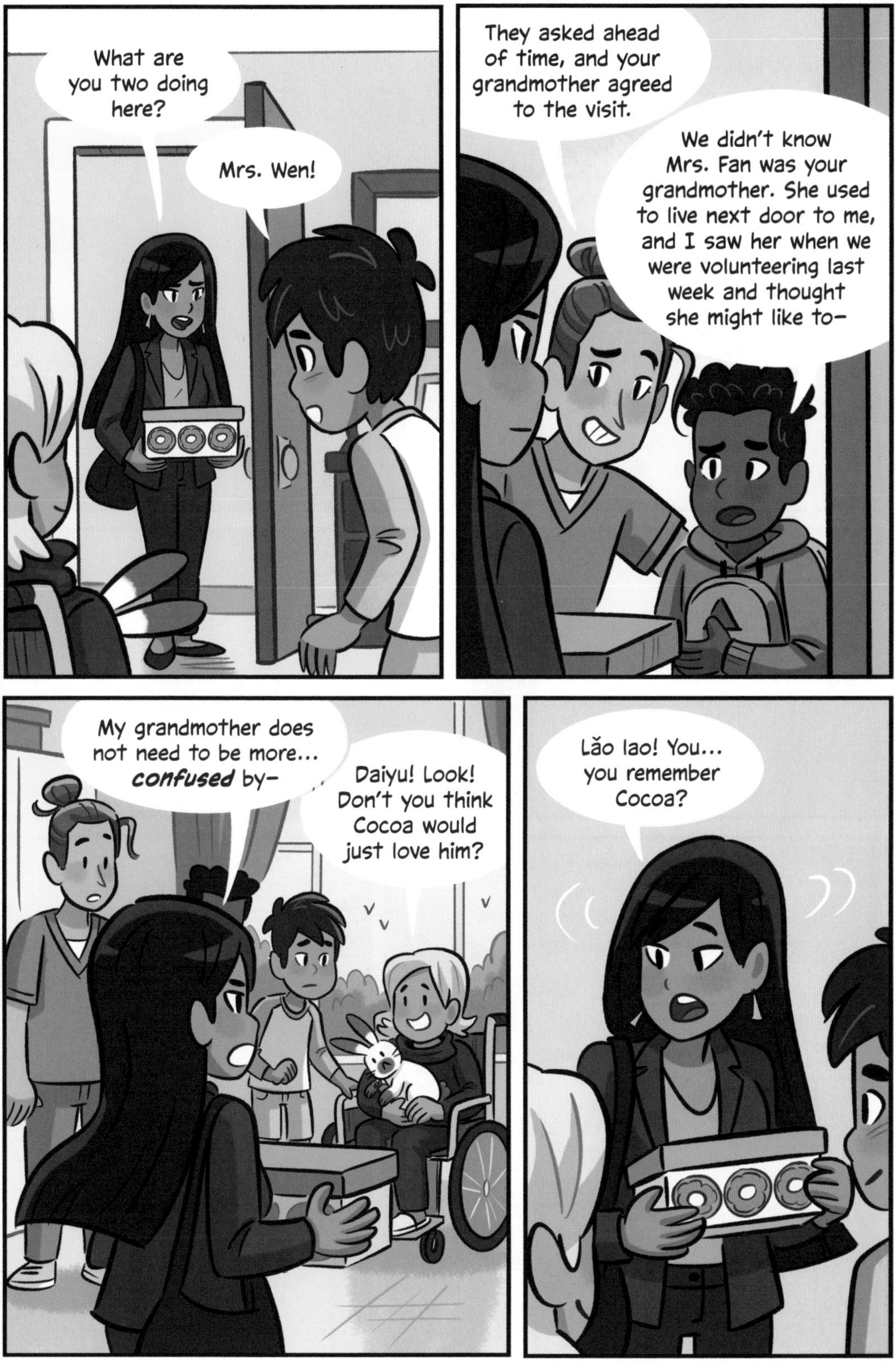
What are you two doing here?
Mrs. Wen!
They asked ahead of time, and your grandmother agreed to the visit.
We didn't know Mrs. Fan was your grandmother. She used to live next door to me, and I saw her when we were volunteering last week and thought she might like to–
My grandmother does not need to be more... *confused* by–
Daiyu! Look! Don't you think Cocoa would just love him?
Lǎo lao! You... you remember Cocoa?

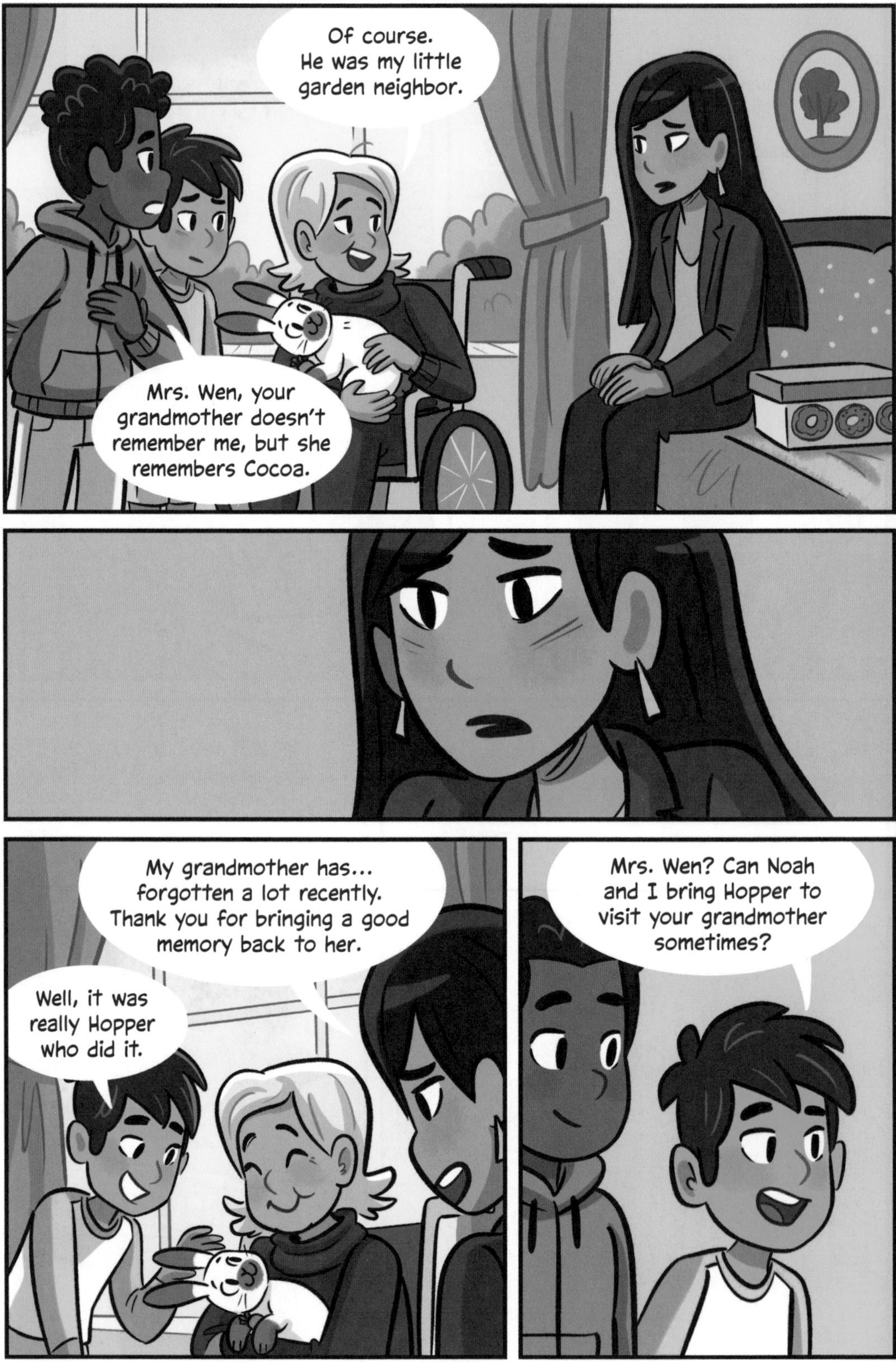
Of course. He was my little garden neighbor.
Mrs. Wen, your grandmother doesn't remember me, but she remembers Cocoa.
My grandmother has... forgotten a lot recently. Thank you for bringing a good memory back to her.
Well, it was really Hopper who did it.
Mrs. Wen? Can Noah and I bring Hopper to visit your grandmother sometimes?

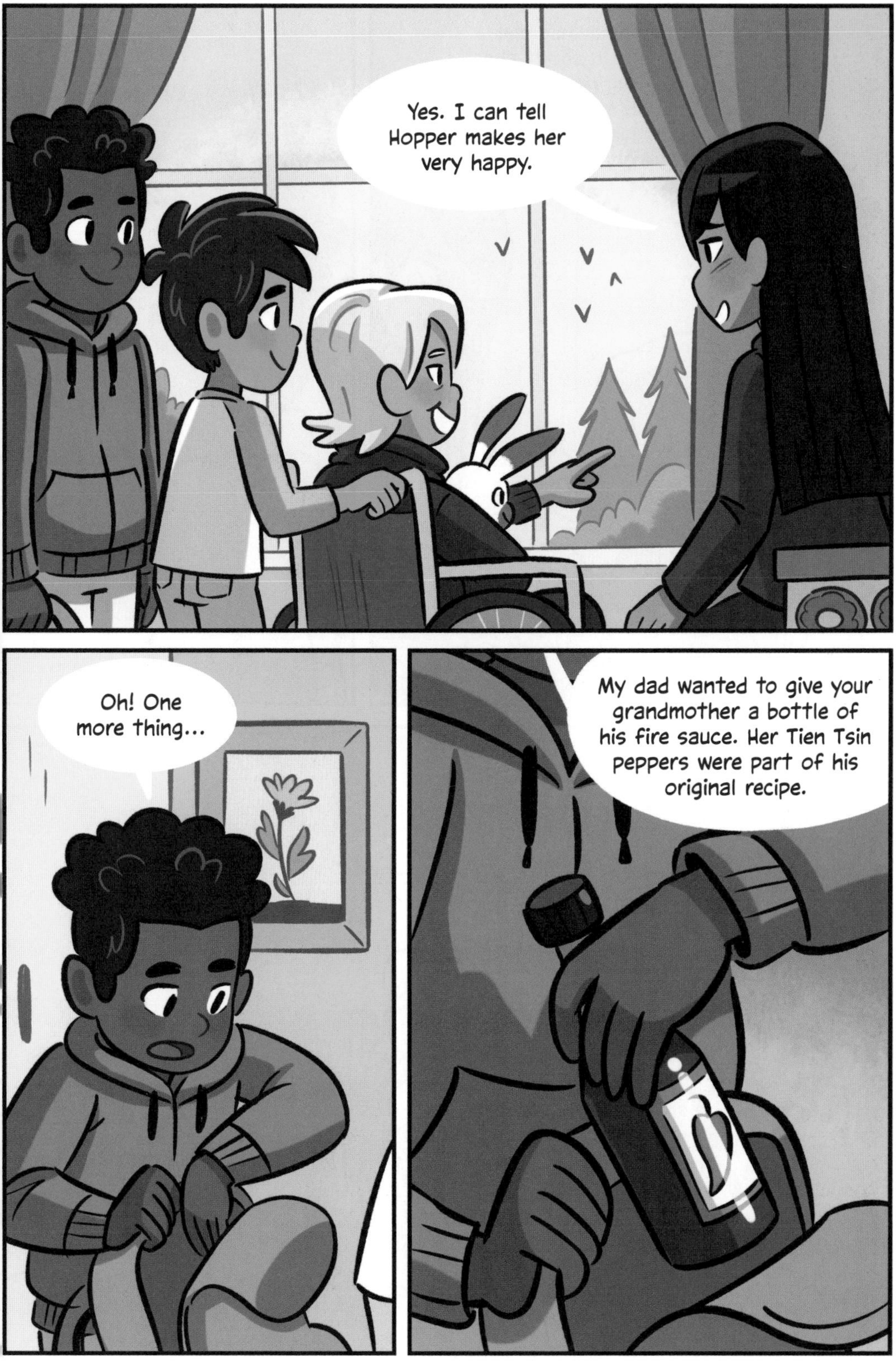
Yes. I can tell Hopper makes her very happy.
Oh! One more thing...
My dad wanted to give your grandmother a bottle of his fire sauce. Her Tien Tsin peppers were part of his original recipe.

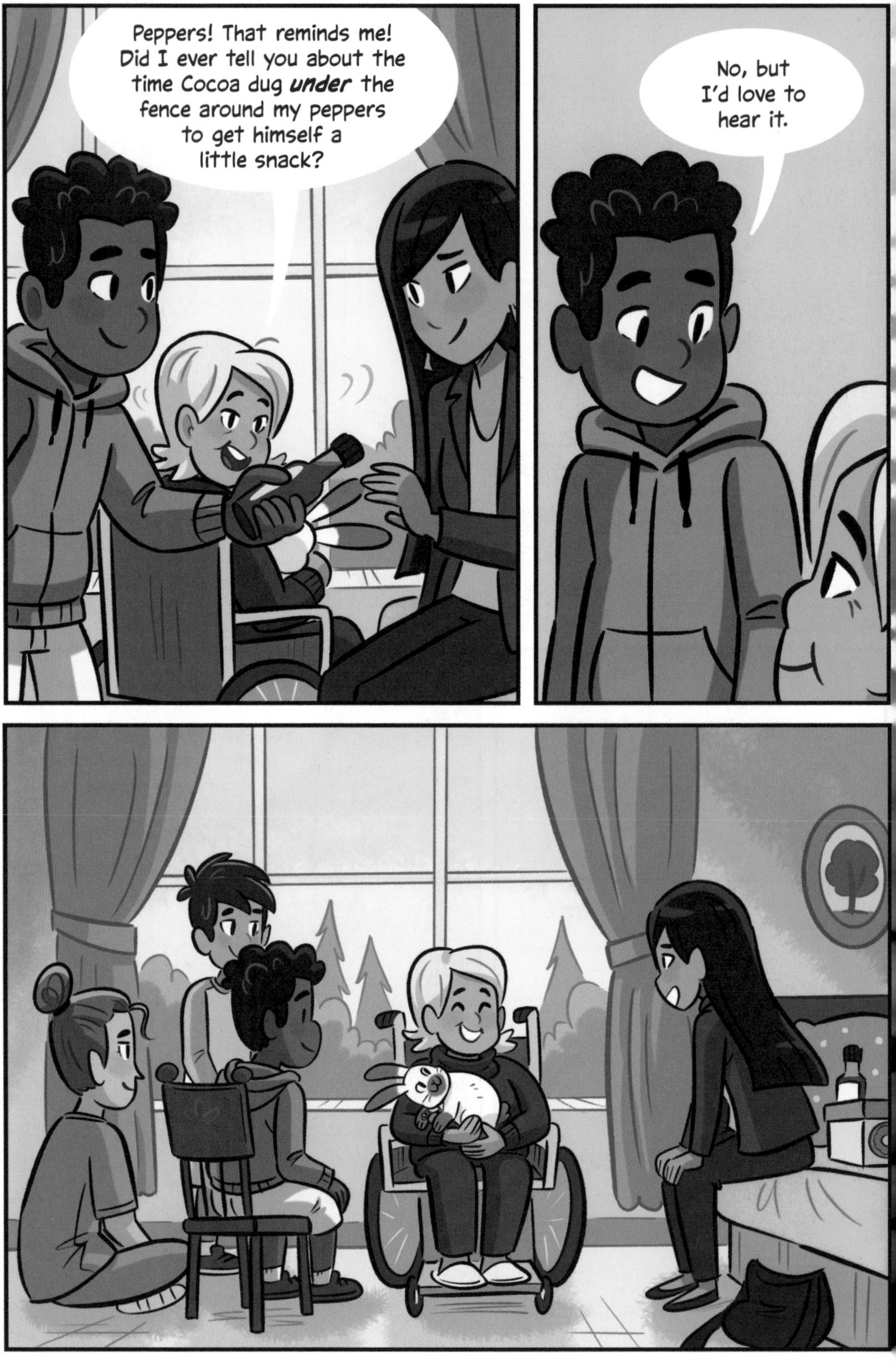
Peppers! That reminds me! Did I ever tell you about the time Cocoa dug ***under*** the fence around my peppers to get himself a little snack?
No, but I'd love to hear it.

Chapter 4

TO FLEE, OR NOT TO FLEE

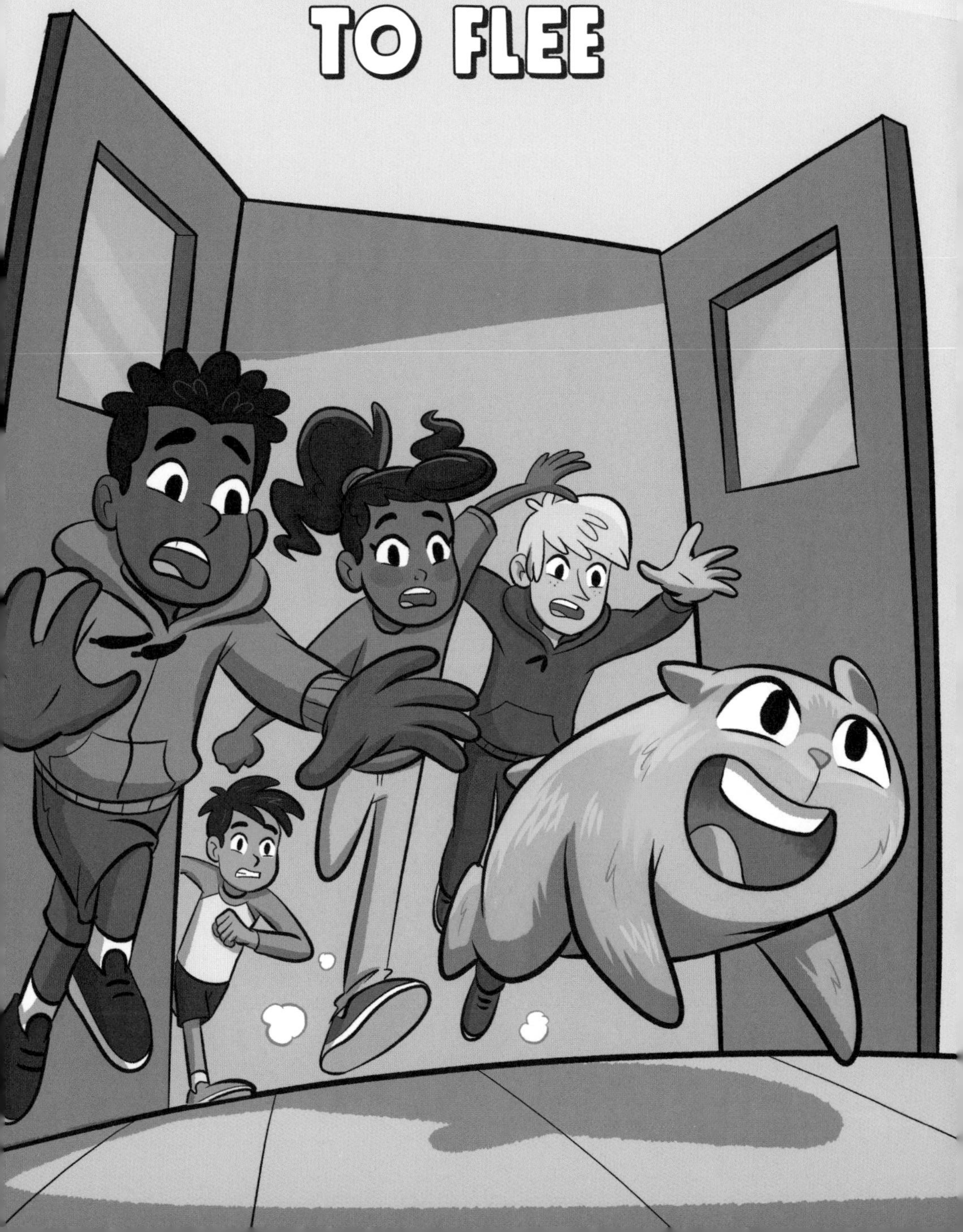

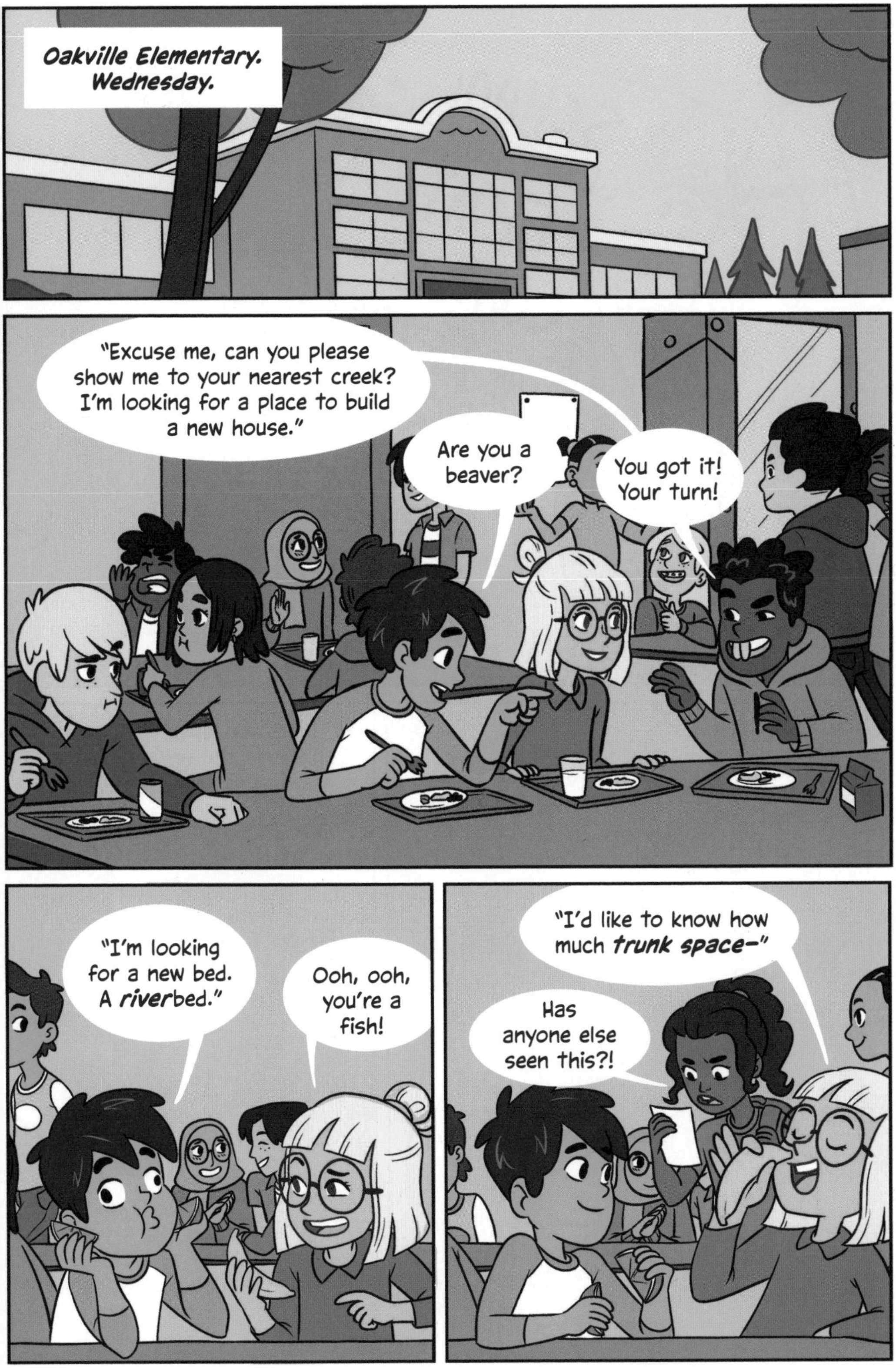
Oakville Elementary. Wednesday.
"Excuse me, can you please show me to your nearest creek? I'm looking for a place to build a new house."
Are you a beaver?
You got it! Your turn!
"I'm looking for a new bed. A *river*bed."
Ooh, ooh, you're a fish!
"I'd like to know how much *trunk space*–"
Has anyone else seen this?!

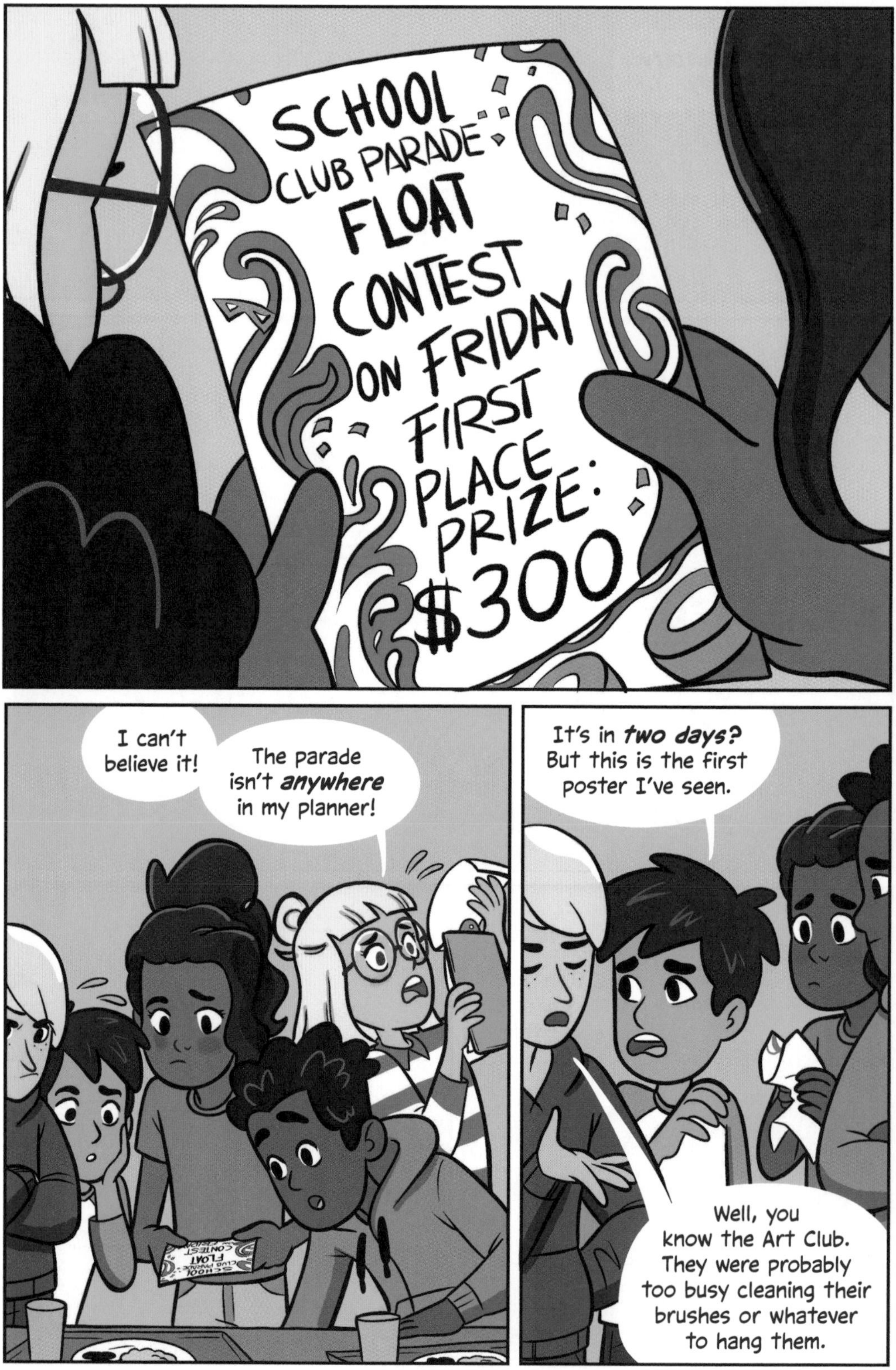
SCHOOL CLUB PARADE FLOAT CONTEST ON FRIDAY FIRST PLACE PRIZE: $300
I can't believe it!
The parade isn't ***anywhere*** in my planner!
SCHOOL CLUB PARADE FLOAT CONTEST
It's in ***two days?*** But this is the first poster I've seen.
Well, you know the Art Club. They were probably too busy cleaning their brushes or whatever to hang them.

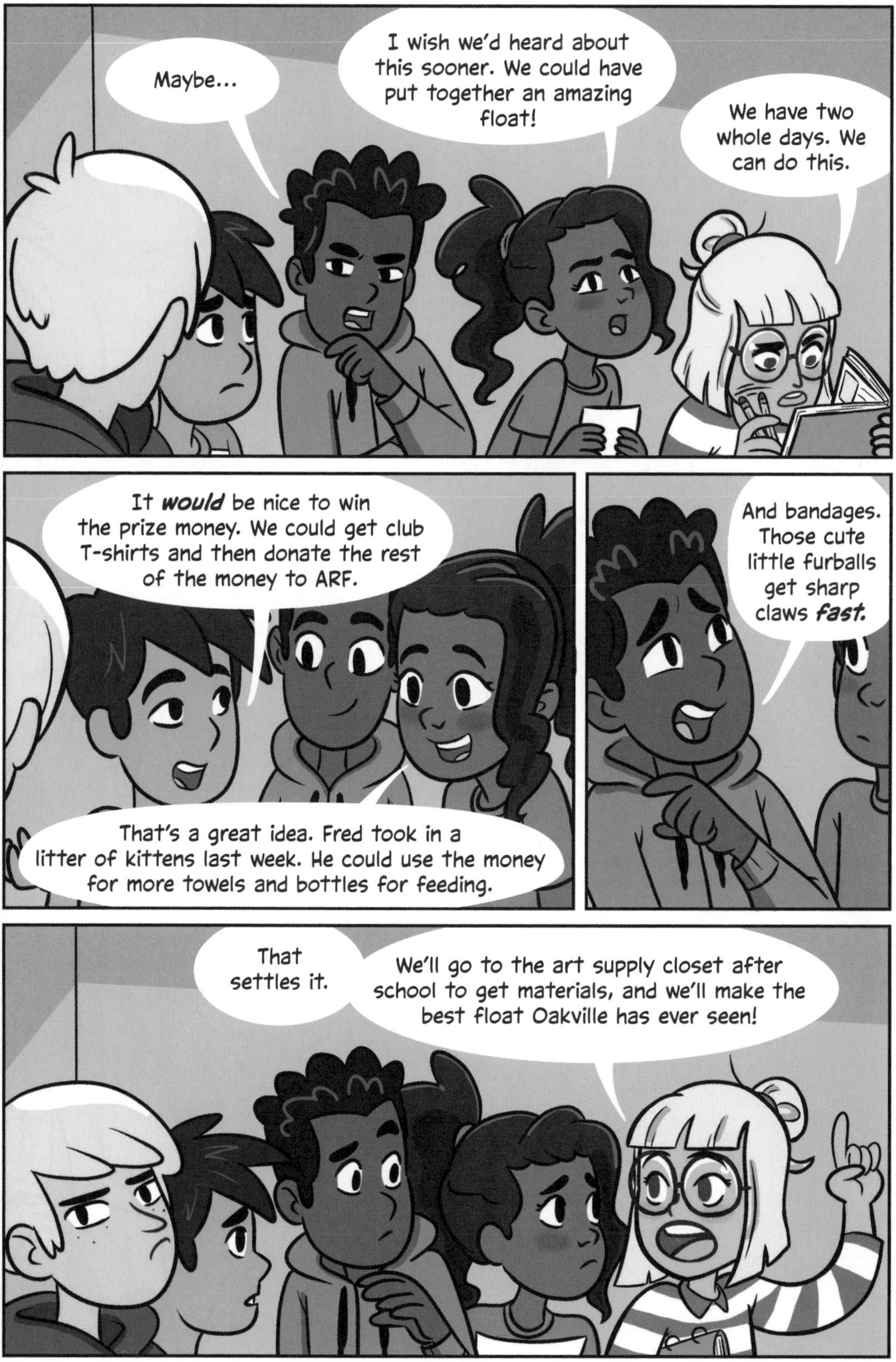
Maybe...
I wish we'd heard about this sooner. We could have put together an amazing float!
We have two whole days. We can do this.
It *would* be nice to win the prize money. We could get club T-shirts and then donate the rest of the money to ARF.
That's a great idea. Fred took in a litter of kittens last week. He could use the money for more towels and bottles for feeding.
And bandages. Those cute little furballs get sharp claws *fast*.
That settles it.
We'll go to the art supply closet after school to get materials, and we'll make the best float Oakville has ever seen!

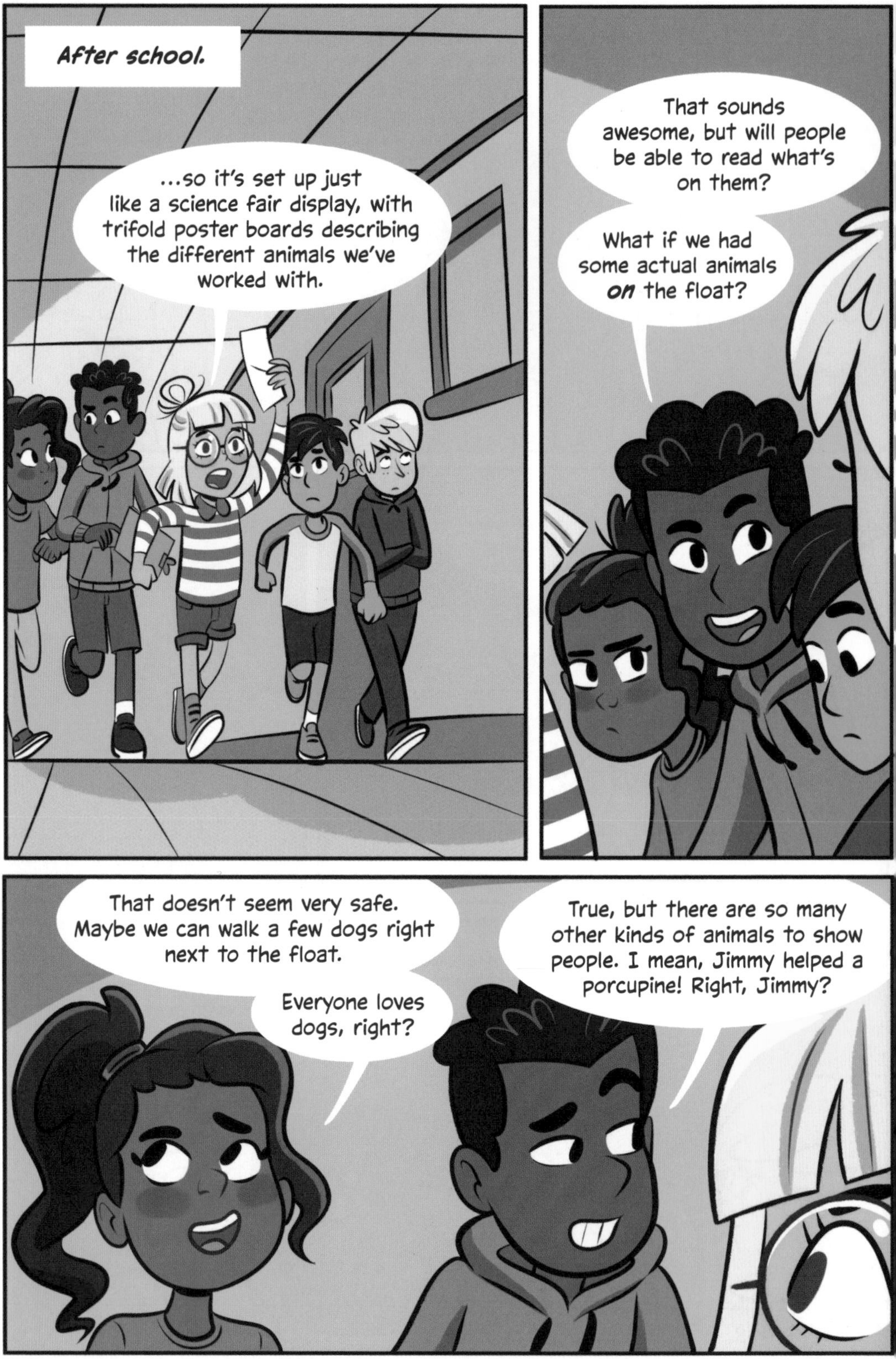
After school.
...so it's set up just like a science fair display, with trifold poster boards describing the different animals we've worked with.
That sounds awesome, but will people be able to read what's on them?
What if we had some actual animals *on* the float?
That doesn't seem very safe. Maybe we can walk a few dogs right next to the float.
Everyone loves dogs, right?
True, but there are so many other kinds of animals to show people. I mean, Jimmy helped a porcupine! Right, Jimmy?

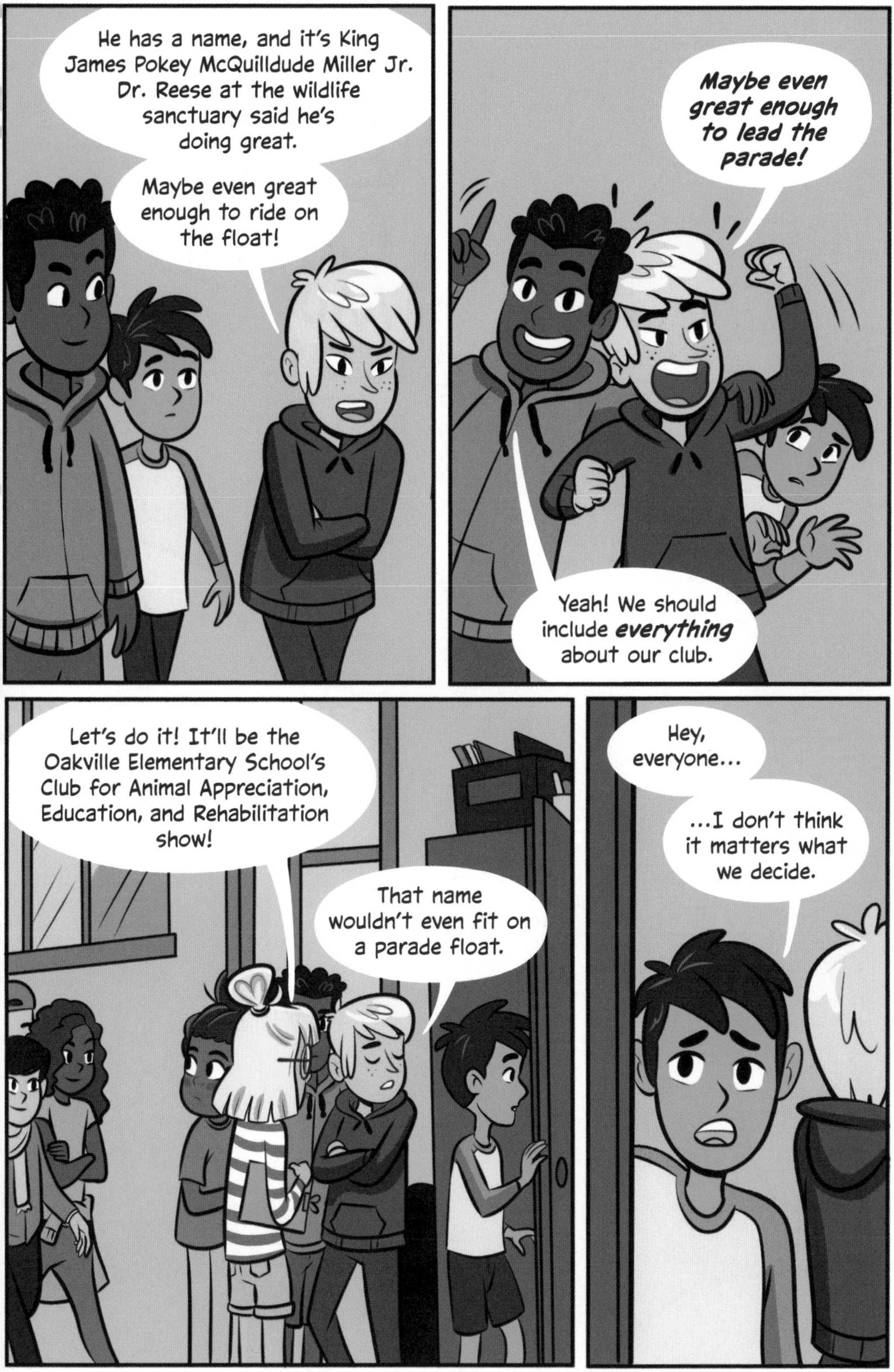
He has a name, and it's King James Pokey McQuilldude Miller Jr. Dr. Reese at the wildlife sanctuary said he's doing great.
Maybe even great enough to ride on the float!
Maybe even great enough to lead the parade!
Yeah! We should include everything about our club.
Let's do it! It'll be the Oakville Elementary School's Club for Animal Appreciation, Education, and Rehabilitation show!
That name wouldn't even fit on a parade float.
Hey, everyone...
...I don't think it matters what we decide.

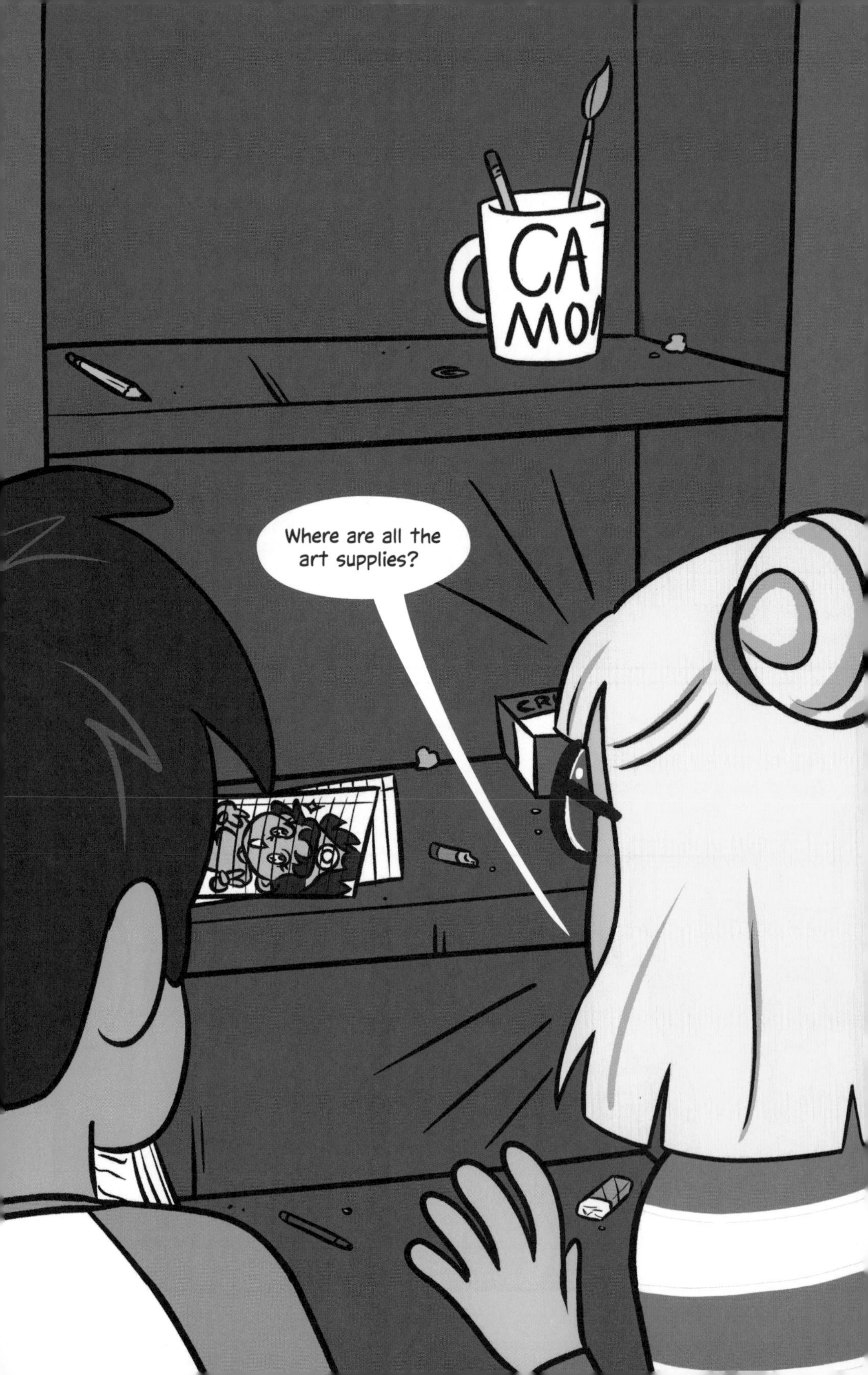
CAT MOM
Where are all the art supplies?

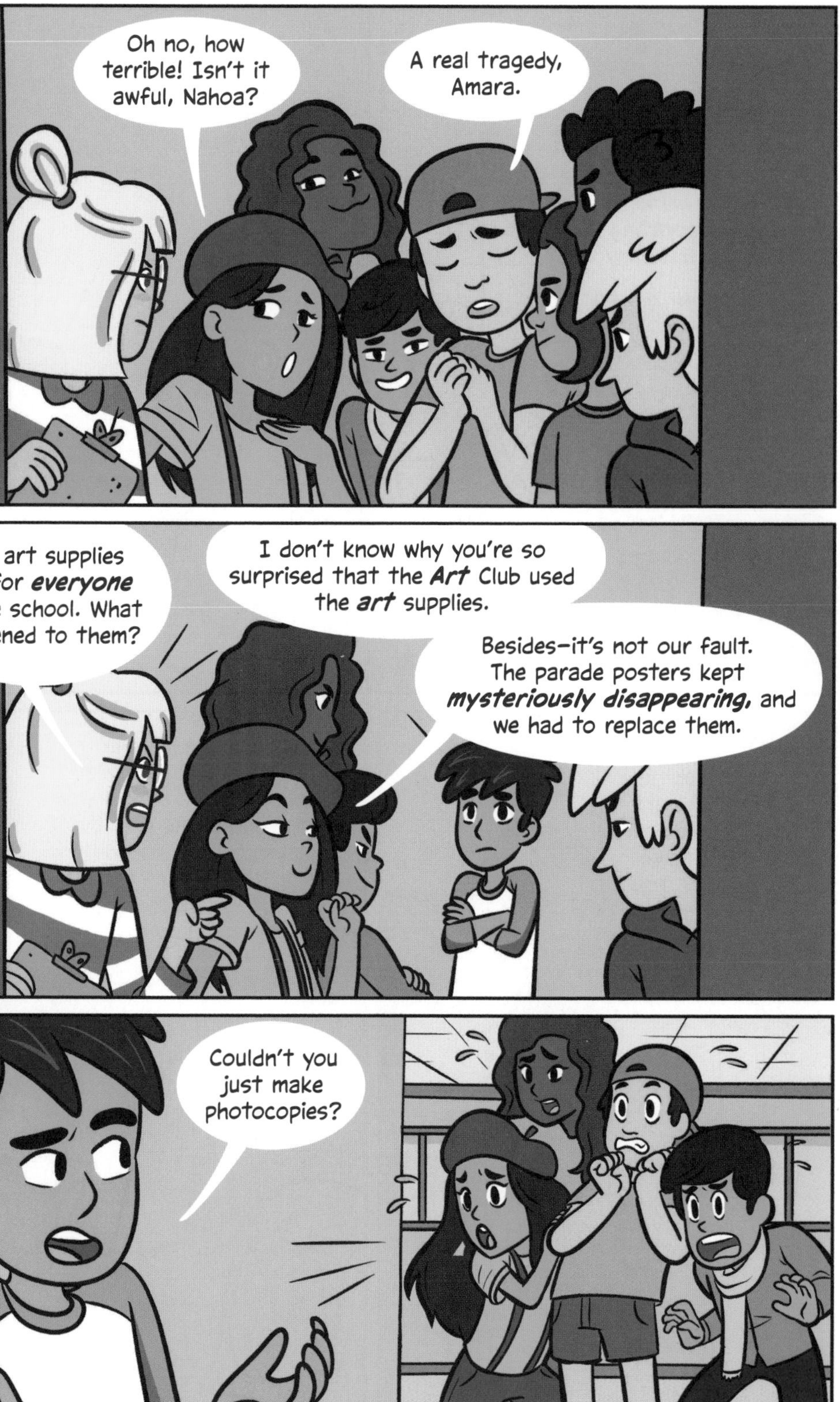
Oh no, how terrible! Isn't it awful, Nahoa?
A real tragedy, Amara.
The art supplies are for **everyone** in the school. What happened to them?
I don't know why you're so surprised that the **Art** Club used the **art** supplies.
Besides—it's not our fault. The parade posters kept **mysteriously disappearing,** and we had to replace them.
Couldn't you just make photocopies?

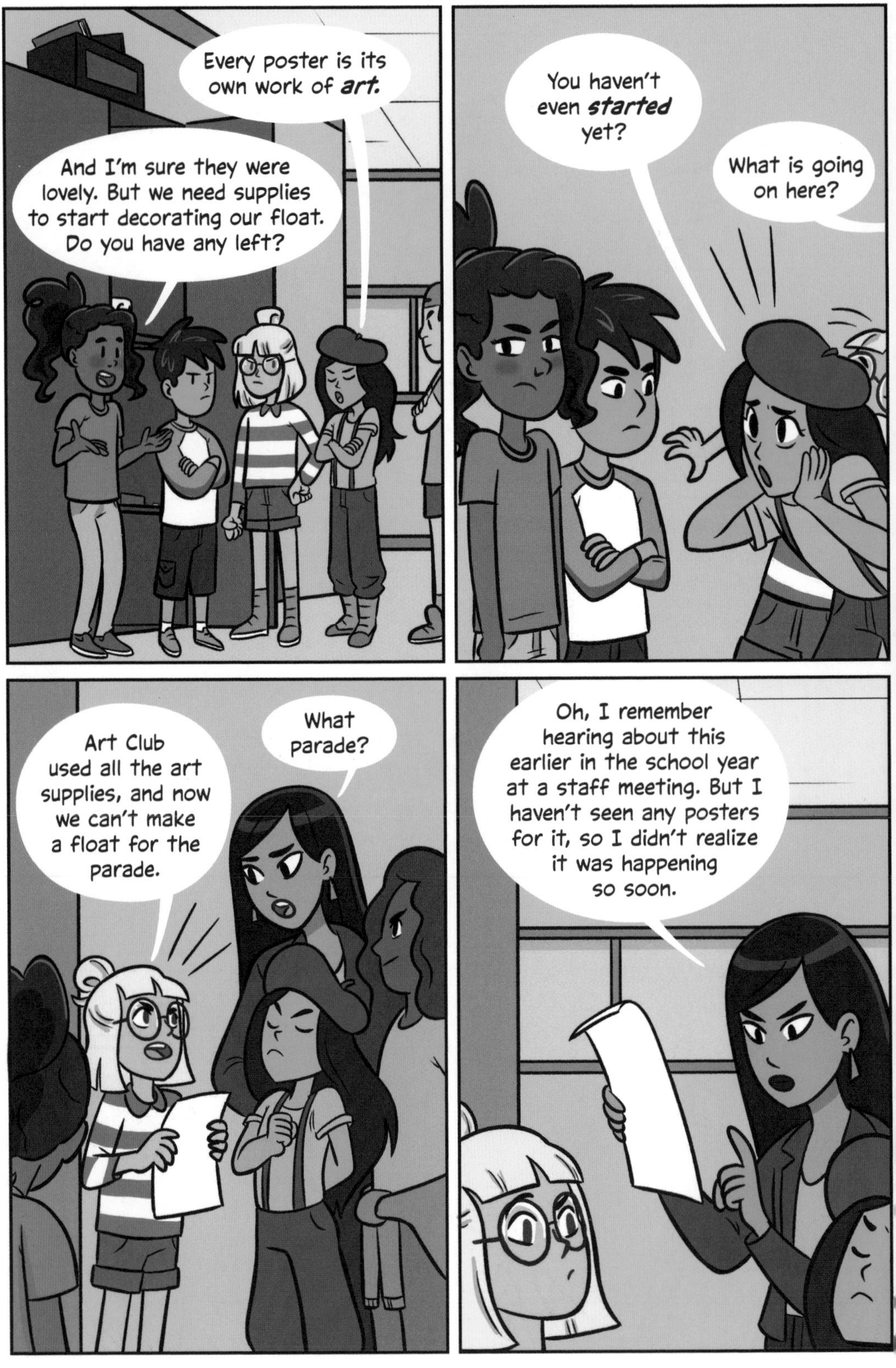
Every poster is its own work of *art.*
And I'm sure they were lovely. But we need supplies to start decorating our float. Do you have any left?
You haven't even *started* yet?
What is going on here?
Art Club used all the art supplies, and now we can't make a float for the parade.
What parade?
Oh, I remember hearing about this earlier in the school year at a staff meeting. But I haven't seen any posters for it, so I didn't realize it was happening so soon.

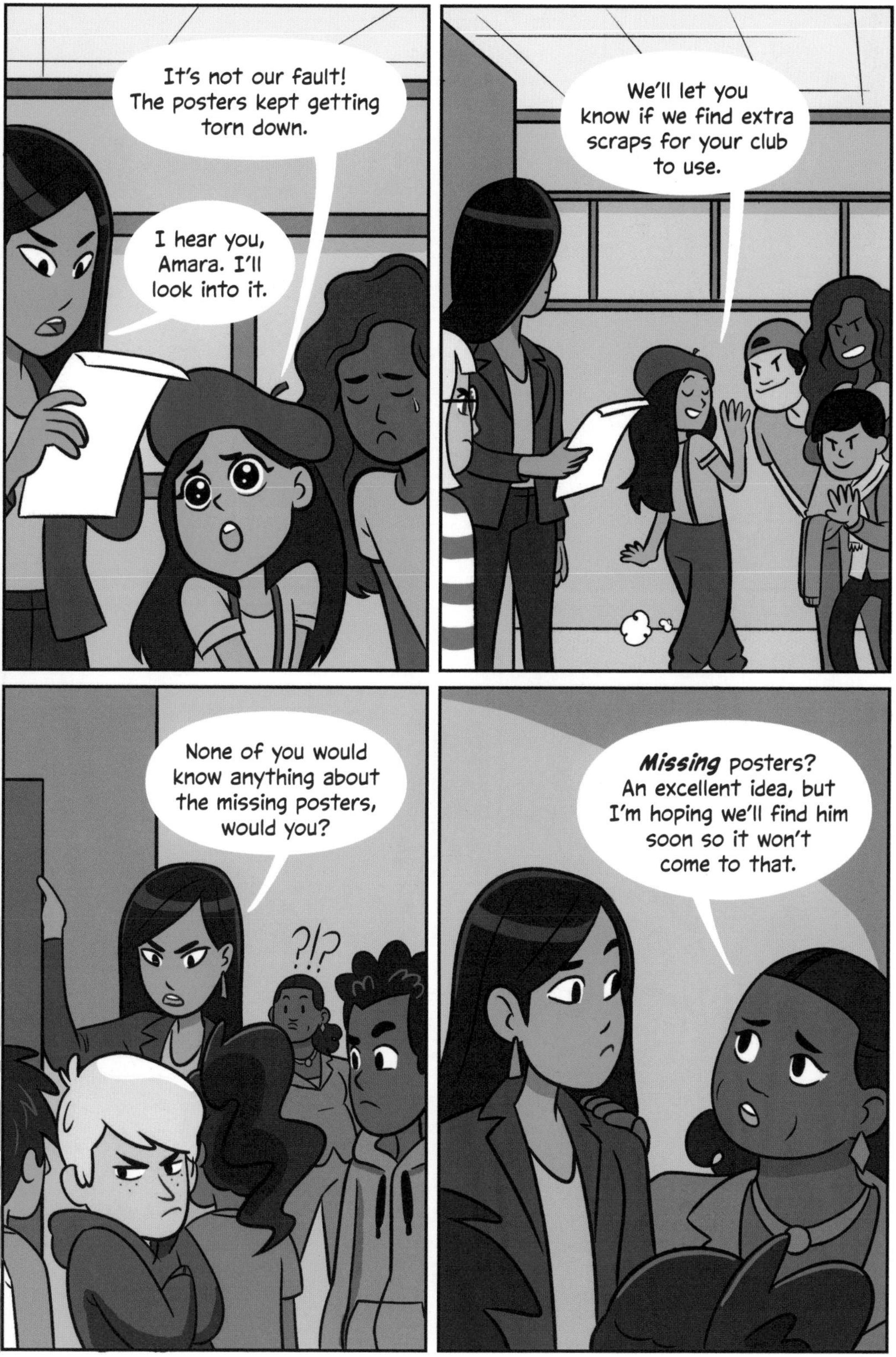
It's not our fault! The posters kept getting torn down.
I hear you, Amara. I'll look into it.
We'll let you know if we find extra scraps for your club to use.
None of you would know anything about the missing posters, would you?
?!?
Missing posters? An excellent idea, but I'm hoping we'll find him soon so it won't come to that.

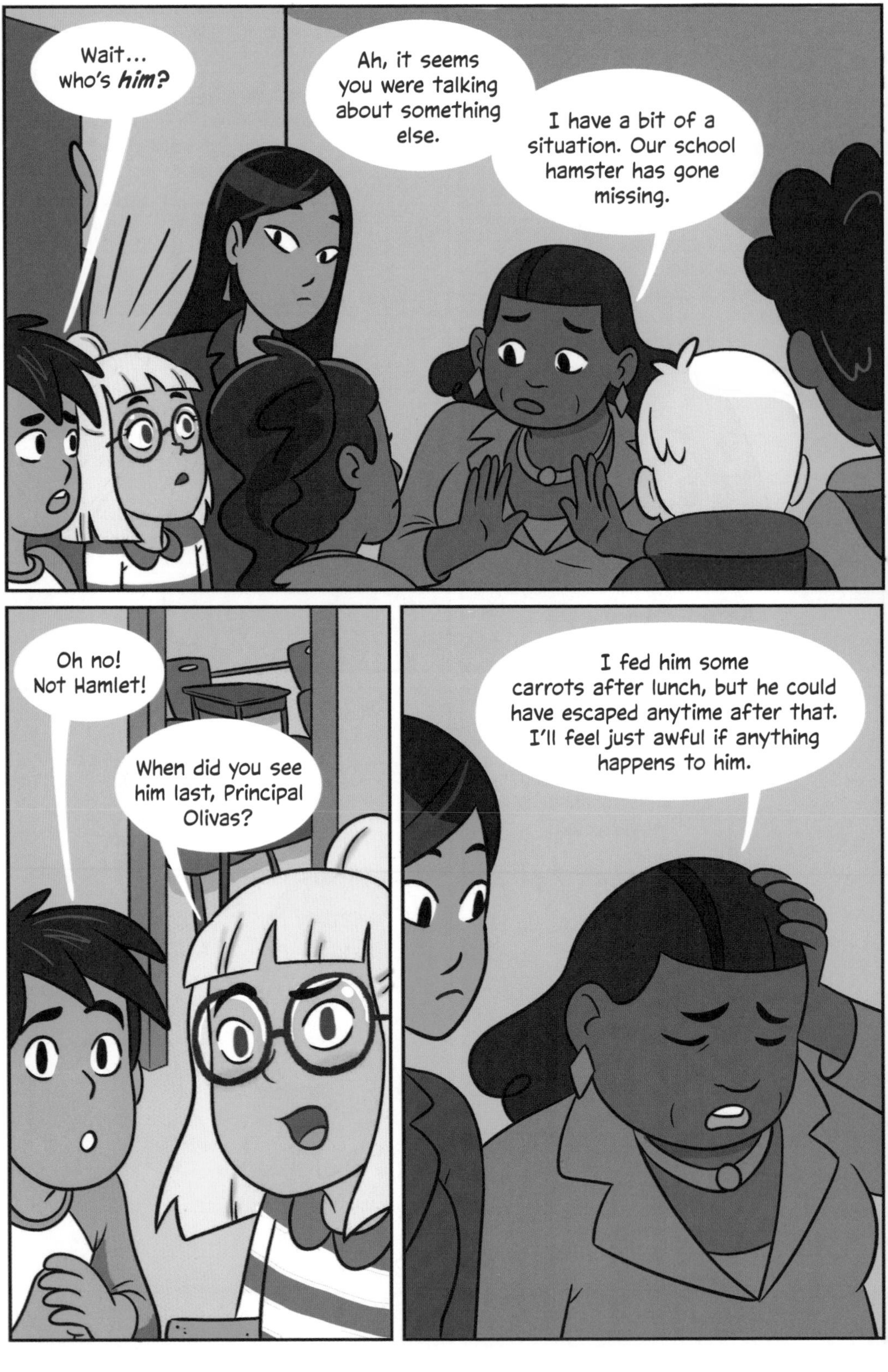
Wait... who's him?
Ah, it seems you were talking about something else.
I have a bit of a situation. Our school hamster has gone missing.
Oh no! Not Hamlet!
When did you see him last, Principal Olivas?
I fed him some carrots after lunch, but he could have escaped anytime after that. I'll feel just awful if anything happens to him.

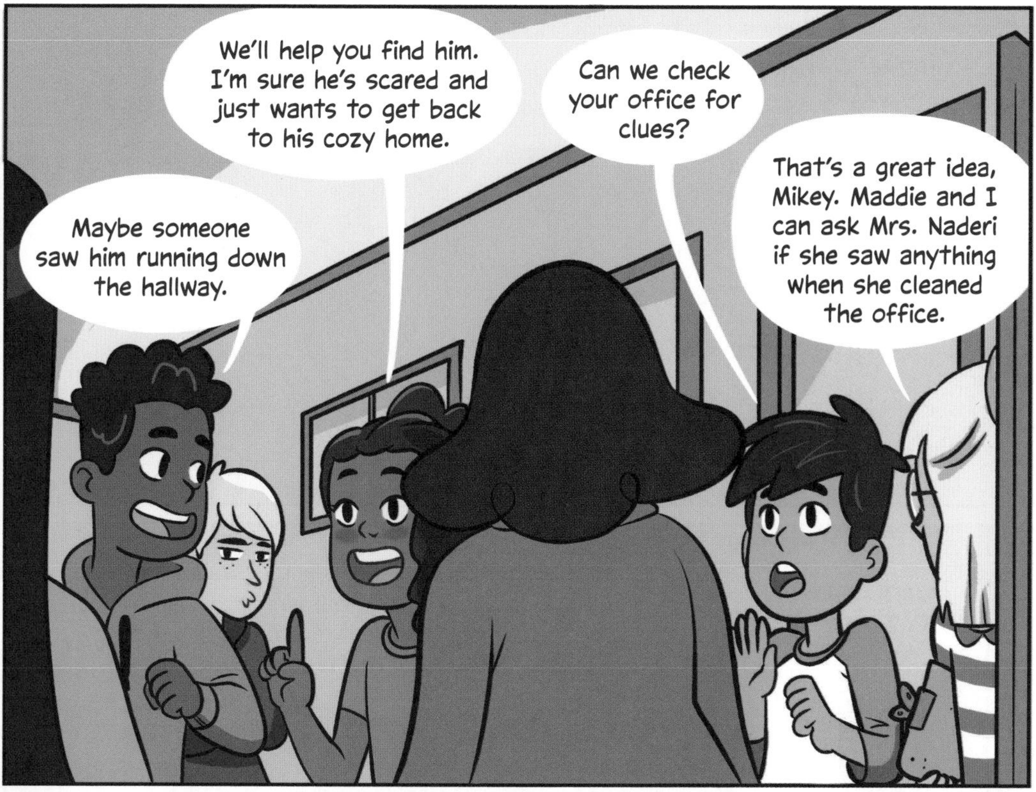
Maybe someone saw him running down the hallway.
We'll help you find him. I'm sure he's scared and just wants to get back to his cozy home.
Can we check your office for clues?
That's a great idea, Mikey. Maddie and I can ask Mrs. Naderi if she saw anything when she cleaned the office.

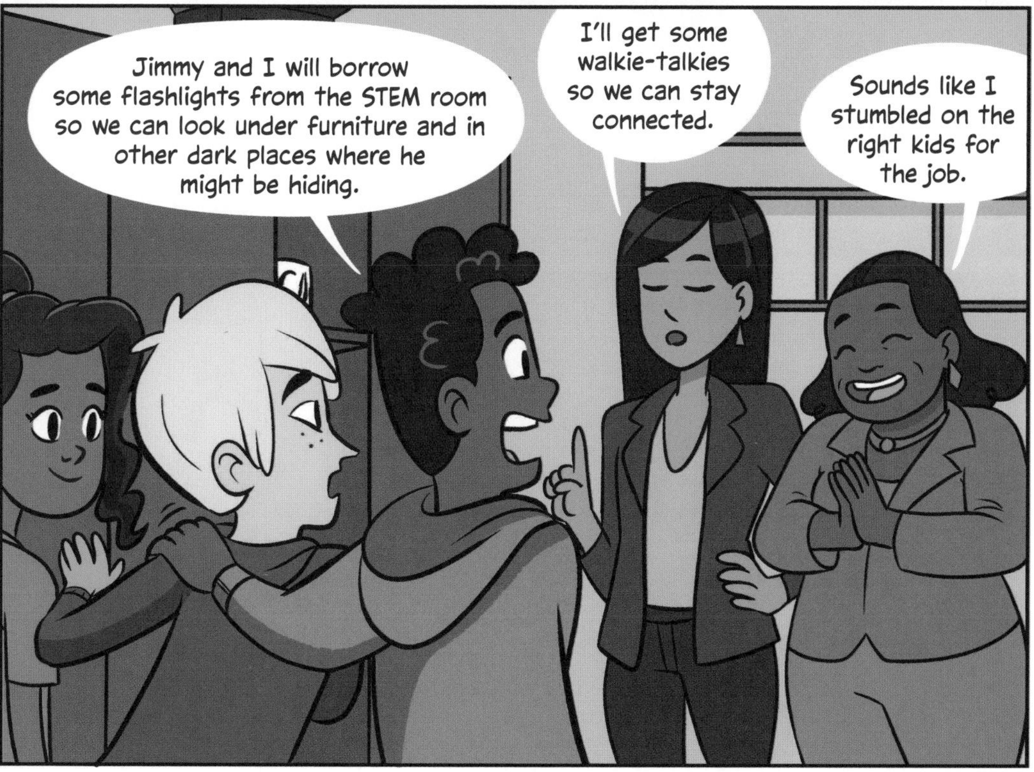
Jimmy and I will borrow some flashlights from the STEM room so we can look under furniture and in other dark places where he might be hiding.
I'll get some walkie-talkies so we can stay connected.
Sounds like I stumbled on the right kids for the job.

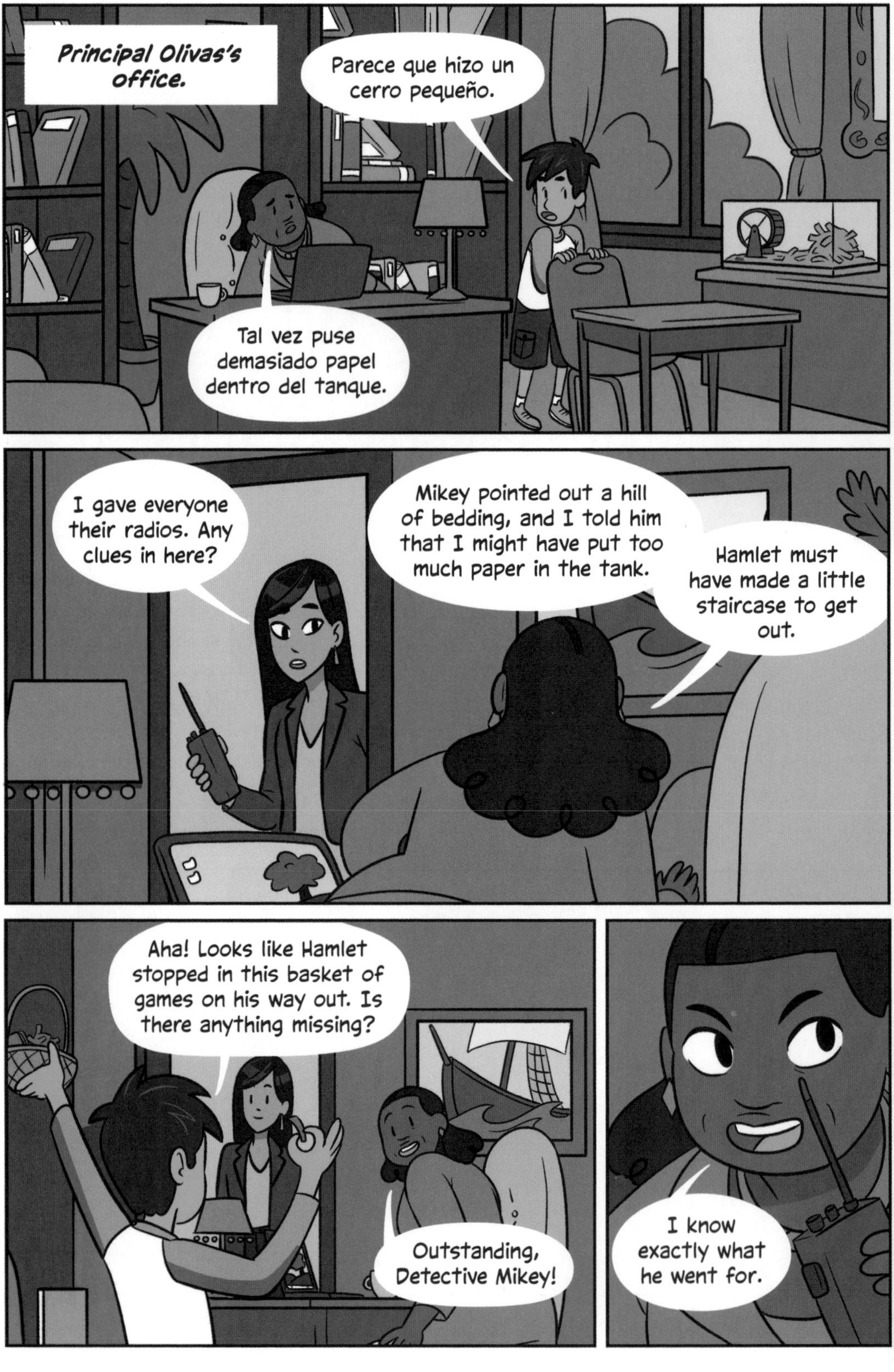

Principal Olivas's office.
Parece que hizo un cerro pequeño.
Tal vez puse demasiado papel dentro del tanque.
I gave everyone their radios. Any clues in here?
Mikey pointed out a hill of bedding, and I told him that I might have put too much paper in the tank.
Hamlet must have made a little staircase to get out.
Aha! Looks like Hamlet stopped in this basket of games on his way out. Is there anything missing?
Outstanding, Detective Mikey!
I know exactly what he went for.

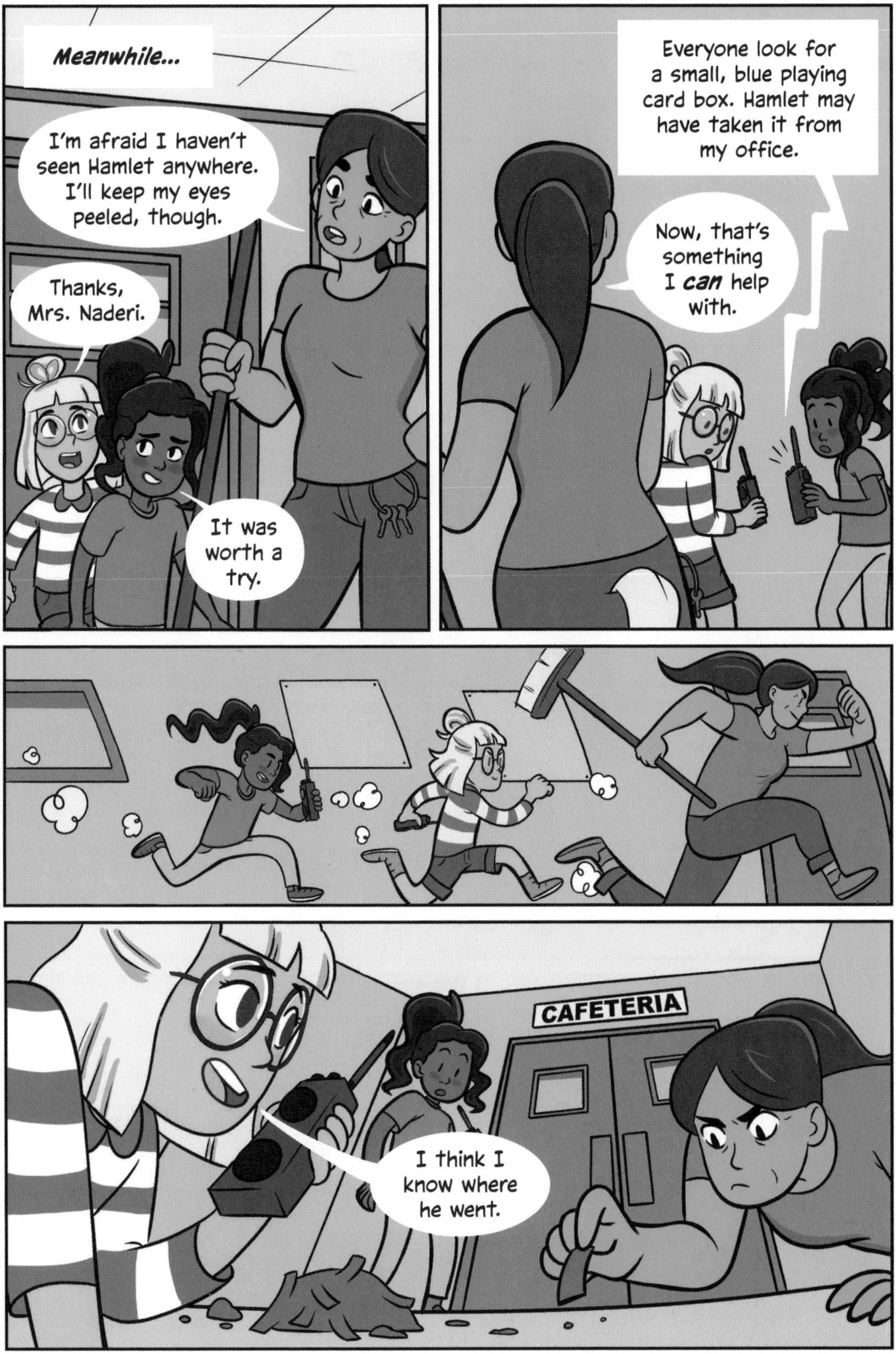

Meanwhile...
I'm afraid I haven't seen Hamlet anywhere. I'll keep my eyes peeled, though.
Thanks, Mrs. Naderi.
It was worth a try.
Everyone look for a small, blue playing card box. Hamlet may have taken it from my office.
Now, that's something I *can* help with.
CAFETERIA
I think I know where he went.

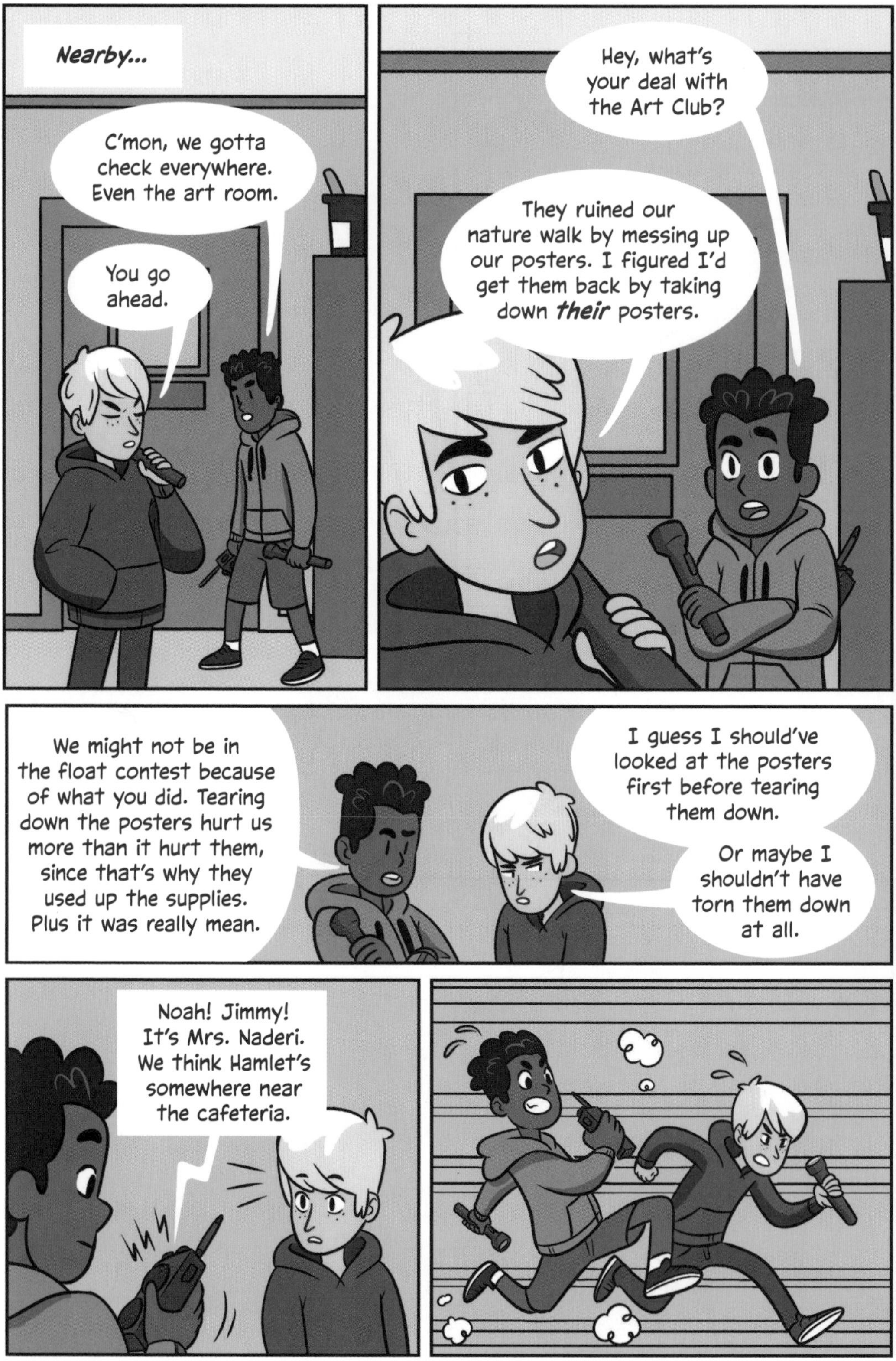
Nearby...
C'mon, we gotta check everywhere. Even the art room.
You go ahead.
Hey, what's your deal with the Art Club?
They ruined our nature walk by messing up our posters. I figured I'd get them back by taking down *their* posters.
We might not be in the float contest because of what you did. Tearing down the posters hurt us more than it hurt them, since that's why they used up the supplies. Plus it was really mean.
I guess I should've looked at the posters first before tearing them down.
Or maybe I shouldn't have torn them down at all.
Noah! Jimmy! It's Mrs. Naderi. We think Hamlet's somewhere near the cafeteria.

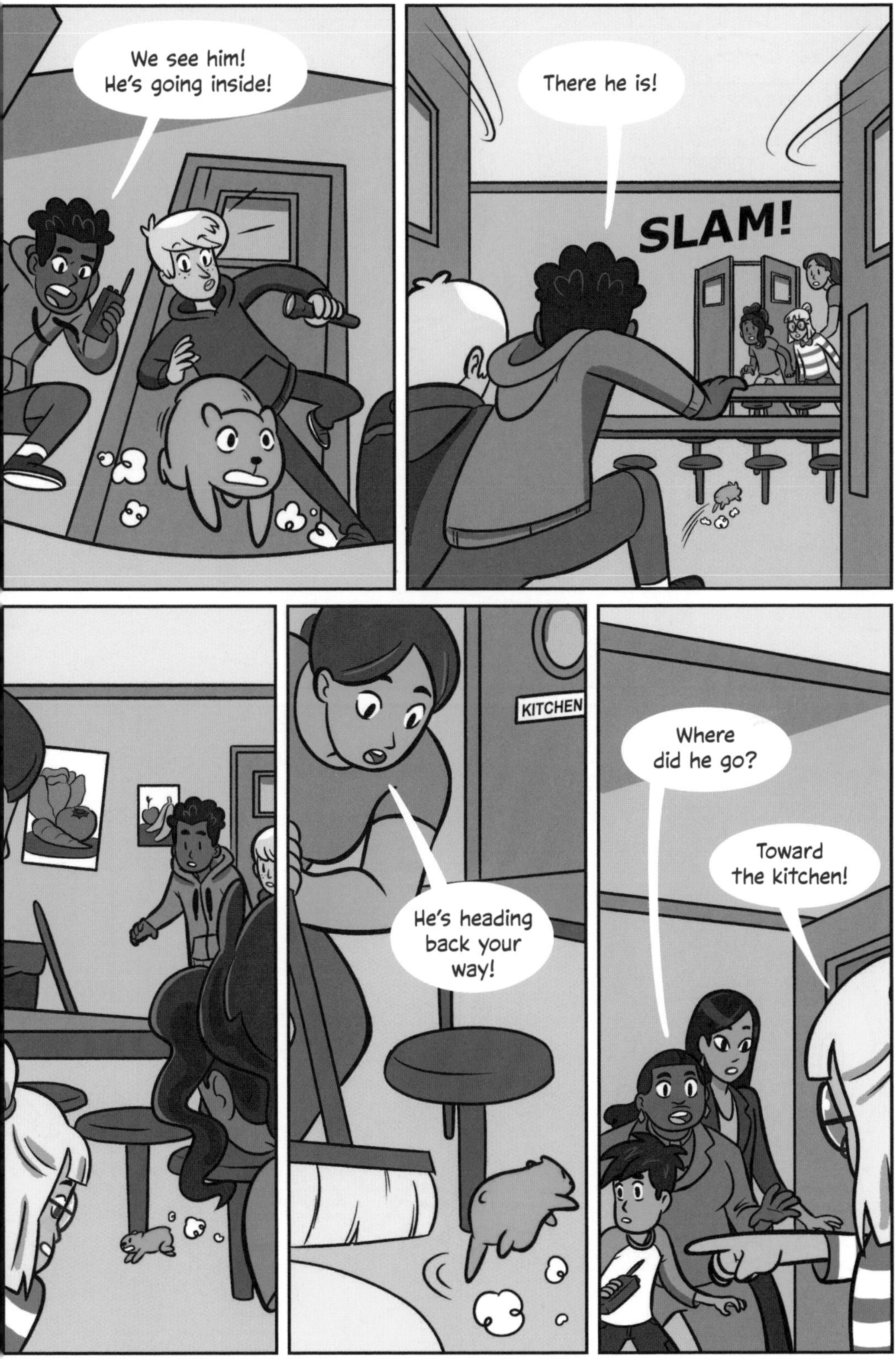
We see him! He's going inside!
There he is!
SLAM!
KITCHEN
He's heading back your way!
Where did he go?
Toward the kitchen!

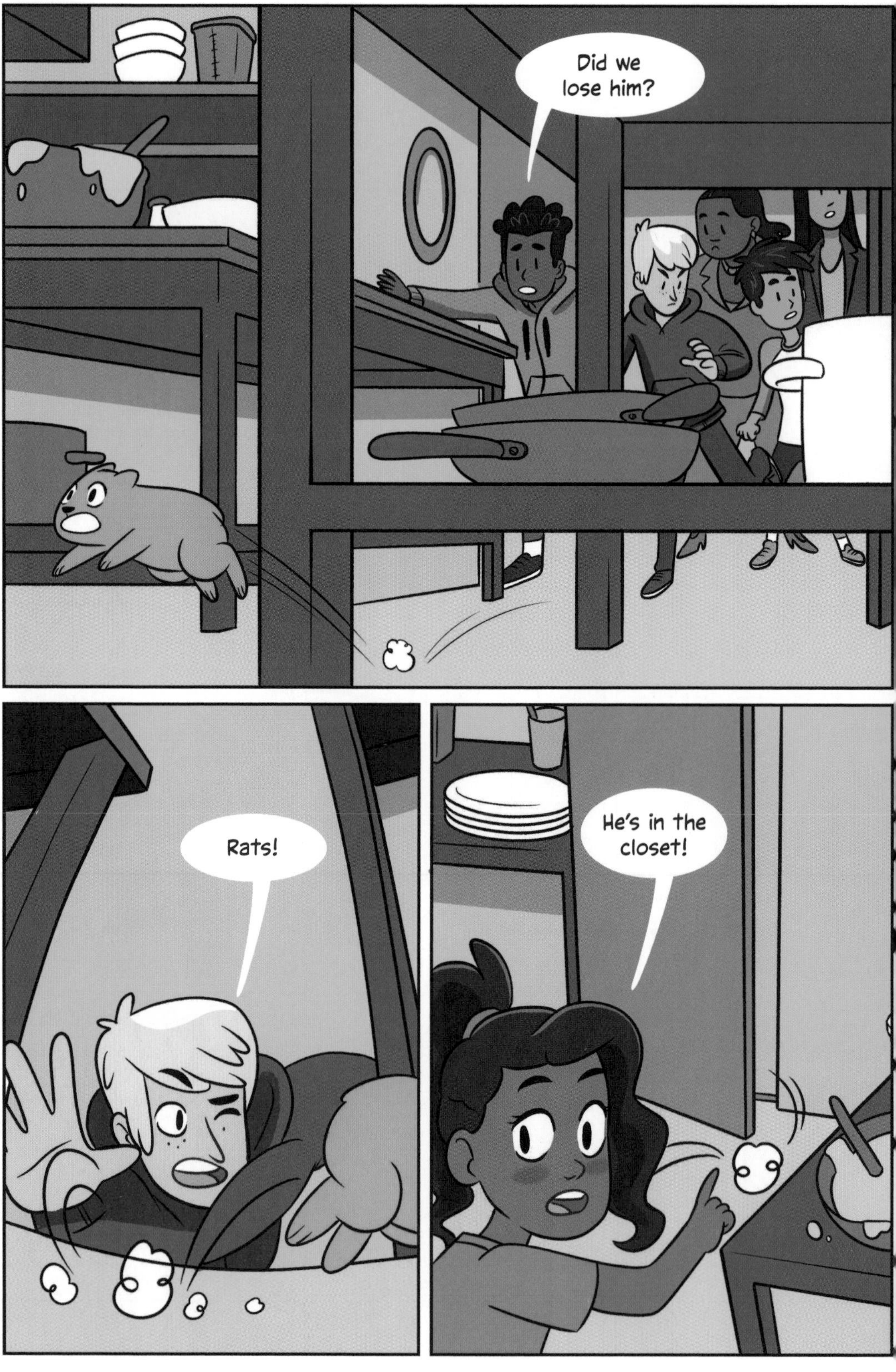
Did we lose him?
Rats!
He's in the closet!

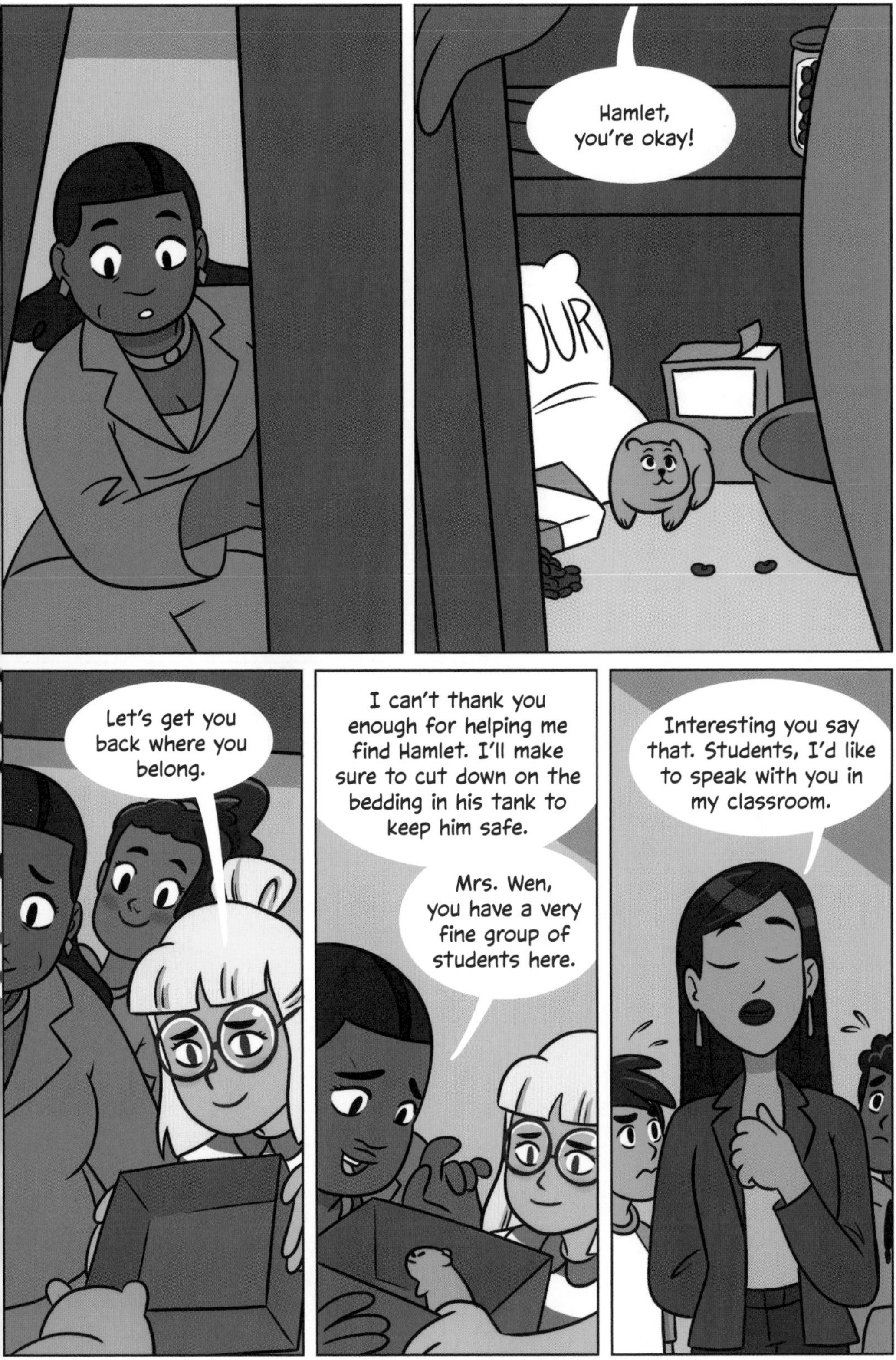
Hamlet, you're okay!
Let's get you back where you belong.
I can't thank you enough for helping me find Hamlet. I'll make sure to cut down on the bedding in his tank to keep him safe.
Mrs. Wen, you have a very fine group of students here.
Interesting you say that. Students, I'd like to speak with you in my classroom.

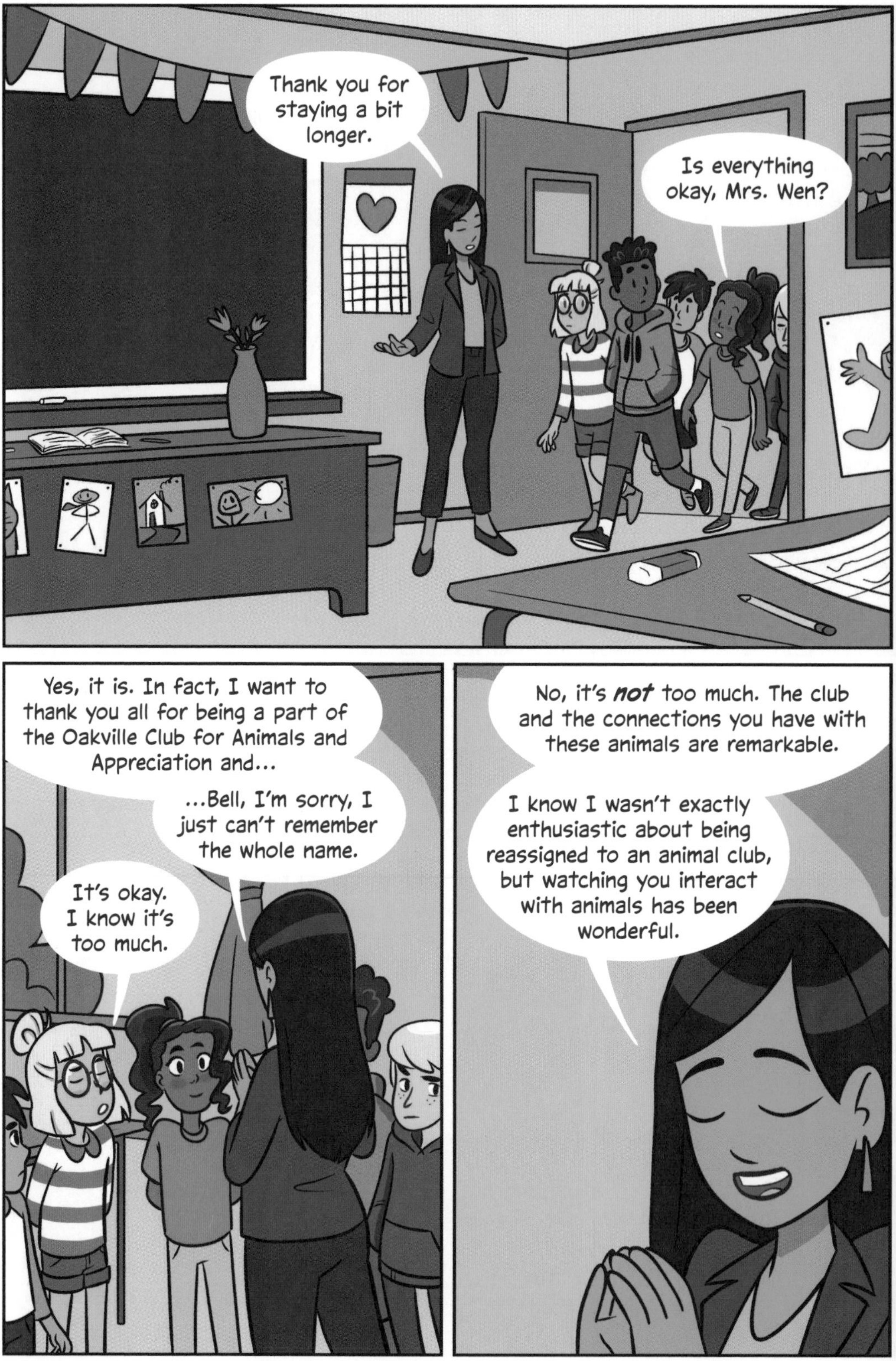
Thank you for staying a bit longer.
Is everything okay, Mrs. Wen?
Yes, it is. In fact, I want to thank you all for being a part of the Oakville Club for Animals and Appreciation and...
...Bell, I'm sorry, I just can't remember the whole name.
It's okay. I know it's too much.
No, it's ***not*** too much. The club and the connections you have with these animals are remarkable.
I know I wasn't exactly enthusiastic about being reassigned to an animal club, but watching you interact with animals has been wonderful.

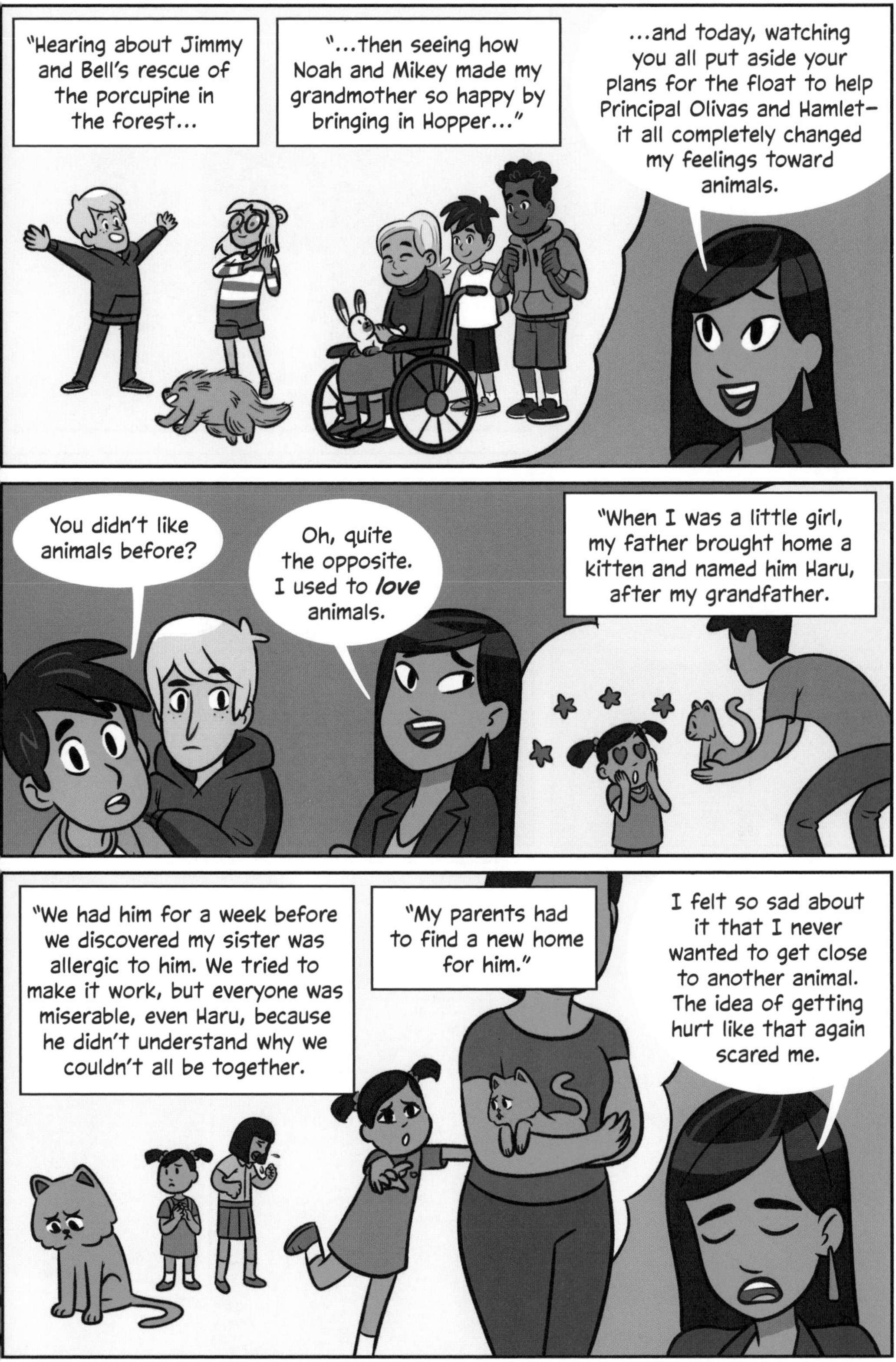
"Hearing about Jimmy and Bell's rescue of the porcupine in the forest...
"...then seeing how Noah and Mikey made my grandmother so happy by bringing in Hopper..."
...and today, watching you all put aside your plans for the float to help Principal Olivas and Hamlet—it all completely changed my feelings toward animals.
You didn't like animals before?
Oh, quite the opposite. I used to *love* animals.
"When I was a little girl, my father brought home a kitten and named him Haru, after my grandfather.
"We had him for a week before we discovered my sister was allergic to him. We tried to make it work, but everyone was miserable, even Haru, because he didn't understand why we couldn't all be together.
"My parents had to find a new home for him."
I felt so sad about it that I never wanted to get close to another animal. The idea of getting hurt like that again scared me.

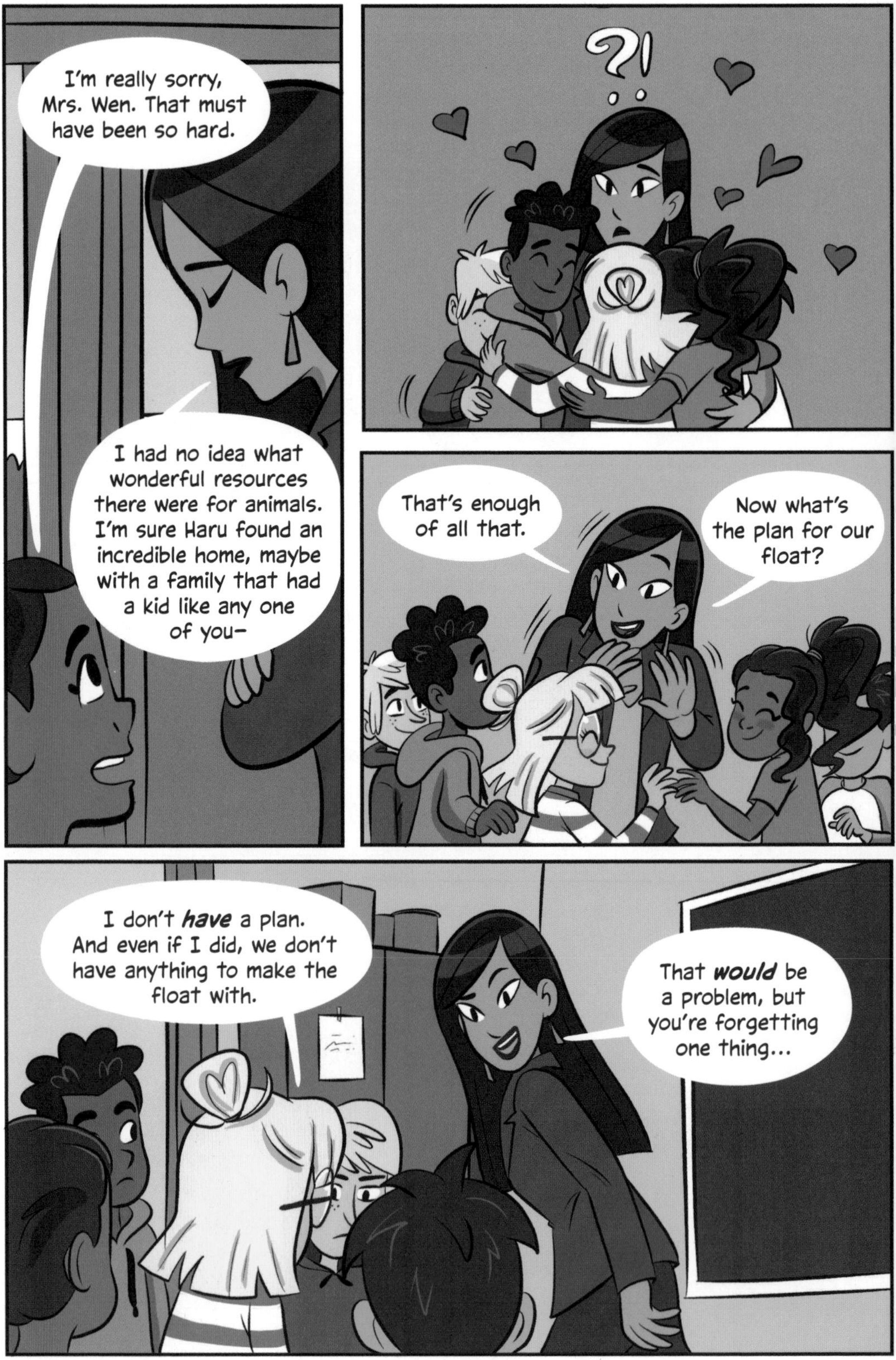
I'm really sorry, Mrs. Wen. That must have been so hard.
I had no idea what wonderful resources there were for animals. I'm sure Haru found an incredible home, maybe with a family that had a kid like any one of you–
?!
That's enough of all that.
Now what's the plan for our float?
I don't *have* a plan. And even if I did, we don't have anything to make the float with.
That *would* be a problem, but you're forgetting one thing...

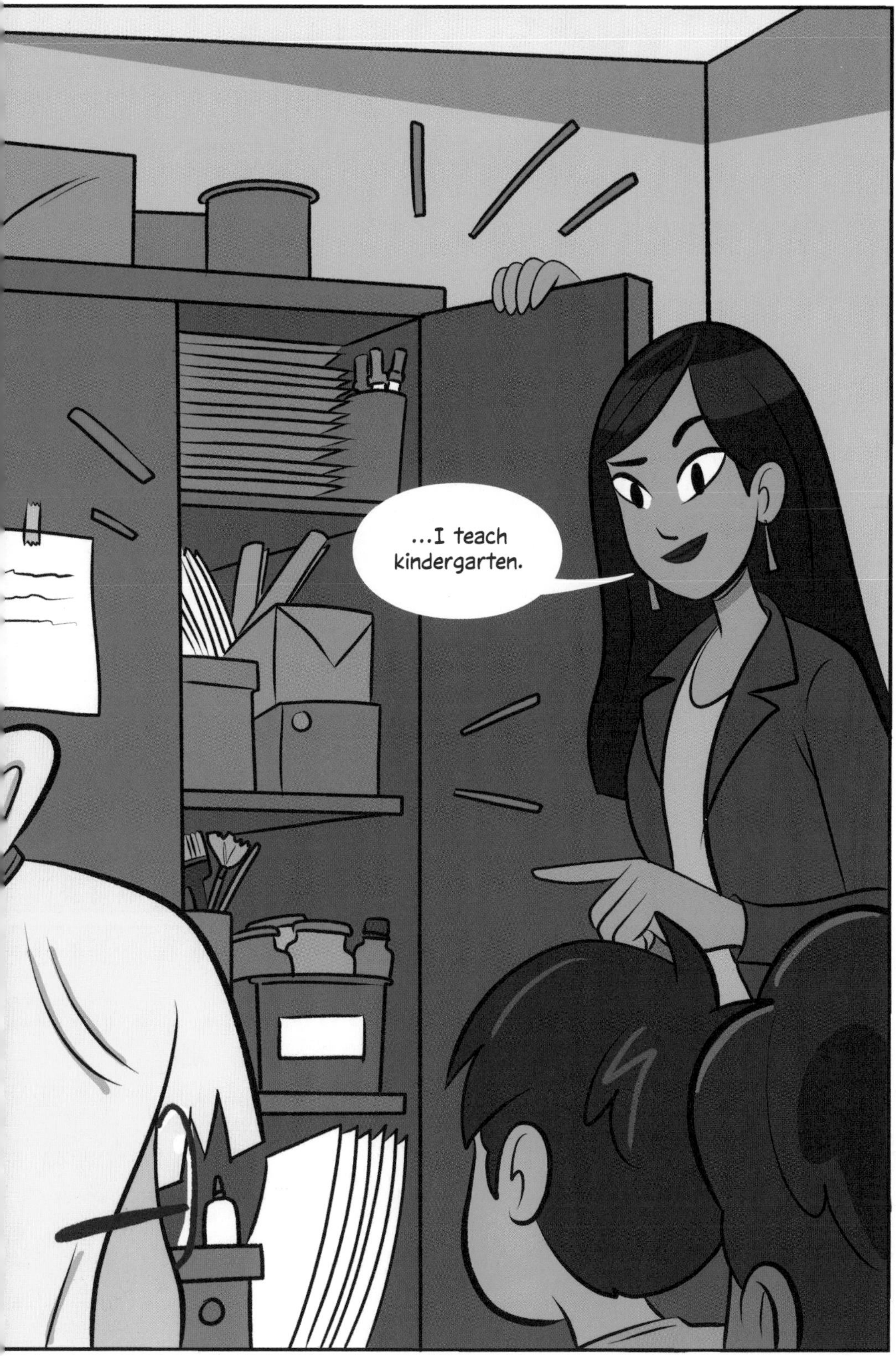
...I teach kindergarten.

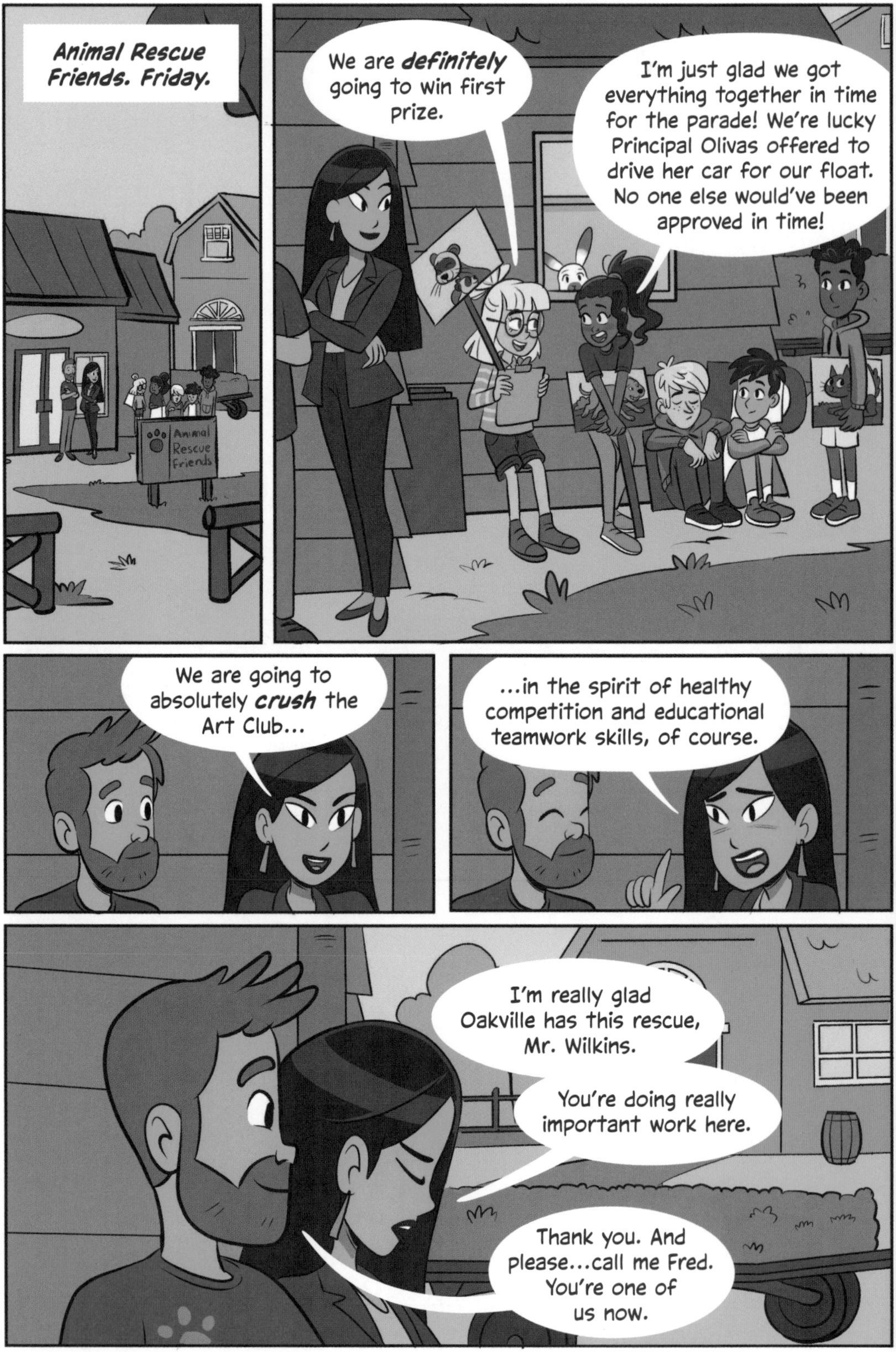
Animal Rescue Friends. Friday.
Animal Rescue Friends
We are *definitely* going to win first prize.
I'm just glad we got everything together in time for the parade! We're lucky Principal Olivas offered to drive her car for our float. No one else would've been approved in time!
We are going to absolutely *crush* the Art Club...
...in the spirit of healthy competition and educational teamwork skills, of course.
I'm really glad Oakville has this rescue, Mr. Wilkins.
You're doing really important work here.
Thank you. And please...call me Fred. You're one of us now.

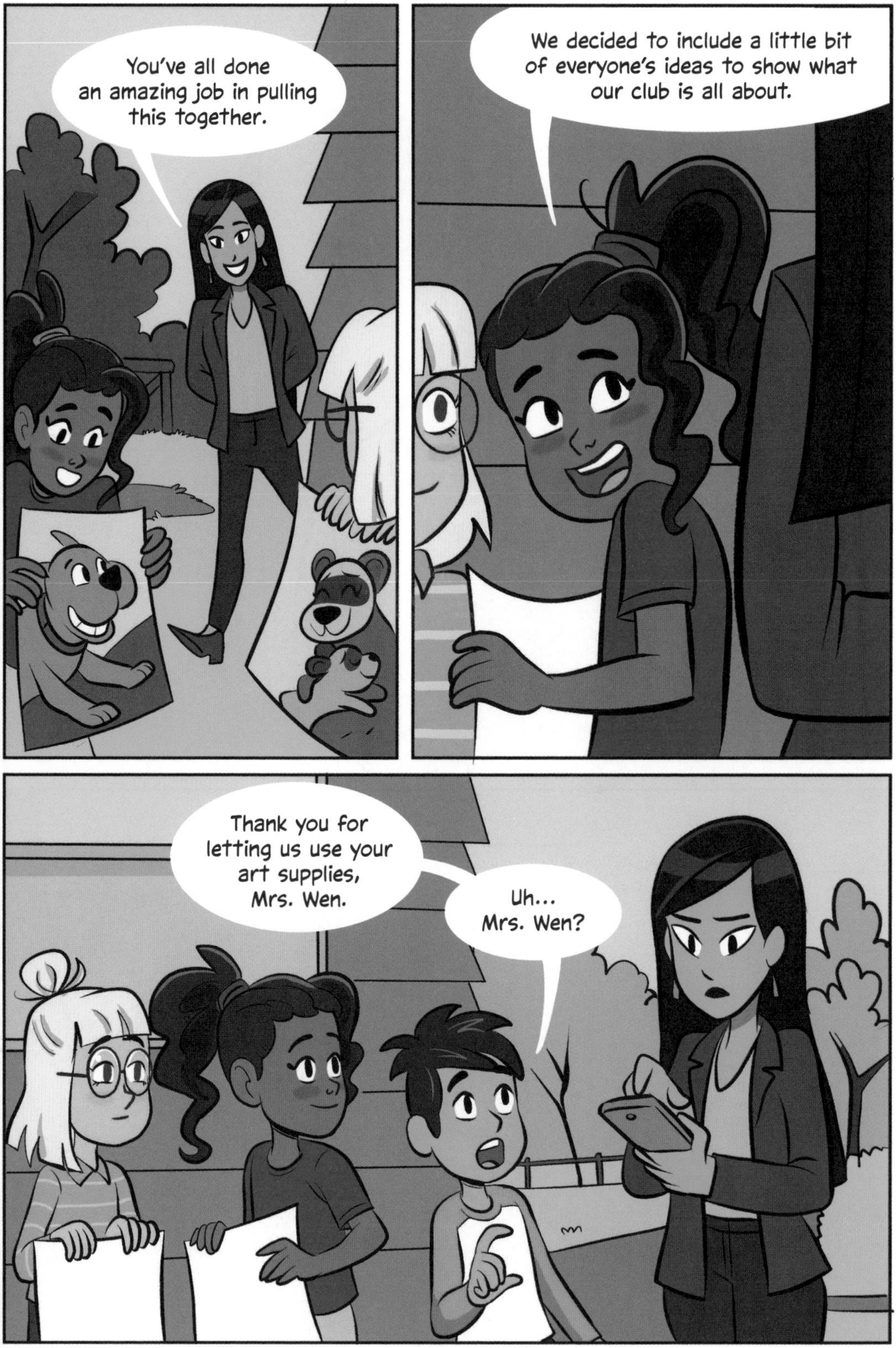
You've all done an amazing job in pulling this together.
We decided to include a little bit of everyone's ideas to show what our club is all about.
Thank you for letting us use your art supplies, Mrs. Wen.
Uh... Mrs. Wen?

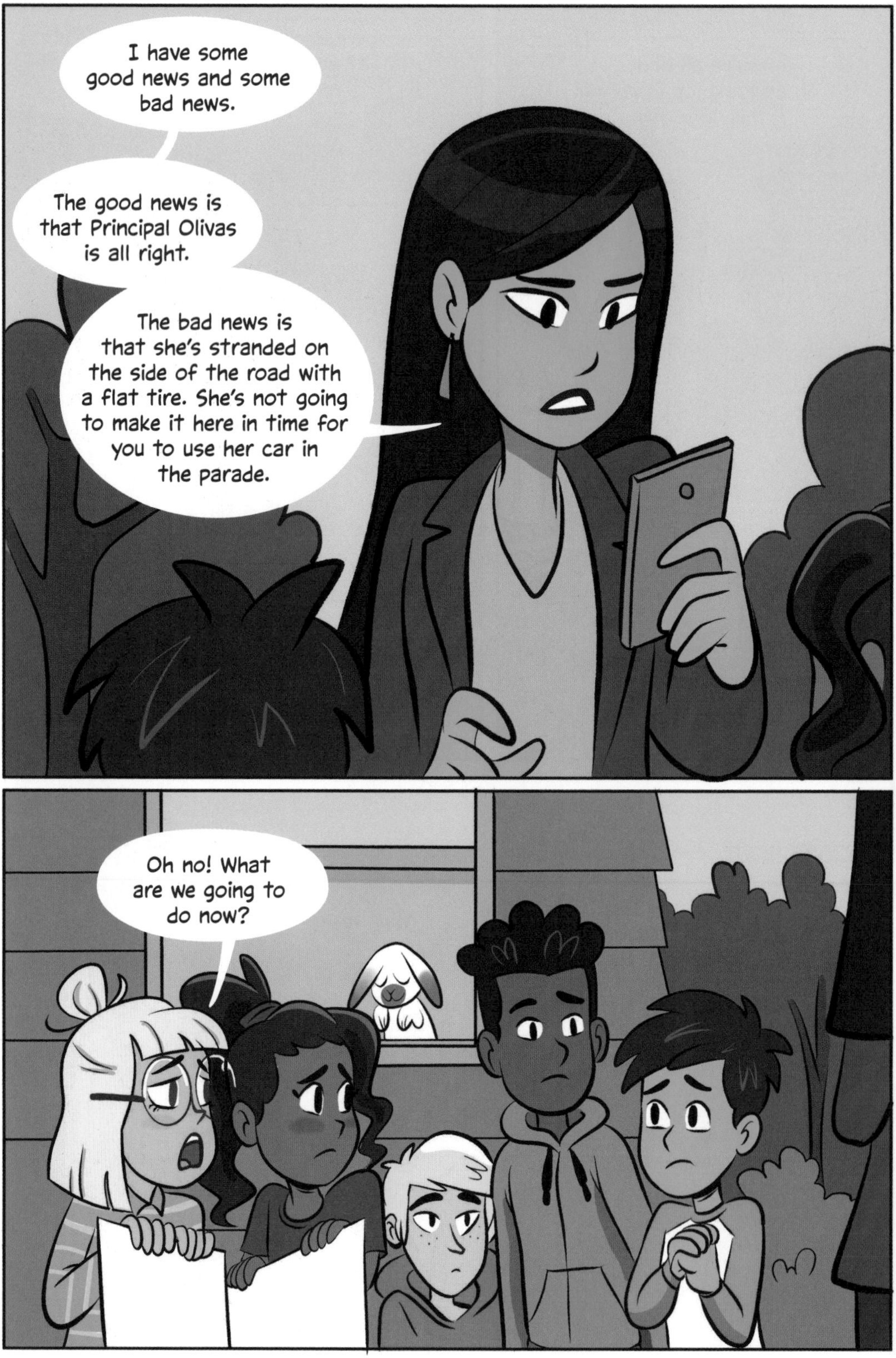
I have some good news and some bad news.
The good news is that Principal Olivas is all right.
The bad news is that she's stranded on the side of the road with a flat tire. She's not going to make it here in time for you to use her car in the parade.
Oh no! What are we going to do now?

Chapter 5

THE MANE EVENT

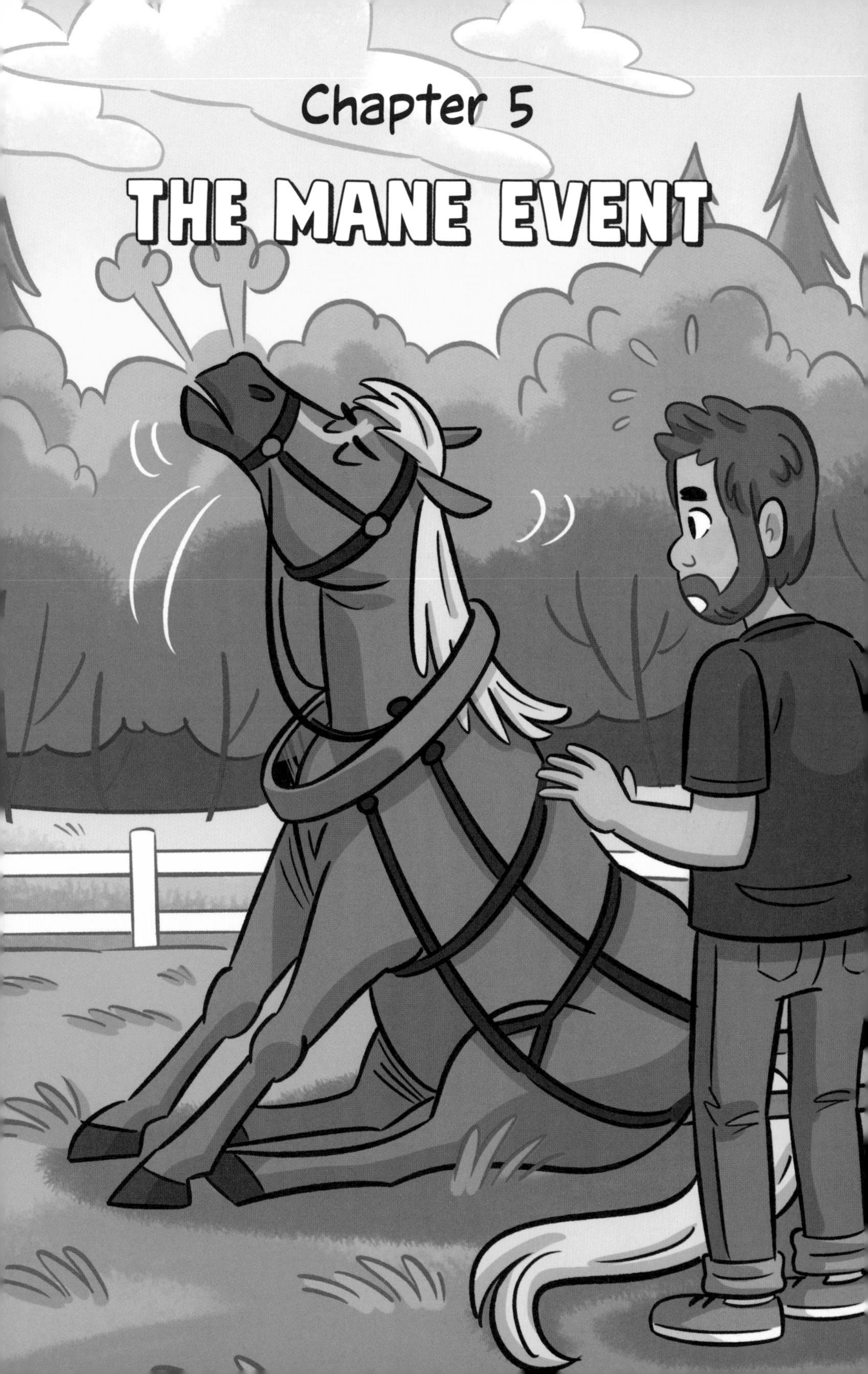

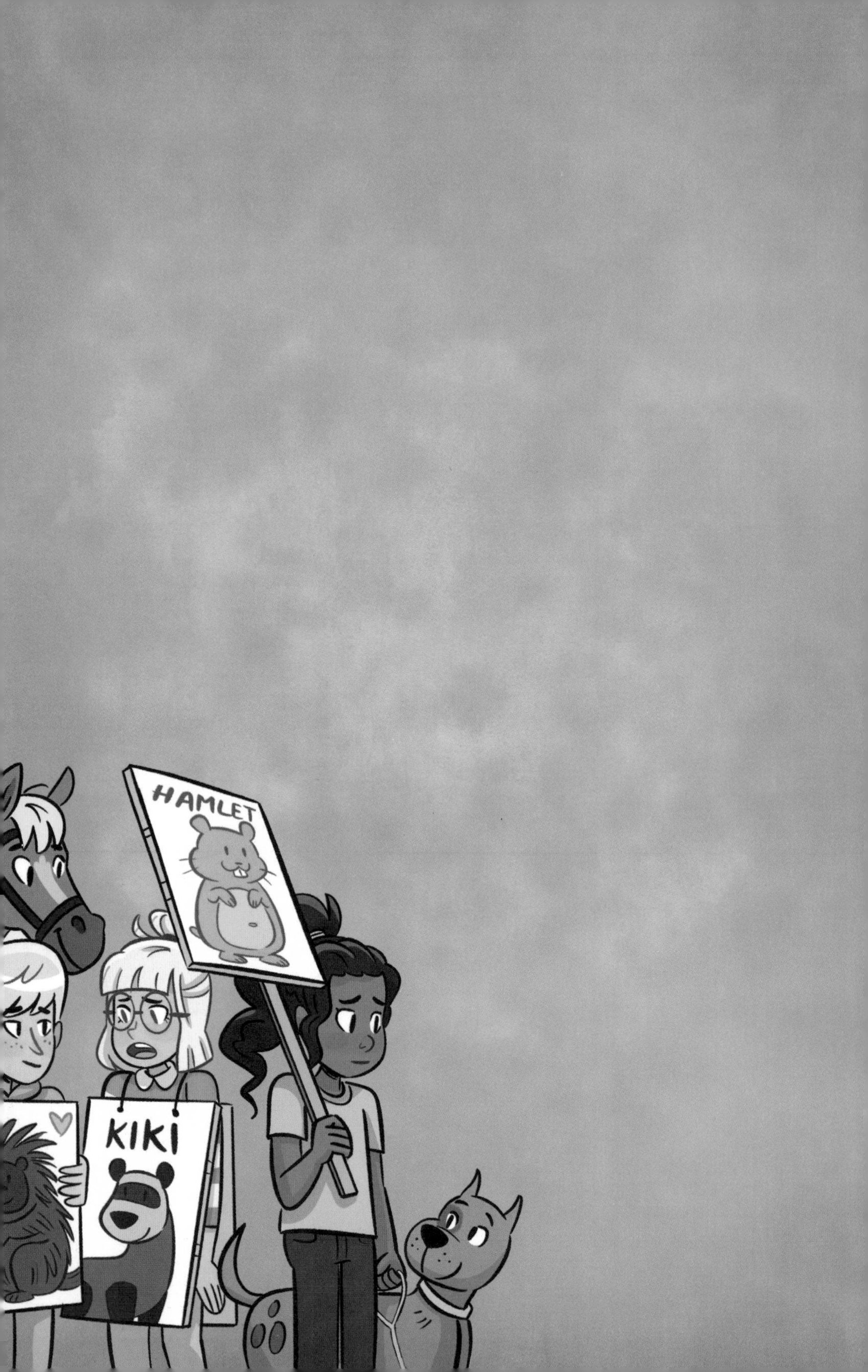
HAMLET
KIKI

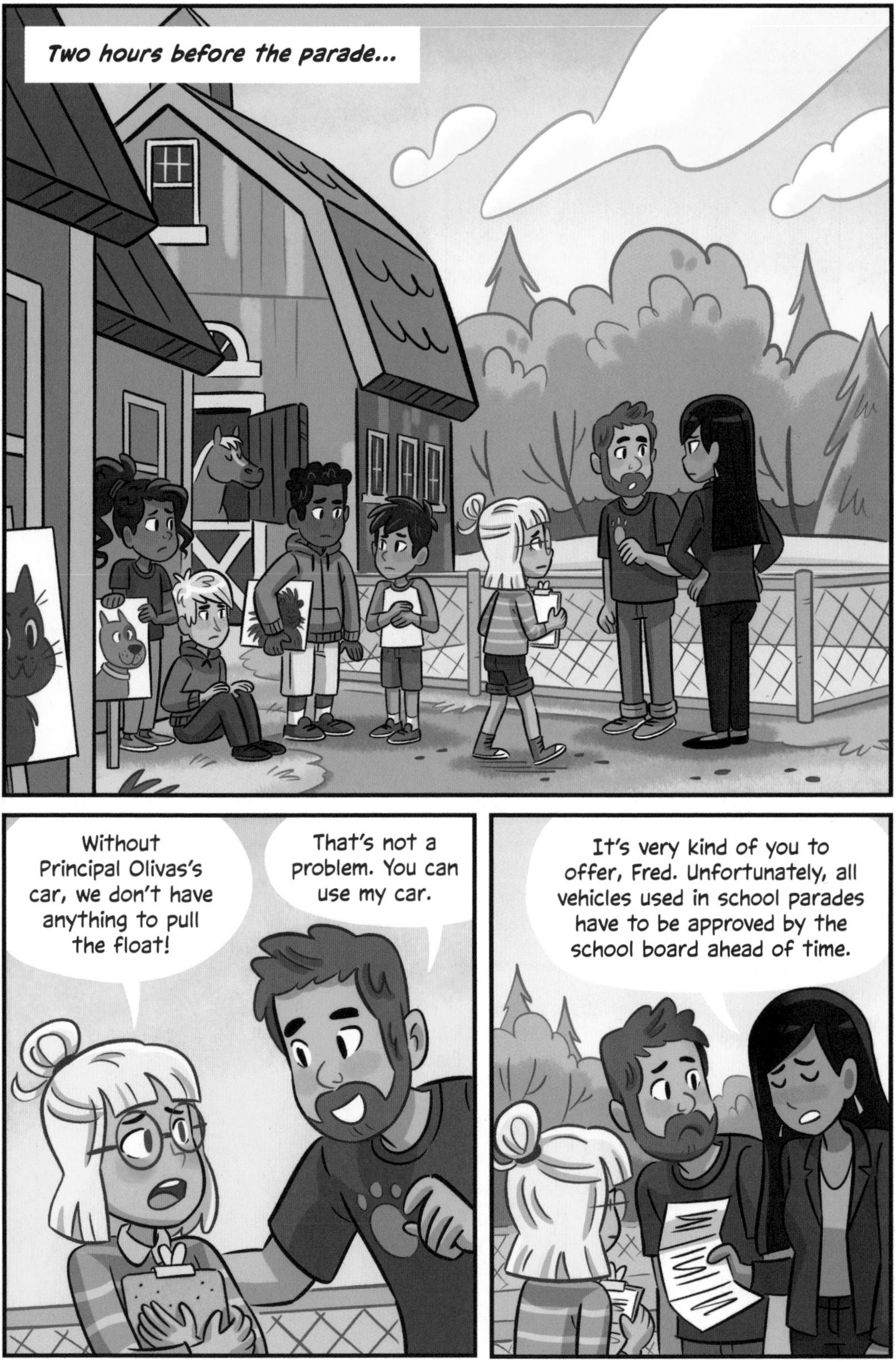
Two hours before the parade...
Without Principal Olivas's car, we don't have anything to pull the float!
That's not a problem. You can use my car.
It's very kind of you to offer, Fred. Unfortunately, all vehicles used in school parades have to be approved by the school board ahead of time.

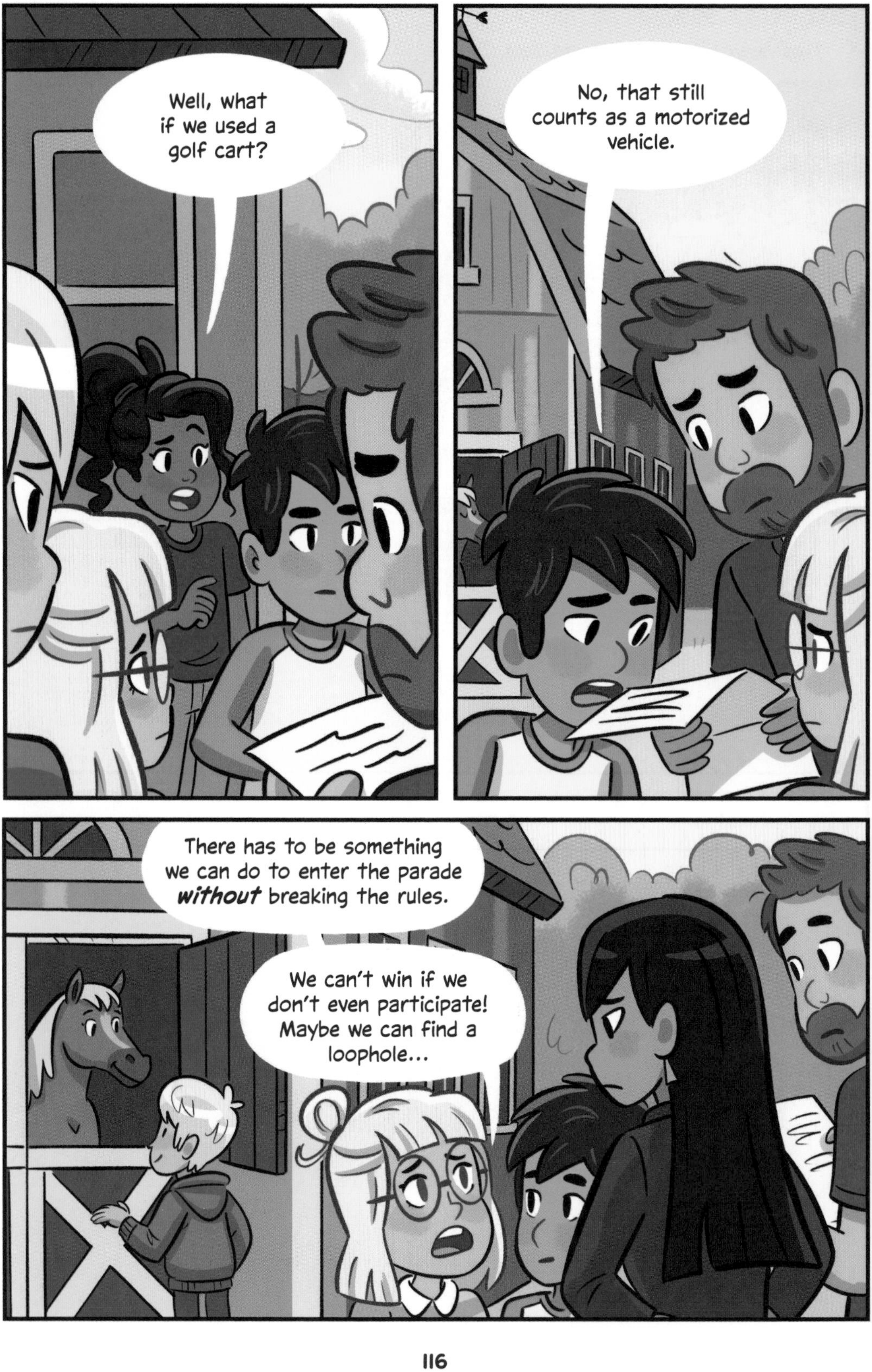
Well, what if we used a golf cart?
No, that still counts as a motorized vehicle.
There has to be something we can do to enter the parade *without* breaking the rules.
We can't win if we don't even participate! Maybe we can find a loophole...

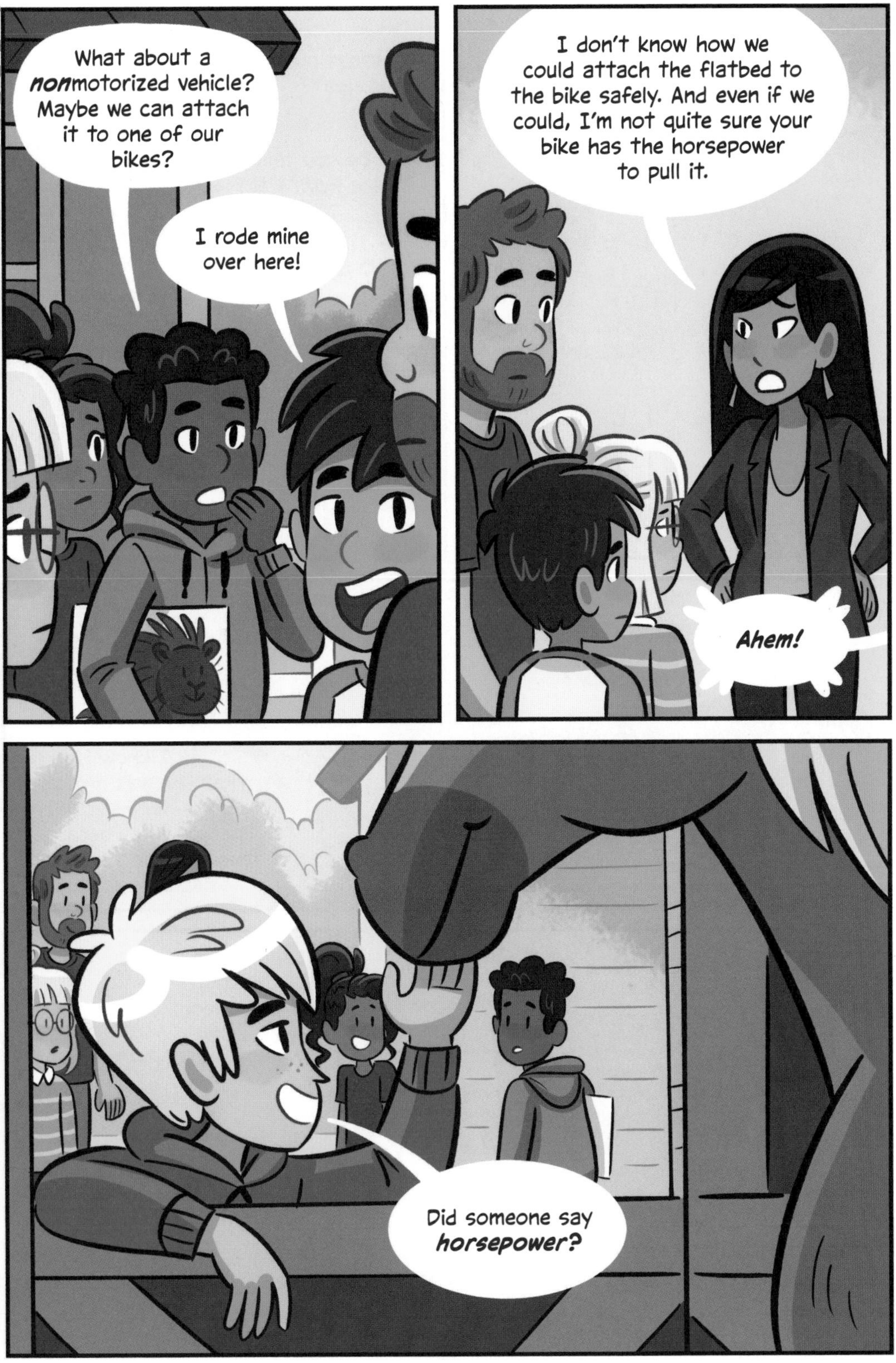
What about a ***non***motorized vehicle? Maybe we can attach it to one of our bikes?
I rode mine over here!
I don't know how we could attach the flatbed to the bike safely. And even if we could, I'm not quite sure your bike has the horsepower to pull it.
Ahem!
Did someone say ***horsepower?***

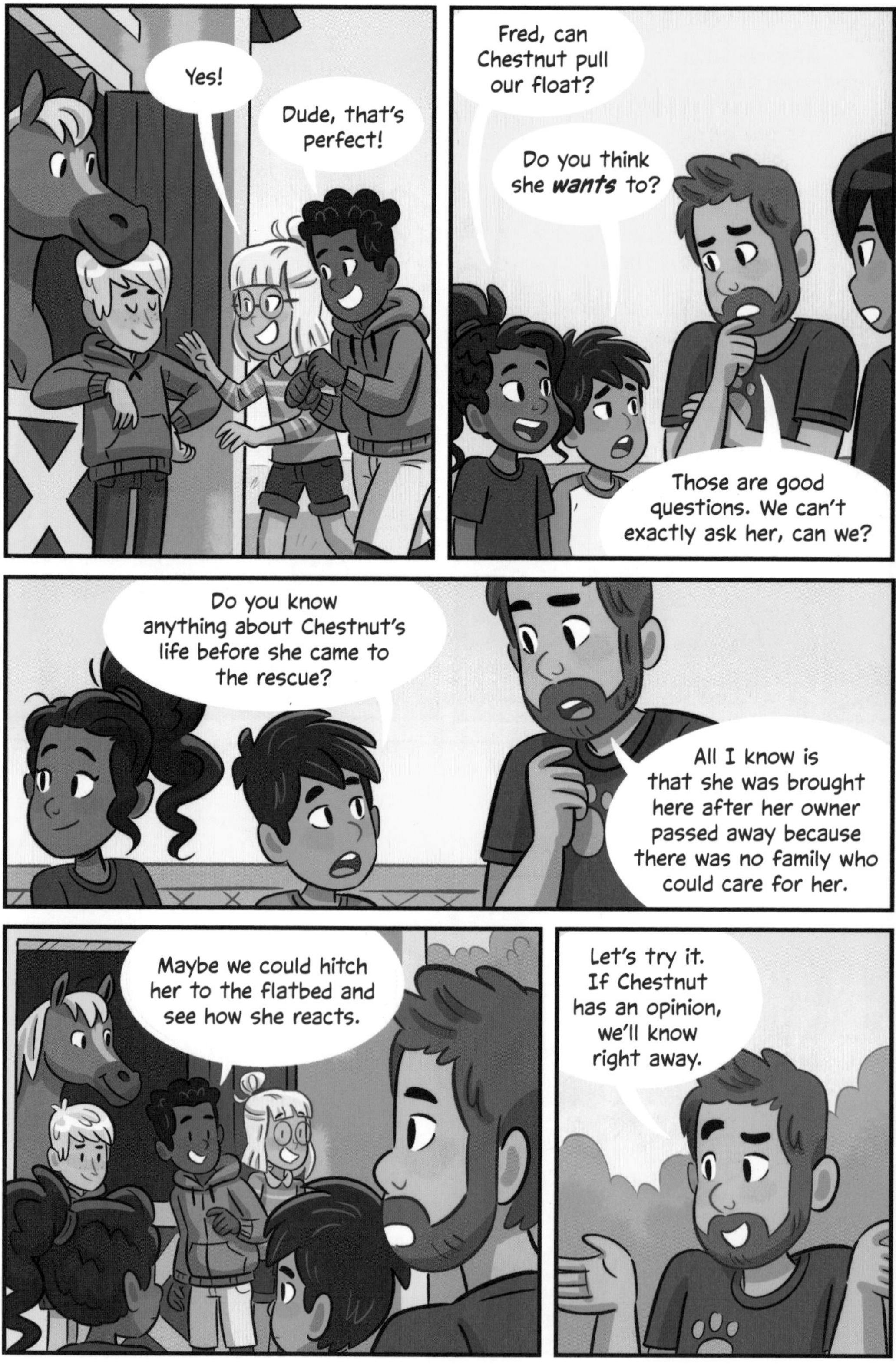
Yes!
Dude, that's perfect!
Fred, can Chestnut pull our float?
Do you think she ***wants*** to?
Those are good questions. We can't exactly ask her, can we?
Do you know anything about Chestnut's life before she came to the rescue?
All I know is that she was brought here after her owner passed away because there was no family who could care for her.
Maybe we could hitch her to the flatbed and see how she reacts.
Let's try it. If Chestnut has an opinion, we'll know right away.

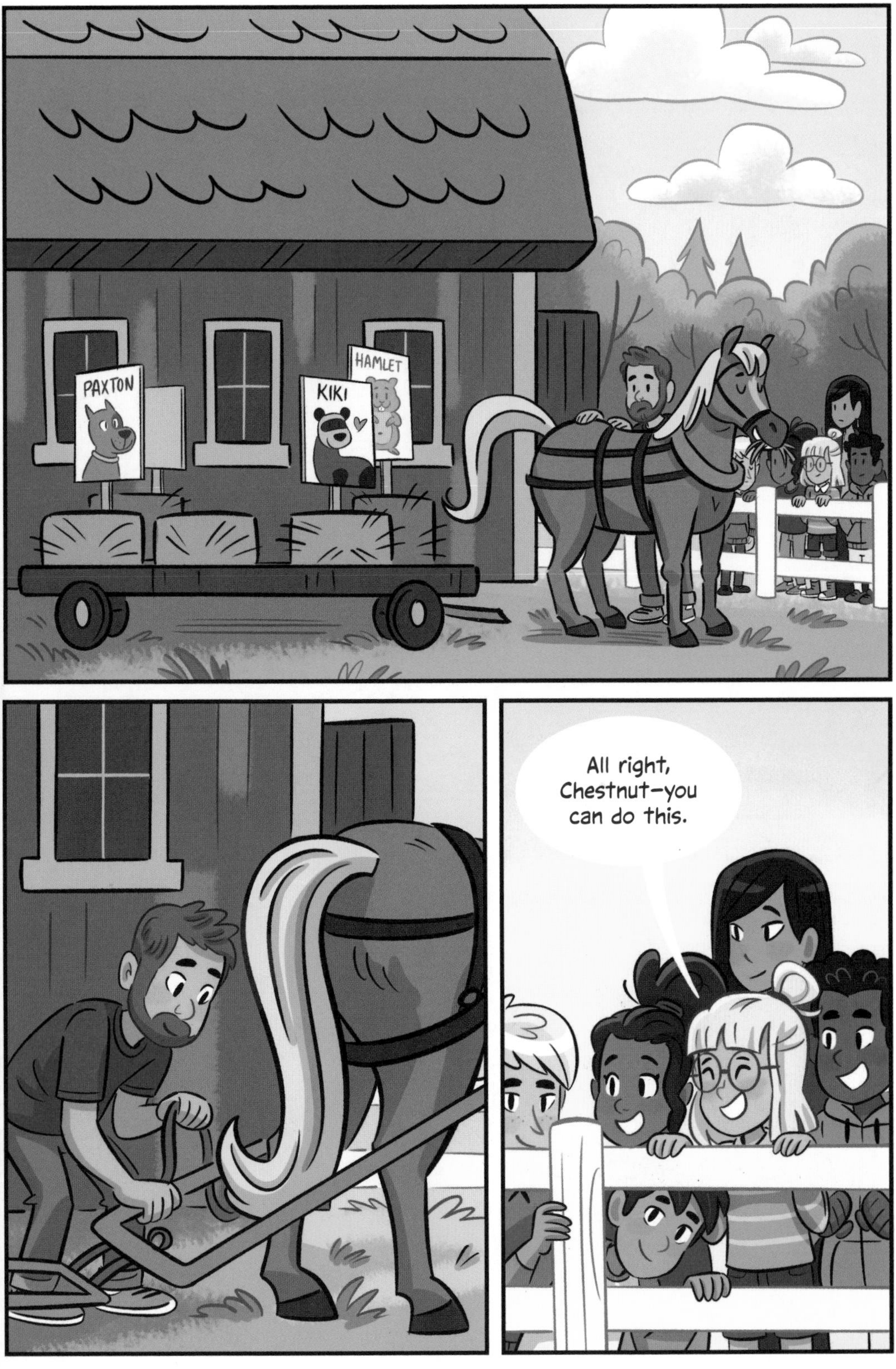
PAXTON
KIKI
HAMLET
All right, Chestnut—you can do this.

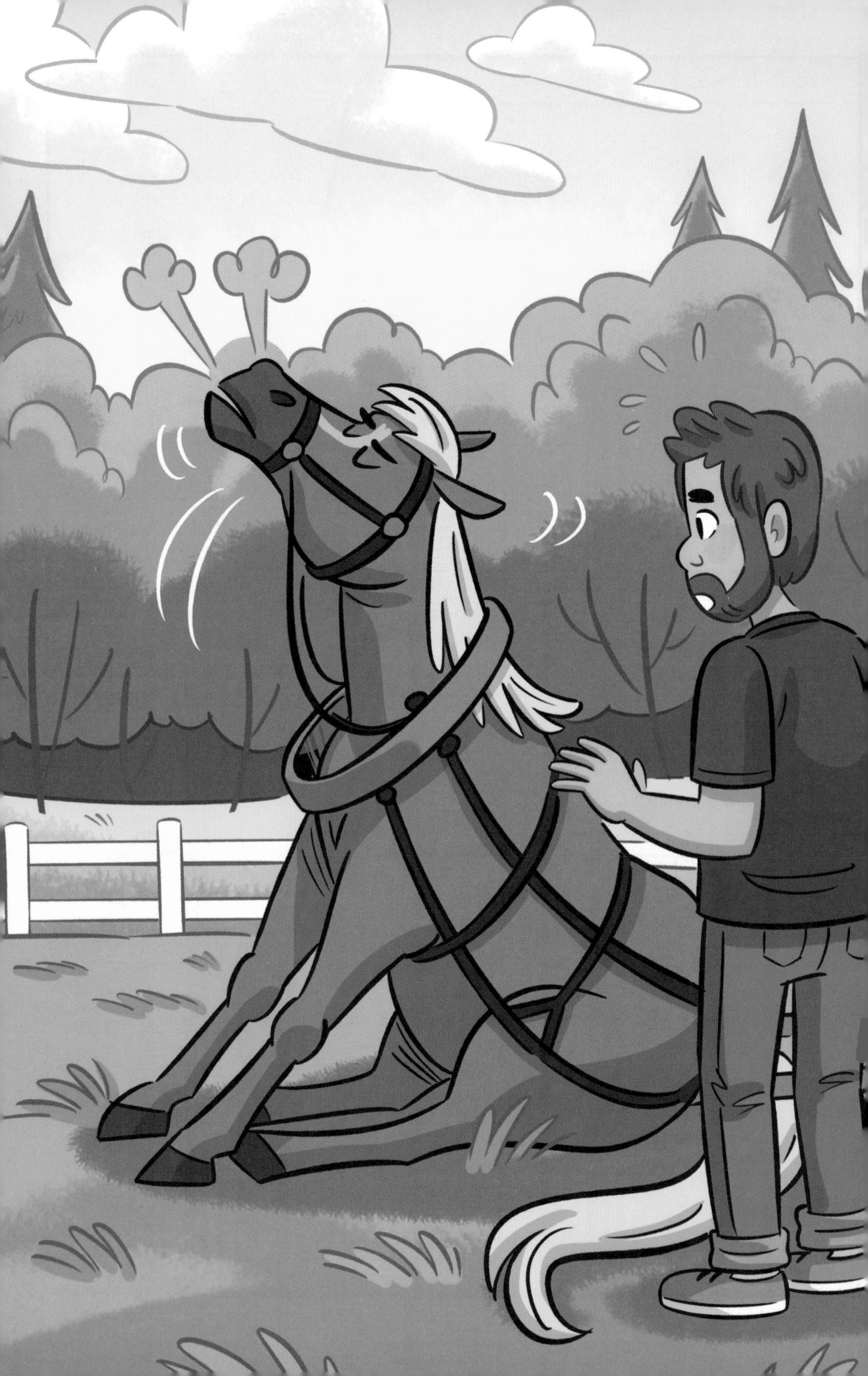

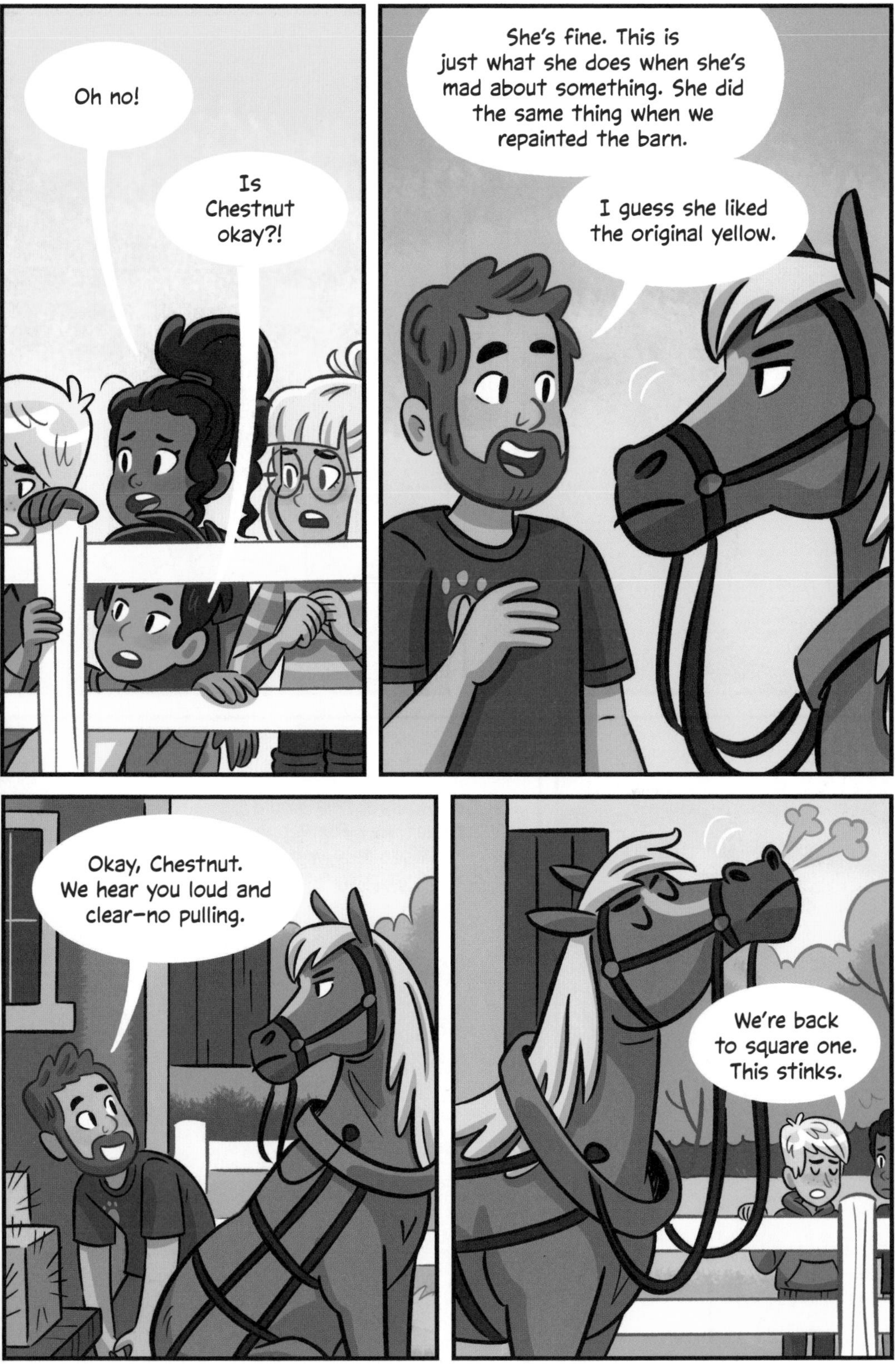
Oh no!
Is Chestnut okay?!
She's fine. This is just what she does when she's mad about something. She did the same thing when we repainted the barn.
I guess she liked the original yellow.
Okay, Chestnut. We hear you loud and clear—no pulling.
We're back to square one. This stinks.

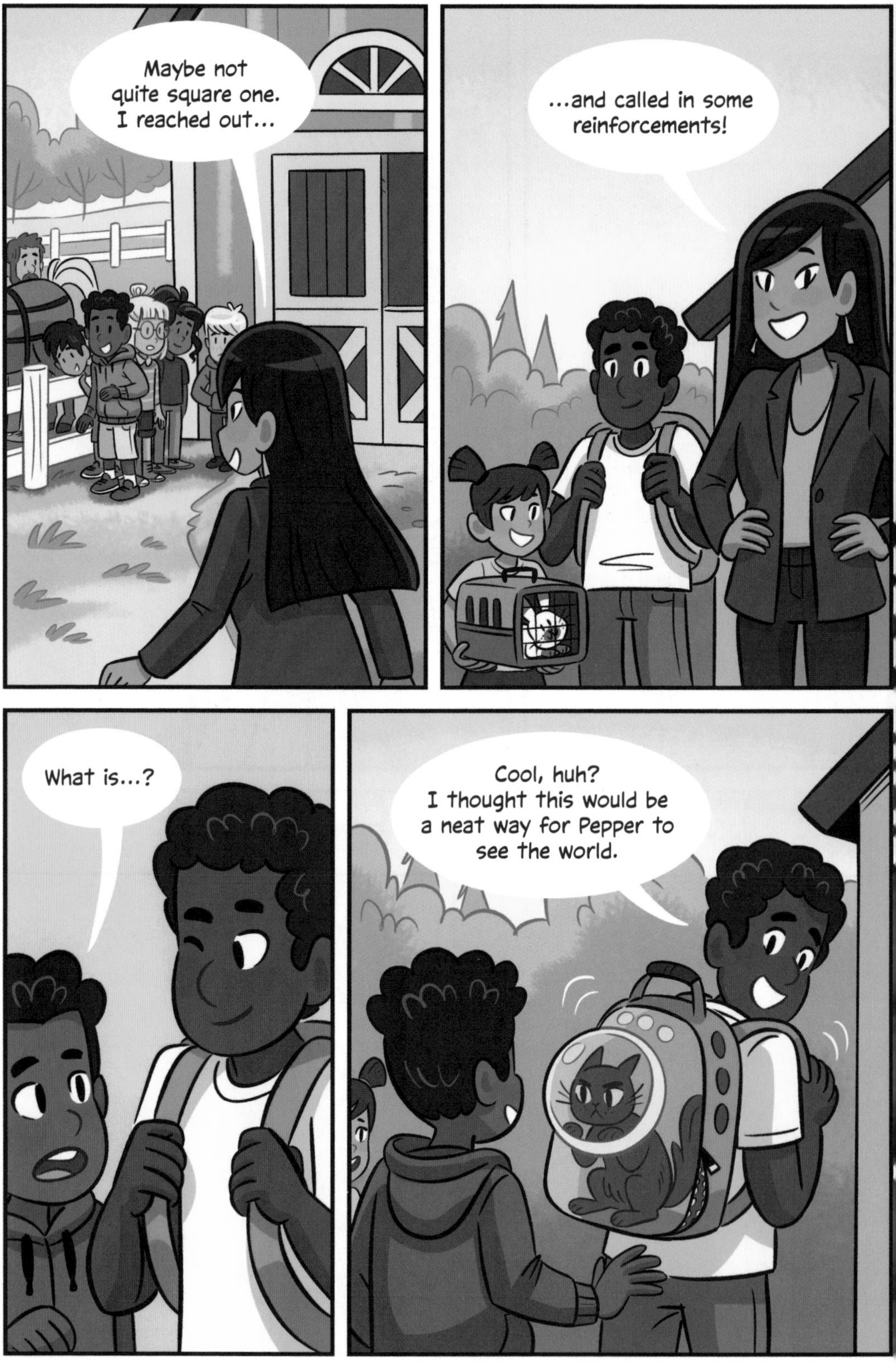
Maybe not quite square one. I reached out...
...and called in some reinforcements!
What is...?
Cool, huh? I thought this would be a neat way for Pepper to see the world.

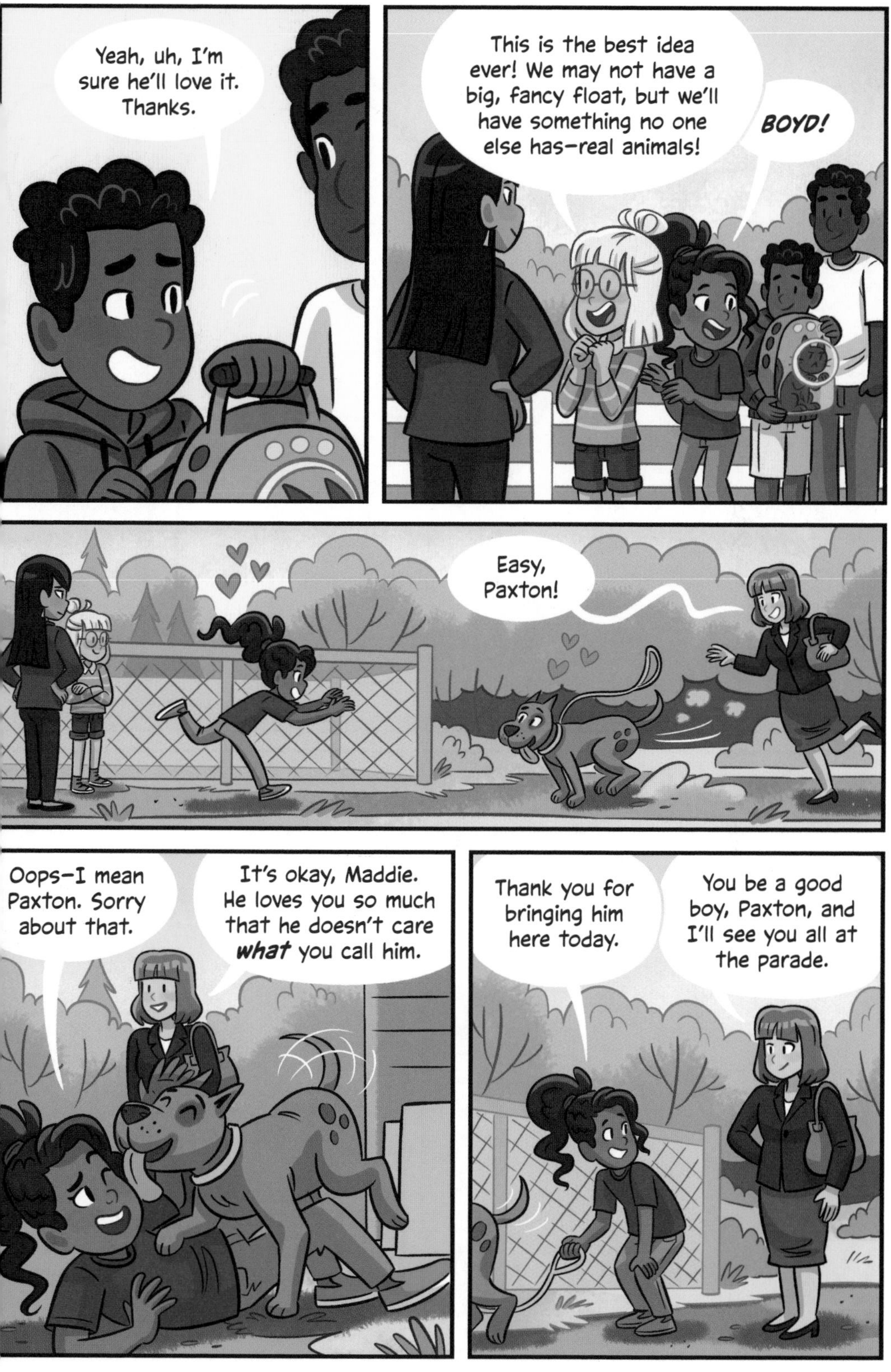
Yeah, uh, I'm sure he'll love it. Thanks.
This is the best idea ever! We may not have a big, fancy float, but we'll have something no one else has—real animals!
BOYD!
Easy, Paxton!
Oops—I mean Paxton. Sorry about that.
It's okay, Maddie. He loves you so much that he doesn't care *what* you call him.
Thank you for bringing him here today.
You be a good boy, Paxton, and I'll see you all at the parade.

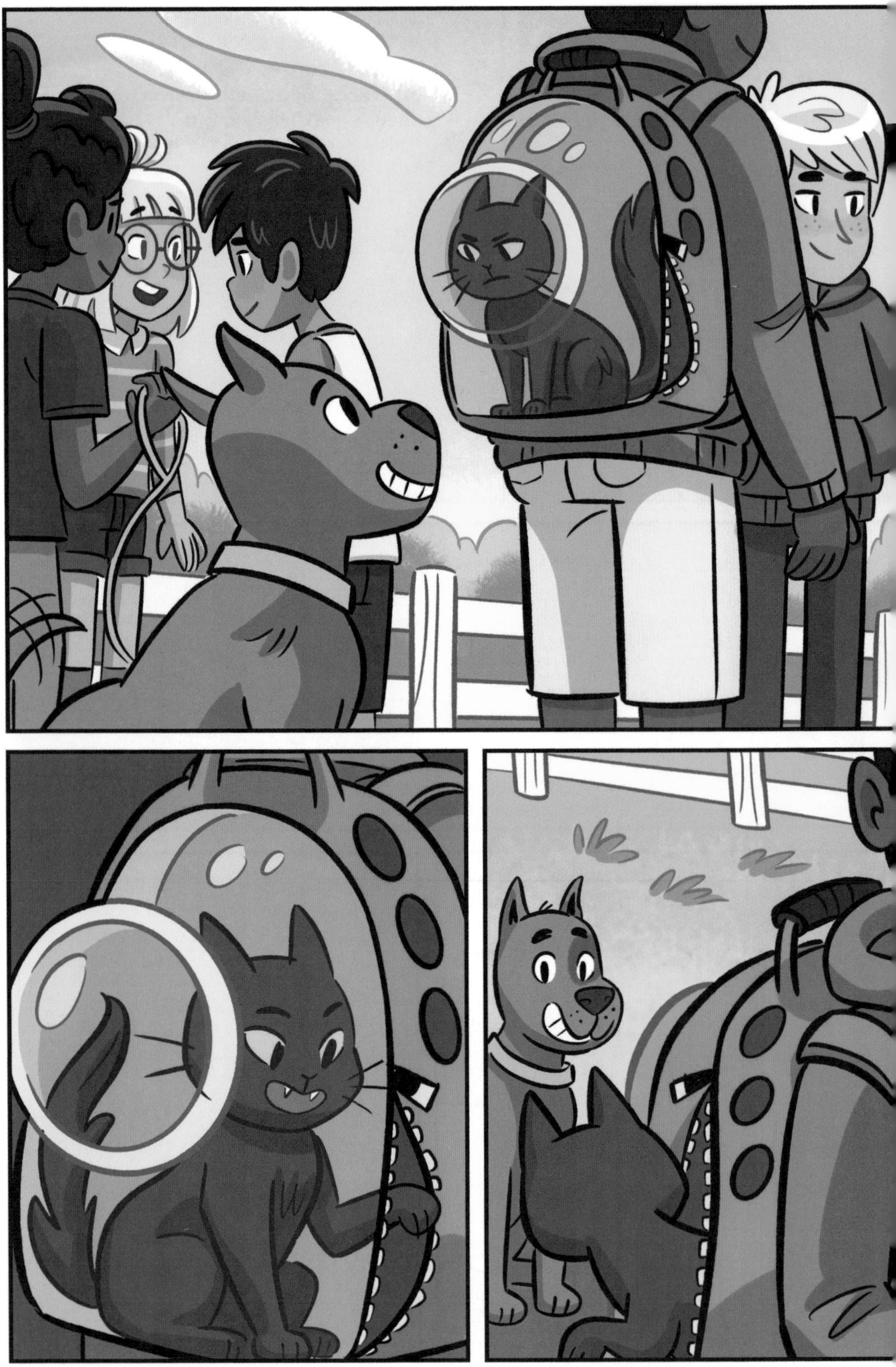

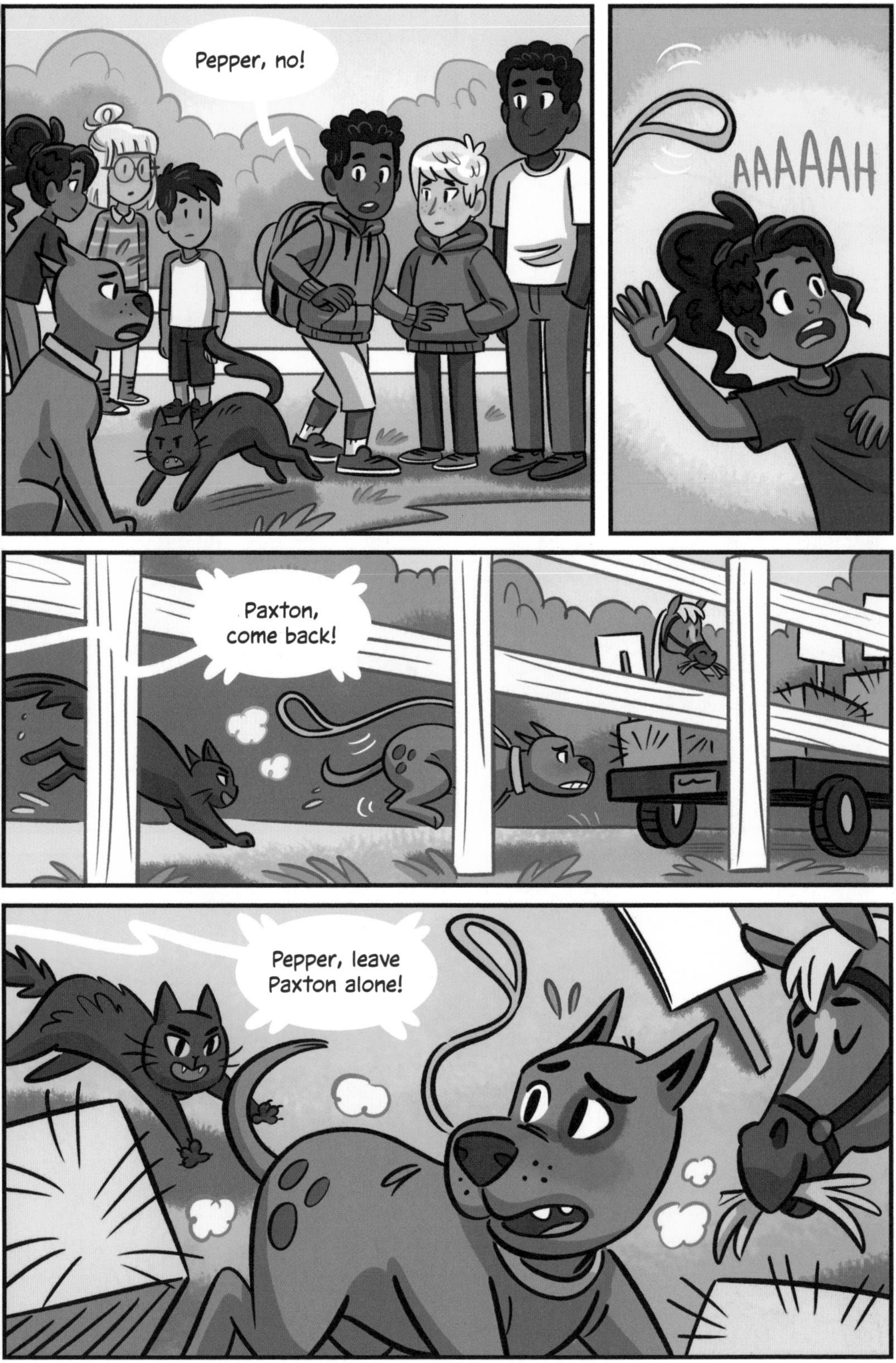
Pepper, no!
AAAAAH
Paxton, come back!
Pepper, leave Paxton alone!

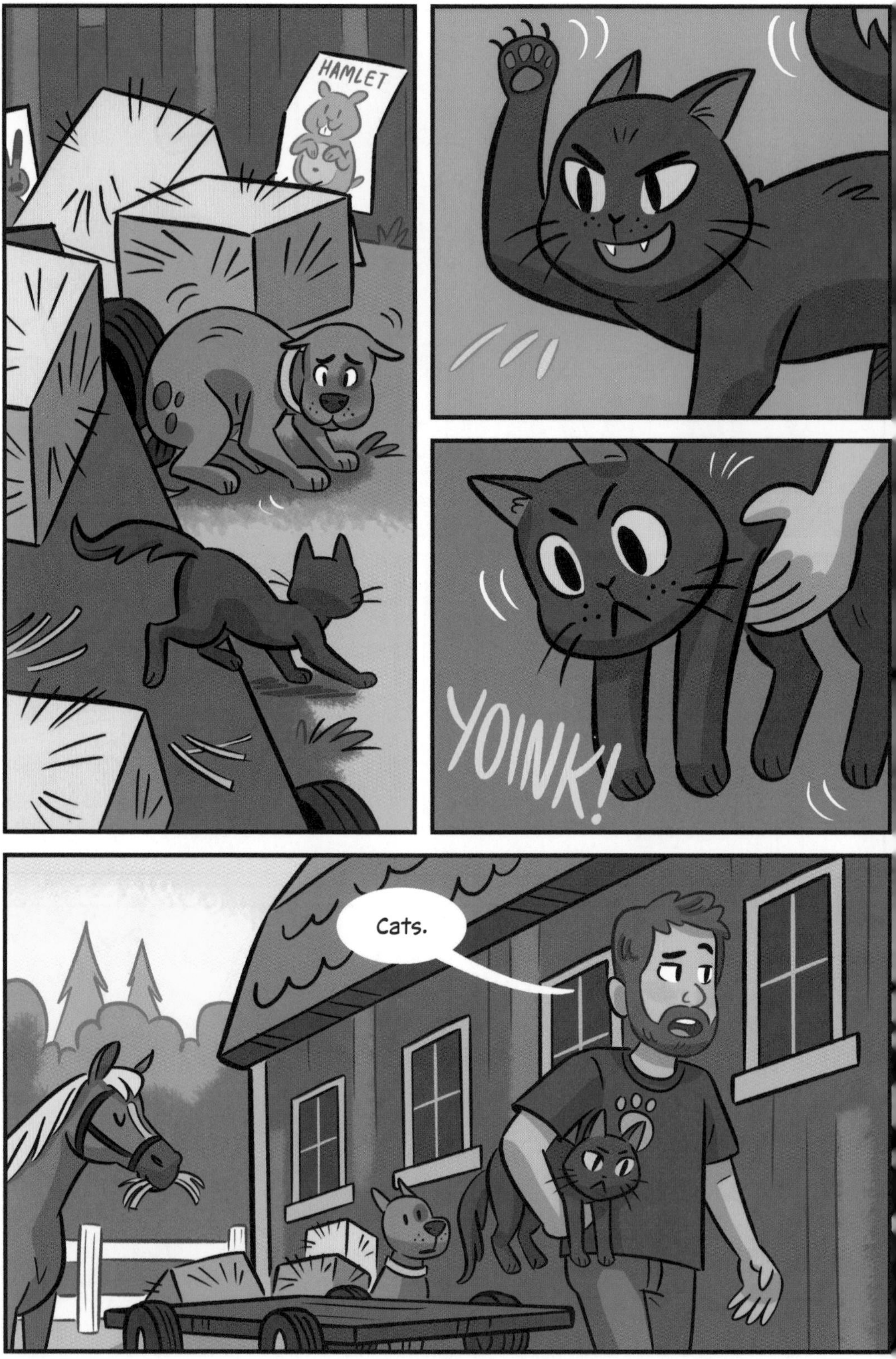
HAMLET
YOINK!
Cats.

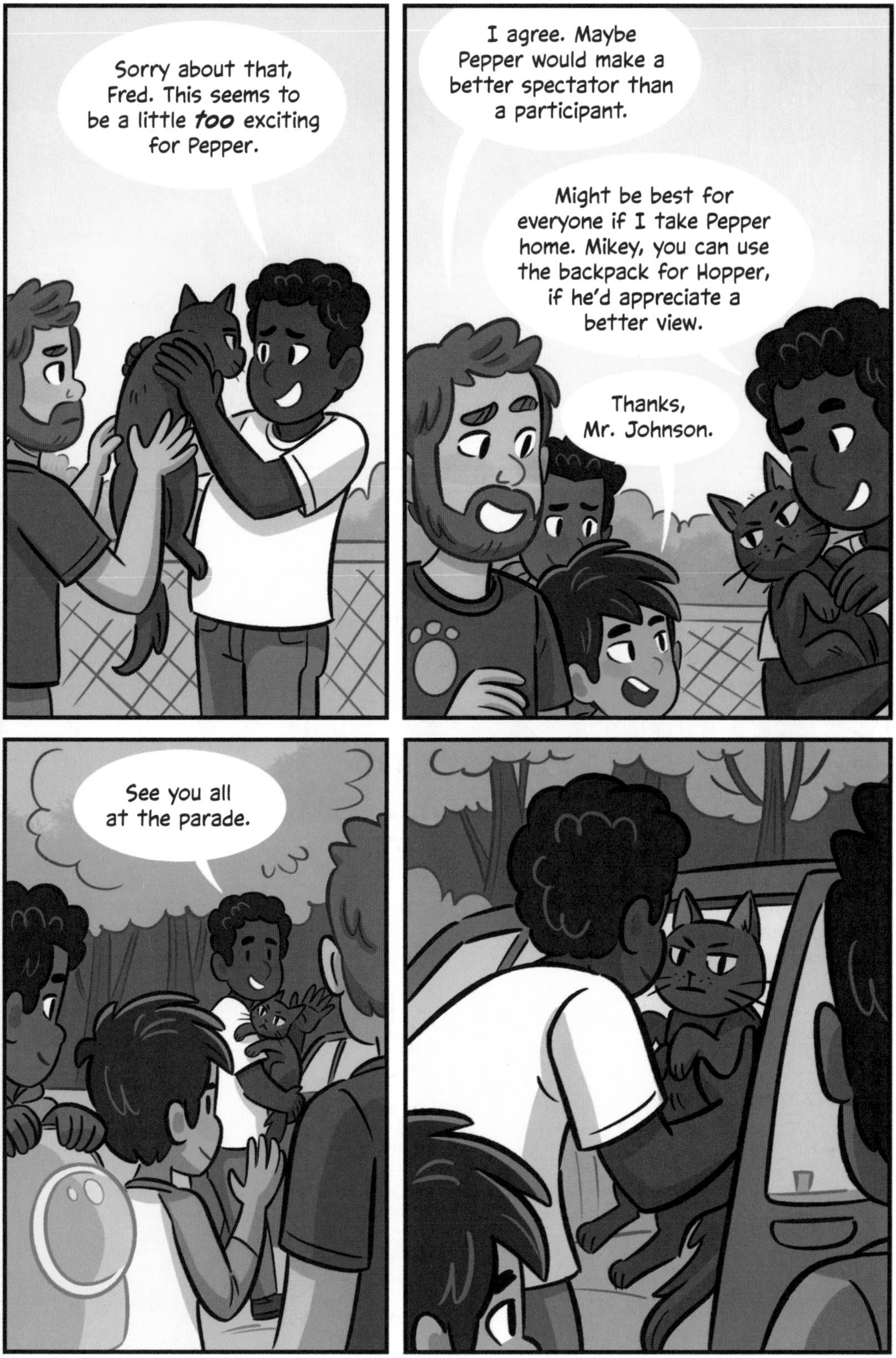
Sorry about that, Fred. This seems to be a little *too* exciting for Pepper.
I agree. Maybe Pepper would make a better spectator than a participant.
Might be best for everyone if I take Pepper home. Mikey, you can use the backpack for Hopper, if he'd appreciate a better view.
Thanks, Mr. Johnson.
See you all at the parade.

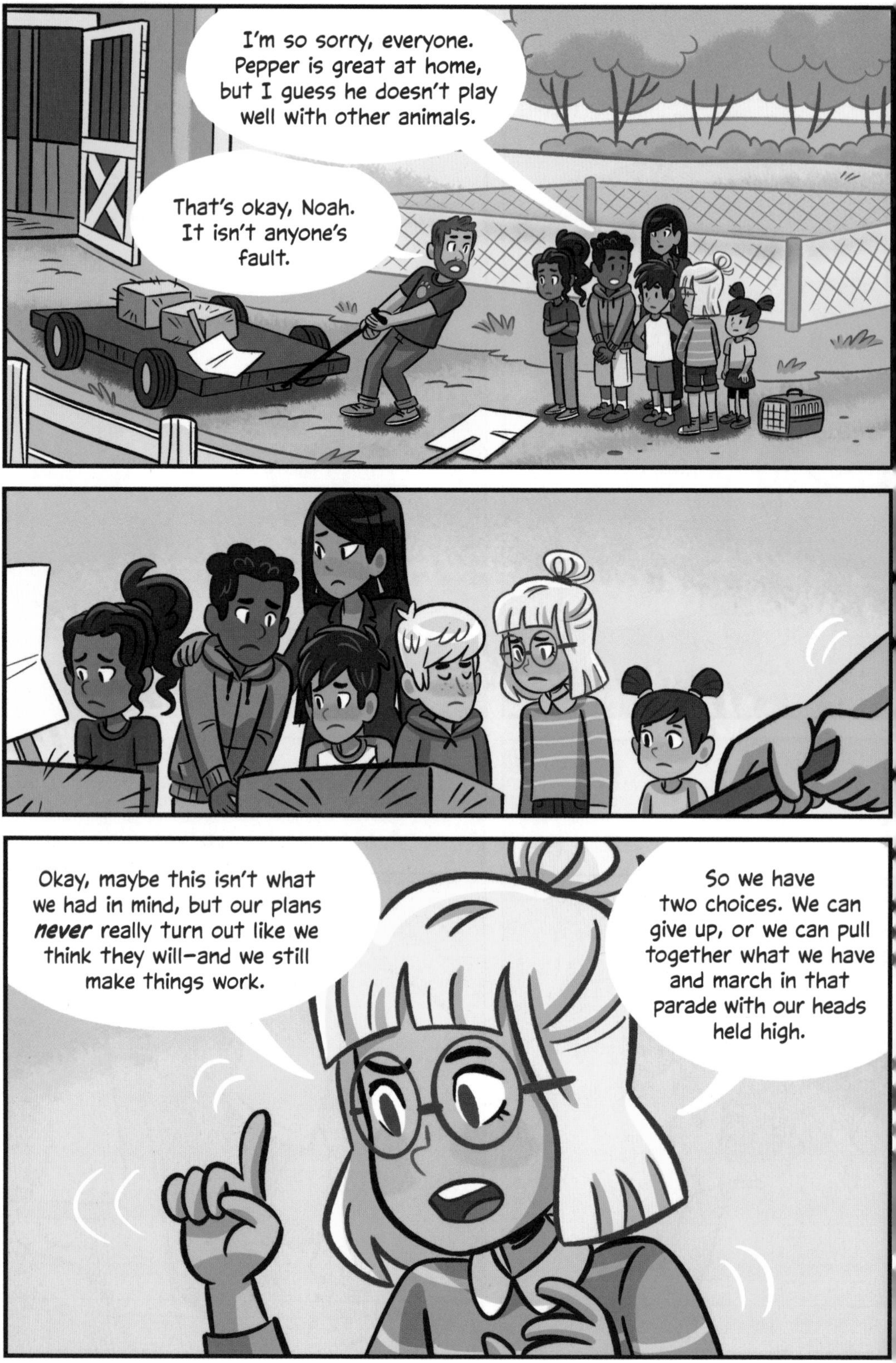
I'm so sorry, everyone. Pepper is great at home, but I guess he doesn't play well with other animals.
That's okay, Noah. It isn't anyone's fault.
Okay, maybe this isn't what we had in mind, but our plans *never* really turn out like we think they will—and we still make things work.
So we have two choices. We can give up, or we can pull together what we have and march in that parade with our heads held high.

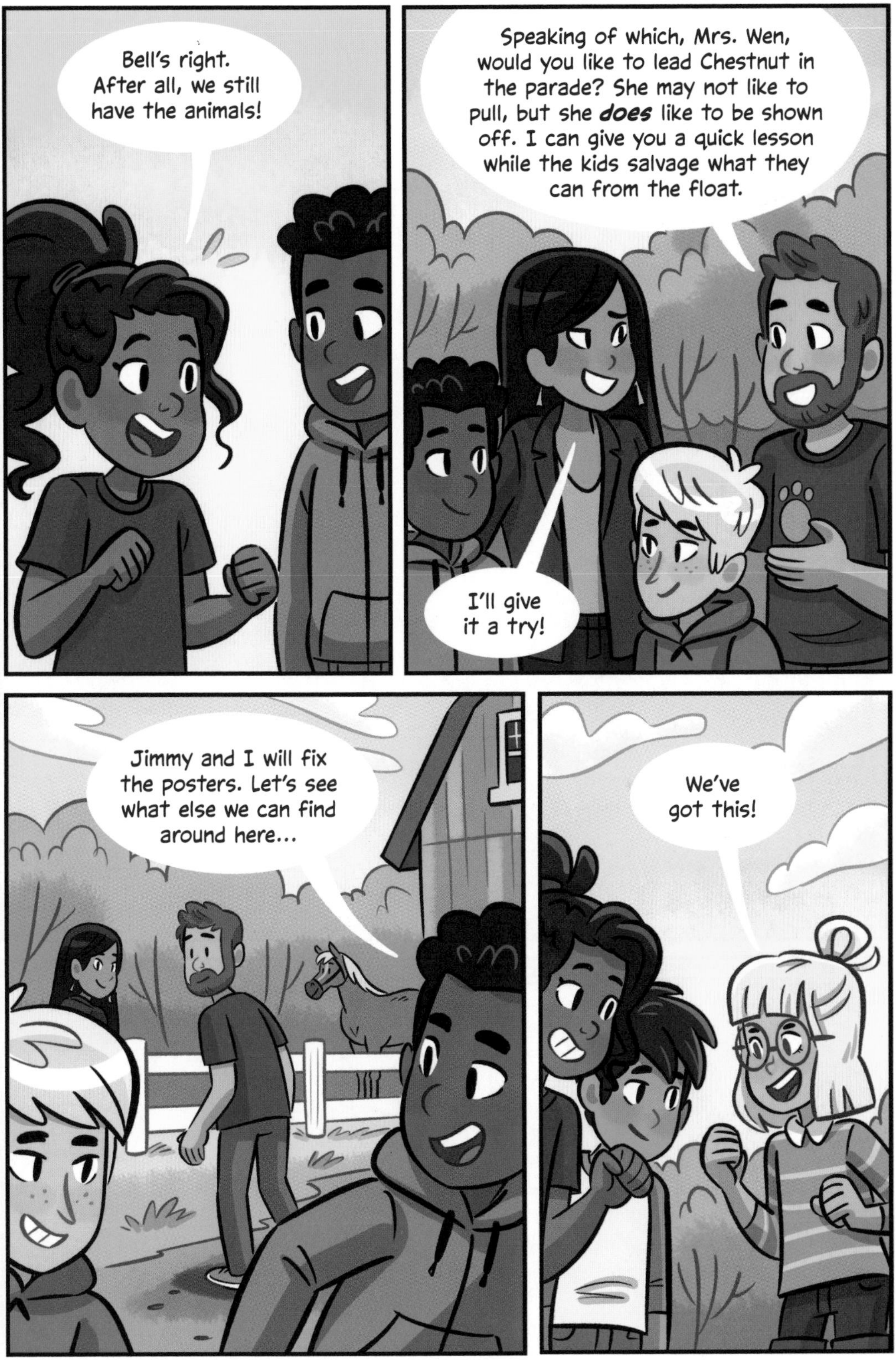
Bell's right. After all, we still have the animals!
Speaking of which, Mrs. Wen, would you like to lead Chestnut in the parade? She may not like to pull, but she ***does*** like to be shown off. I can give you a quick lesson while the kids salvage what they can from the float.
I'll give it a try!
Jimmy and I will fix the posters. Let's see what else we can find around here...
We've got this!

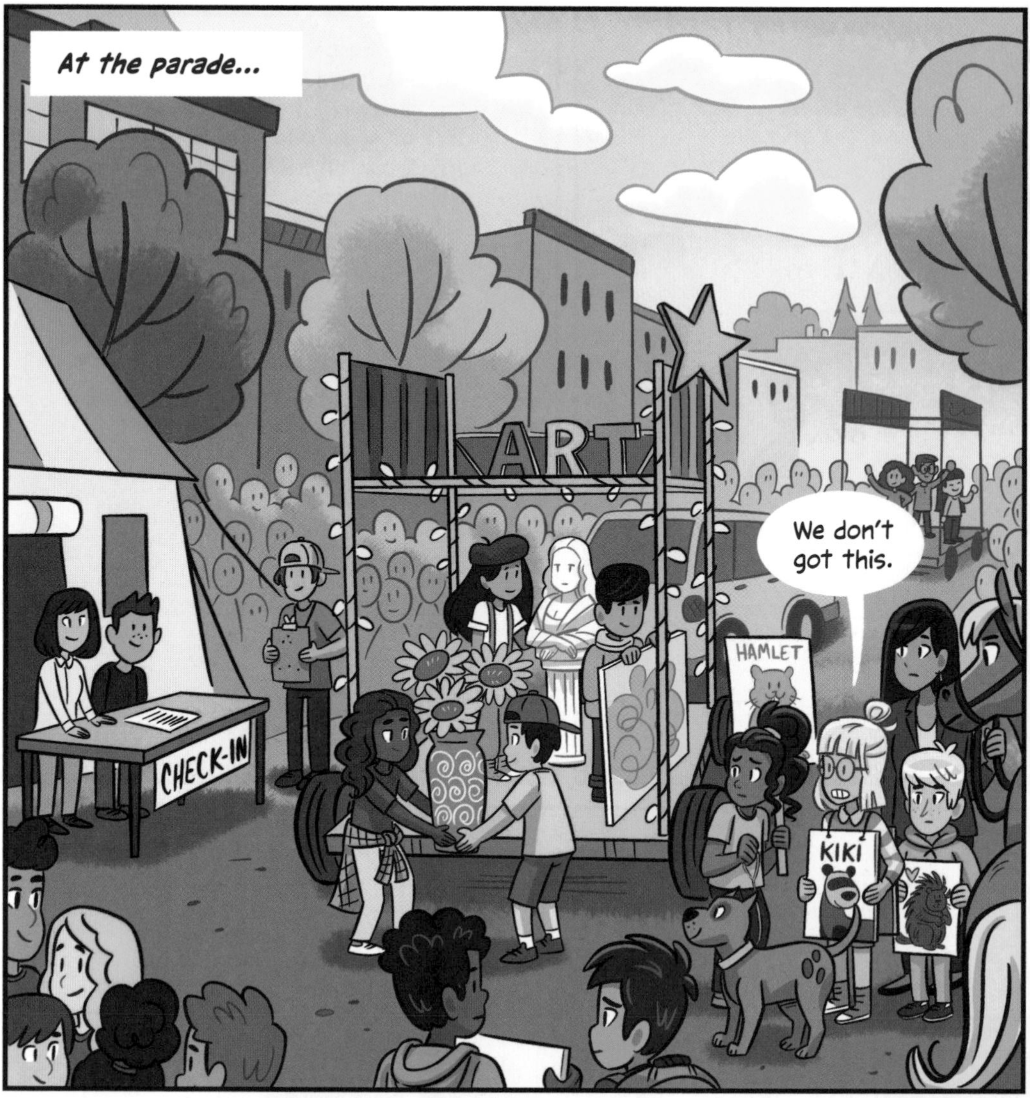
At the parade...
ART
CHECK-IN
HAMLET
KIKI
We don't got this.

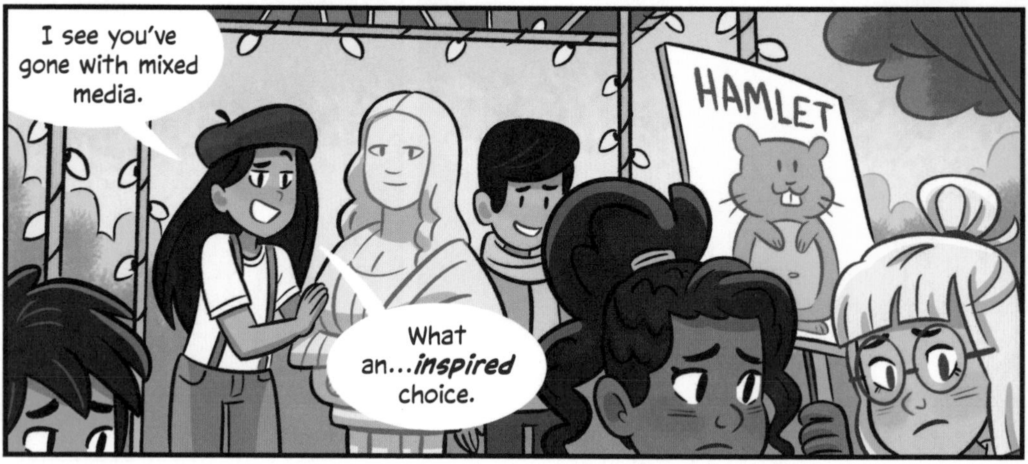
I see you've gone with mixed media.
What an...*inspired* choice.
HAMLET

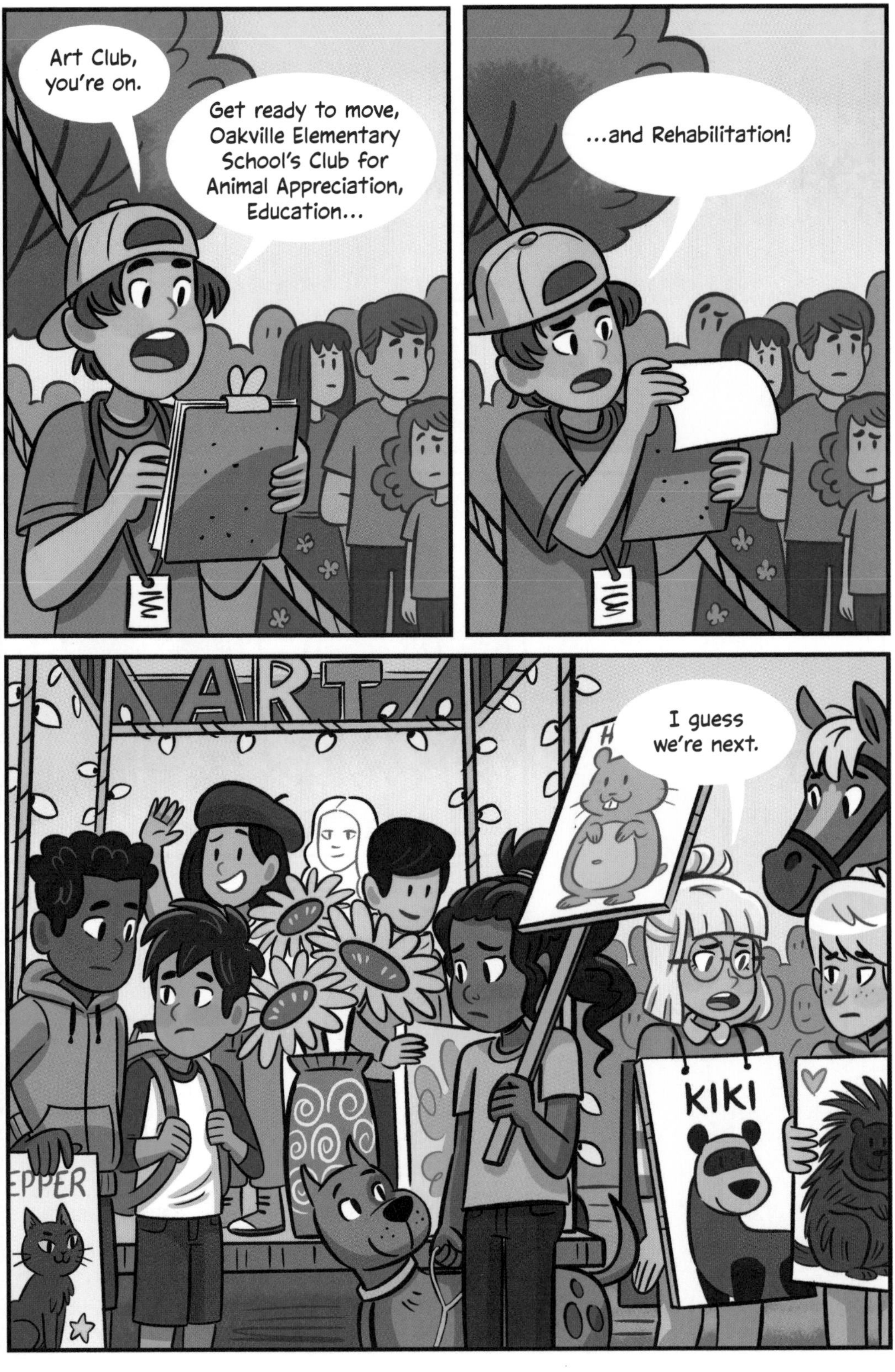
Art Club, you're on.
Get ready to move, Oakville Elementary School's Club for Animal Appreciation, Education...
...and Rehabilitation!
ART
I guess we're next.
KIKI
EPPER

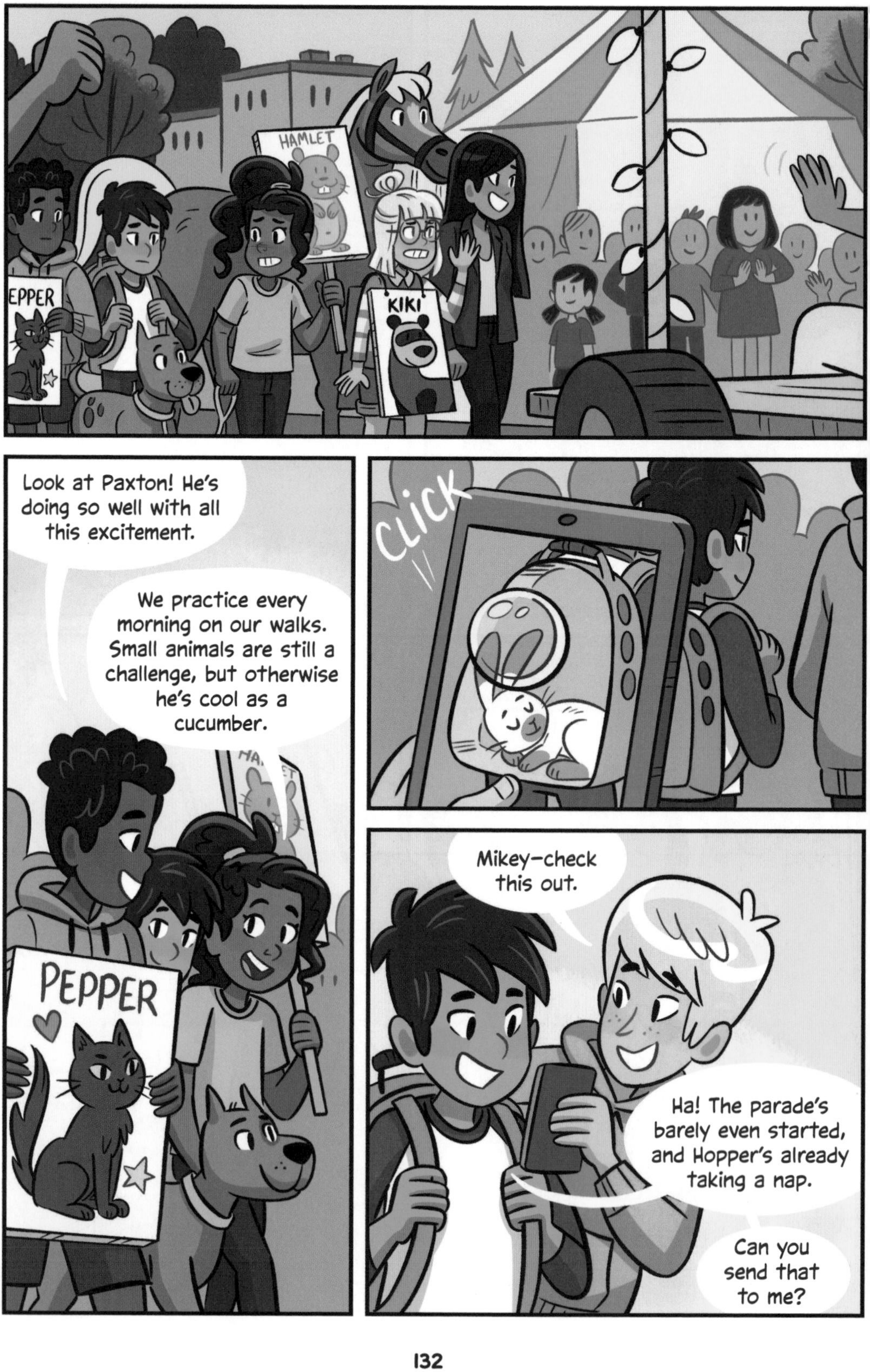
EPPER
HAMLET
KIKI
Look at Paxton! He's doing so well with all this excitement.
We practice every morning on our walks. Small animals are still a challenge, but otherwise he's cool as a cucumber.
PEPPER
CLICK
Mikey—check this out.
Ha! The parade's barely even started, and Hopper's already taking a nap.
Can you send that to me?

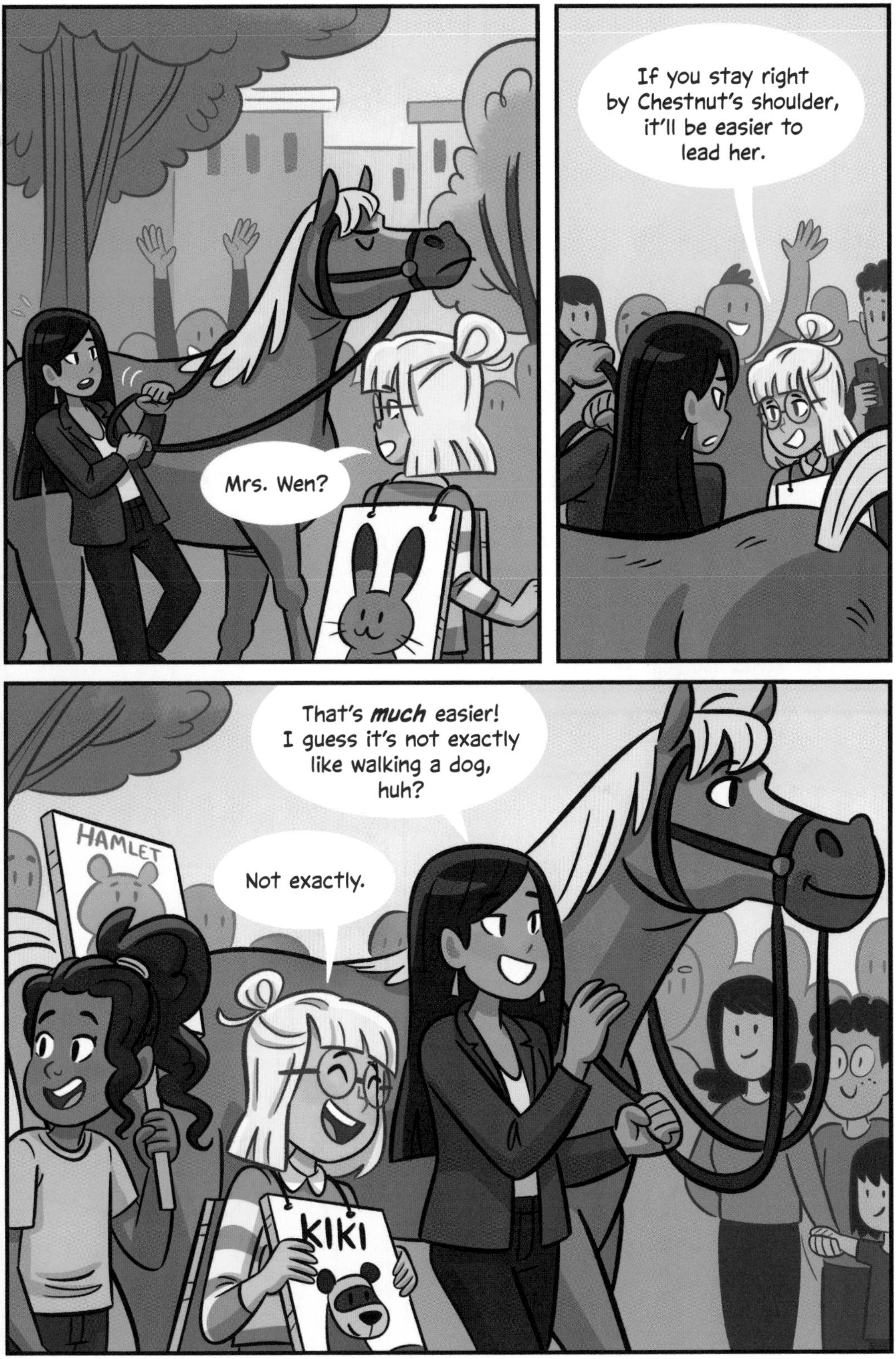
Mrs. Wen?
If you stay right by Chestnut's shoulder, it'll be easier to lead her.
That's **much** easier! I guess it's not exactly like walking a dog, huh?
Not exactly.
HAMLET
KIKI

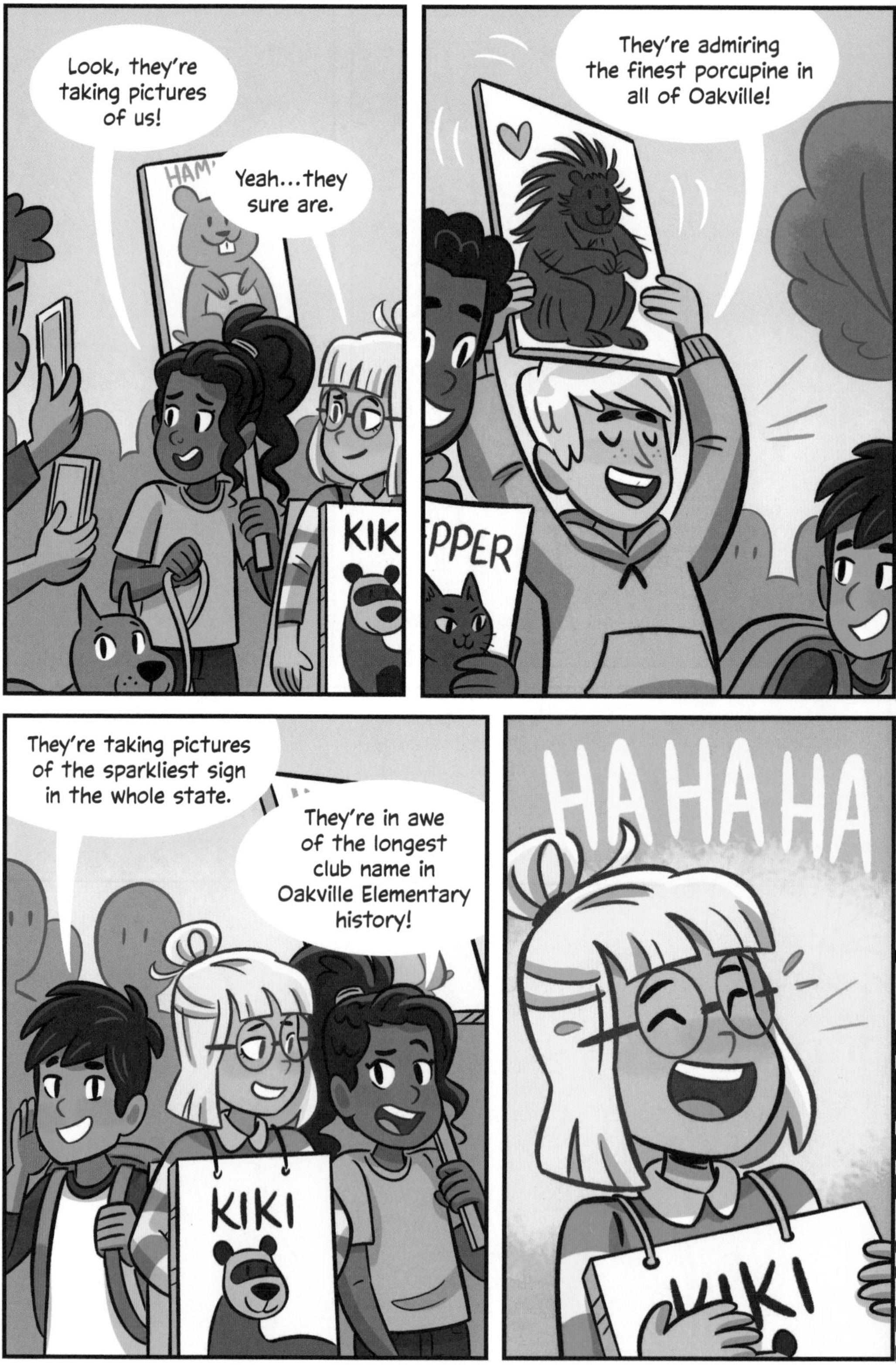
Look, they're taking pictures of us!
Yeah...they sure are.
HAM
KIK
They're admiring the finest porcupine in all of Oakville!
PPER
They're taking pictures of the sparkliest sign in the whole state.
They're in awe of the longest club name in Oakville Elementary history!
KIKI
HA HA HA HA

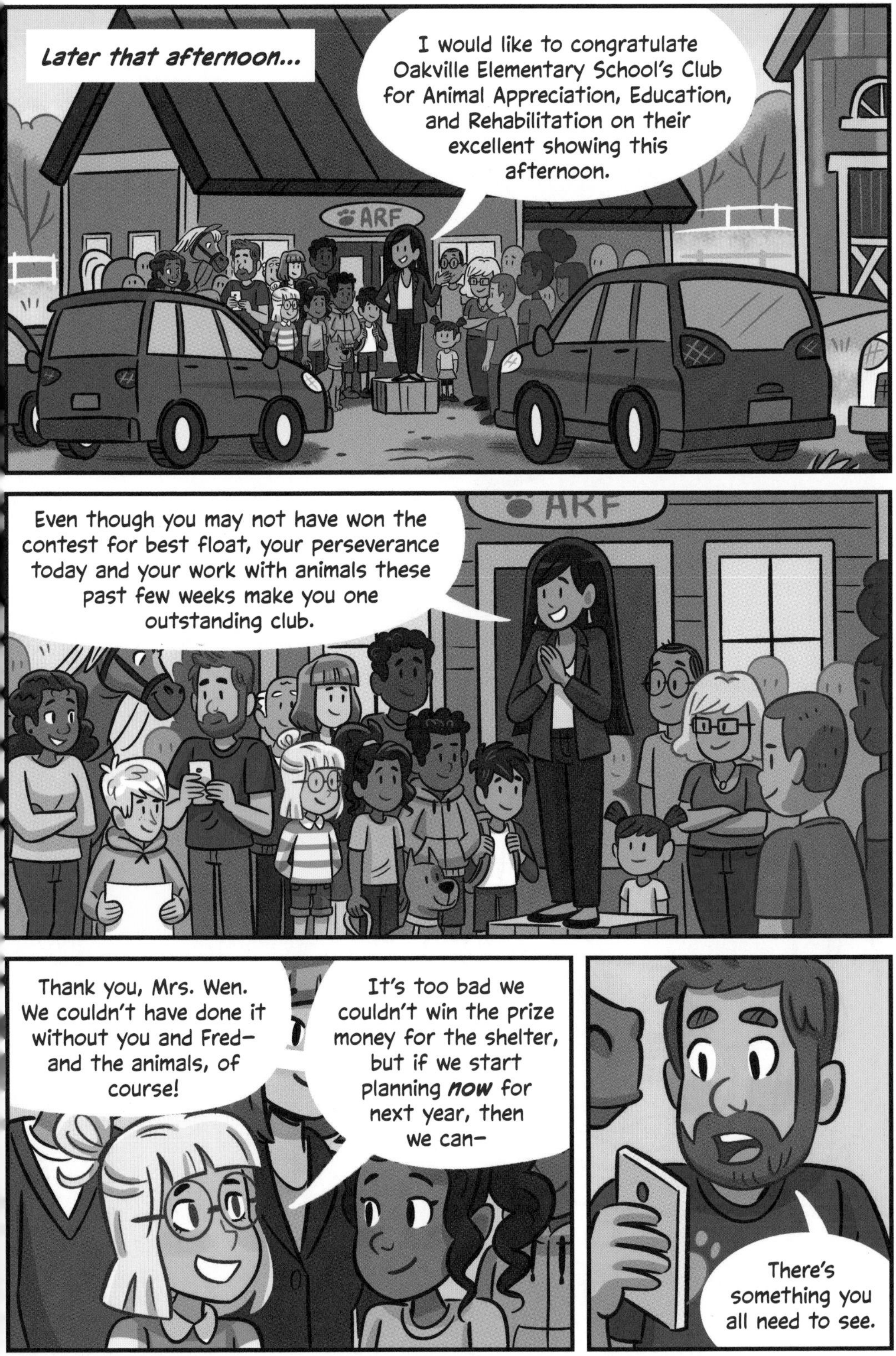
Later that afternoon...
I would like to congratulate Oakville Elementary School's Club for Animal Appreciation, Education, and Rehabilitation on their excellent showing this afternoon.
ARF
ARF
Even though you may not have won the contest for best float, your perseverance today and your work with animals these past few weeks make you one outstanding club.
Thank you, Mrs. Wen. We couldn't have done it without you and Fred— and the animals, of course!
It's too bad we couldn't win the prize money for the shelter, but if we start planning *now* for next year, then we can—
There's something you all need to see.

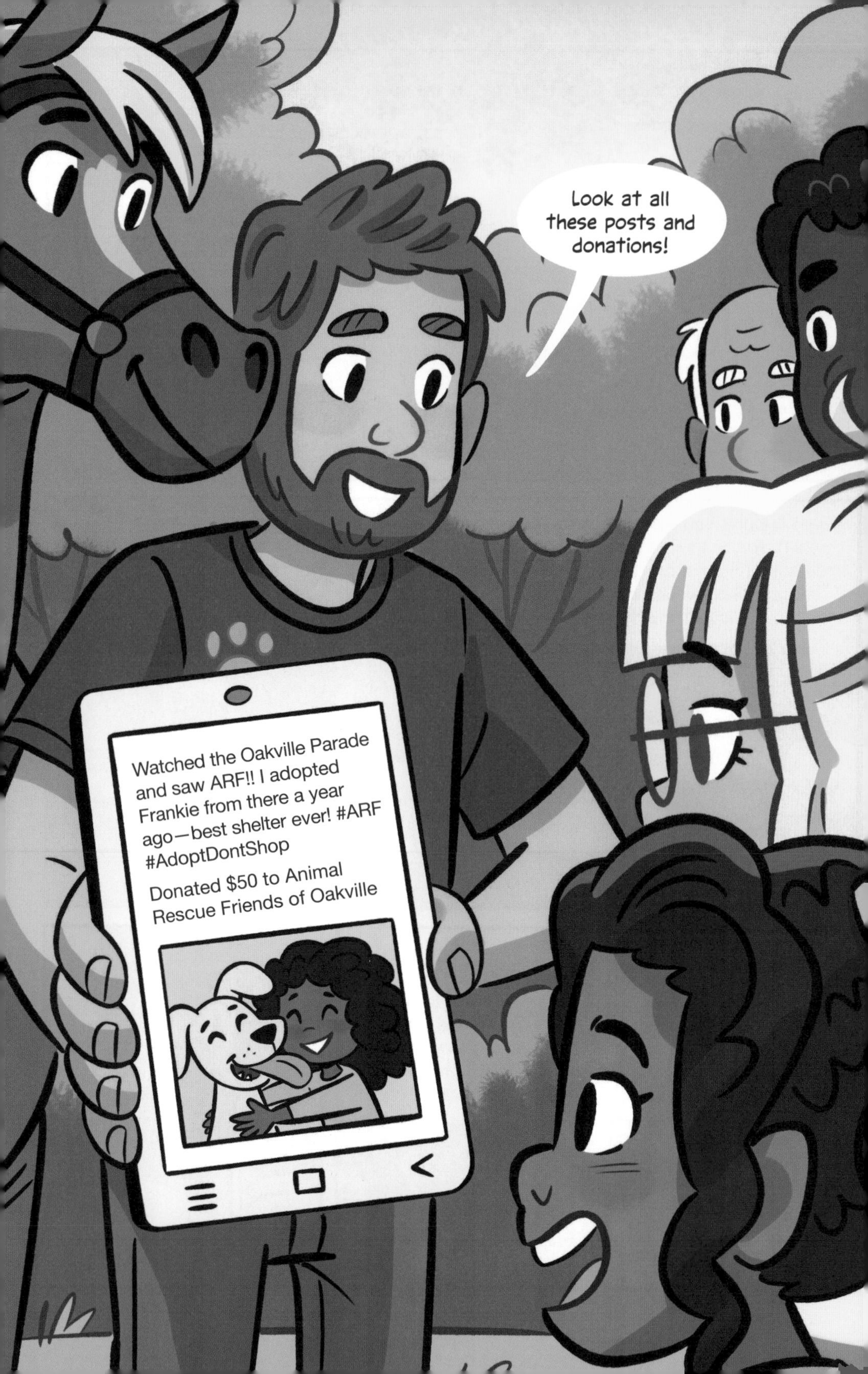
Look at all these posts and donations!
Watched the Oakville Parade and saw ARF!! I adopted Frankie from there a year ago—best shelter ever! #ARF #AdoptDontShop
Donated $50 to Animal Rescue Friends of Oakville

The kids at ARF helped me find a buddy when I moved back home to Oakville. Love from Miles & Scooter!

Donated $75 to Animal Rescue Friends of Oakville

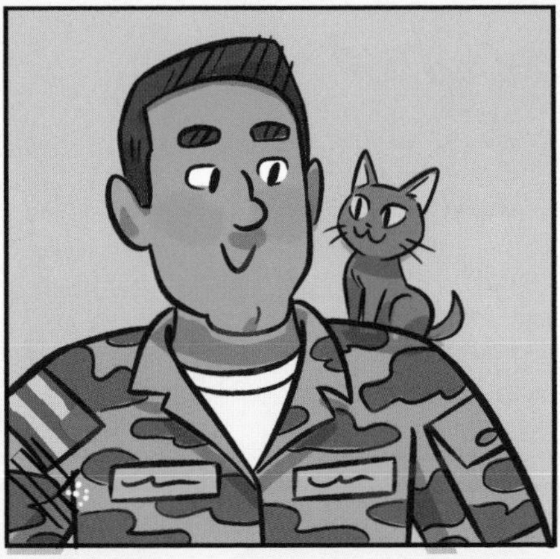

Pendleton and Pickles are best friends! Thanks, ARF!

Donated $100 to Animal Rescue Friends of Oakville

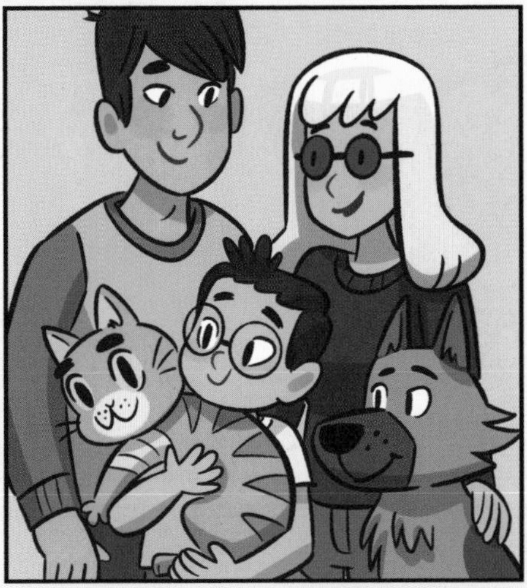

ARF is the best! Thanx 4 helping me w/ Monster. Skipping pizza nite this week 2 give 2 ARF! #ARF

Donated $20 to Animal Rescue Friends of Oakville

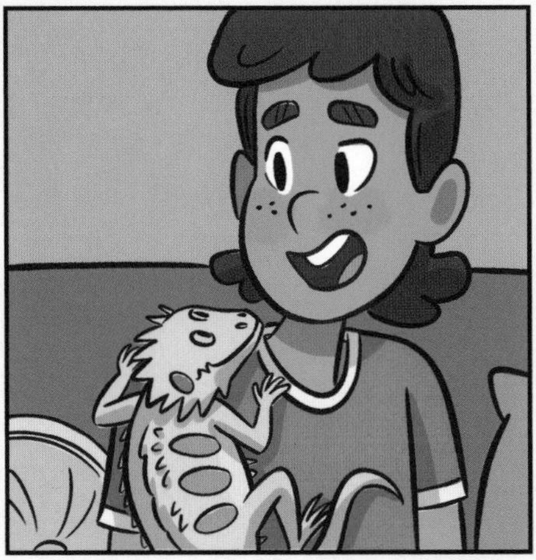

With love from Art Club

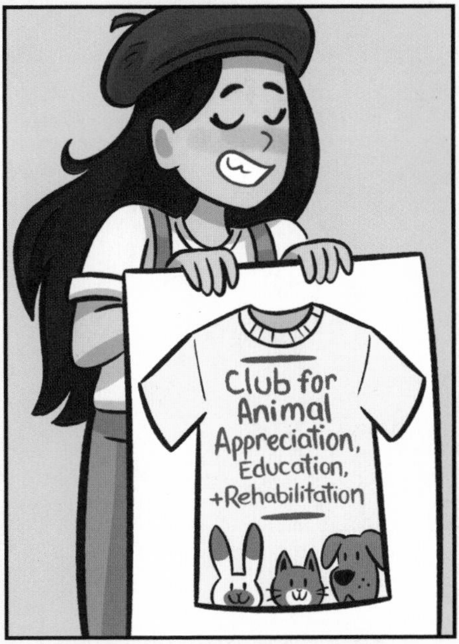
Club for Animal Appreciation, Education, +Rehabilitation

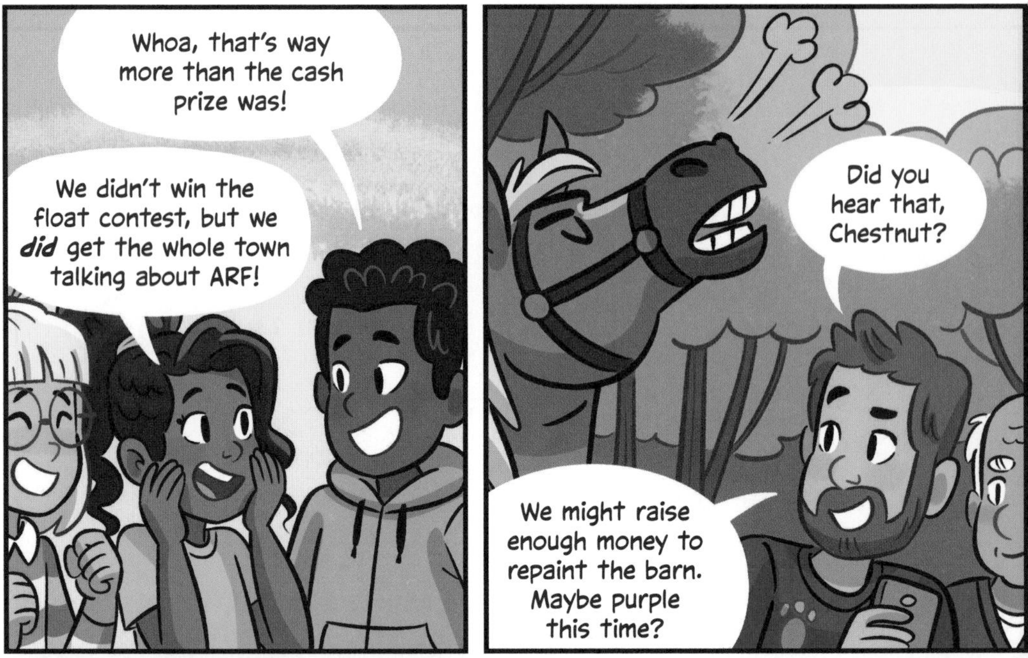
Whoa, that's way more than the cash prize was!
We didn't win the float contest, but we ***did*** get the whole town talking about ARF!
Did you hear that, Chestnut?
We might raise enough money to repaint the barn. Maybe purple this time?

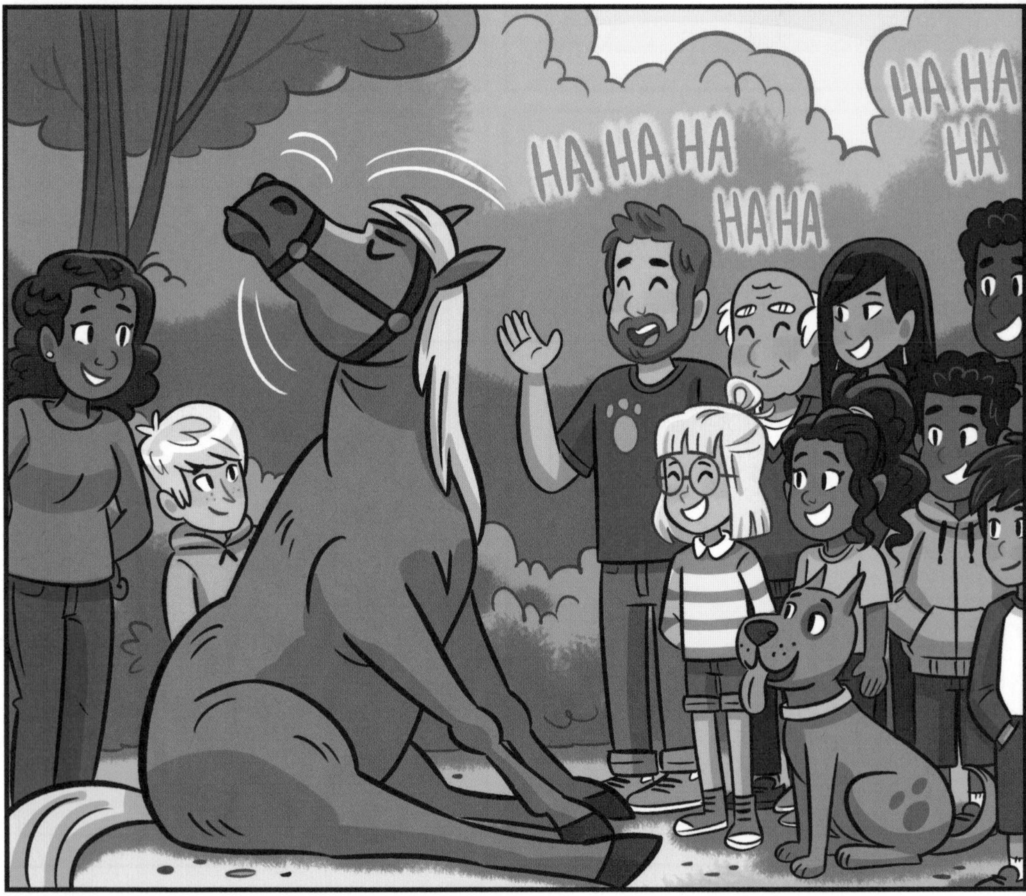
HA HA HA
HA HA
HA HA HA

MADDIE AND PENDLETON

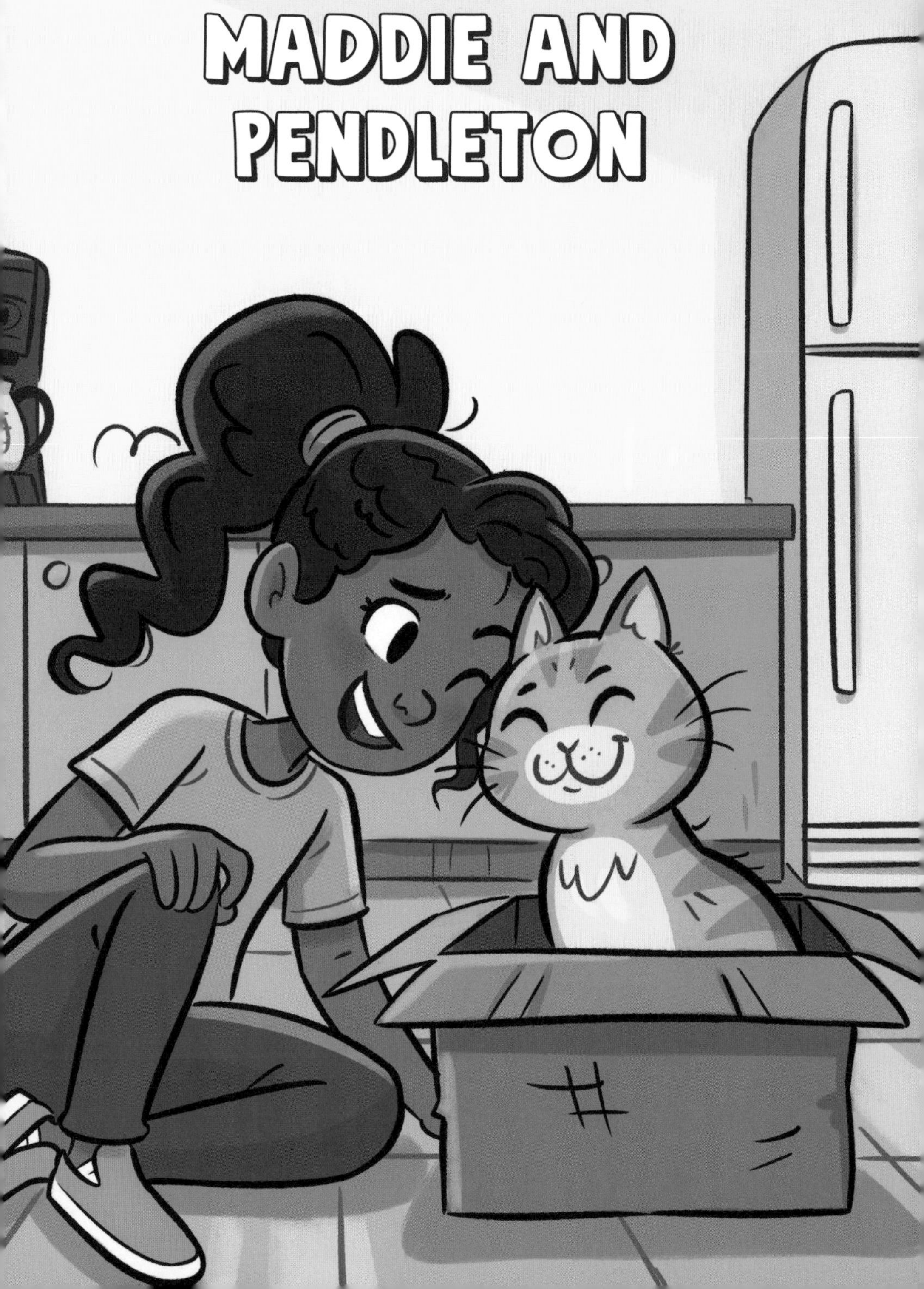

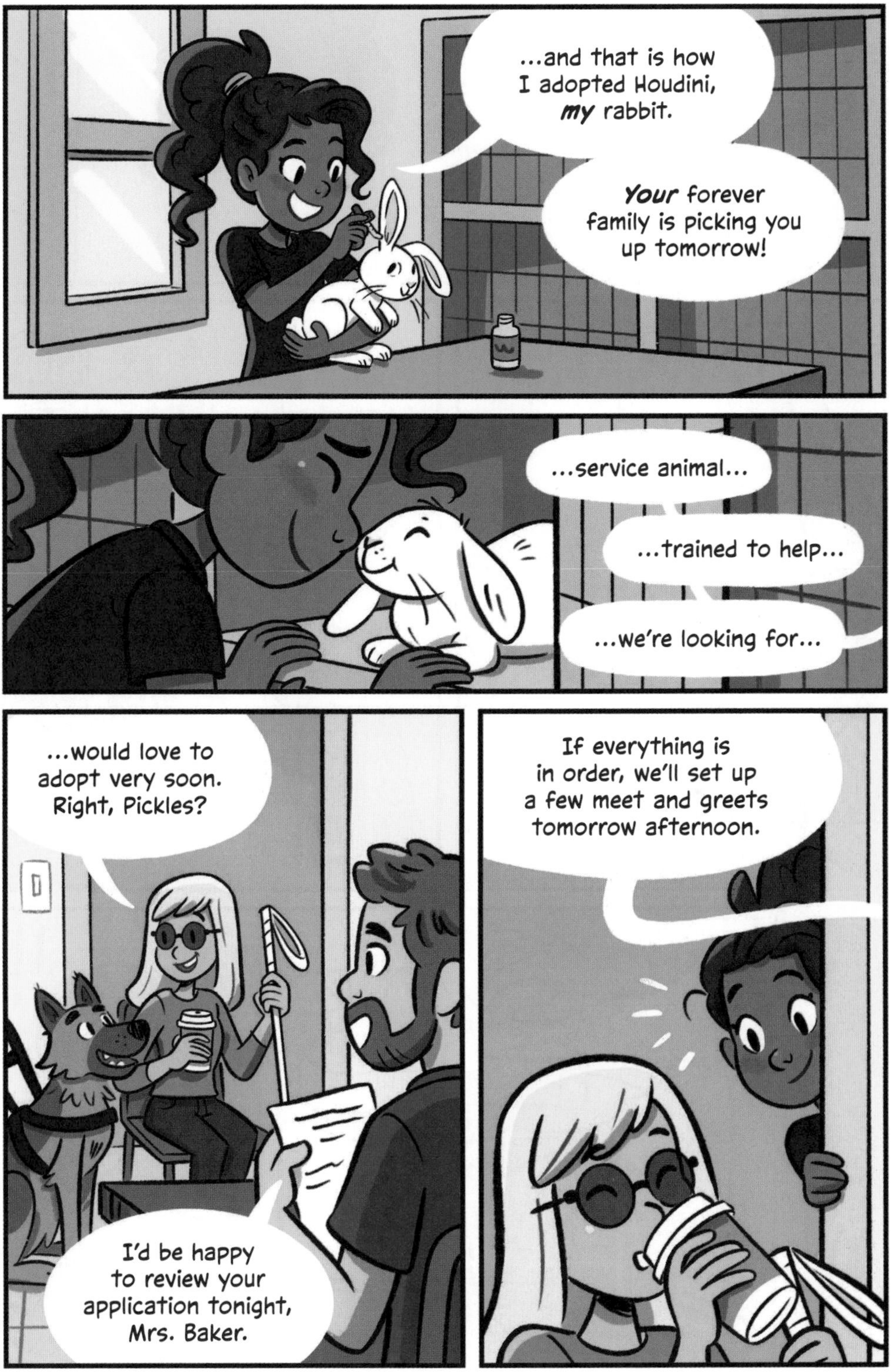
...and that is how I adopted Houdini, *my* rabbit.
Your forever family is picking you up tomorrow!
...service animal...
...trained to help...
...we're looking for...
...would love to adopt very soon. Right, Pickles?
I'd be happy to review your application tonight, Mrs. Baker.
If everything is in order, we'll set up a few meet and greets tomorrow afternoon.

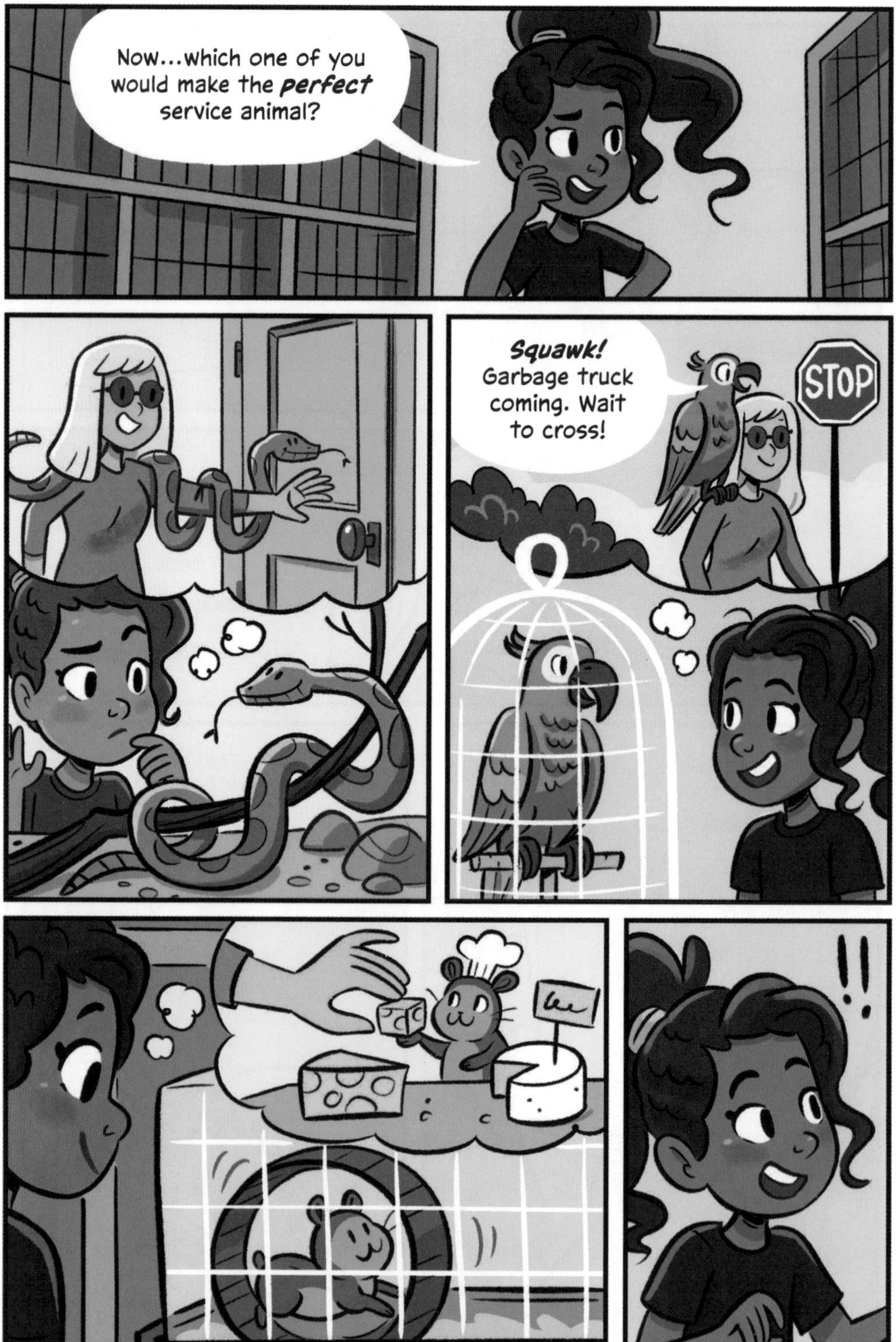
Now...which one of you would make the *perfect* service animal?
Squawk! Garbage truck coming. Wait to cross!
STOP
!!

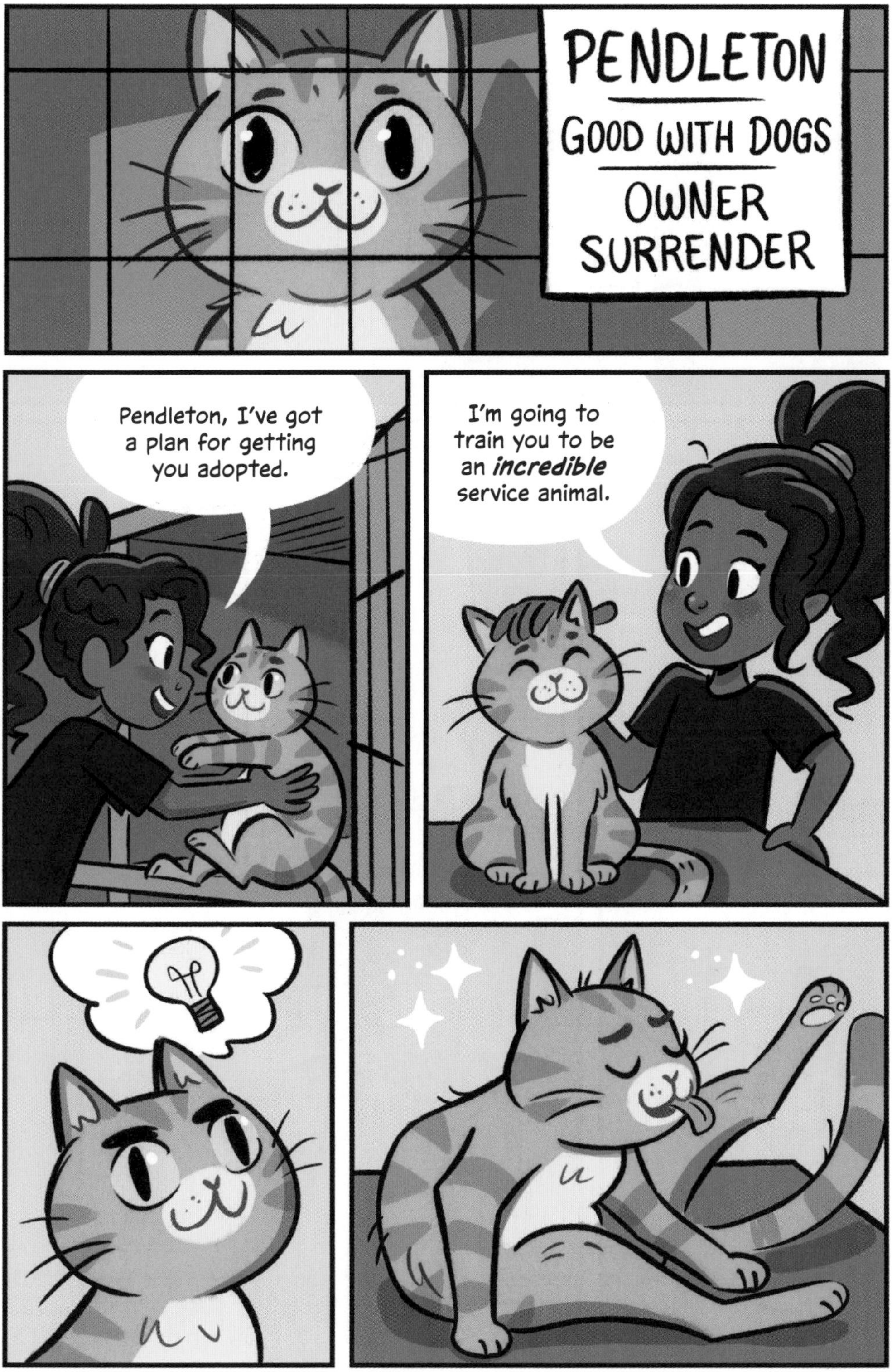
PENDLETON
GOOD WITH DOGS
OWNER SURRENDER
Pendleton, I've got a plan for getting you adopted.
I'm going to train you to be an *incredible* service animal.

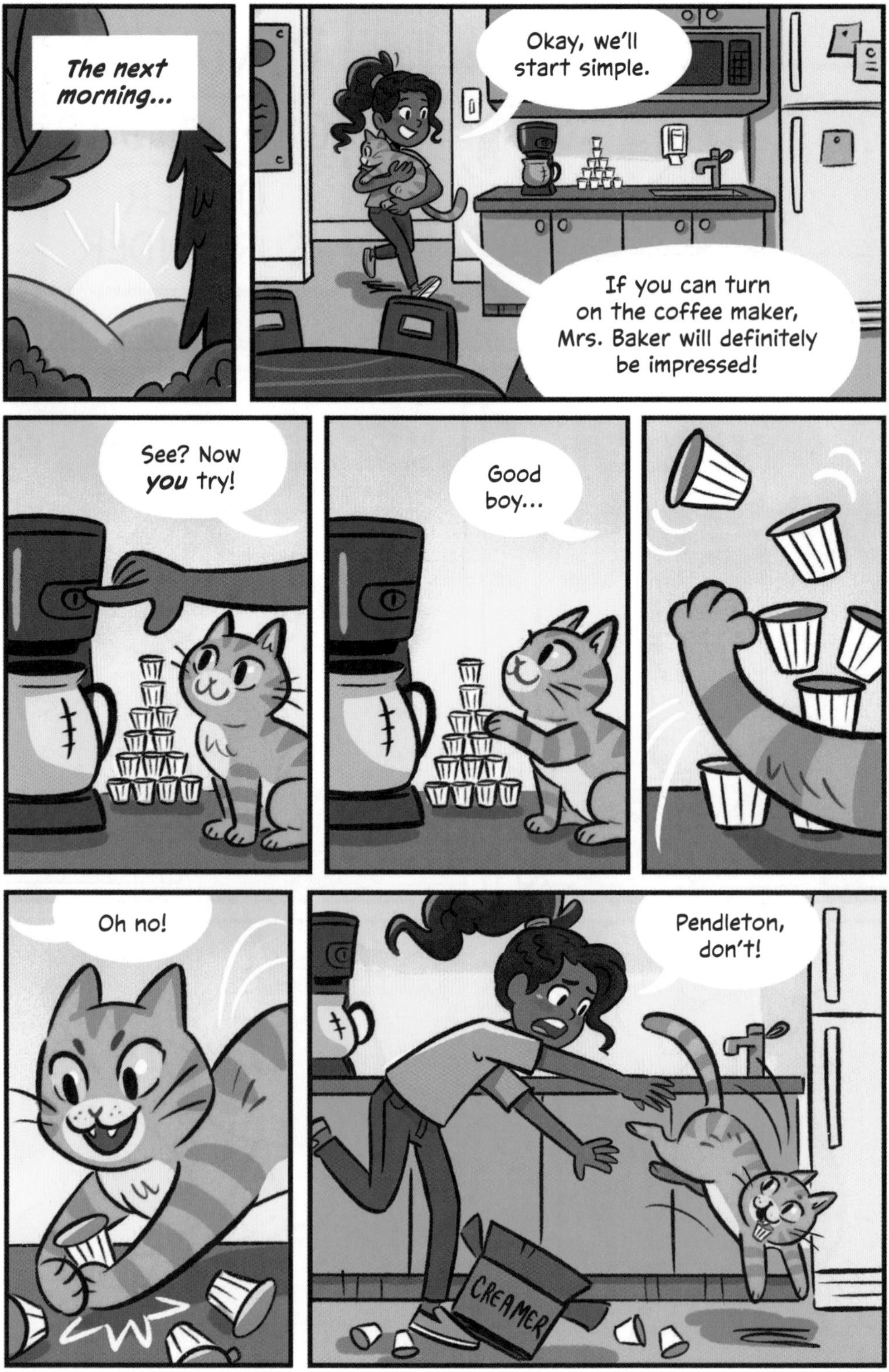

The next morning...
Okay, we'll start simple.
If you can turn on the coffee maker, Mrs. Baker will definitely be impressed!
See? Now *you* try!
Good boy...
Oh no!
Pendleton, don't!
CREAMER

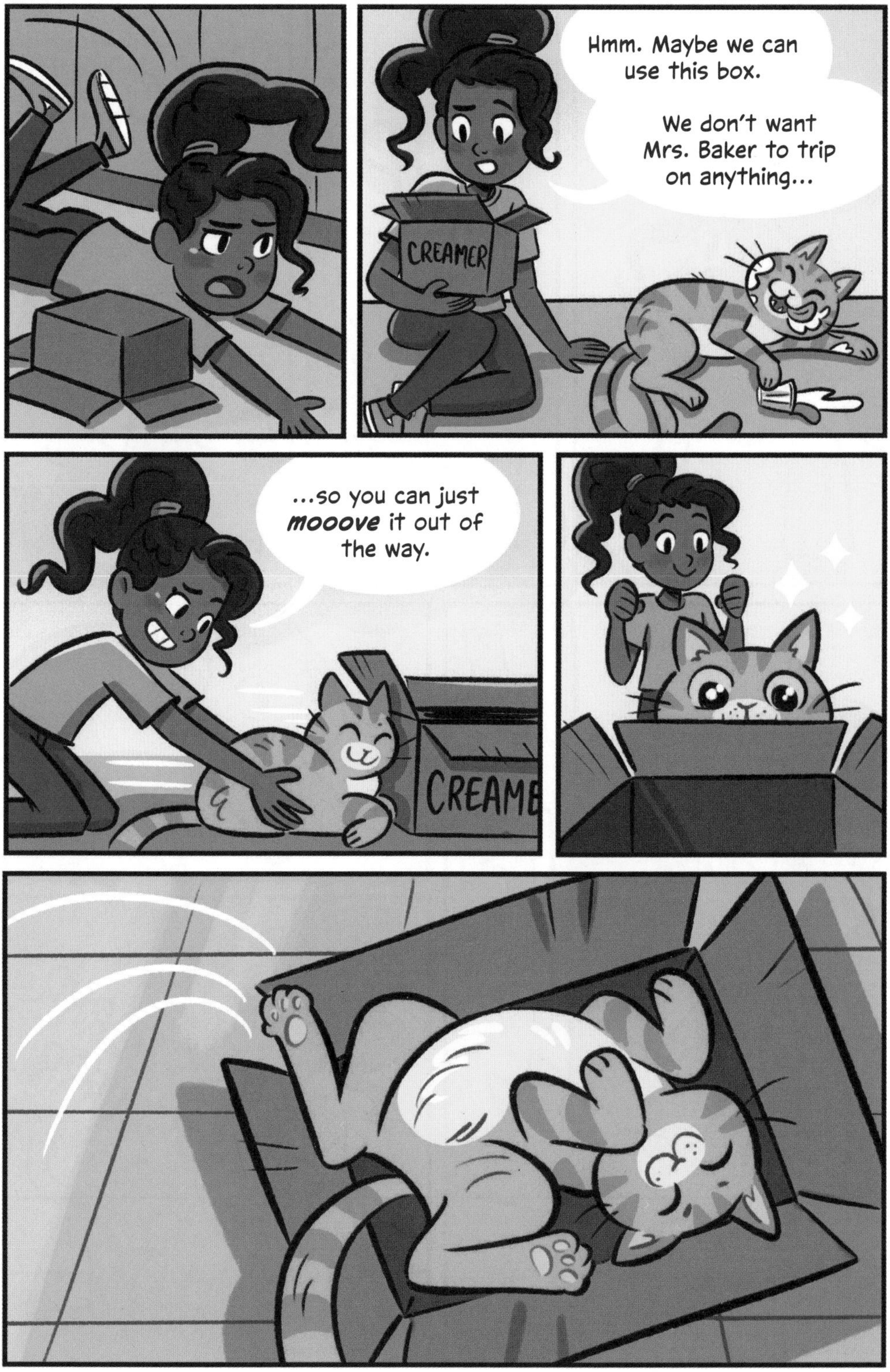
Hmm. Maybe we can use this box.
We don't want Mrs. Baker to trip on anything...
CREAMER
...so you can just *mooove* it out of the way.
CREAMB

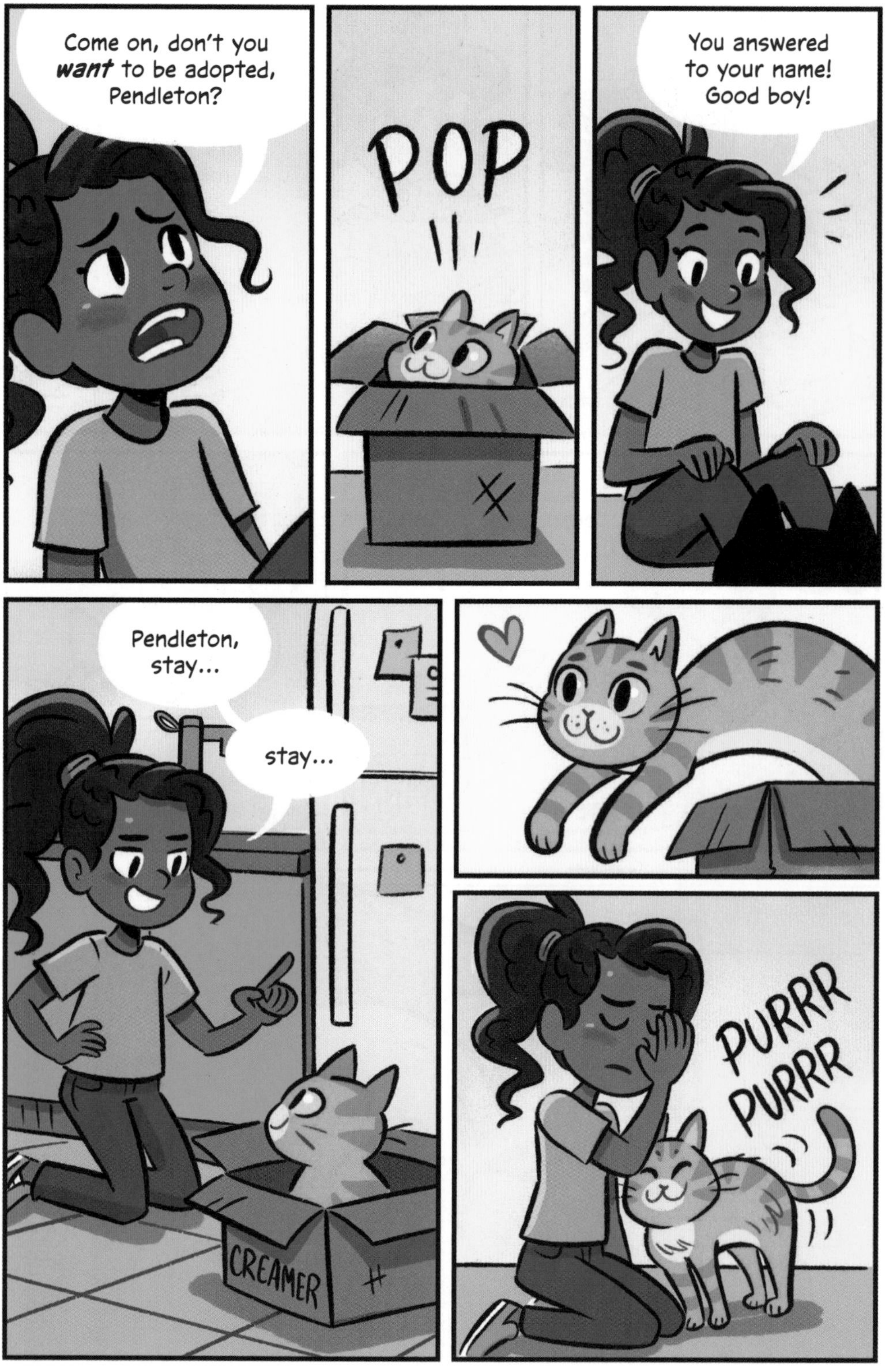
Come on, don't you *want* to be adopted, Pendleton?
POP
You answered to your name! Good boy!
Pendleton, stay...
stay...
CREAMER
PURRR
PURRR

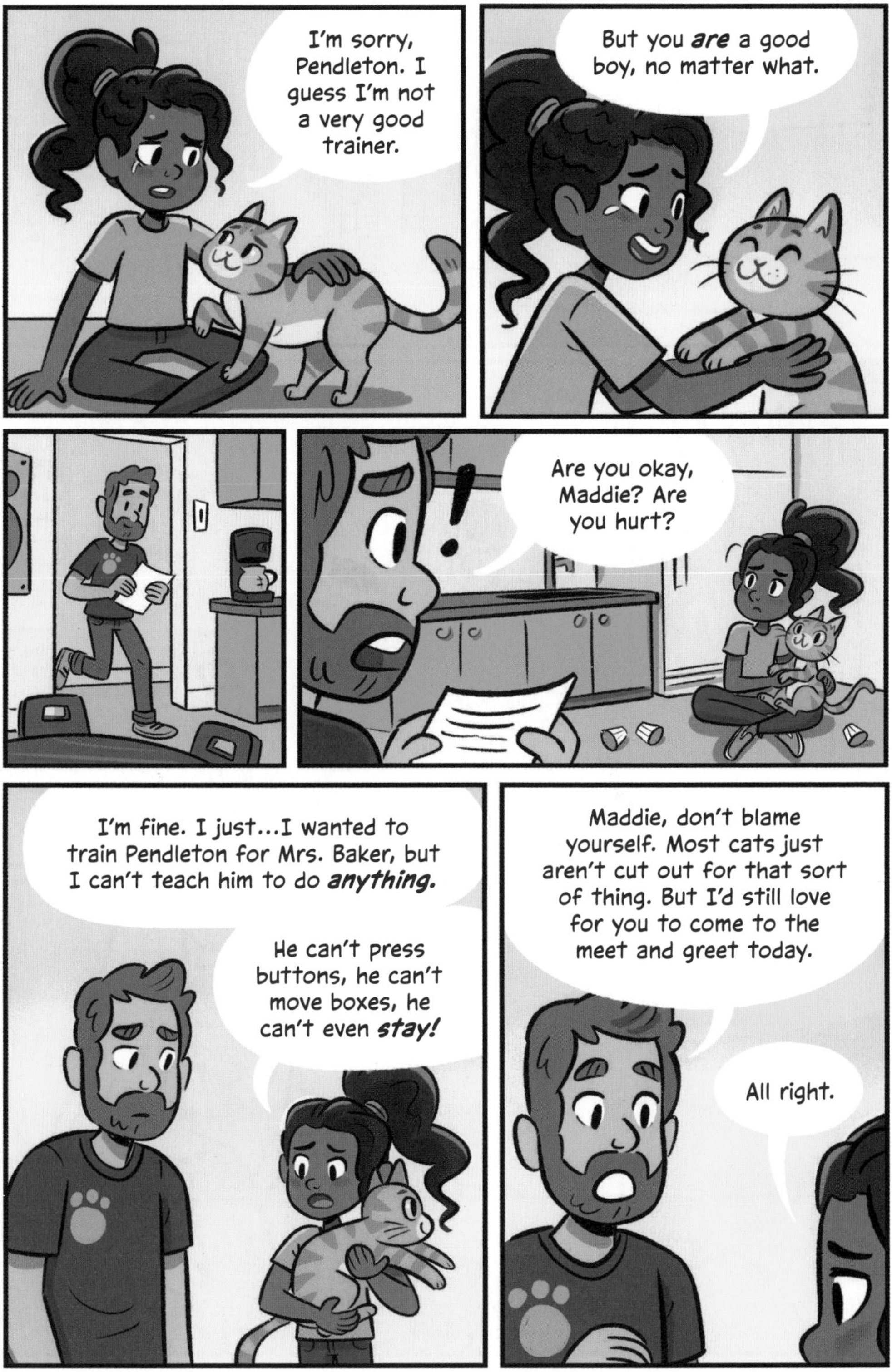
I'm sorry, Pendleton. I guess I'm not a very good trainer.
But you *are* a good boy, no matter what.
!
Are you okay, Maddie? Are you hurt?
I'm fine. I just...I wanted to train Pendleton for Mrs. Baker, but I can't teach him to do *anything.*
He can't press buttons, he can't move boxes, he can't even *stay!*
Maddie, don't blame yourself. Most cats just aren't cut out for that sort of thing. But I'd still love for you to come to the meet and greet today.
All right.

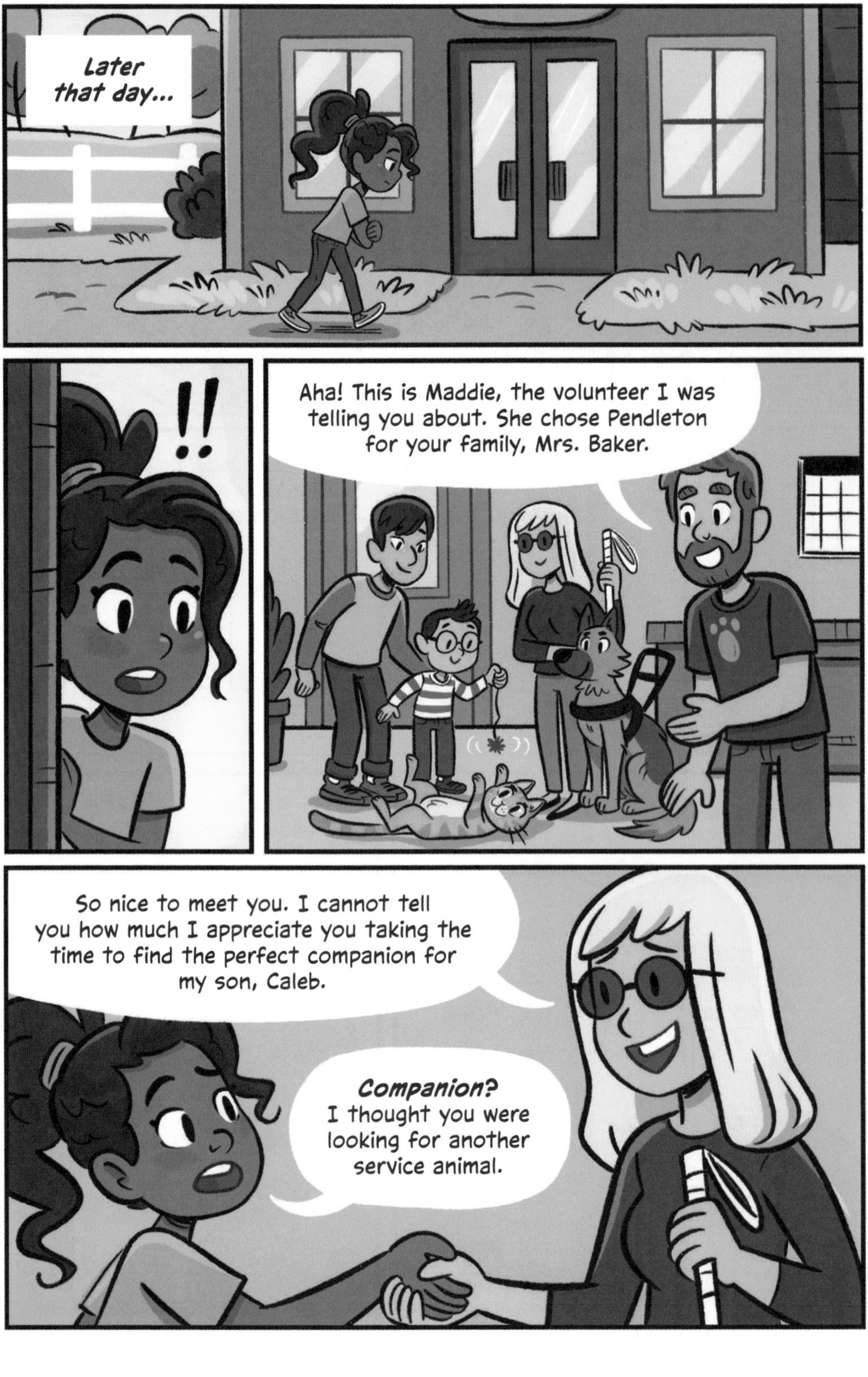
Later that day...
!!
Aha! This is Maddie, the volunteer I was telling you about. She chose Pendleton for your family, Mrs. Baker.
So nice to meet you. I cannot tell you how much I appreciate you taking the time to find the perfect companion for my son, Caleb.
Companion? I thought you were looking for another service animal.

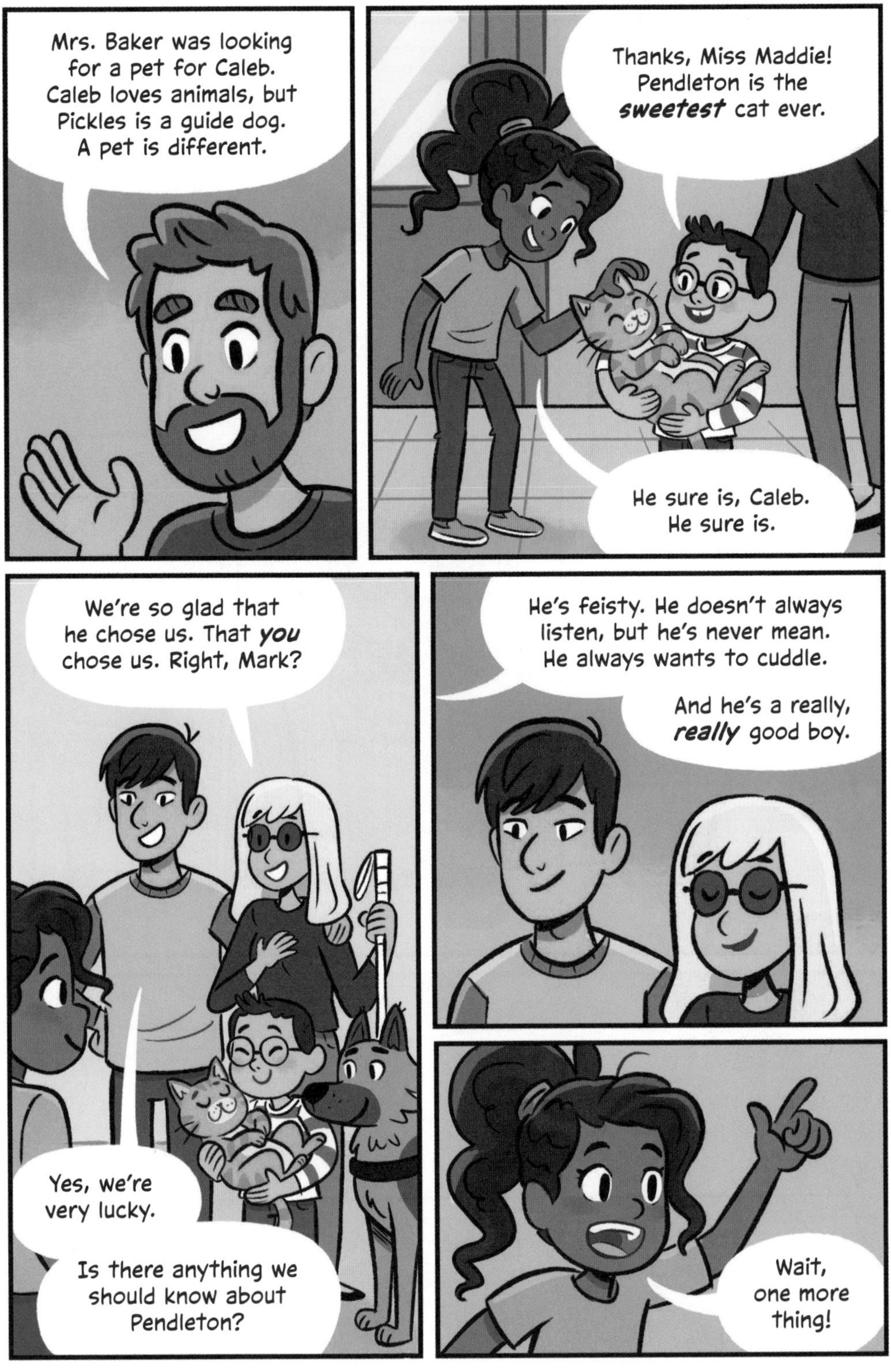
Mrs. Baker was looking for a pet for Caleb. Caleb loves animals, but Pickles is a guide dog. A pet is different.
Thanks, Miss Maddie! Pendleton is the *sweetest* cat ever.
He sure is, Caleb. He sure is.
We're so glad that he chose us. That *you* chose us. Right, Mark?
Yes, we're very lucky.
Is there anything we should know about Pendleton?
He's feisty. He doesn't always listen, but he's never mean. He always wants to cuddle.
And he's a really, *really* good boy.
Wait, one more thing!

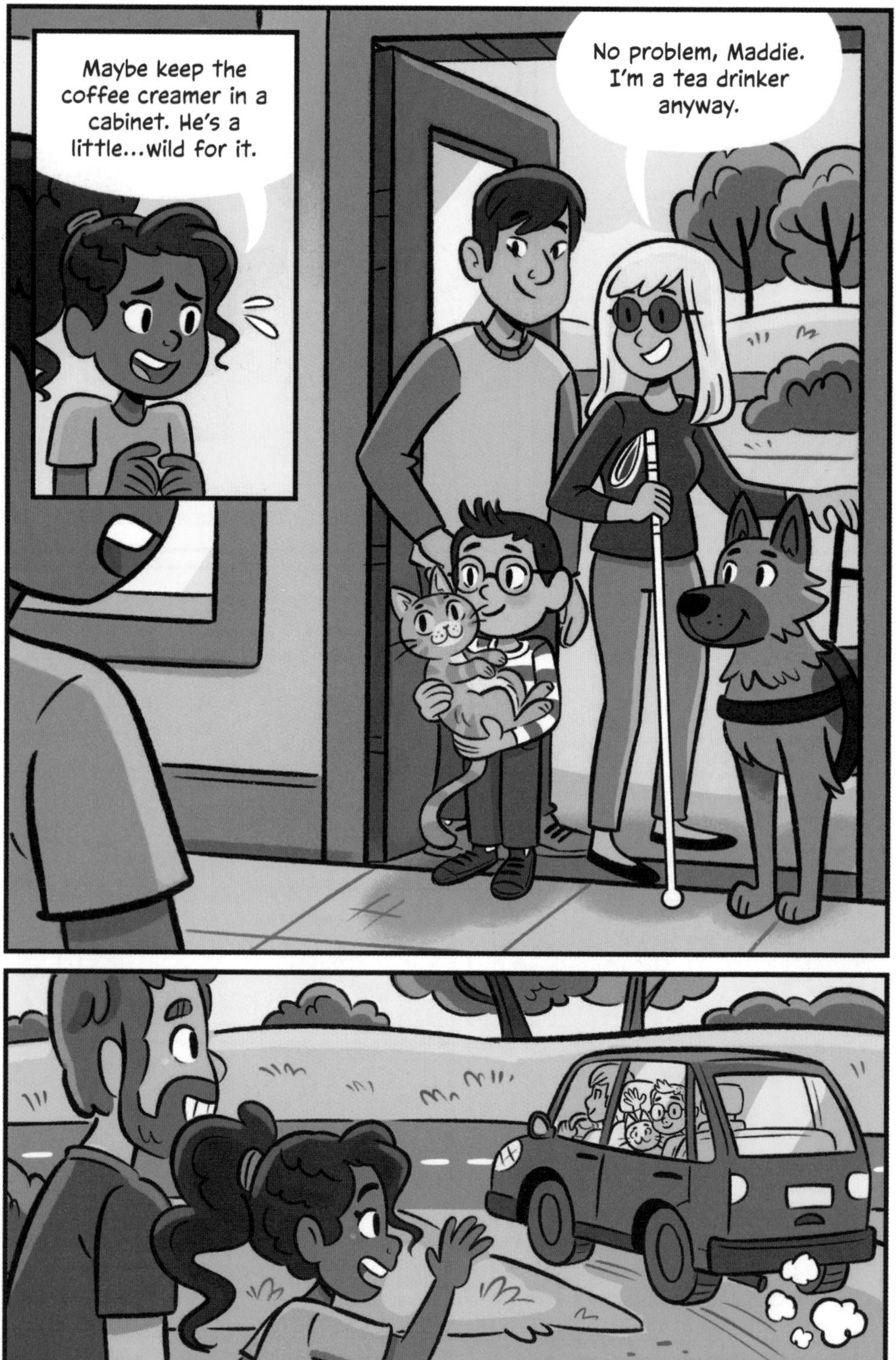
Maybe keep the coffee creamer in a cabinet. He's a little...wild for it.
No problem, Maddie. I'm a tea drinker anyway.

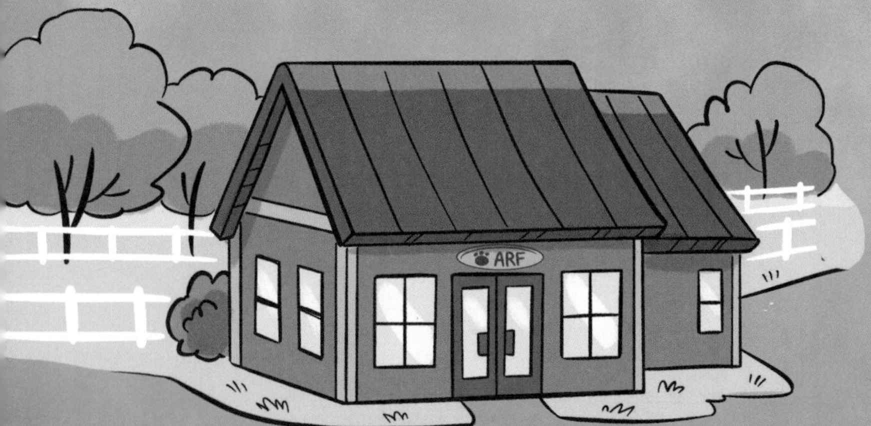
ARF

ABOUT THE AUTHOR AND ILLUSTRATORS

Jana Tropper, MS, CCC-SLP/L, is a speech-language pathologist at a public elementary school in the Midwest. When she's not with students or writing, she reads, plays video games, and serves as the director of literacy for Reading With Pictures, a nonprofit organization dedicated to supporting the use of comics in education. She lives with her husband, Josh, and their own three rescue dogs: Ripley, Newt, and Sandy.

Genevieve Kote is an illustrator living in Montreal, Canada. She loves reading manga and graphic novels. View more of her work at genevievekote.com.

Leo Trinidad is an illustrator and storyboard artist from Costa Rica. For 15 years he has been creating content for children's books and TV shows. He has worked on productions for Cartoon Network, Disney, Sony Pictures, and DreamWorks.